PORTSMOUTH
POLICE

0333

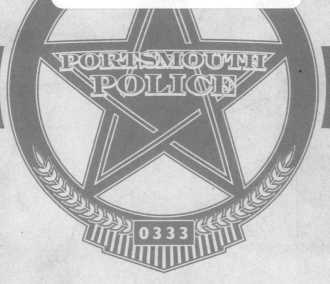

BLACK MAGICK ™

Created by Greg Rucka and Nicola Scott

VOLUME 3: "ASCENSION I"

Writer: **GREG RUCKA**

Artist: **NICOLA SCOTT**

Color Assists: CHIARA ARENA

Letterer: JODI WYNNE

Cover: NICOLA SCOTT
       (with ERIC TRAUTMANN)

Follow Greg on Twitter: @ruckawriter • Follow Nicola on Twitter: @NicolaScottArt
Follow Alejandro on Twitter: @alejandrobot • Follow Eric on Twitter: @mercuryeric

IMAGE COMICS, INC.
Todd McFarlane—President
Jim Valentino—Vice-President
Marc Silvestri—Chief Executive Officer
Erik Larsen—Chief Financial Officer
Robert Kirkman—Chief Operating Officer
Eric Stephenson—Publisher / Chief Creative Officer
Shanna Matuszak—Editorial Coordinator
Marla Eizik—Talent Liaison
Nicole Lapalme—Controller
Leanna Caunter—Accounting Analyst
Sue Korpela—Accounting & HR Manager
Jeff Boison—Director of Sales & Publishing Planning
Dirk Wood—Director of International Sales & Licensing
Alex Cox—Director of Direct Market & Specialty Sales
Chloe Ramos-Peterson—Book Market & Library Sales Manager
Emilio Bautista—Digital Sales Coordinator
Kat Salazar—Director of PR & Marketing
Drew Fitzgerald—Marketing Content Associate
Heather Doornink—Production Director
Drew Gill—Art Director
Hilary DiLoreto—Print Manager
Tricia Ramos—Traffic Manager
Erika Schnatz—Senior Production Artist
Ryan Brewer—Production Artist
Deanna Phelps—Production Artist
IMAGECOMICS.COM

Editor: ALEJANDRO ARBONA

Book and Logo Designer, cover colors: ERIC TRAUTMANN

http://blackmagickcomic.tumblr.com

BLACK MAGICK VOLUME 3: ASCENSION I.

First printing. January 2021. Published by Image Comics, Inc. Office of publication: PO BOX 14457, Portland, OR 97293.

For international rights, contact: foreignlicensing@imagecomics.com.

ISBN: 978-1-5343-1373-6.

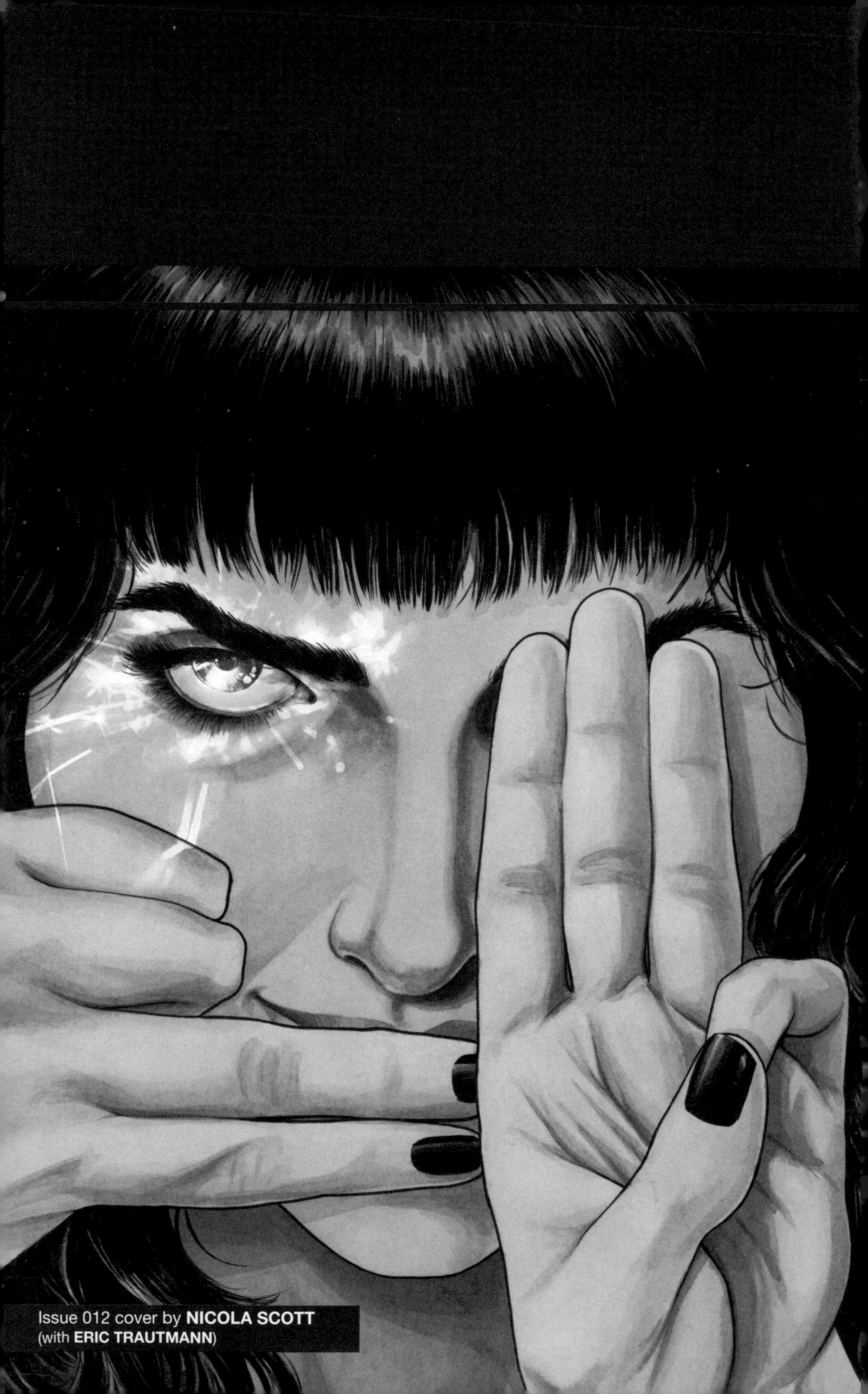

Issue 012 cover by **NICOLA SCOTT**
(with **ERIC TRAUTMANN**)

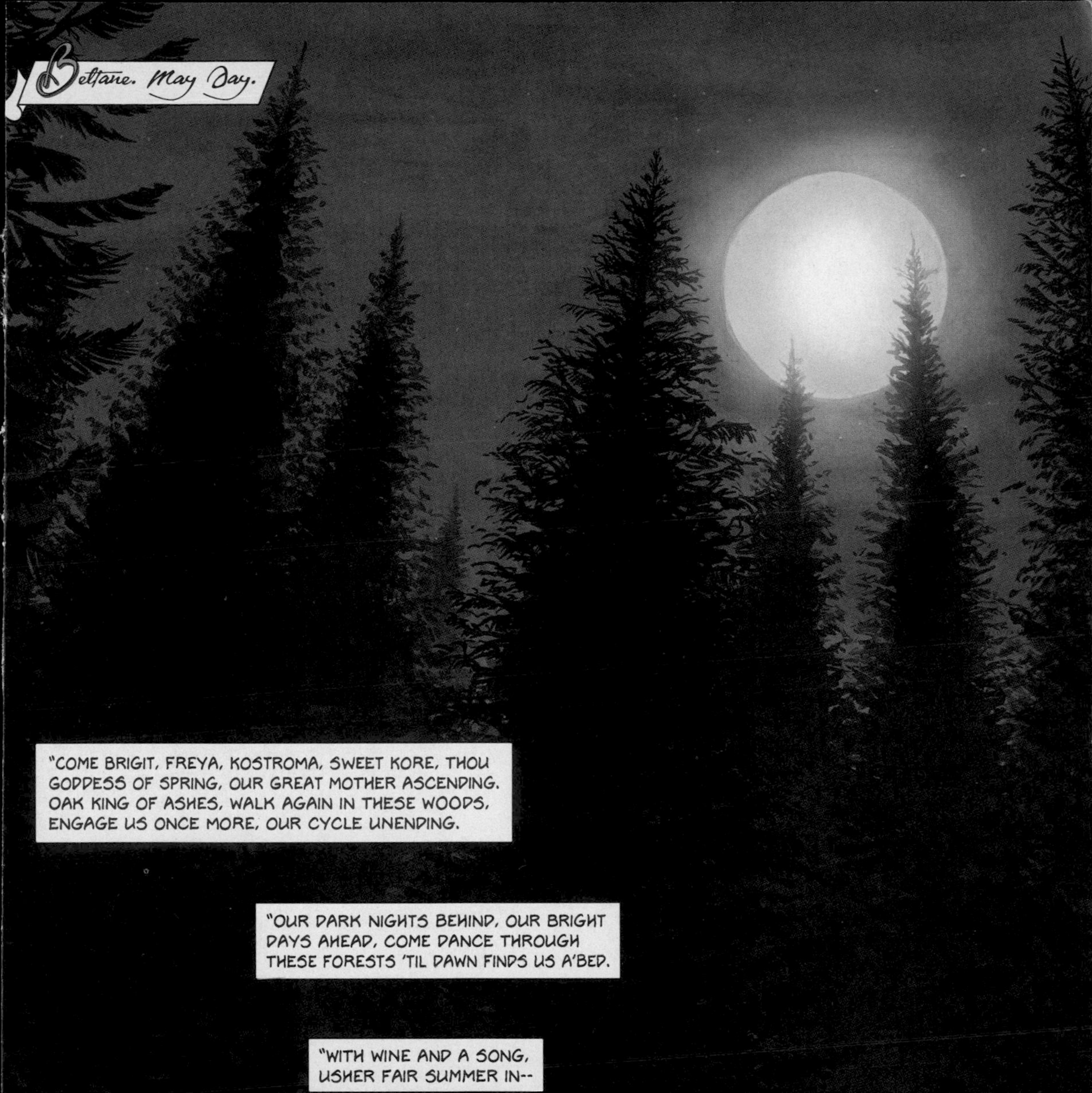
Beltane. May Day.
"COME BRIGIT, FREYA, KOSTROMA, SWEET KORE, THOU GODDESS OF SPRING, OUR GREAT MOTHER ASCENDING. OAK KING OF ASHES, WALK AGAIN IN THESE WOODS, ENGAGE US ONCE MORE, OUR CYCLE UNENDING.
"OUR DARK NIGHTS BEHIND, OUR BRIGHT DAYS AHEAD, COME DANCE THROUGH THESE FORESTS 'TIL DAWN FINDS US A'BED.
"WITH WINE AND A SONG, USHER FAIR SUMMER IN--

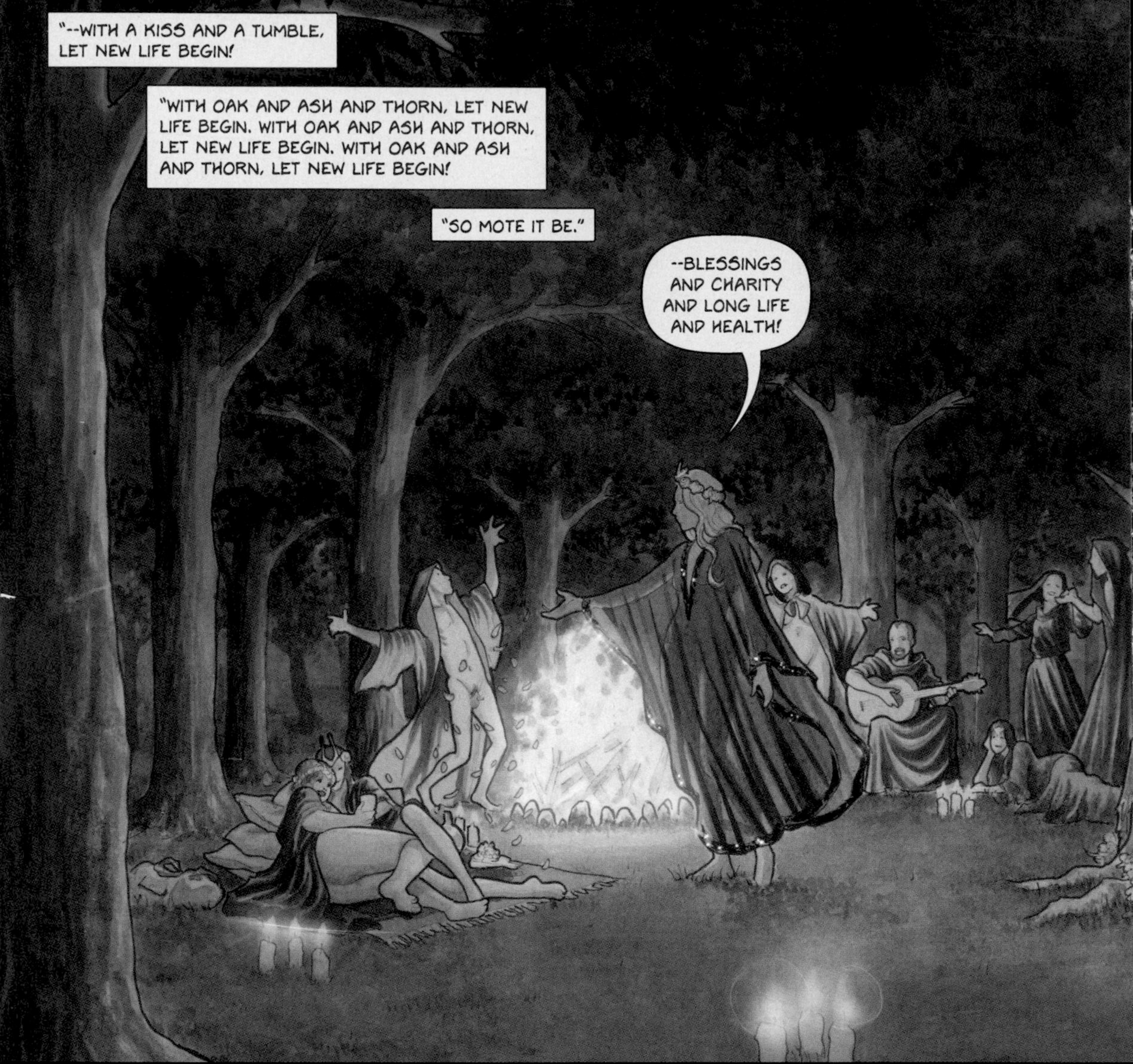
"--WITH A KISS AND A TUMBLE, LET NEW LIFE BEGIN!
"WITH OAK AND ASH AND THORN, LET NEW LIFE BEGIN. WITH OAK AND ASH AND THORN, LET NEW LIFE BEGIN. WITH OAK AND ASH AND THORN, LET NEW LIFE BEGIN!
"SO MOTE IT BE."
--BLESSINGS AND CHARITY AND LONG LIFE AND HEALTH!

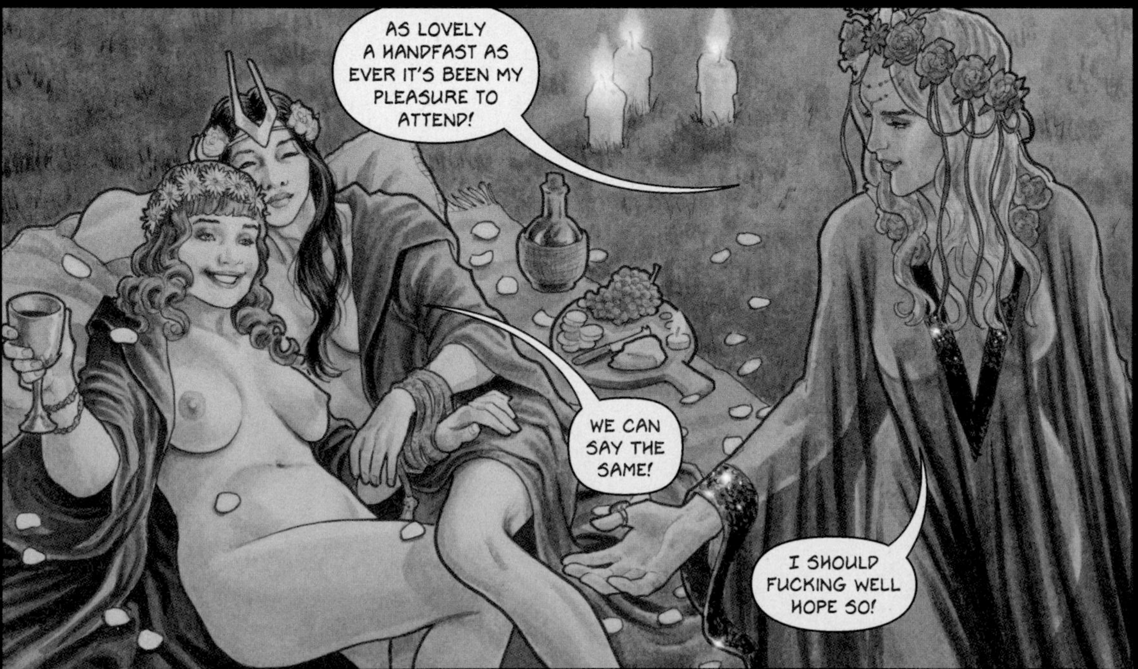
AS LOVELY A HANDFAST AS EVER IT'S BEEN MY PLEASURE TO ATTEND!
WE CAN SAY THE SAME!
I SHOULD FUCKING WELL HOPE SO!

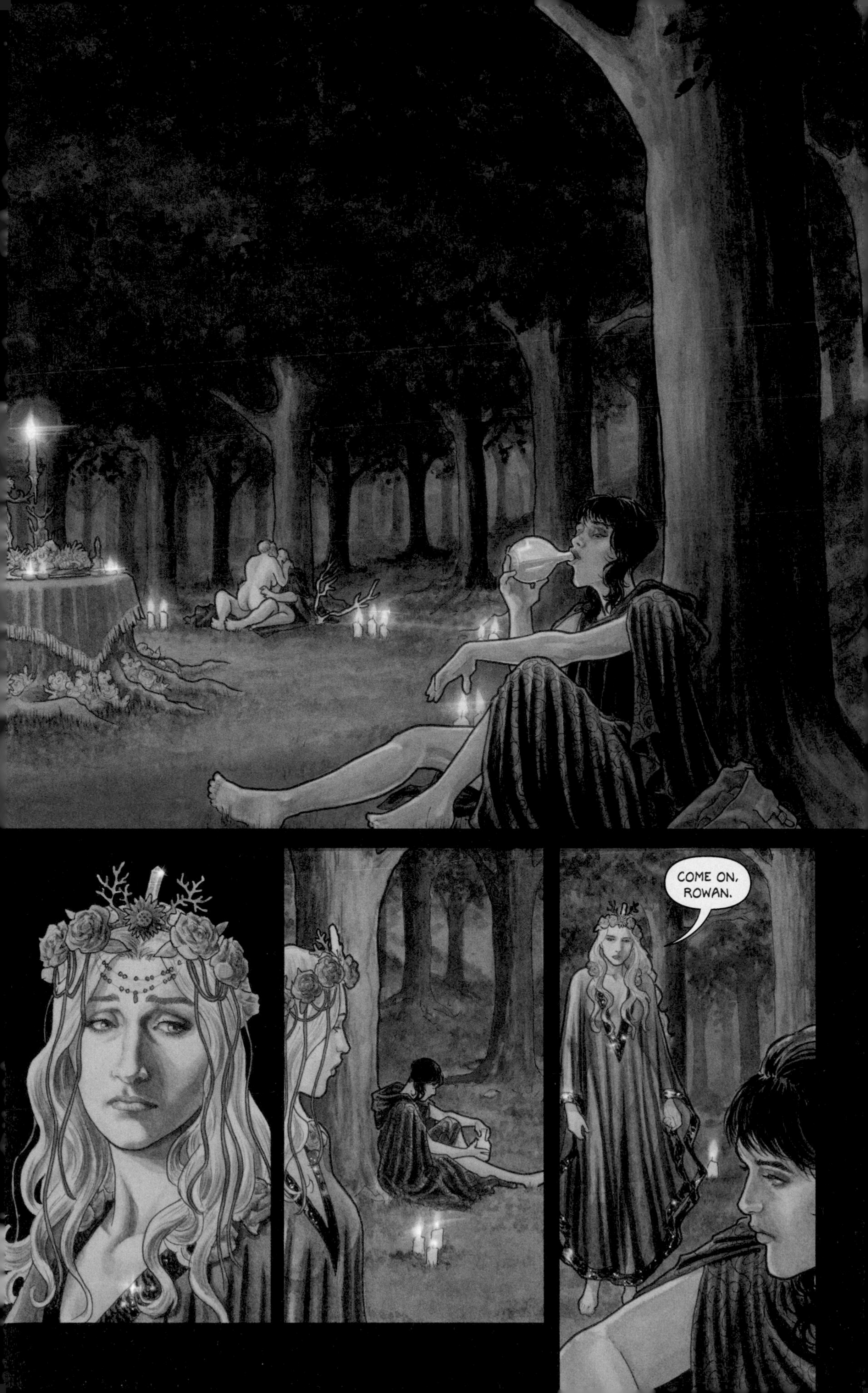
COME ON, ROWAN.

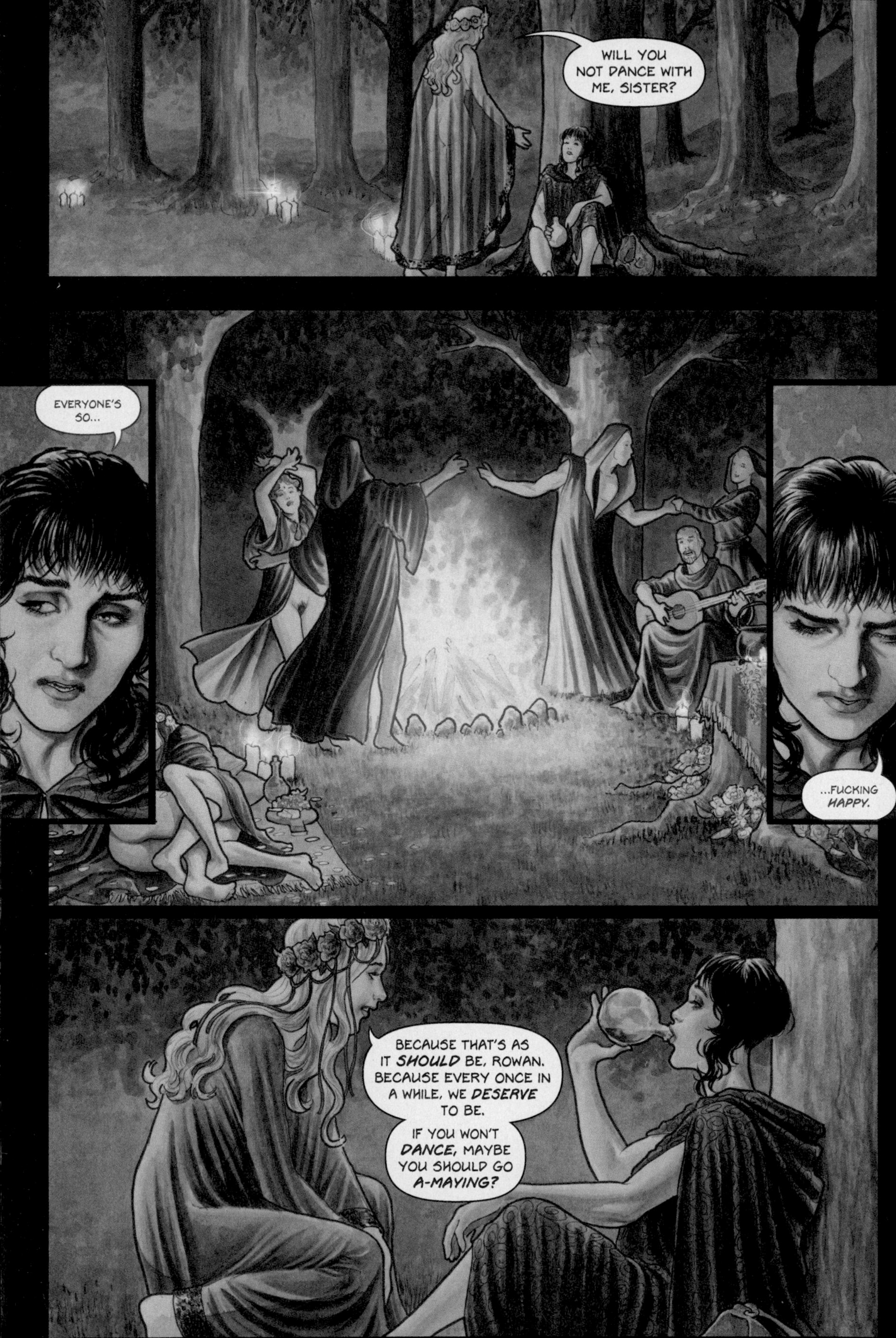
WILL YOU NOT DANCE WITH ME, SISTER?
EVERYONE'S SO...
...FUCKING *HAPPY.*
BECAUSE THAT'S AS IT *SHOULD* BE, ROWAN. BECAUSE EVERY ONCE IN A WHILE, WE *DESERVE* TO BE.
IF YOU WON'T *DANCE*, MAYBE YOU SHOULD GO *A-MAYING?*

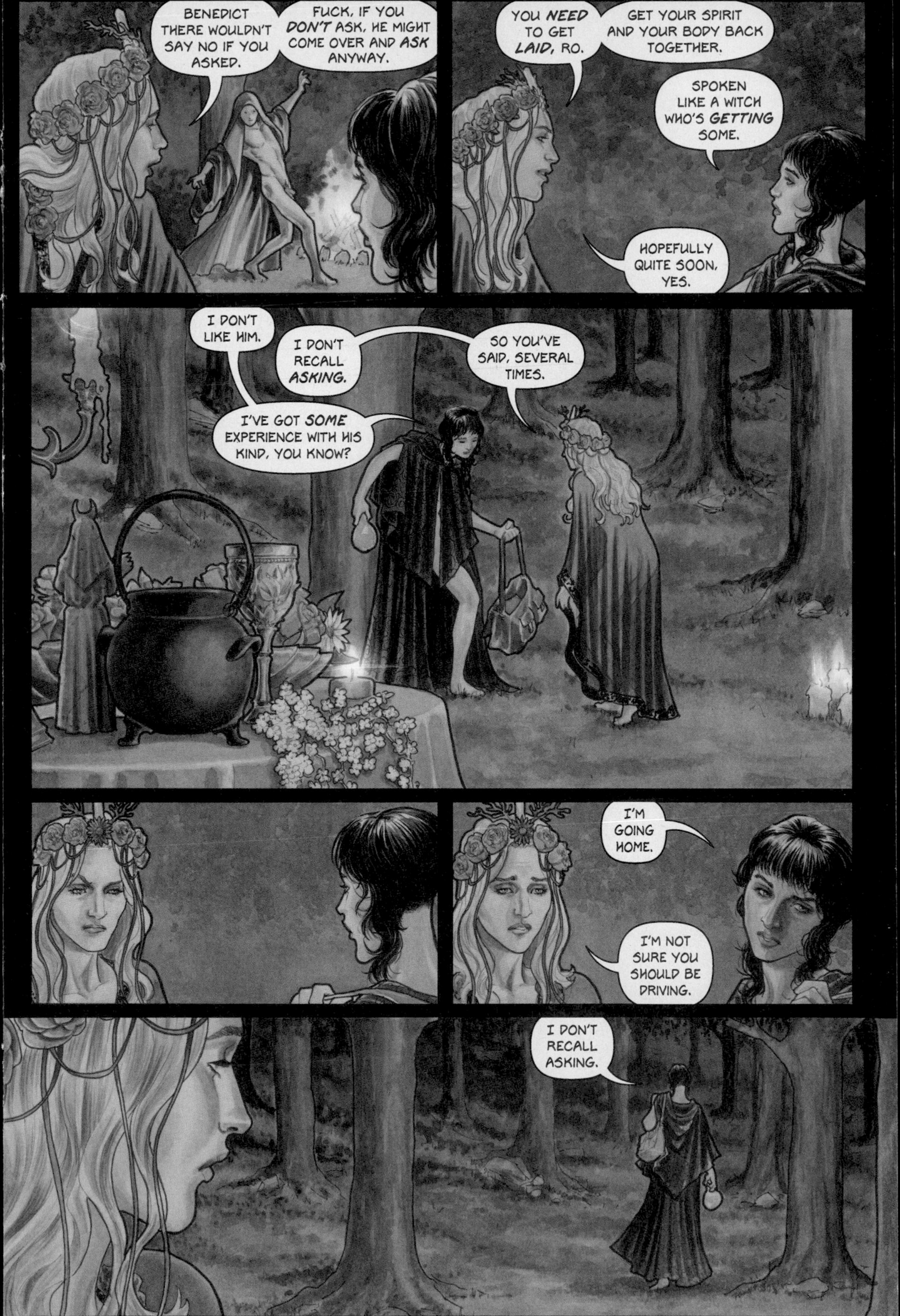
BENEDICT THERE WOULDN'T SAY NO IF YOU ASKED.
FUCK, IF YOU DON'T ASK, HE MIGHT COME OVER AND ASK ANYWAY.
YOU NEED TO GET LAID, RO.
GET YOUR SPIRIT AND YOUR BODY BACK TOGETHER.
SPOKEN LIKE A WITCH WHO'S GETTING SOME.
HOPEFULLY QUITE SOON, YES.
I DON'T LIKE HIM.
I DON'T RECALL ASKING.
SO YOU'VE SAID, SEVERAL TIMES.
I'VE GOT SOME EXPERIENCE WITH HIS KIND, YOU KNOW?
I'M GOING HOME.
I'M NOT SURE YOU SHOULD BE DRIVING.
I DON'T RECALL ASKING.

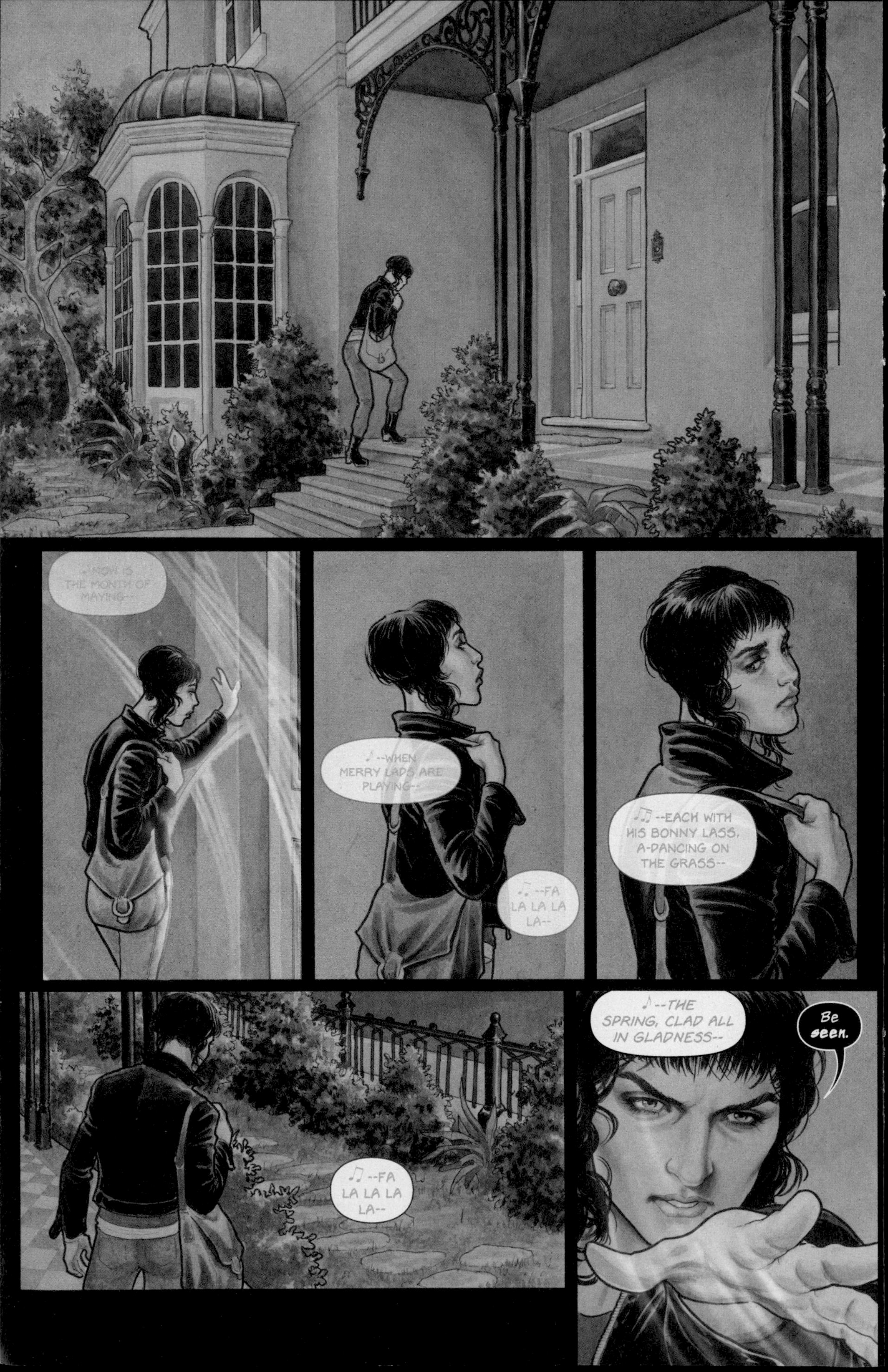
NOW IS THE MONTH OF MAYING--
♪--WHEN MERRY LADS ARE PLAYING--
♪--FA LA LA LA LA--
♫--EACH WITH HIS BONNY LASS, A-DANCING ON THE GRASS--
♫--FA LA LA LA LA--
♪--THE SPRING, CLAD ALL IN GLADNESS--
Be seen.

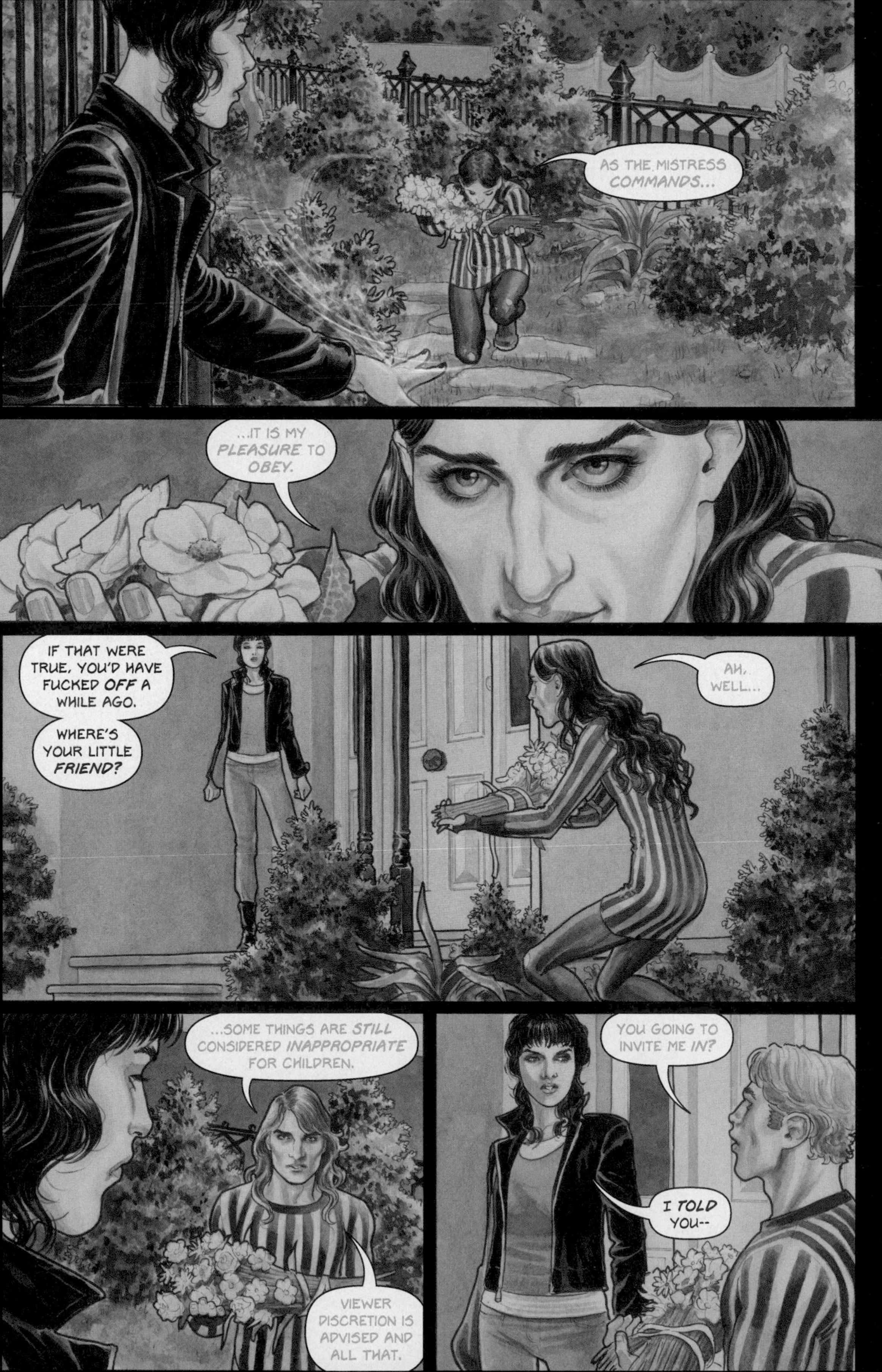
AS THE MISTRESS COMMANDS...
...IT IS MY PLEASURE TO OBEY.
IF THAT WERE TRUE, YOU'D HAVE FUCKED OFF A WHILE AGO.
WHERE'S YOUR LITTLE FRIEND?
AH, WELL...
...SOME THINGS ARE STILL CONSIDERED INAPPROPRIATE FOR CHILDREN.
VIEWER DISCRETION IS ADVISED AND ALL THAT.
YOU GOING TO INVITE ME IN?
I TOLD YOU--

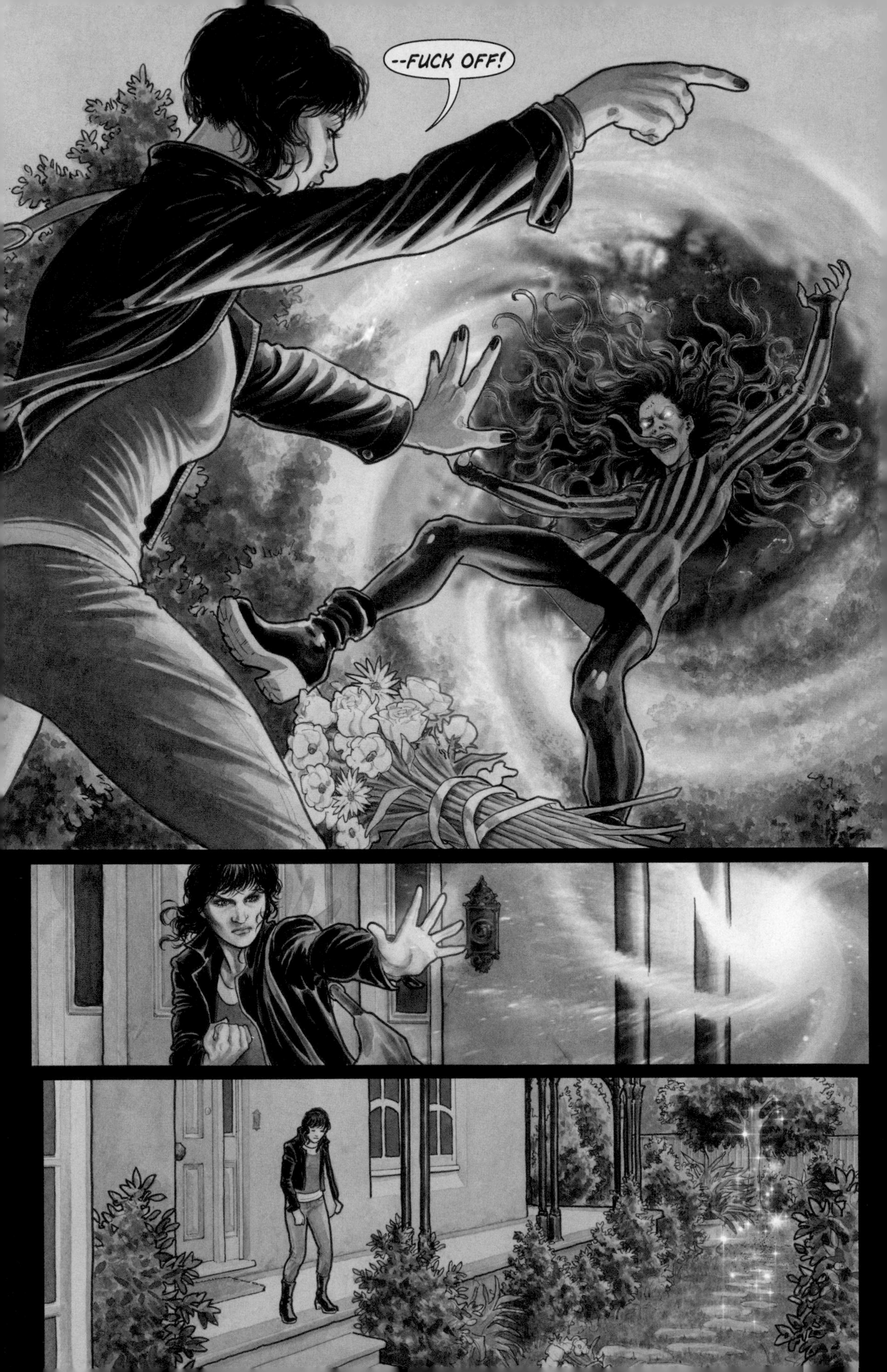
--FUCK OFF!

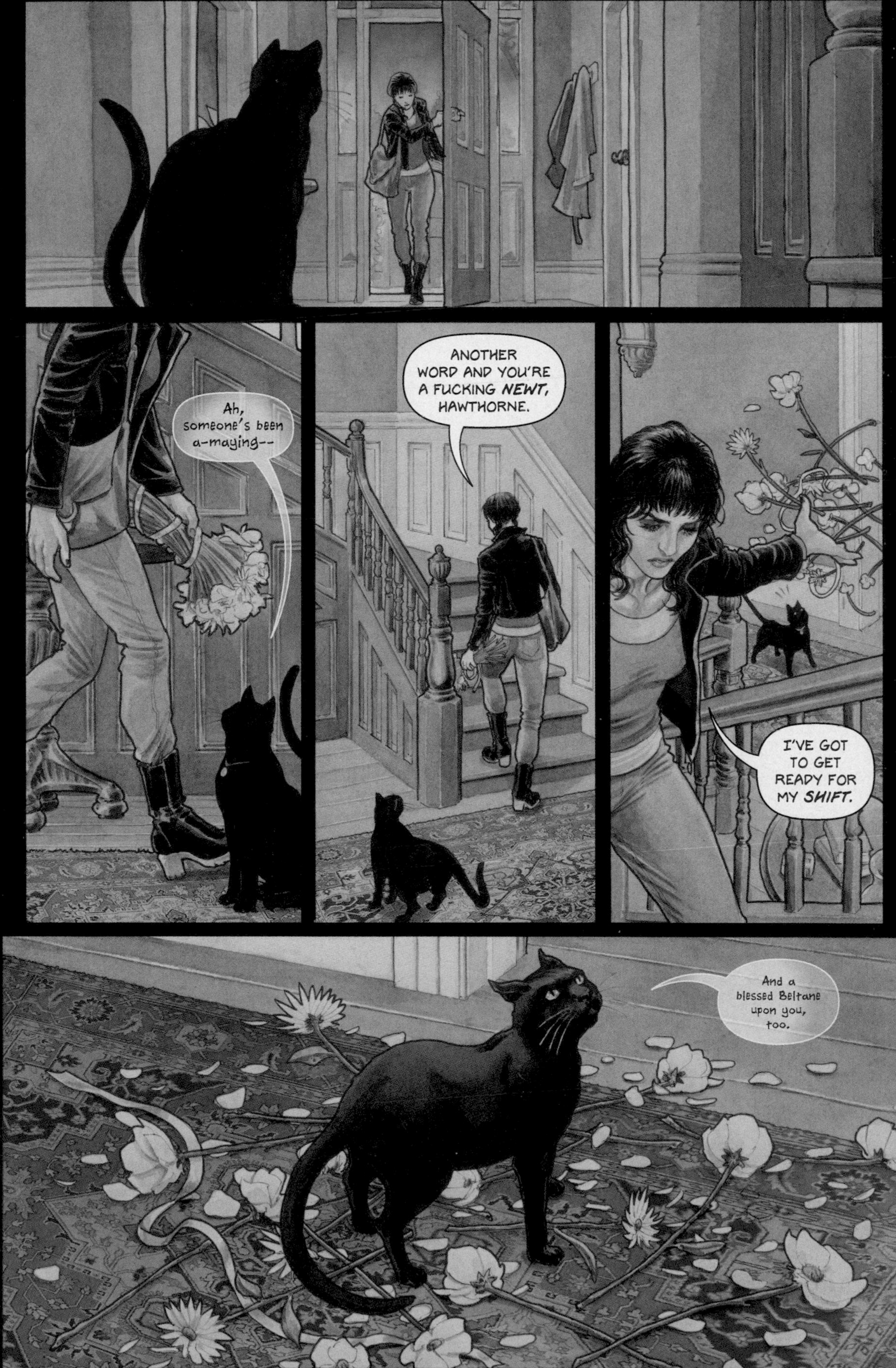
Ah, someone's been a-maying--
ANOTHER WORD AND YOU'RE A FUCKING NEWT, HAWTHORNE.
I'VE GOT TO GET READY FOR MY SHIFT.
And a blessed Beltane upon you, too.

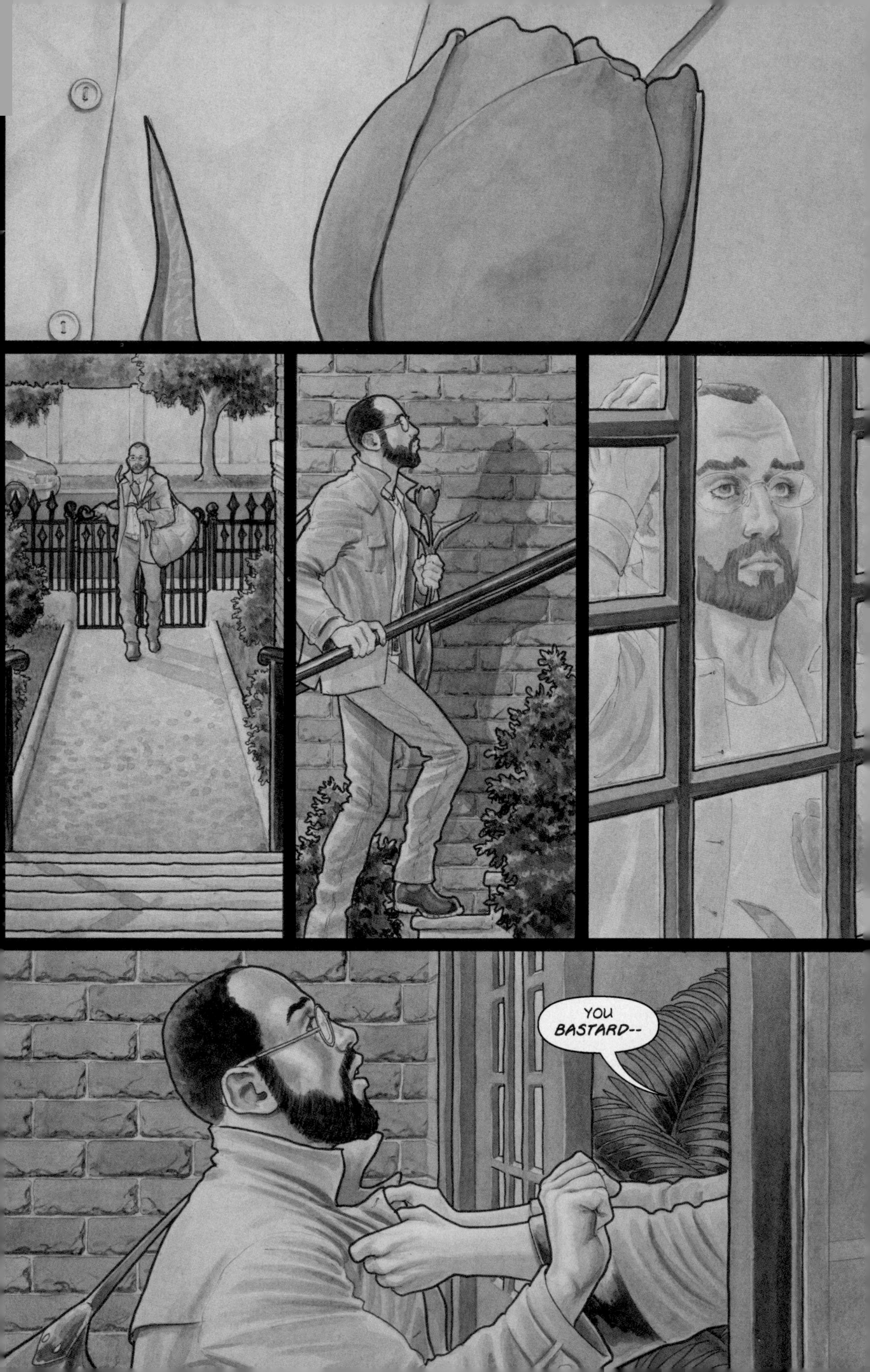
YOU BASTARD--

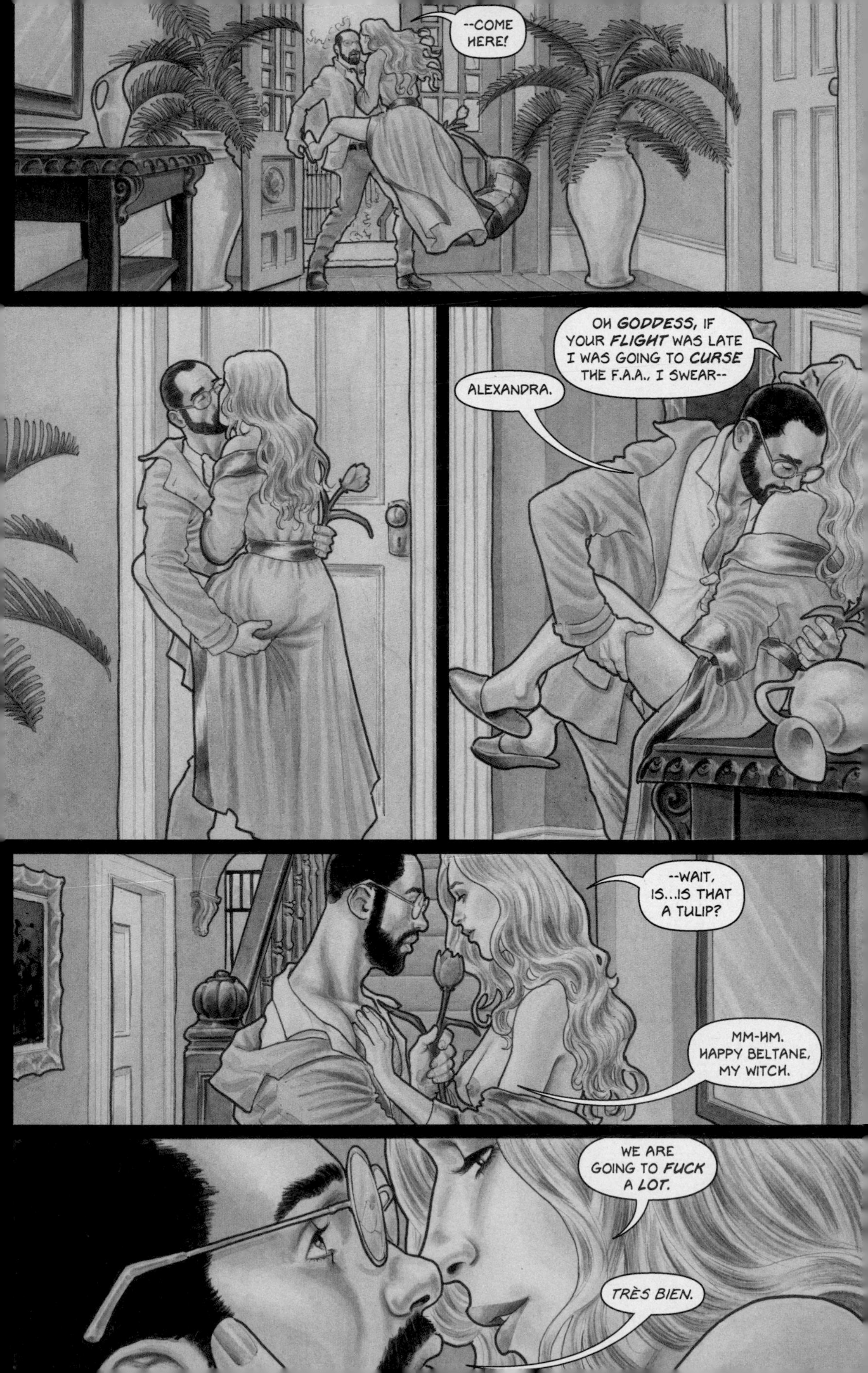
--COME HERE!
OH GODDESS, IF YOUR FLIGHT WAS LATE I WAS GOING TO CURSE THE F.A.A., I SWEAR--
ALEXANDRA.
--WAIT, IS...IS THAT A TULIP?
MM-HM. HAPPY BELTANE, MY WITCH.
WE ARE GOING TO FUCK A LOT.
TRÈS BIEN.

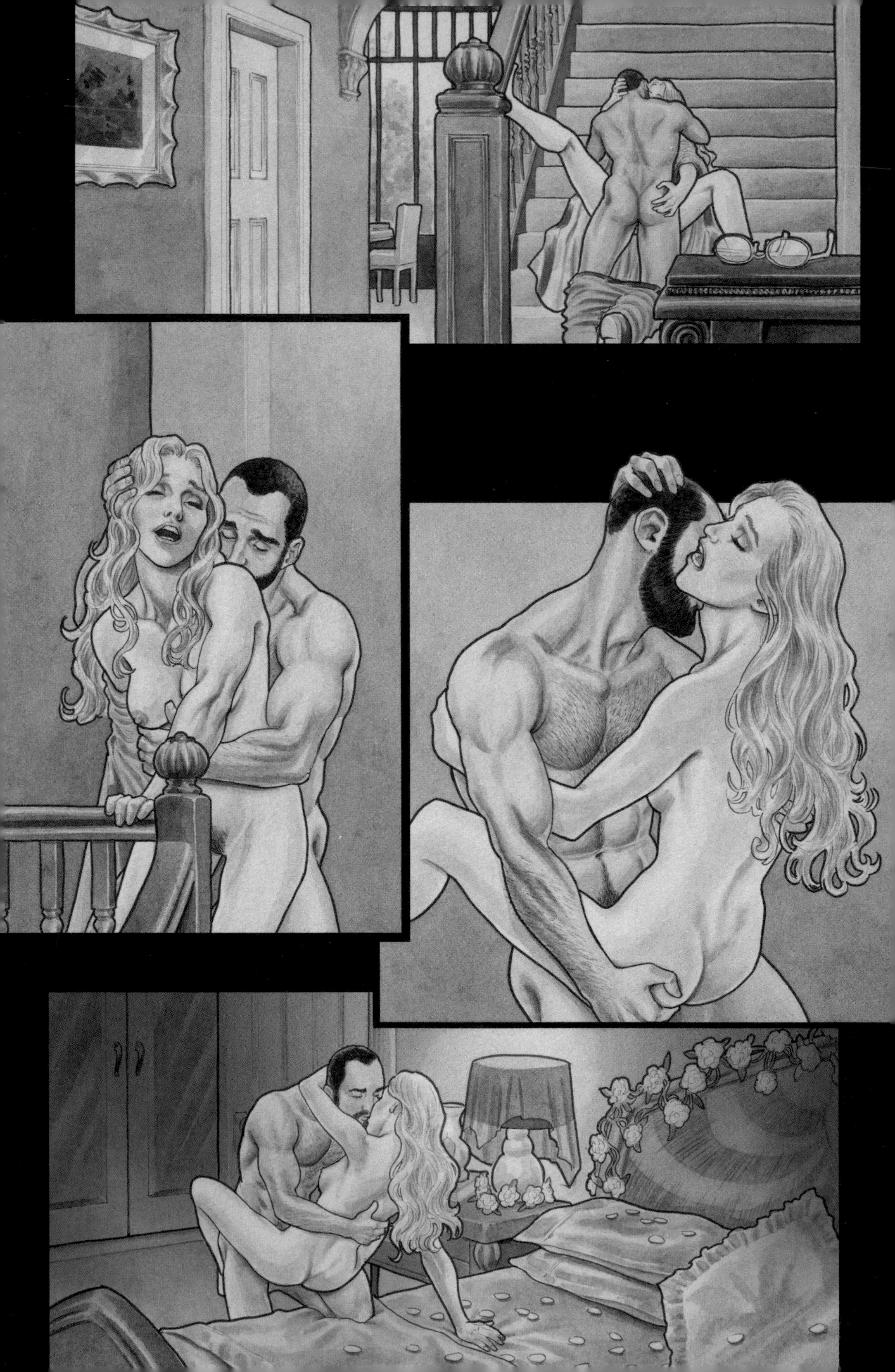

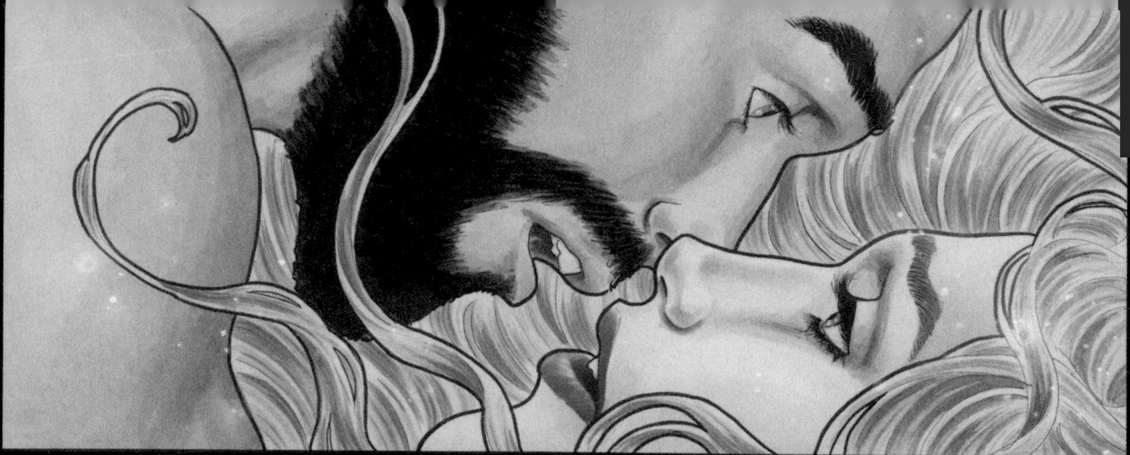

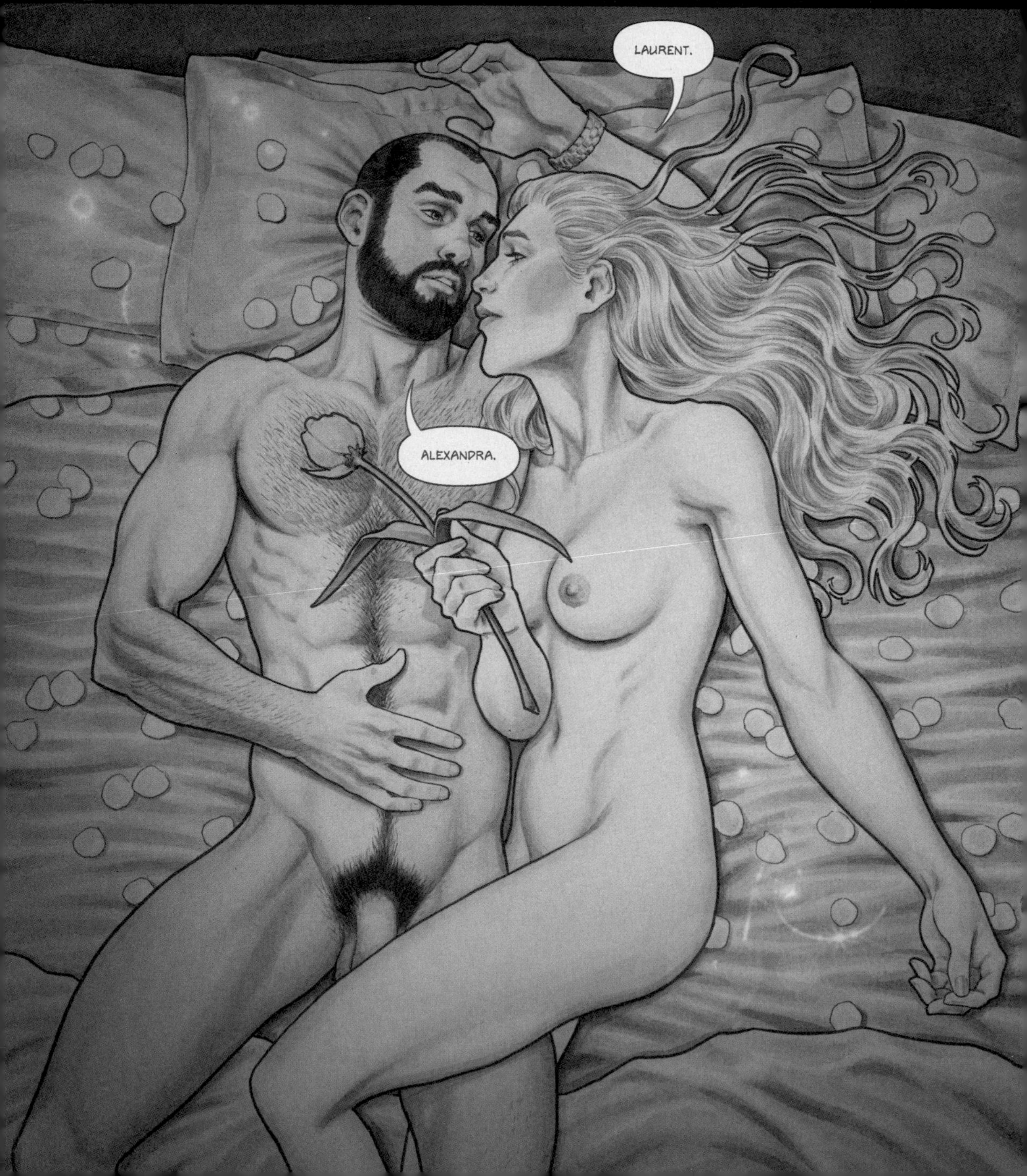
LAURENT.
ALEXANDRA.

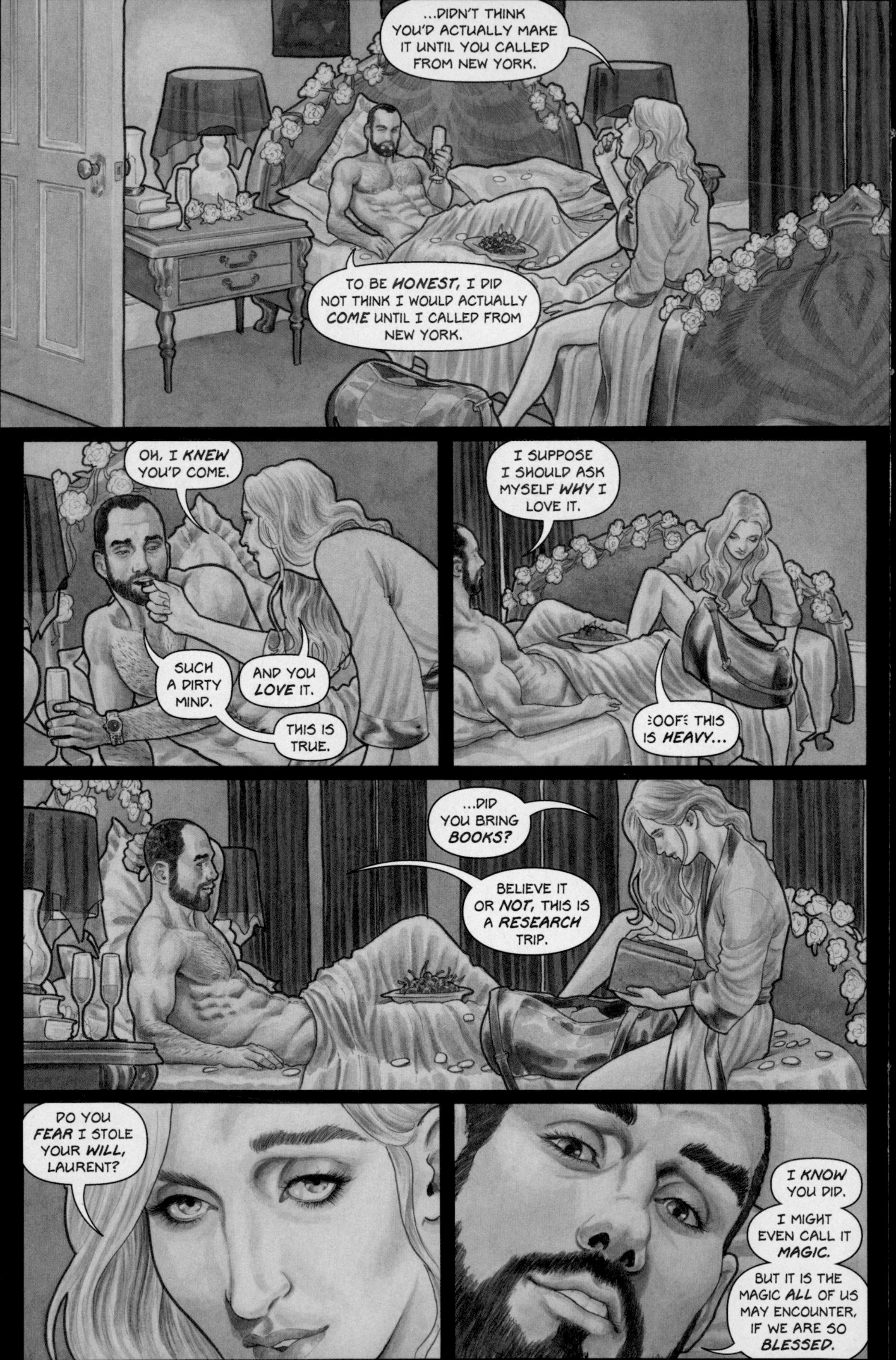
...DIDN'T THINK YOU'D ACTUALLY MAKE IT UNTIL YOU CALLED FROM NEW YORK.
TO BE *HONEST,* I DID NOT THINK I WOULD ACTUALLY *COME* UNTIL I CALLED FROM NEW YORK.
OH, I *KNEW* YOU'D COME.
SUCH A DIRTY MIND.
AND YOU *LOVE* IT.
THIS IS TRUE.
I SUPPOSE I SHOULD ASK MYSELF *WHY* I LOVE IT.
OOF THIS IS *HEAVY...*
...DID YOU BRING *BOOKS?*
BELIEVE IT OR *NOT,* THIS IS A *RESEARCH* TRIP.
DO YOU *FEAR* I STOLE YOUR *WILL,* LAURENT?
I *KNOW* YOU DID.
I MIGHT EVEN CALL IT *MAGIC.*
BUT IT IS THE MAGIC *ALL* OF US MAY ENCOUNTER, IF WE ARE SO *BLESSED.*

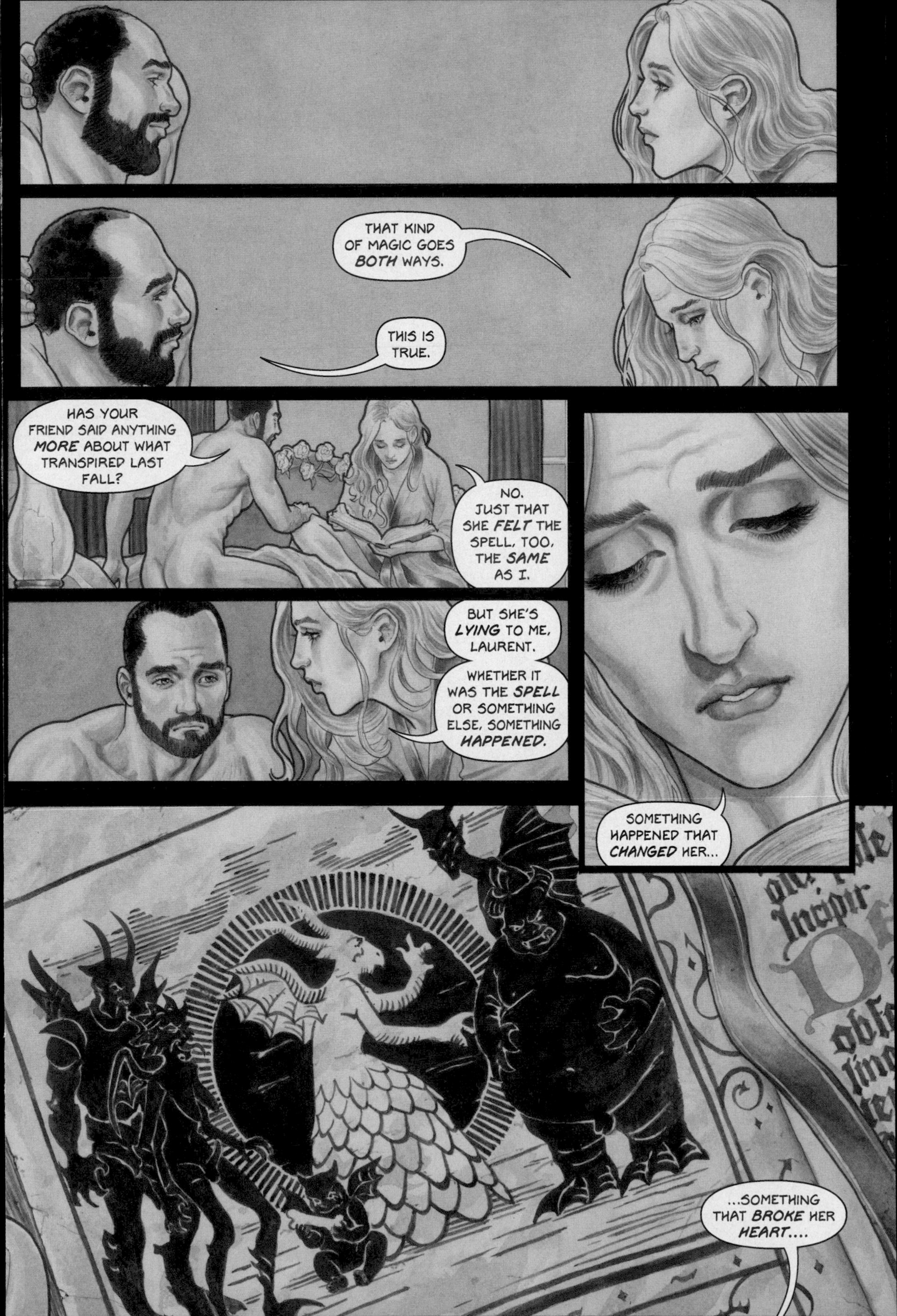
THAT KIND OF MAGIC GOES *BOTH* WAYS.
THIS IS TRUE.
HAS YOUR FRIEND SAID ANYTHING *MORE* ABOUT WHAT TRANSPIRED LAST FALL?
NO. JUST THAT SHE *FELT* THE SPELL, TOO, THE *SAME* AS I.
BUT SHE'S *LYING* TO ME, LAURENT.
WHETHER IT WAS THE *SPELL* OR SOMETHING ELSE, SOMETHING *HAPPENED*.
SOMETHING HAPPENED THAT *CHANGED* HER...
...SOMETHING THAT *BROKE* HER *HEART*....

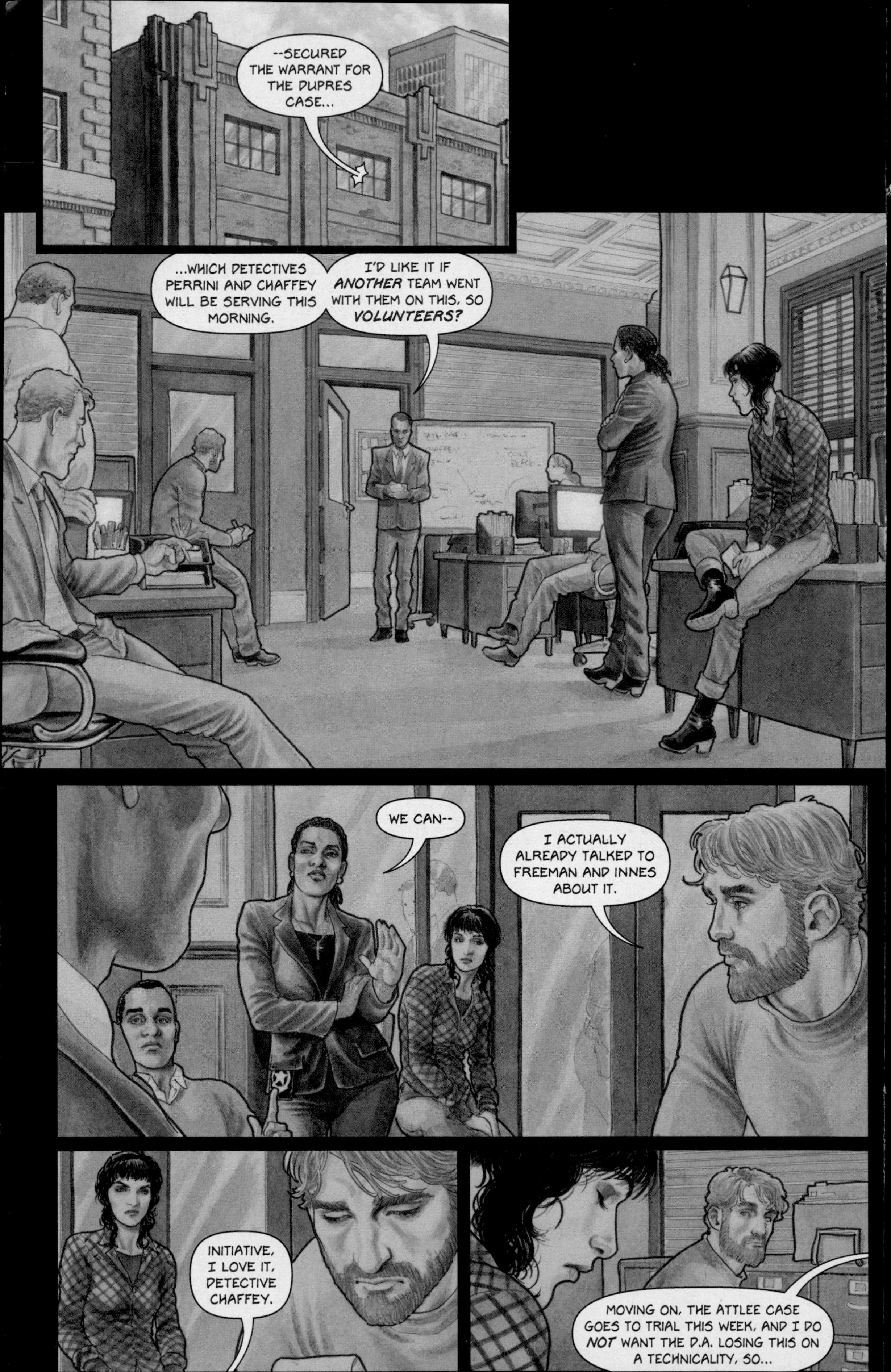
--SECURED THE WARRANT FOR THE DUPRES CASE...
...WHICH DETECTIVES PERRINI AND CHAFFEY WILL BE SERVING THIS MORNING.
I'D LIKE IT IF *ANOTHER* TEAM WENT WITH THEM ON THIS, SO *VOLUNTEERS?*
WE CAN--
I ACTUALLY ALREADY TALKED TO FREEMAN AND INNES ABOUT IT.
INITIATIVE, I LOVE IT, DETECTIVE CHAFFEY.
MOVING ON, THE ATTLEE CASE GOES TO TRIAL THIS WEEK, AND I DO *NOT* WANT THE D.A. LOSING THIS ON A TECHNICALITY, SO...

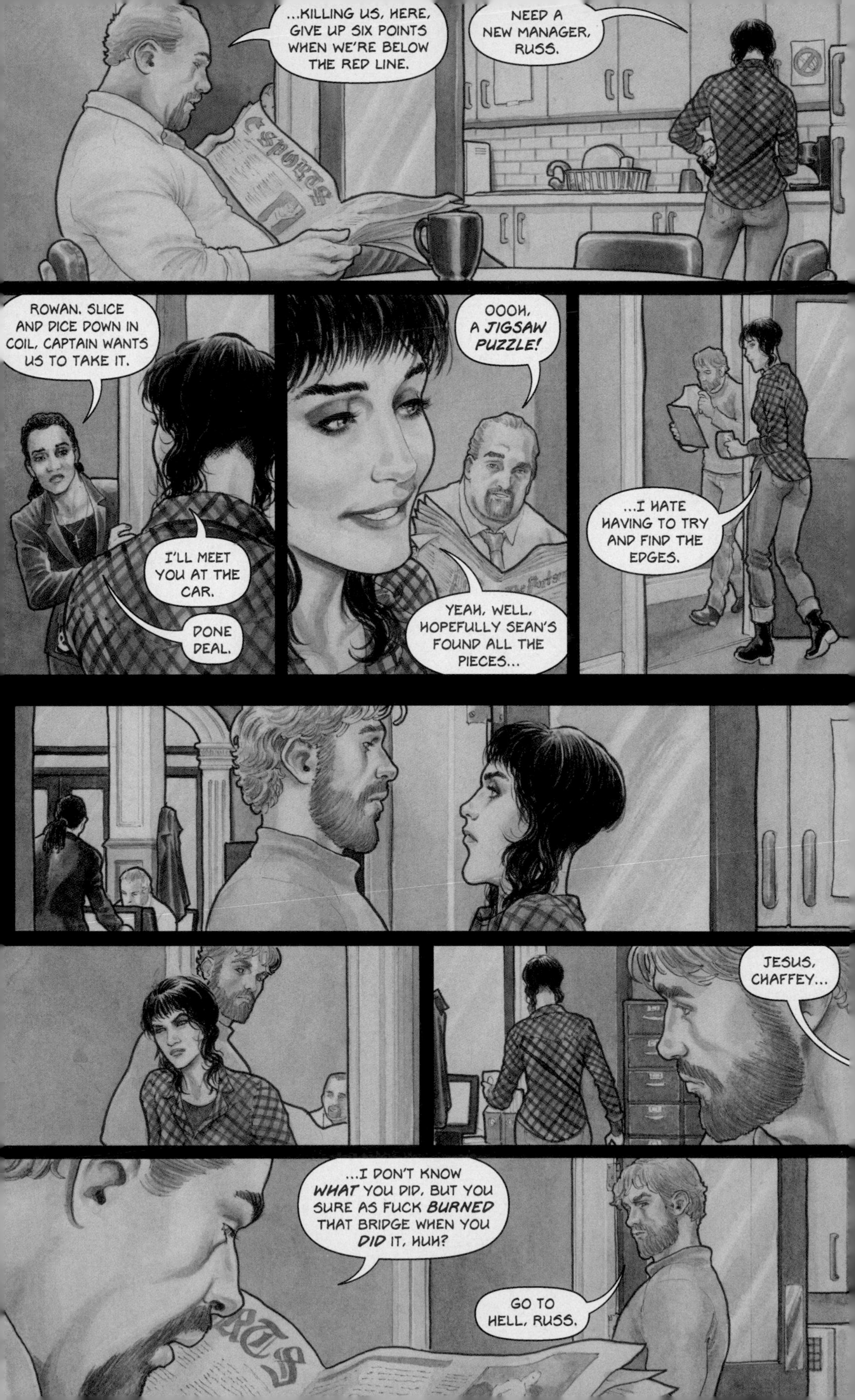

...KILLING US, HERE, GIVE UP SIX POINTS WHEN WE'RE BELOW THE RED LINE.
NEED A NEW MANAGER, RUSS.
ROWAN. SLICE AND DICE DOWN IN COIL, CAPTAIN WANTS US TO TAKE IT.
I'LL MEET YOU AT THE CAR.
DONE DEAL.
OOOH, A *JIGSAW PUZZLE!*
YEAH, WELL, HOPEFULLY SEAN'S FOUND ALL THE PIECES...
...I HATE HAVING TO TRY AND FIND THE EDGES.
JESUS, CHAFFEY...
...I DON'T KNOW ***WHAT*** YOU DID, BUT YOU SURE AS FUCK ***BURNED*** THAT BRIDGE WHEN YOU ***DID*** IT, HUH?
GO TO HELL, RUSS.

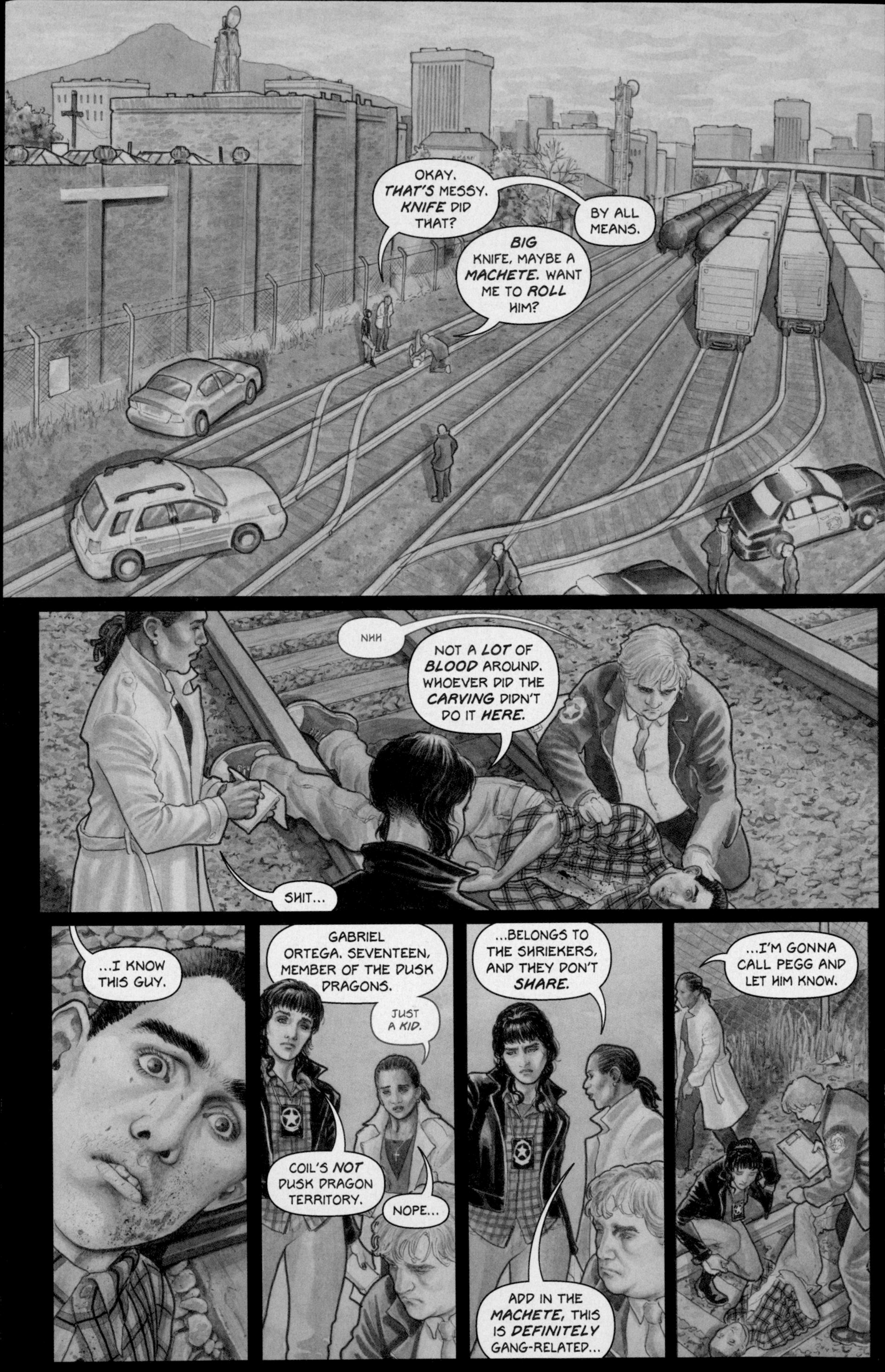
OKAY. THAT'S MESSY. KNIFE DID THAT?
BY ALL MEANS.
BIG KNIFE, MAYBE A MACHETE. WANT ME TO ROLL HIM?
NHH
NOT A LOT OF BLOOD AROUND. WHOEVER DID THE CARVING DIDN'T DO IT HERE.
SHIT...
...I KNOW THIS GUY.
GABRIEL ORTEGA. SEVENTEEN, MEMBER OF THE DUSK DRAGONS.
JUST A KID.
COIL'S NOT DUSK DRAGON TERRITORY.
NOPE...
...BELONGS TO THE SHRIEKERS, AND THEY DON'T SHARE.
ADD IN THE MACHETE, THIS IS DEFINITELY GANG-RELATED...
...I'M GONNA CALL PEGG AND LET HIM KNOW.

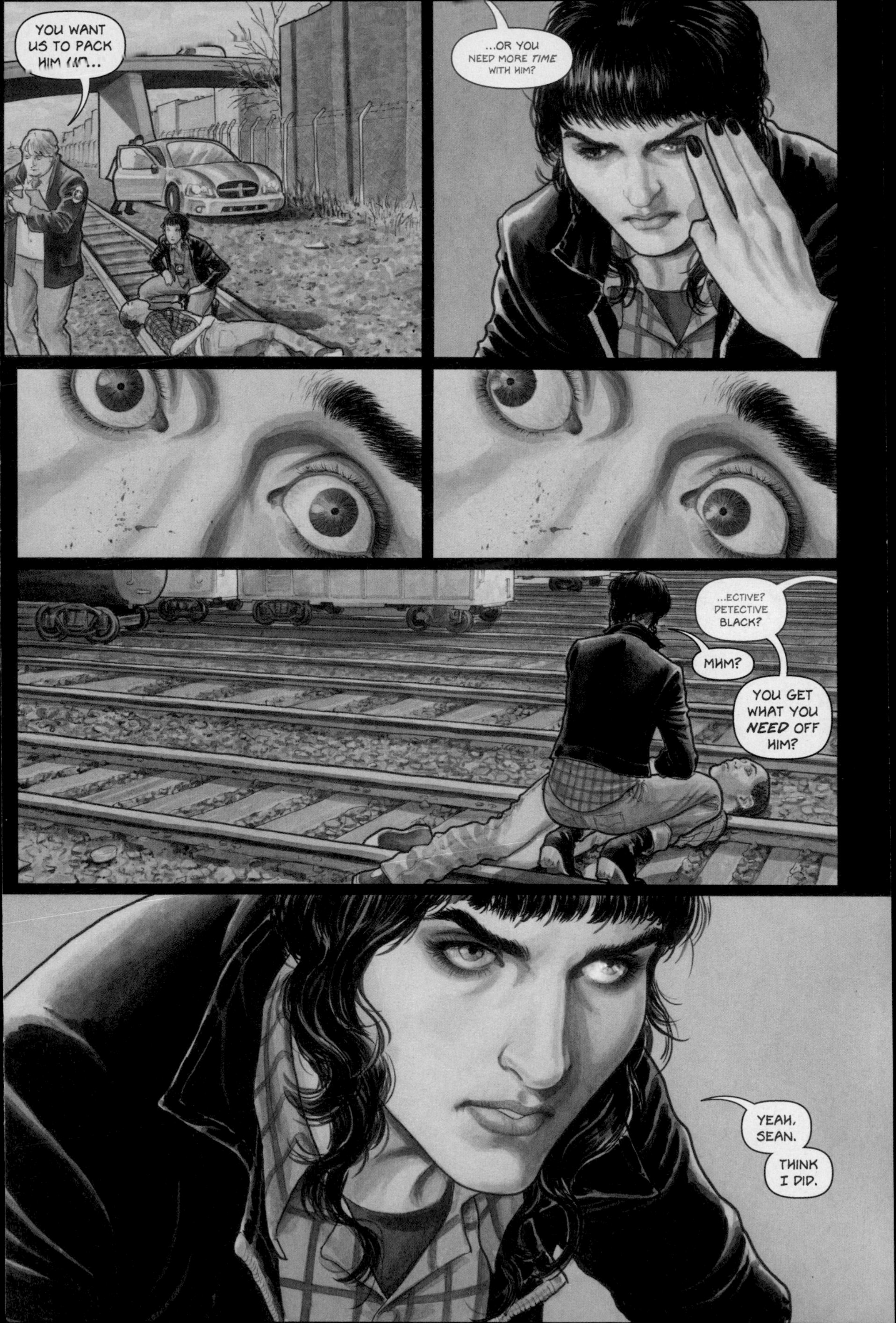
YOU WANT US TO PACK HIM UP...
...OR YOU NEED MORE *TIME* WITH HIM?
...ECTIVE? DETECTIVE BLACK?
MHM?
YOU GET WHAT YOU ***NEED*** OFF HIM?
YEAH, SEAN.
THINK I DID.

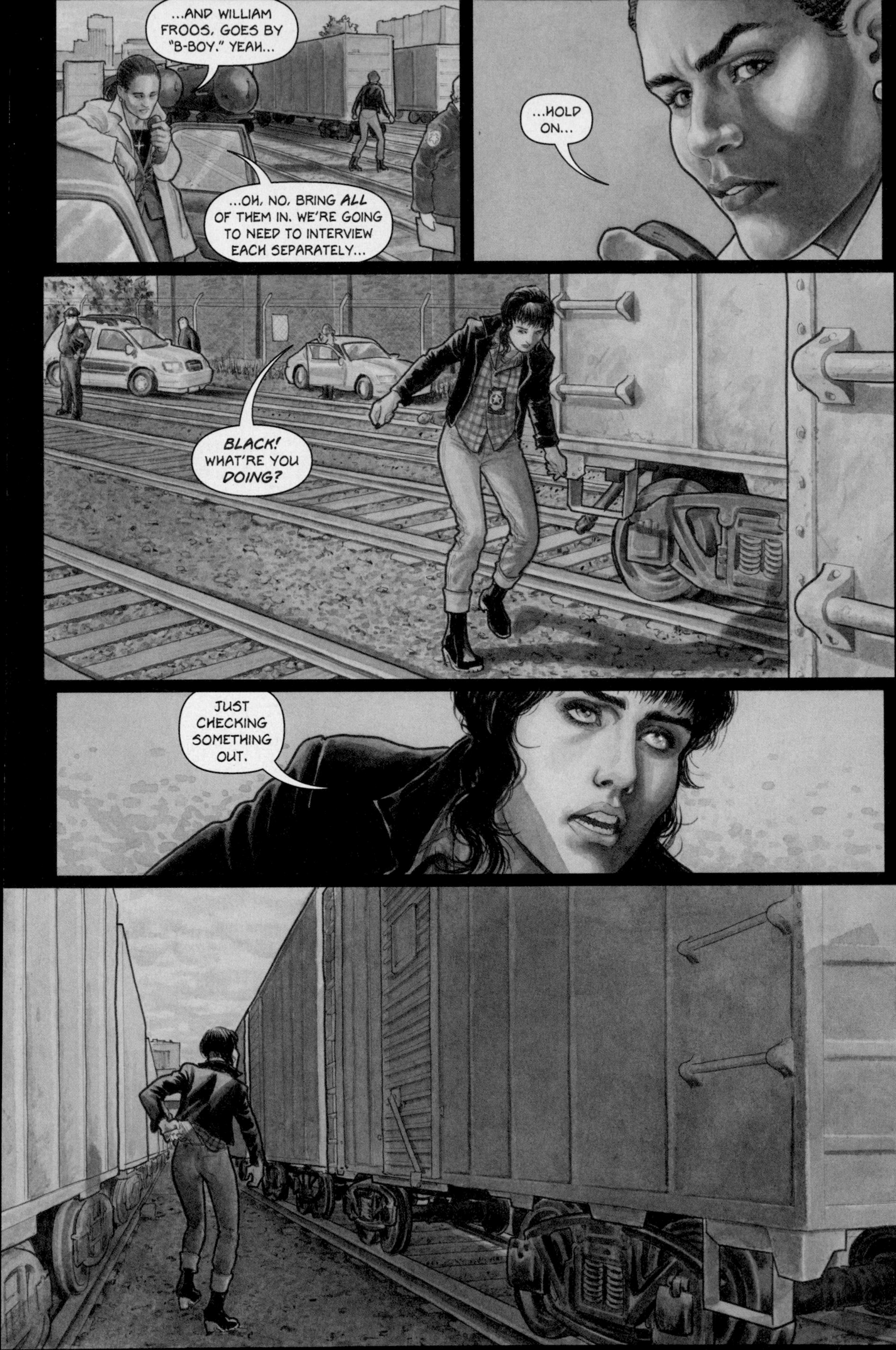
...AND WILLIAM FROOS, GOES BY "B-BOY." YEAH...
...OH, NO, BRING ALL OF THEM IN. WE'RE GOING TO NEED TO INTERVIEW EACH SEPARATELY...
...HOLD ON...
BLACK! WHAT'RE YOU DOING?
JUST CHECKING SOMETHING OUT.

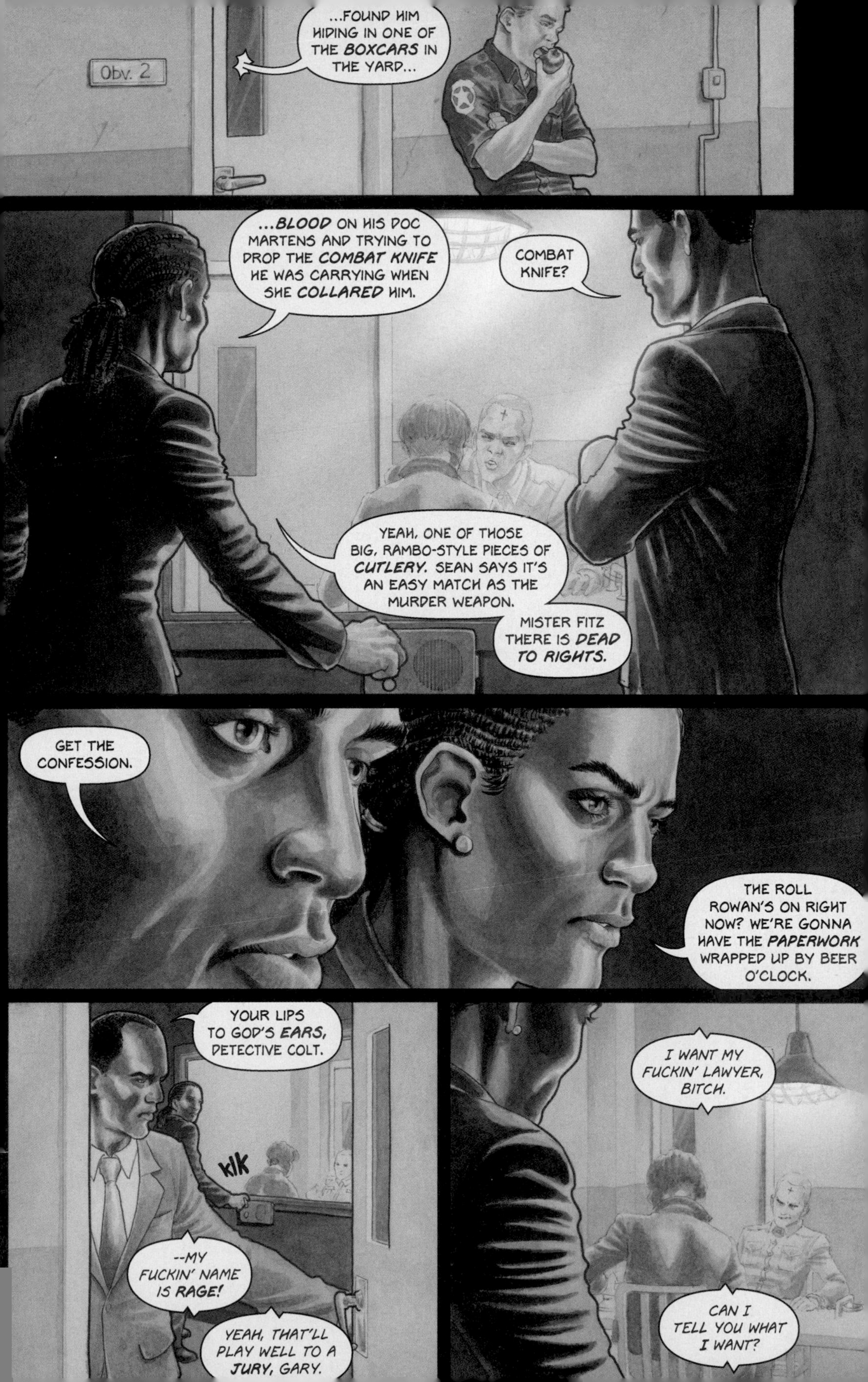
Obv. 2
...FOUND HIM HIDING IN ONE OF THE BOXCARS IN THE YARD...
...BLOOD ON HIS DOC MARTENS AND TRYING TO DROP THE COMBAT KNIFE HE WAS CARRYING WHEN SHE COLLARED HIM.
COMBAT KNIFE?
YEAH, ONE OF THOSE BIG, RAMBO-STYLE PIECES OF CUTLERY. SEAN SAYS IT'S AN EASY MATCH AS THE MURDER WEAPON.
MISTER FITZ THERE IS DEAD TO RIGHTS.
GET THE CONFESSION.
THE ROLL ROWAN'S ON RIGHT NOW? WE'RE GONNA HAVE THE PAPERWORK WRAPPED UP BY BEER O'CLOCK.
YOUR LIPS TO GOD'S EARS, DETECTIVE COLT.
KLIK
--MY FUCKIN' NAME IS RAGE!
YEAH, THAT'LL PLAY WELL TO A JURY, GARY.
I WANT MY FUCKIN' LAWYER, BITCH.
CAN I TELL YOU WHAT I WANT?

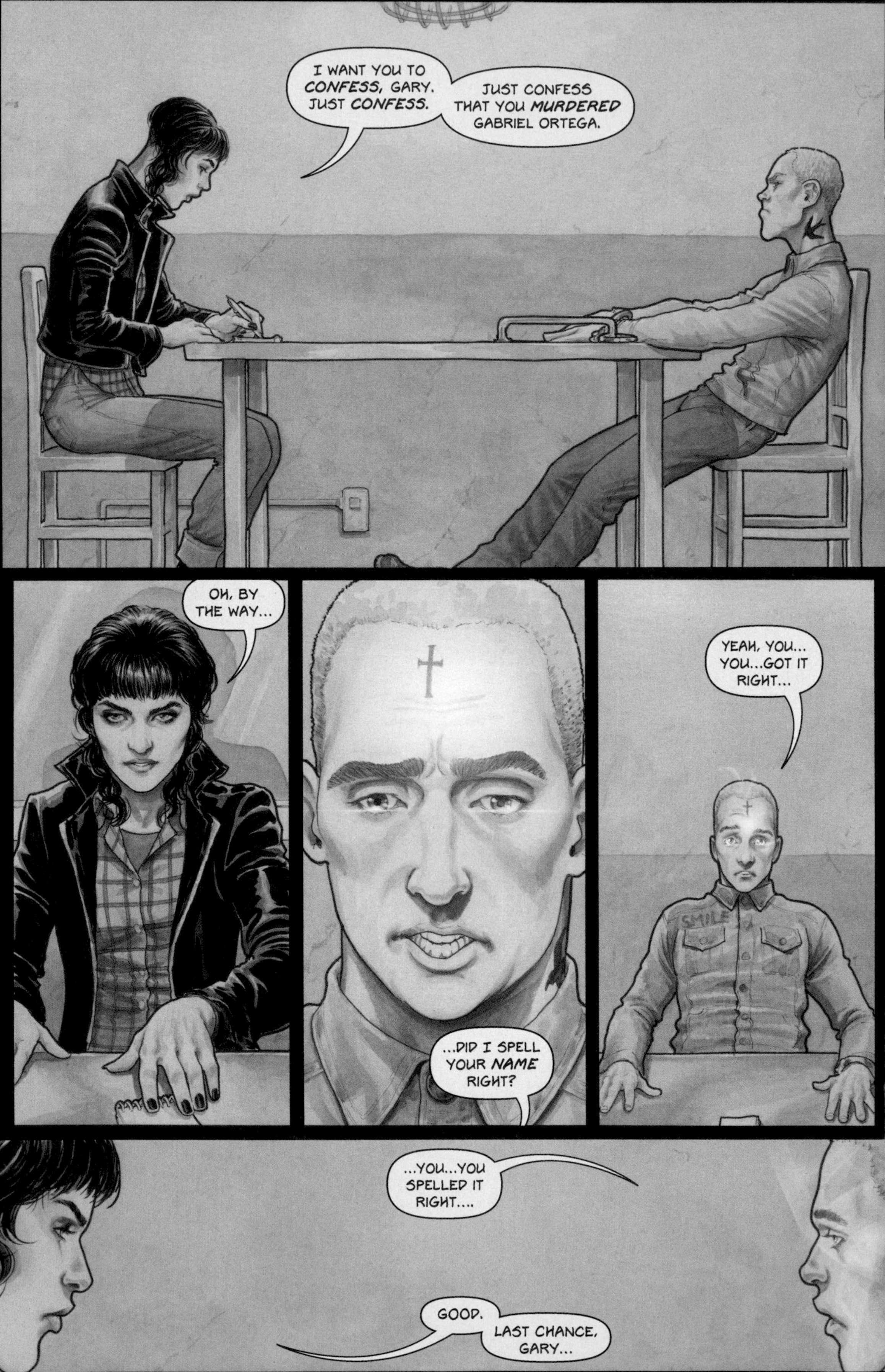

I WANT YOU TO CONFESS, GARY. JUST CONFESS.
JUST CONFESS THAT YOU MURDERED GABRIEL ORTEGA.
OH, BY THE WAY...
...DID I SPELL YOUR NAME RIGHT?
YEAH, YOU... YOU...GOT IT RIGHT...
...YOU...YOU SPELLED IT RIGHT....
GOOD.
LAST CHANCE, GARY...

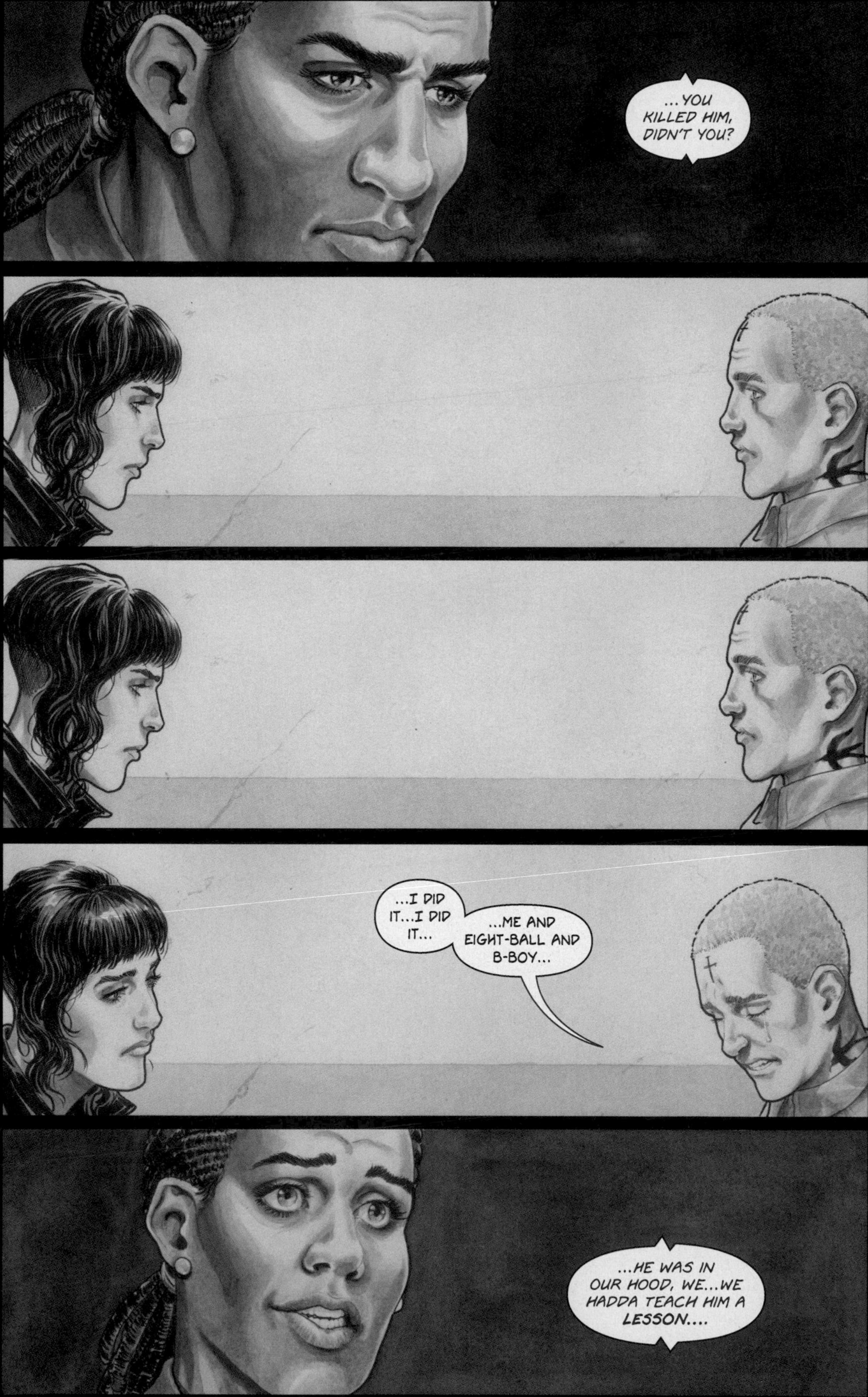
...YOU KILLED HIM, DIDN'T YOU?
...I DID IT...I DID IT...
...ME AND EIGHT-BALL AND B-BOY...
...HE WAS IN OUR HOOD, WE...WE HADDA TEACH HIM A LESSON....

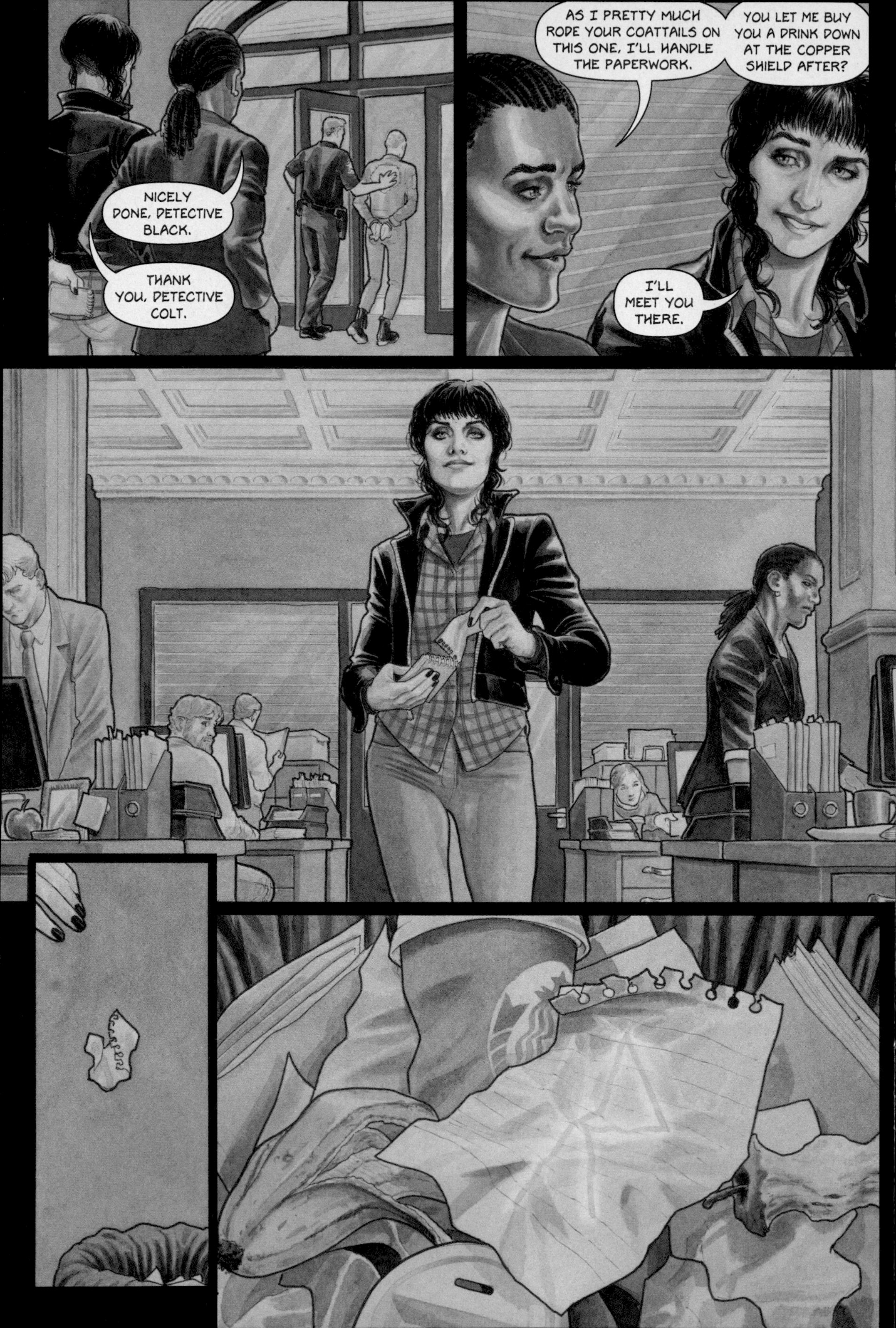
NICELY DONE, DETECTIVE BLACK.
THANK YOU, DETECTIVE COLT.
AS I PRETTY MUCH RODE YOUR COATTAILS ON THIS ONE, I'LL HANDLE THE PAPERWORK.
YOU LET ME BUY YOU A DRINK DOWN AT THE COPPER SHIELD AFTER?
I'LL MEET YOU THERE.

EPARTMENT

CITY OF PORTSMO

| ON KILLED | FIRST NAME | MIDDLE NAME | RACE | SEX | AGE | RESIDENCE OF PERSON KILLED | | OFFENSE SERIAL |

| | | TITLE OR RELATIONSHIP | RACE | SEX | AGE | ADDRESS OF PERSON KILLED | | PHONE OF PERSO |

| D (CRIME) | | | | | | AFTER INVESTIGATION CHANGED TO | | |

| NCE — STREET AND NUMBER OR INTERSECTION | | DIVISION | PLATOON | BEAT | OFFICER MAKING REPORT | I.D. NO. | NAME |

| TE OF OCCURENCE | TIME OF DAY | DATE REPORTED | TIME REPORTED | REPORT RECEIVED BY | | RECEIVED — TIME — TYPED |

DESCRIPTION OF DEAD PERSON

| WEIGHT | EYES | HAIR | BEARD | COMPLEXION | | SCARS, MARKS, ETC. | CLOTHING |

| NAME OF CORONER ATTENDING | TIME OF ARRIVAL | | | | PROSECUTOR ATTENDING — TIME OF ARRIVAL |

| D BY PHYSICIAN | | PERSON WITH WHOM ACCUSED LIVED OR ASSOCIATED |

| E (GIVE CIRCUMSTANCES OF OCCURENCE OF OFFENSE AND ITS INVESTIGATION) | USE OTHER SIDE OF THIS SHEET |

| CUSTODY | ADDRESS | WITNESS TAKEN INTO CUSTODY | ADDRESS |

| OR POSSIBLE MOTIVES | |

DESCRIPTION OF SUSPECTS OR PERSONS WANTED

| | ALIAS | ADDRESS | | RACE | AGE | HEIGHT | WEIGHT | EYES | HAIR | COMPLEXION |

| OCCUPATION | DRESS AND OTHER MARKS | CAUSE FOR SUSPICION | | | | | | | | |

| | ALIAS | ADDRESS | | RACE | AGE | HEIGHT | WEIGHT | EYES | HAIR | COMPLEXION |

| OCCUPATION | DRESS AND OTHER MARKS | CAUSE FOR SUSPICION | | | | | | | | |

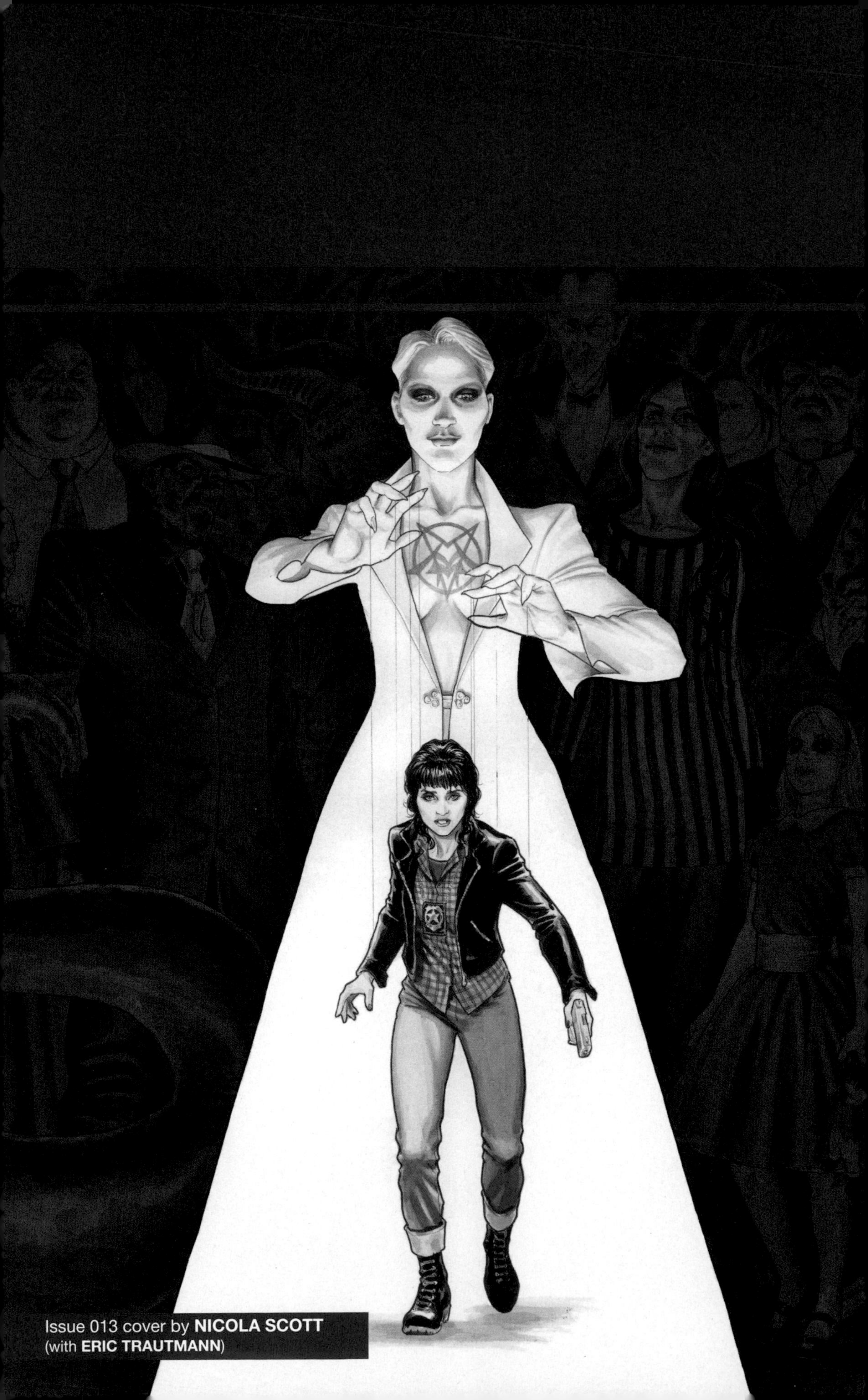

Issue 013 cover by **NICOLA SCOTT**
(with **ERIC TRAUTMANN**)

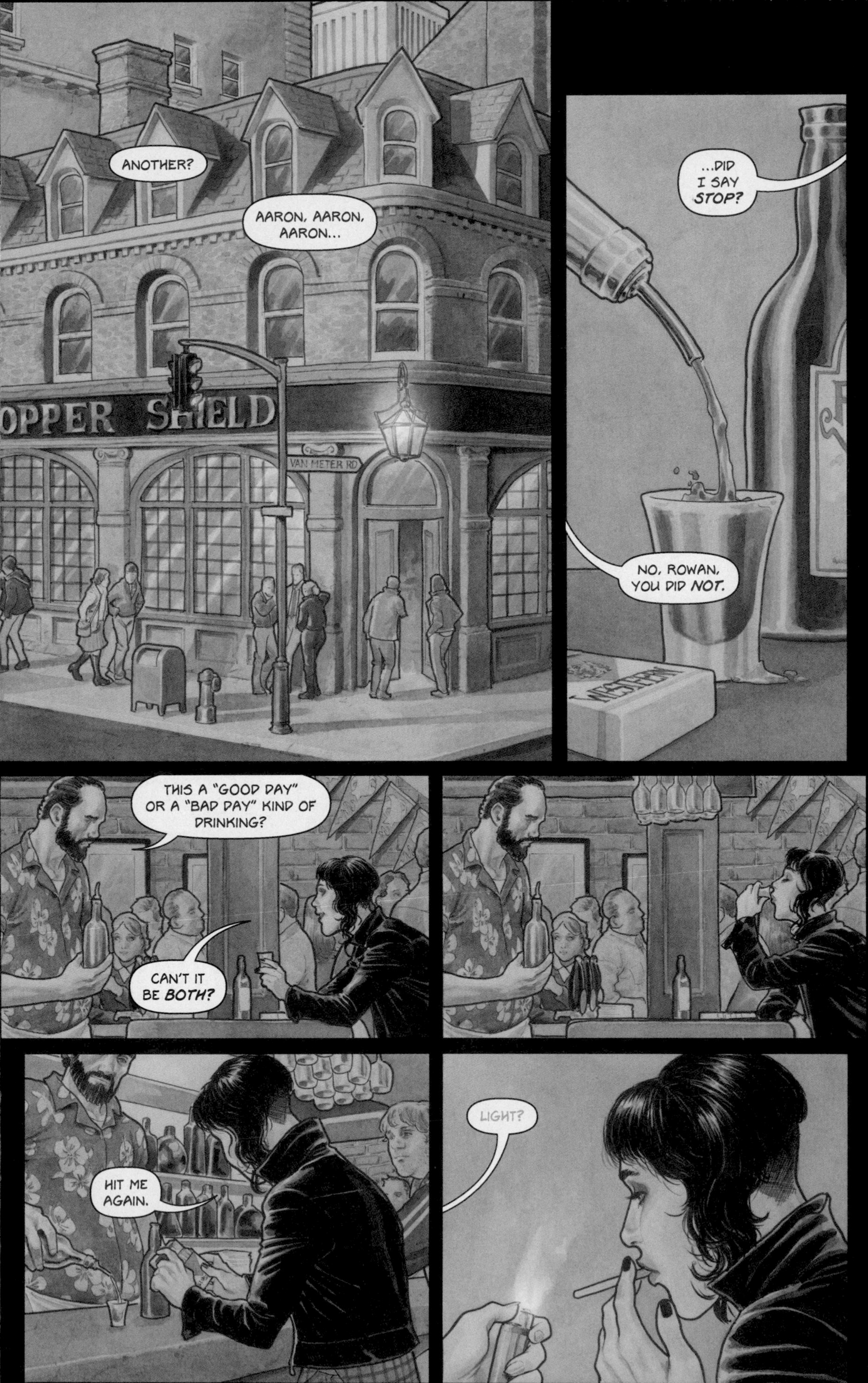
ANOTHER?
AARON, AARON, AARON...
COPPER SHIELD
VAN METER RD
...DID I SAY *STOP?*
NO, ROWAN, YOU DID *NOT*.
THIS A "GOOD DAY" OR A "BAD DAY" KIND OF DRINKING?
CAN'T IT BE *BOTH?*
HIT ME AGAIN.
LIGHT?

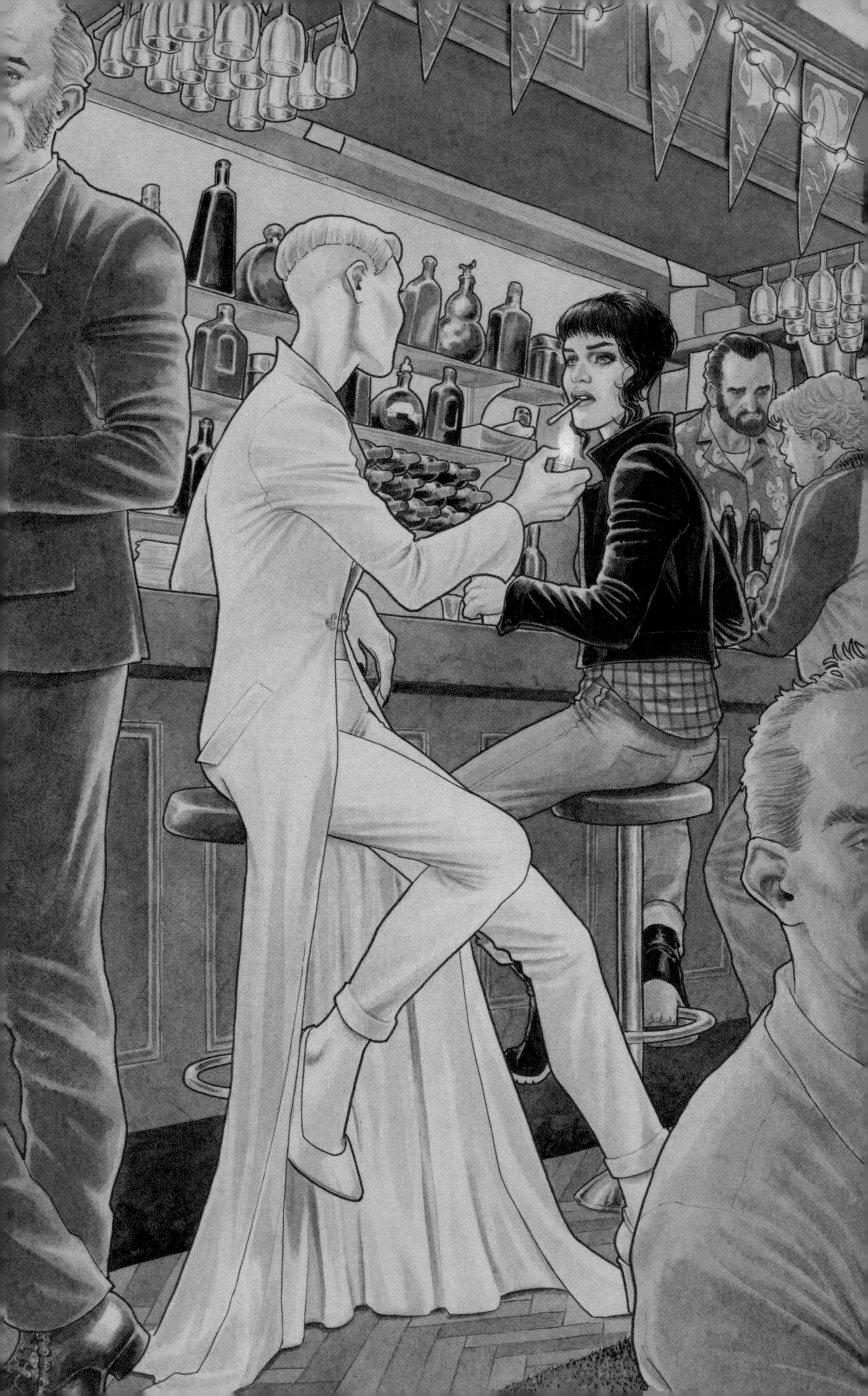

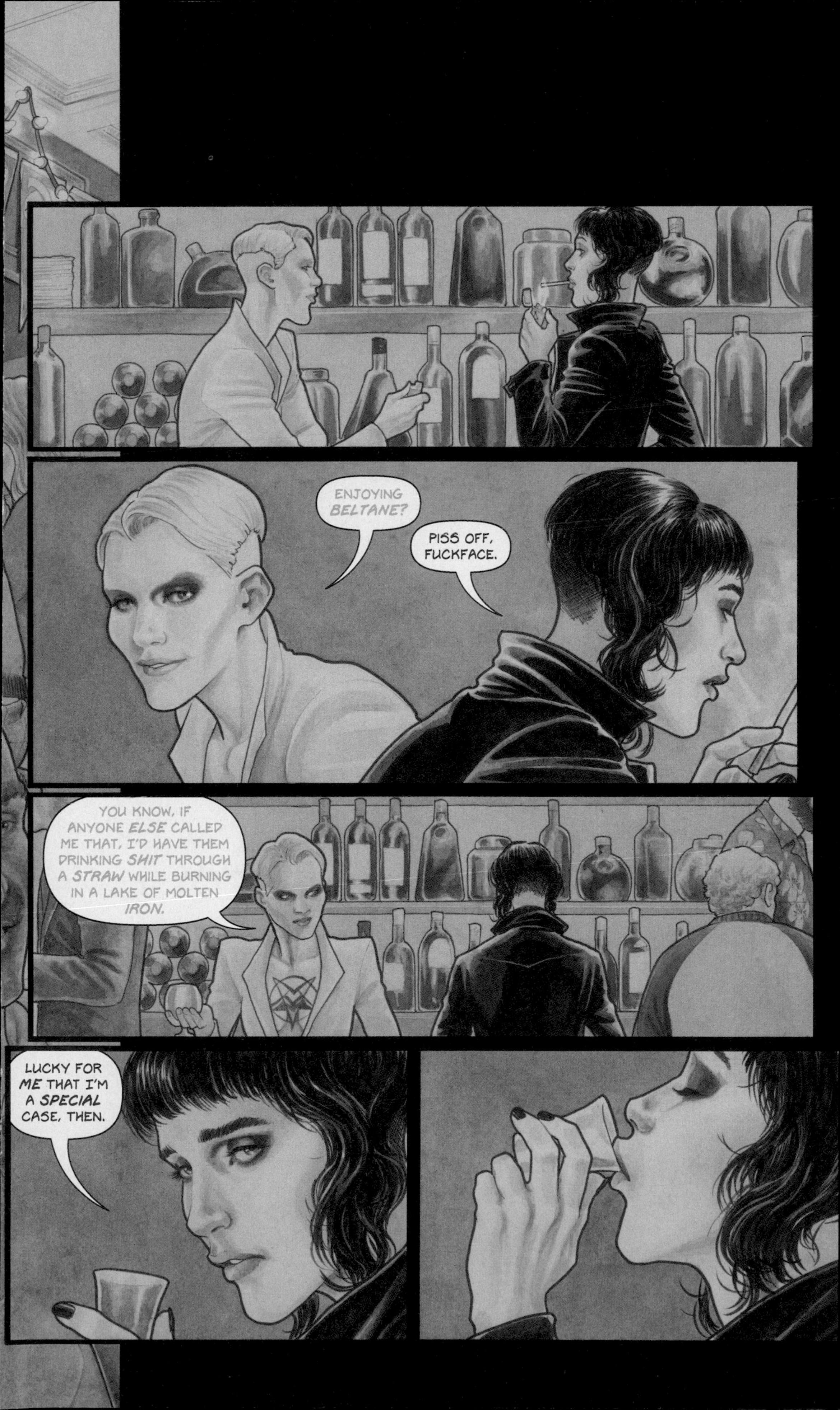
ENJOYING BELTANE?
PISS OFF, FUCKFACE.
YOU KNOW, IF ANYONE ELSE CALLED ME THAT, I'D HAVE THEM DRINKING SHIT THROUGH A STRAW WHILE BURNING IN A LAKE OF MOLTEN IRON.
LUCKY FOR ME THAT I'M A SPECIAL CASE, THEN.

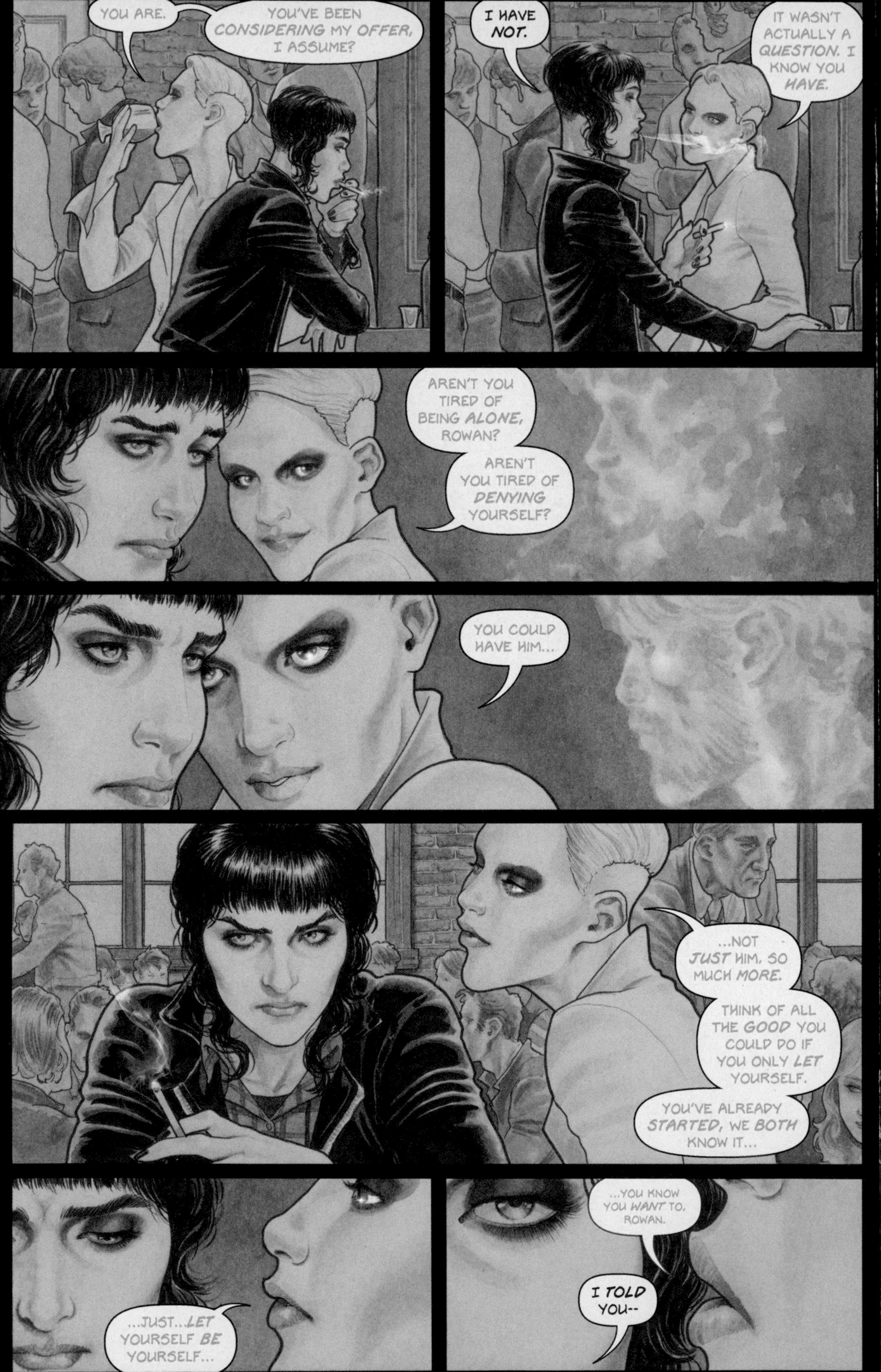

YOU ARE.
YOU'VE BEEN CONSIDERING MY OFFER, I ASSUME?
I HAVE NOT.
IT WASN'T ACTUALLY A QUESTION. I KNOW YOU HAVE.
AREN'T YOU TIRED OF BEING ALONE, ROWAN?
AREN'T YOU TIRED OF DENYING YOURSELF?
YOU COULD HAVE HIM...
...NOT JUST HIM. SO MUCH MORE.
THINK OF ALL THE GOOD YOU COULD DO IF YOU ONLY LET YOURSELF.
YOU'VE ALREADY STARTED, WE BOTH KNOW IT...
...JUST...LET YOURSELF BE YOURSELF...
...YOU KNOW YOU WANT TO, ROWAN.
I TOLD YOU--

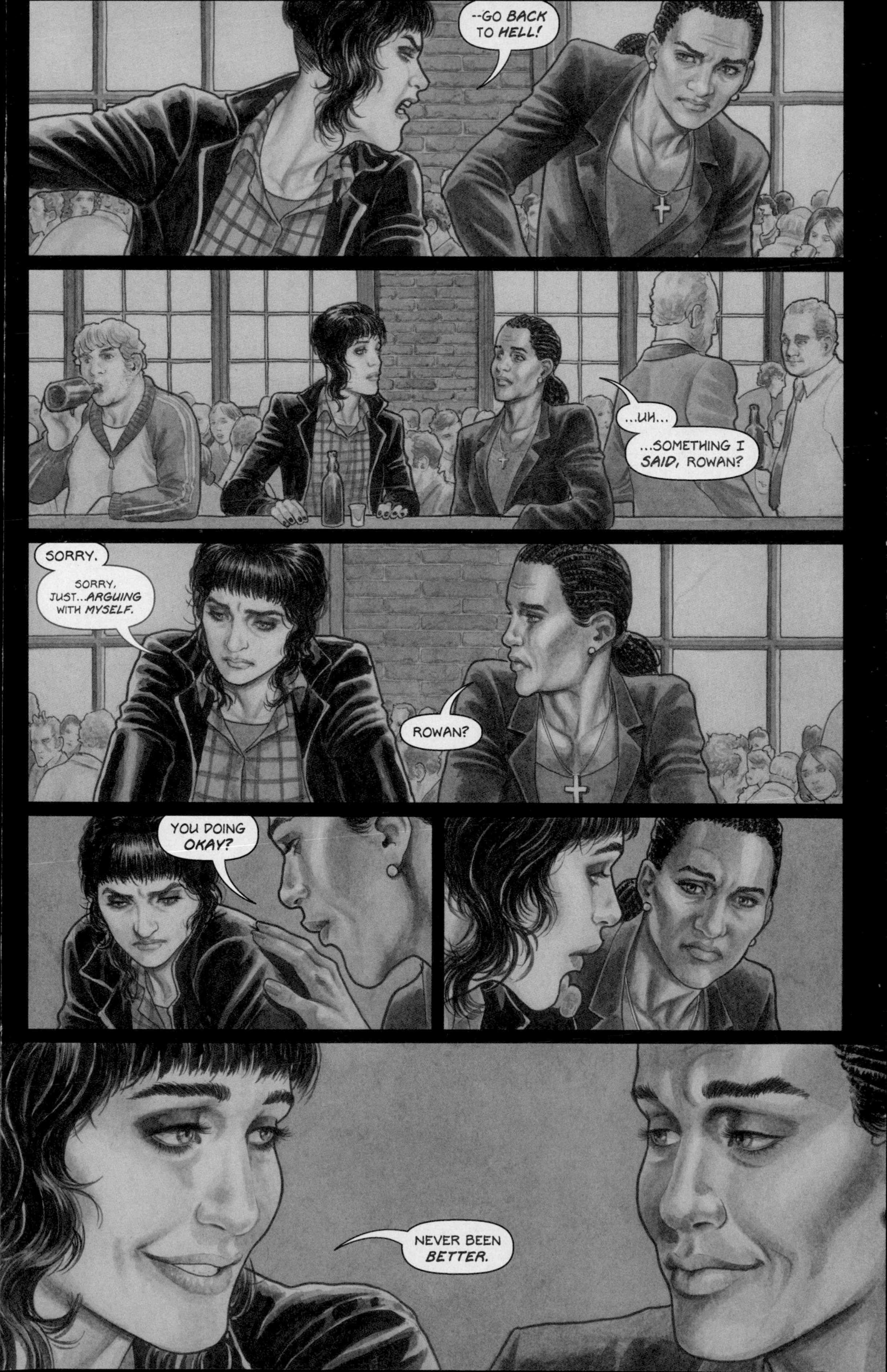
--GO BACK TO HELL!
...UH...
...SOMETHING I SAID, ROWAN?
SORRY.
SORRY, JUST...ARGUING WITH MYSELF.
ROWAN?
YOU DOING OKAY?
NEVER BEEN BETTER.

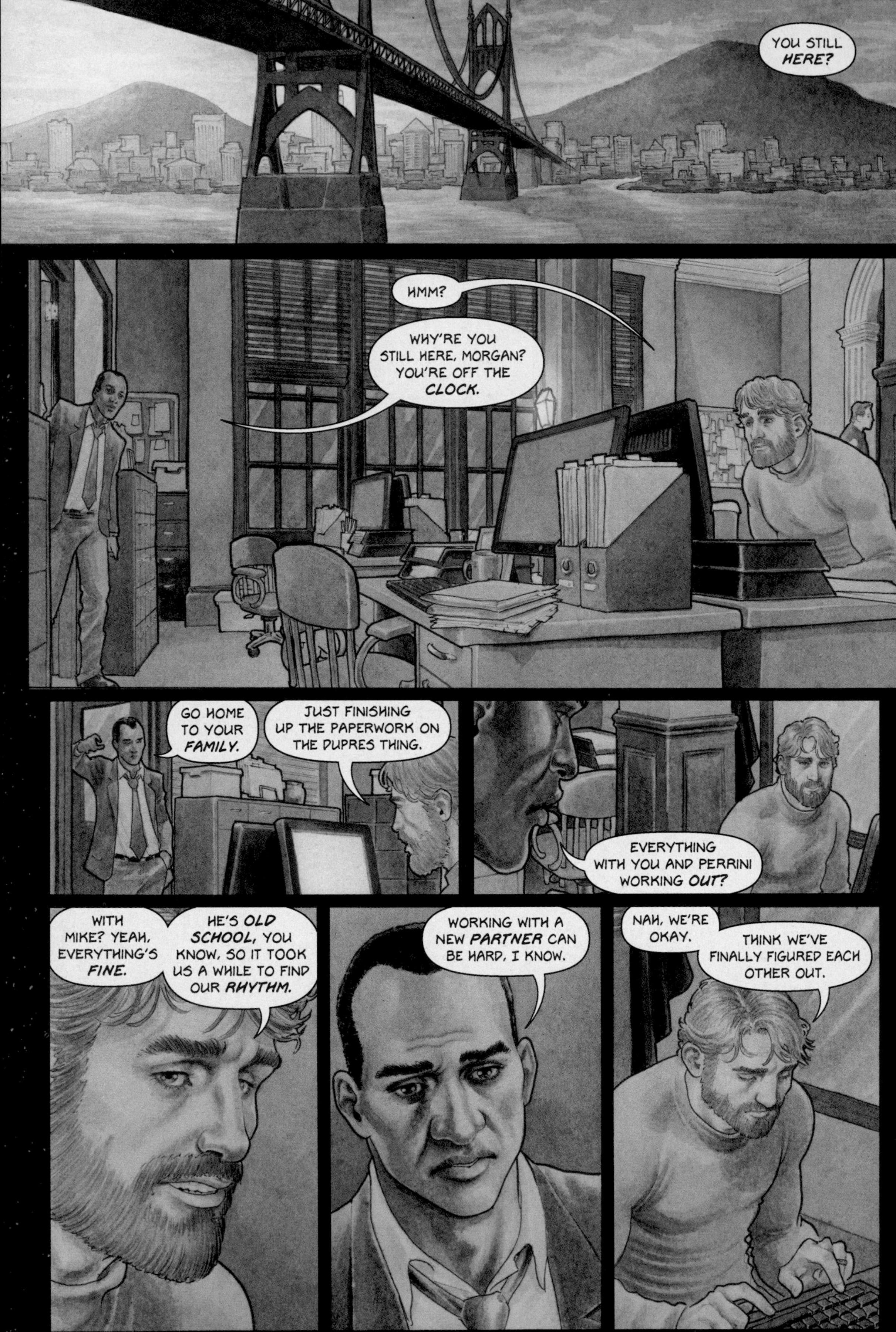
YOU STILL HERE?
HMM?
WHY'RE YOU STILL HERE, MORGAN? YOU'RE OFF THE CLOCK.
GO HOME TO YOUR FAMILY.
JUST FINISHING UP THE PAPERWORK ON THE DUPRES THING.
EVERYTHING WITH YOU AND PERRINI WORKING OUT?
WITH MIKE? YEAH, EVERYTHING'S FINE.
HE'S OLD SCHOOL, YOU KNOW, SO IT TOOK US A WHILE TO FIND OUR RHYTHM.
WORKING WITH A NEW PARTNER CAN BE HARD, I KNOW.
NAH, WE'RE OKAY.
THINK WE'VE FINALLY FIGURED EACH OTHER OUT.

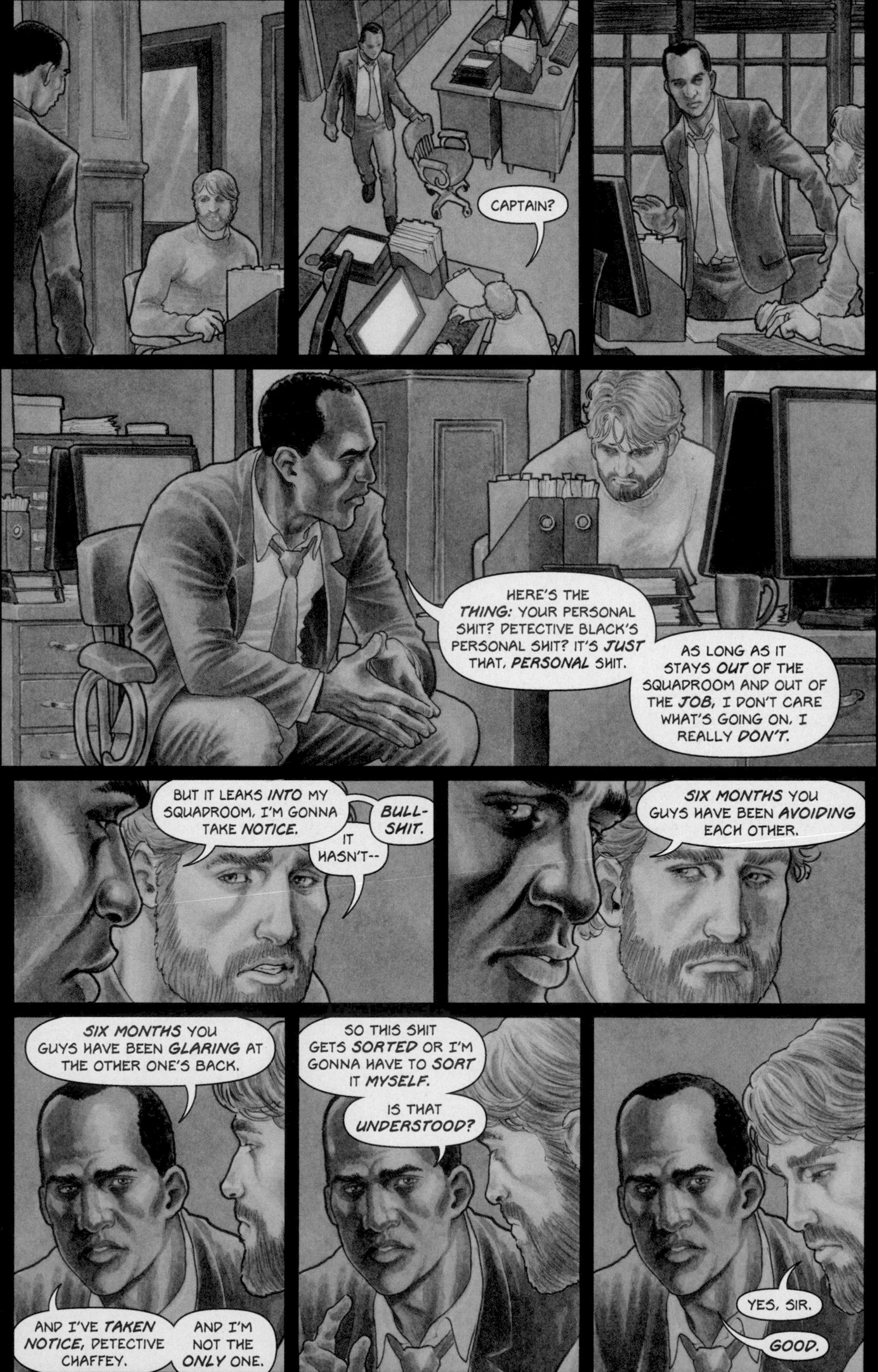
CAPTAIN?
HERE'S THE THING: YOUR PERSONAL SHIT? DETECTIVE BLACK'S PERSONAL SHIT? IT'S JUST THAT, PERSONAL SHIT.
AS LONG AS IT STAYS OUT OF THE SQUADROOM AND OUT OF THE JOB, I DON'T CARE WHAT'S GOING ON, I REALLY DON'T.
BUT IT LEAKS INTO MY SQUADROOM, I'M GONNA TAKE NOTICE.
IT HASN'T--
BULLSHIT.
SIX MONTHS YOU GUYS HAVE BEEN AVOIDING EACH OTHER.
SIX MONTHS YOU GUYS HAVE BEEN GLARING AT THE OTHER ONE'S BACK.
AND I'VE TAKEN NOTICE, DETECTIVE CHAFFEY.
AND I'M NOT THE ONLY ONE.
SO THIS SHIT GETS SORTED OR I'M GONNA HAVE TO SORT IT MYSELF.
IS THAT UNDERSTOOD?
YES, SIR.
GOOD.

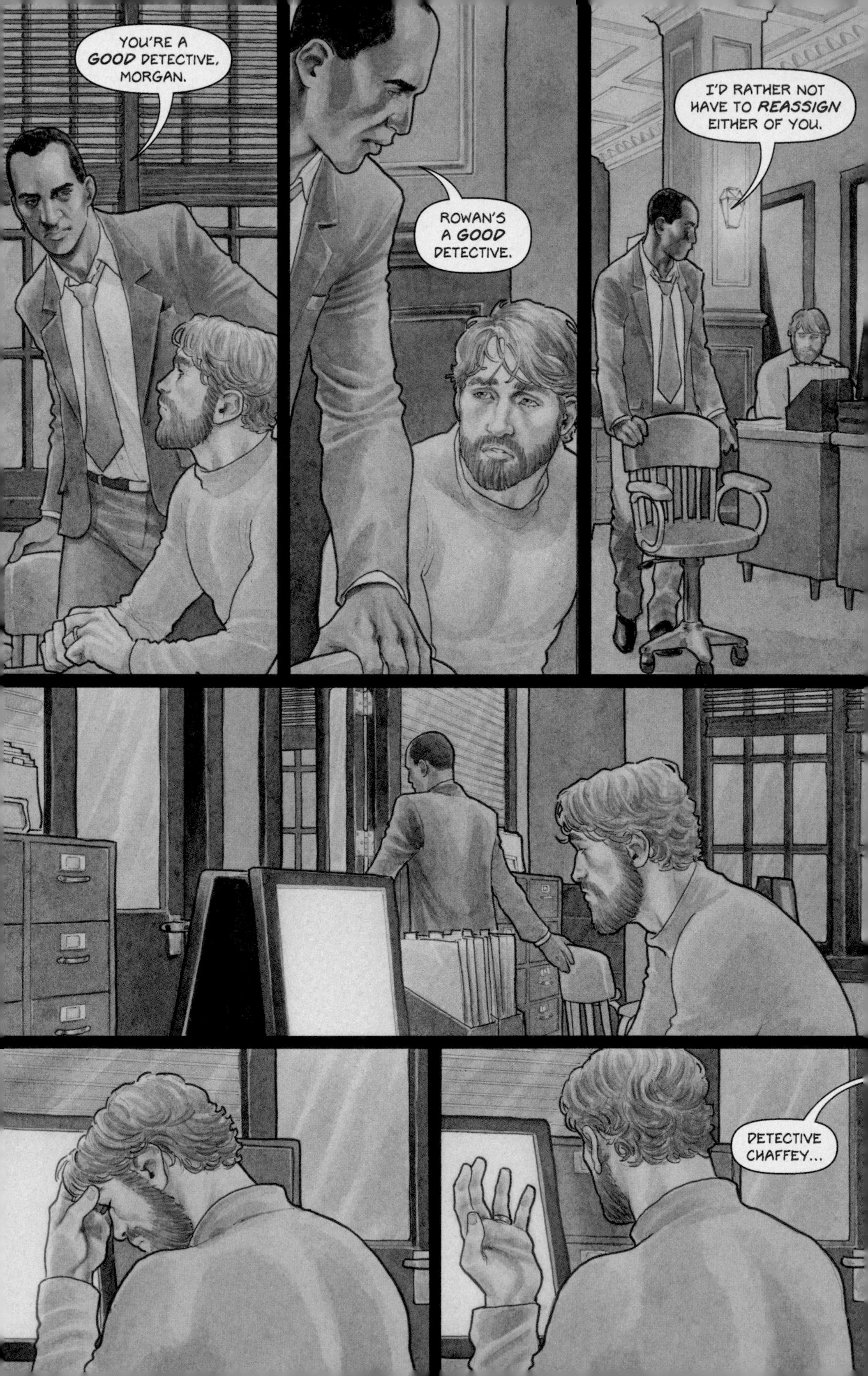
YOU'RE A GOOD DETECTIVE, MORGAN.
ROWAN'S A GOOD DETECTIVE.
I'D RATHER NOT HAVE TO REASSIGN EITHER OF YOU.
DETECTIVE CHAFFEY...

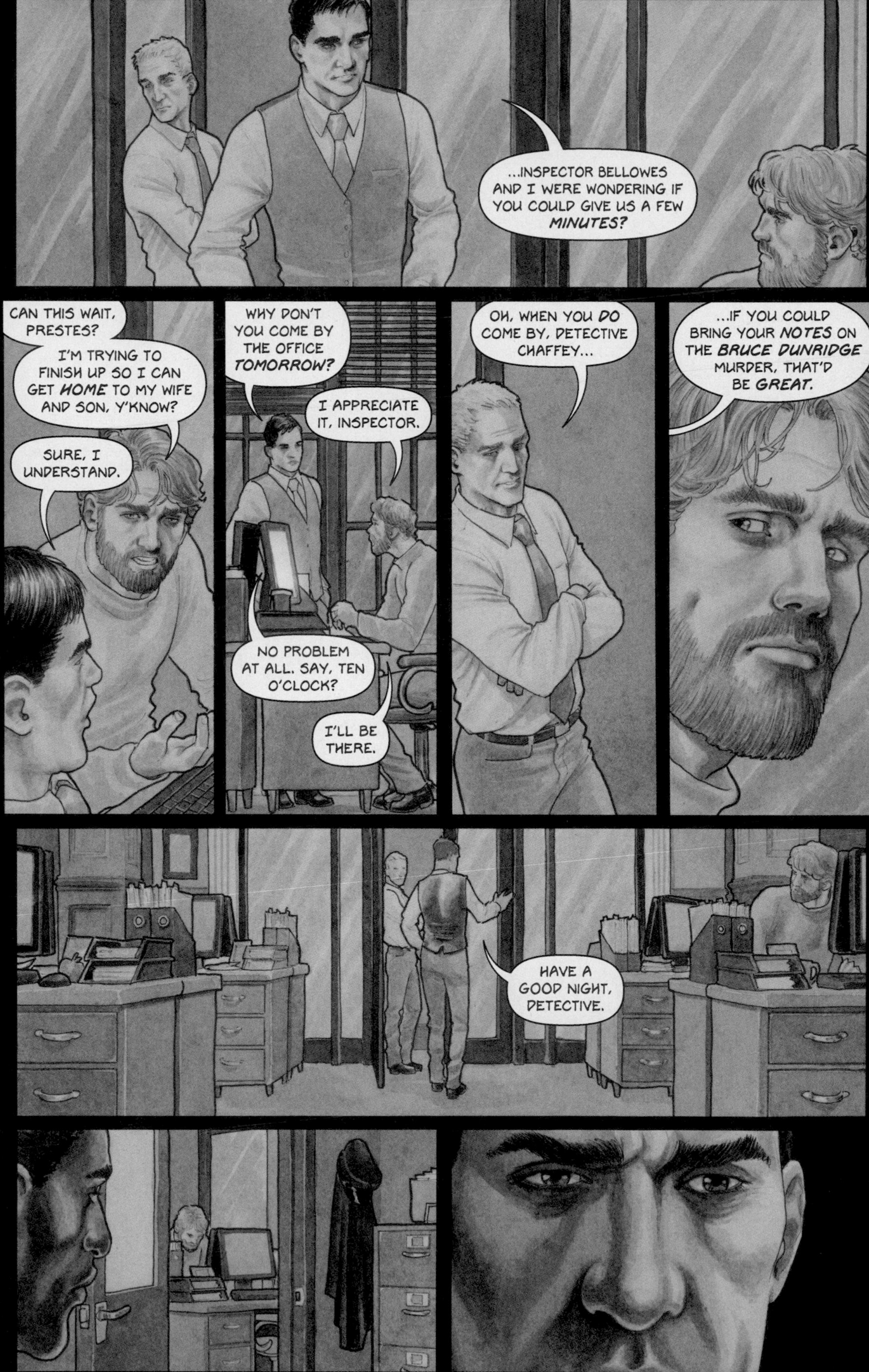
...INSPECTOR BELLOWES AND I WERE WONDERING IF YOU COULD GIVE US A FEW *MINUTES?*
CAN THIS WAIT, PRESTES?
I'M TRYING TO FINISH UP SO I CAN GET *HOME* TO MY WIFE AND SON, Y'KNOW?
SURE, I UNDERSTAND.
WHY DON'T YOU COME BY THE OFFICE *TOMORROW?*
I APPRECIATE IT, INSPECTOR.
NO PROBLEM AT ALL. SAY, TEN O'CLOCK?
I'LL BE THERE.
OH, WHEN YOU *DO* COME BY, DETECTIVE CHAFFEY...
...IF YOU COULD BRING YOUR *NOTES* ON THE *BRUCE DUNRIDGE* MURDER, THAT'D BE *GREAT.*
HAVE A GOOD NIGHT, DETECTIVE.

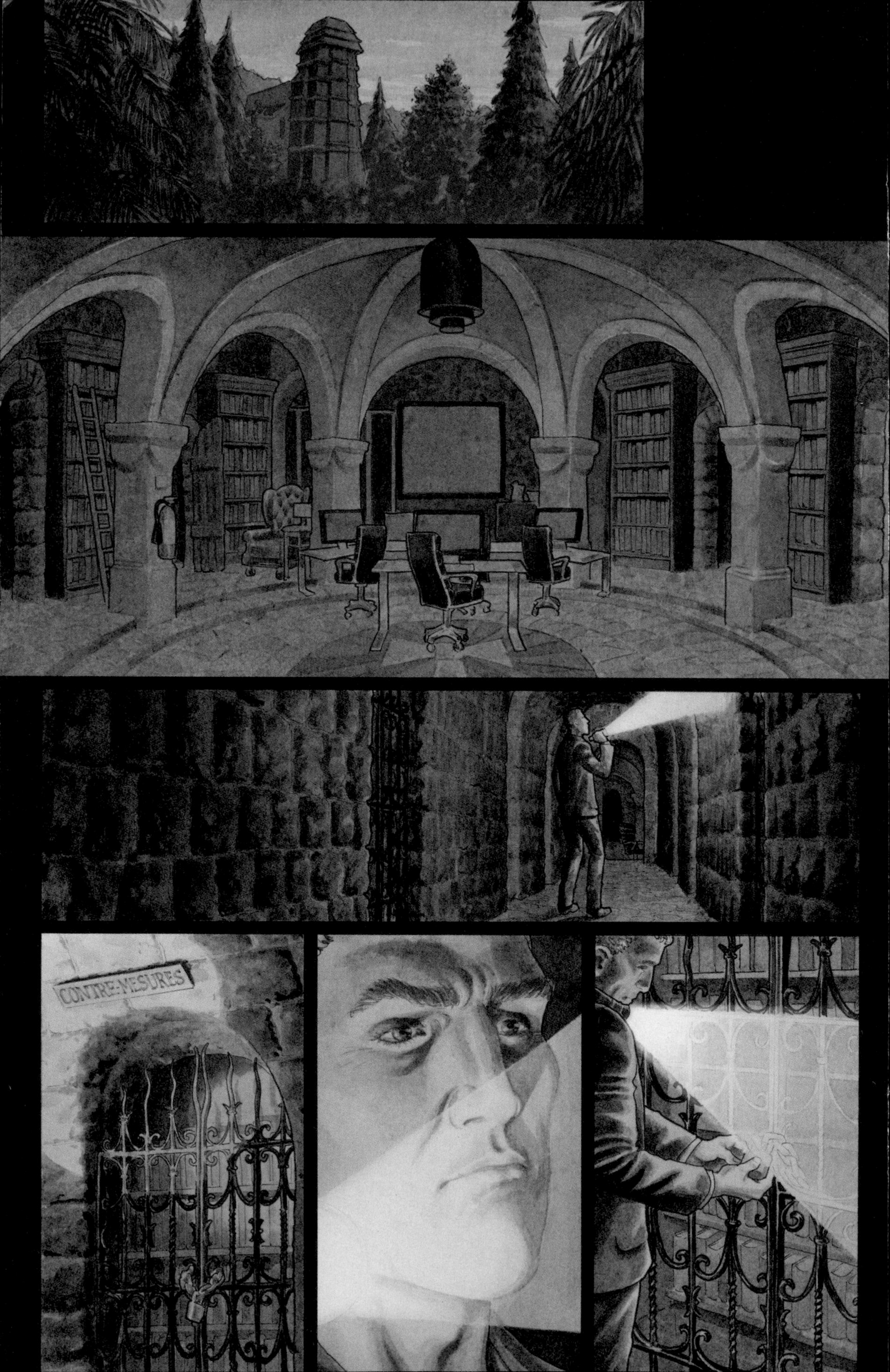
CONTRE-MESURES

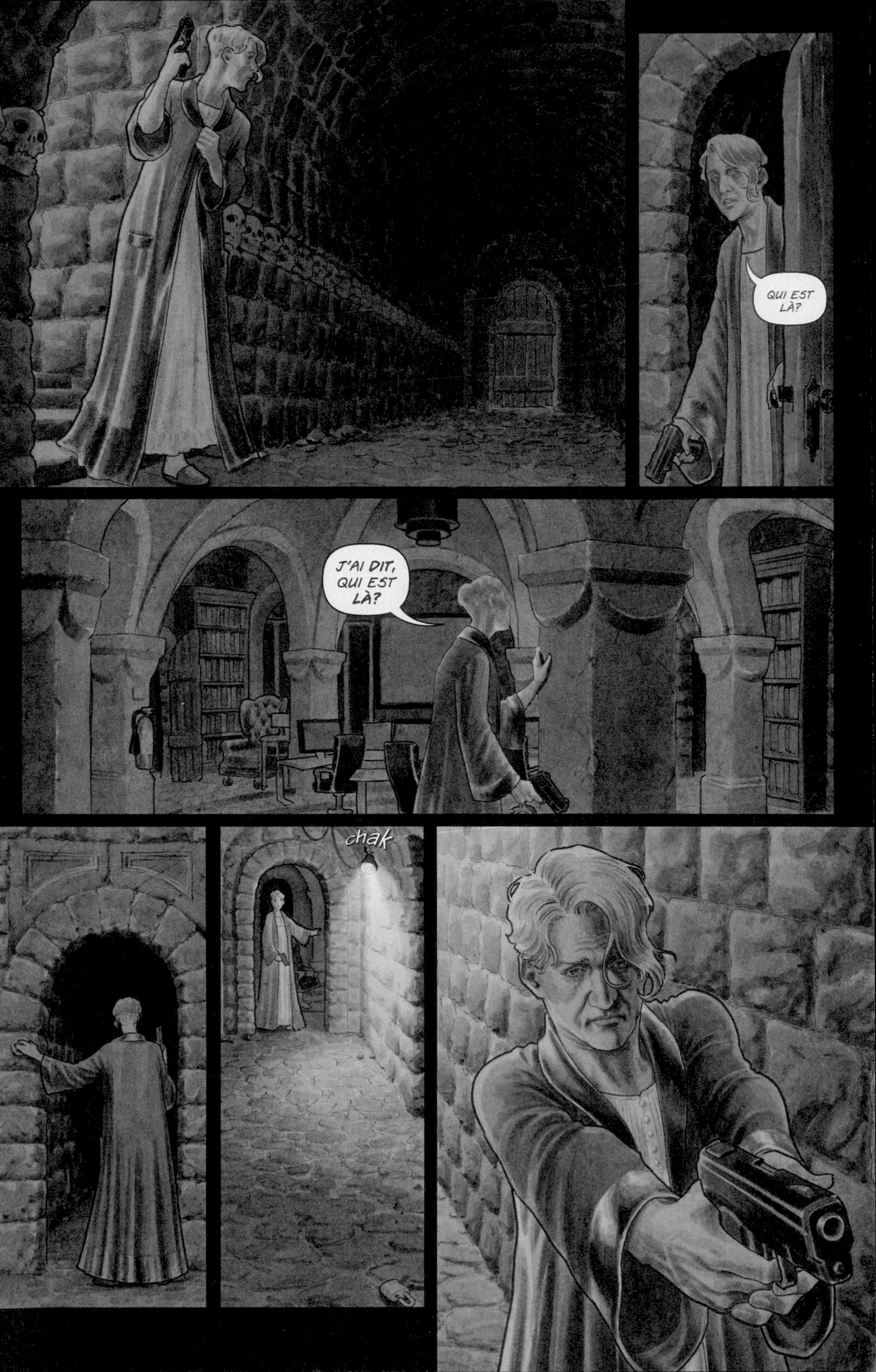
QUI EST LÀ?
J'AI DIT, QUI EST LÀ?
chak

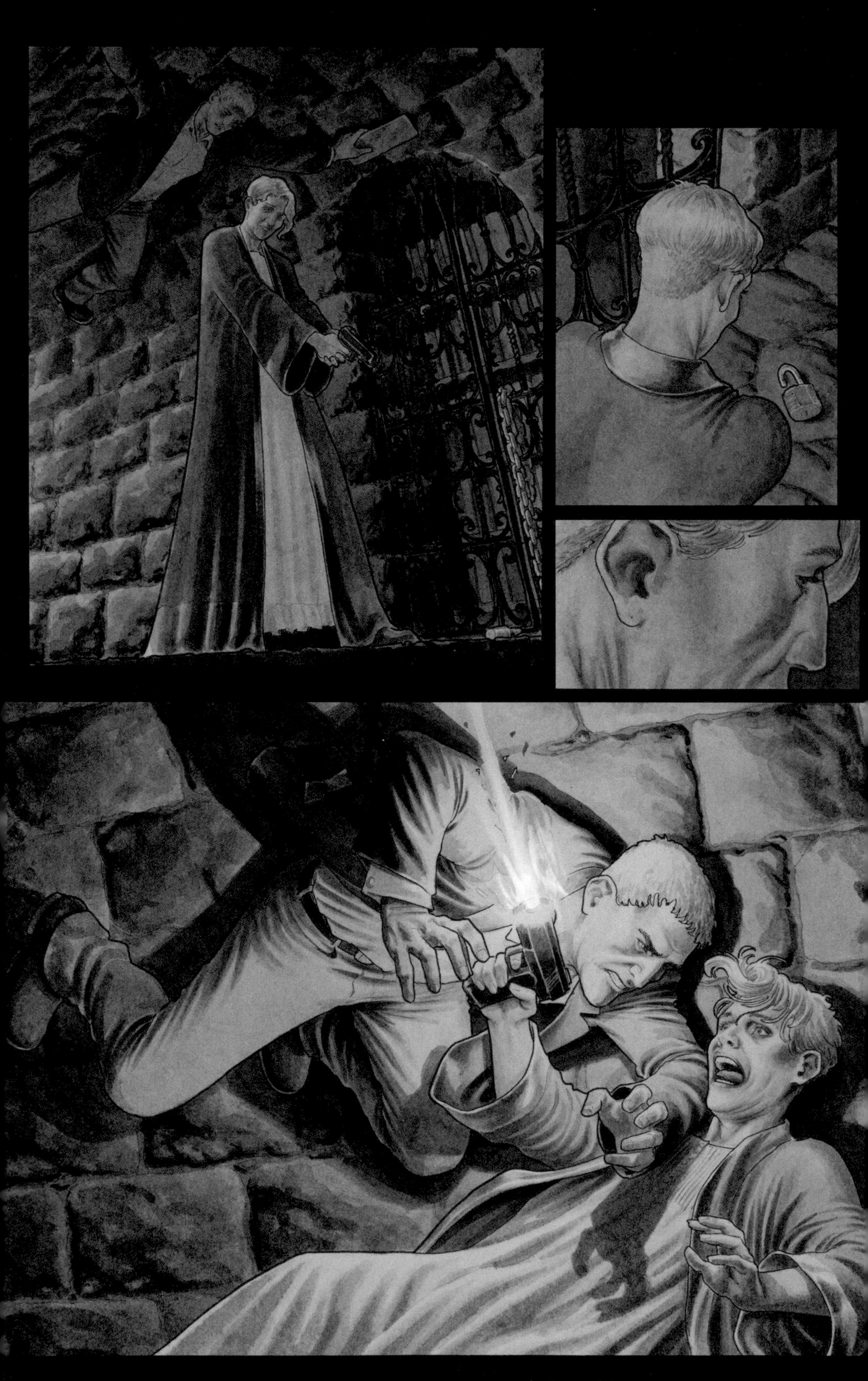

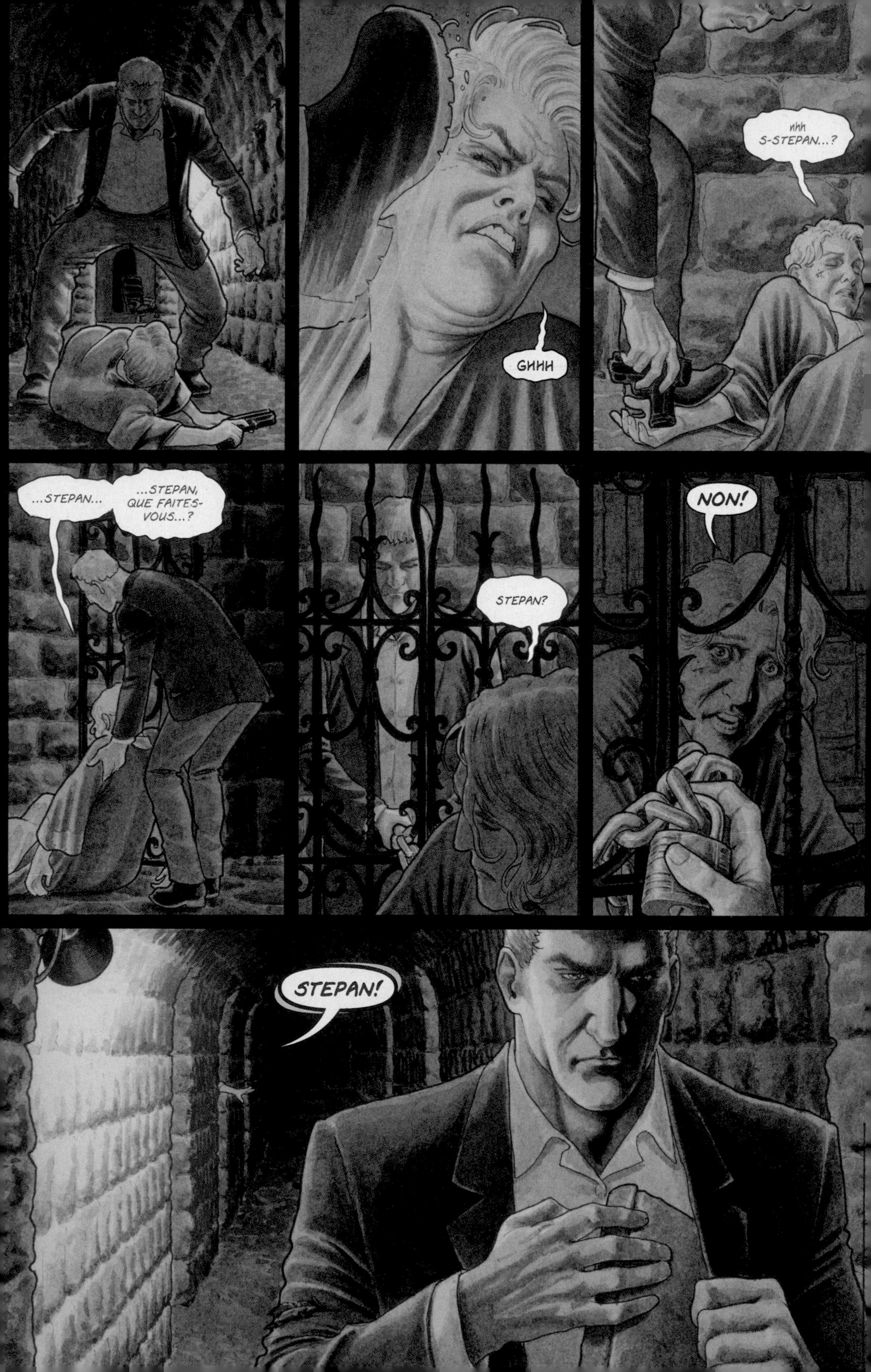
GHHH
nhh S-STEPAN...?
...STEPAN...
...STEPAN, QUE FAITES-VOUS...?
STEPAN?
NON!
STEPAN!

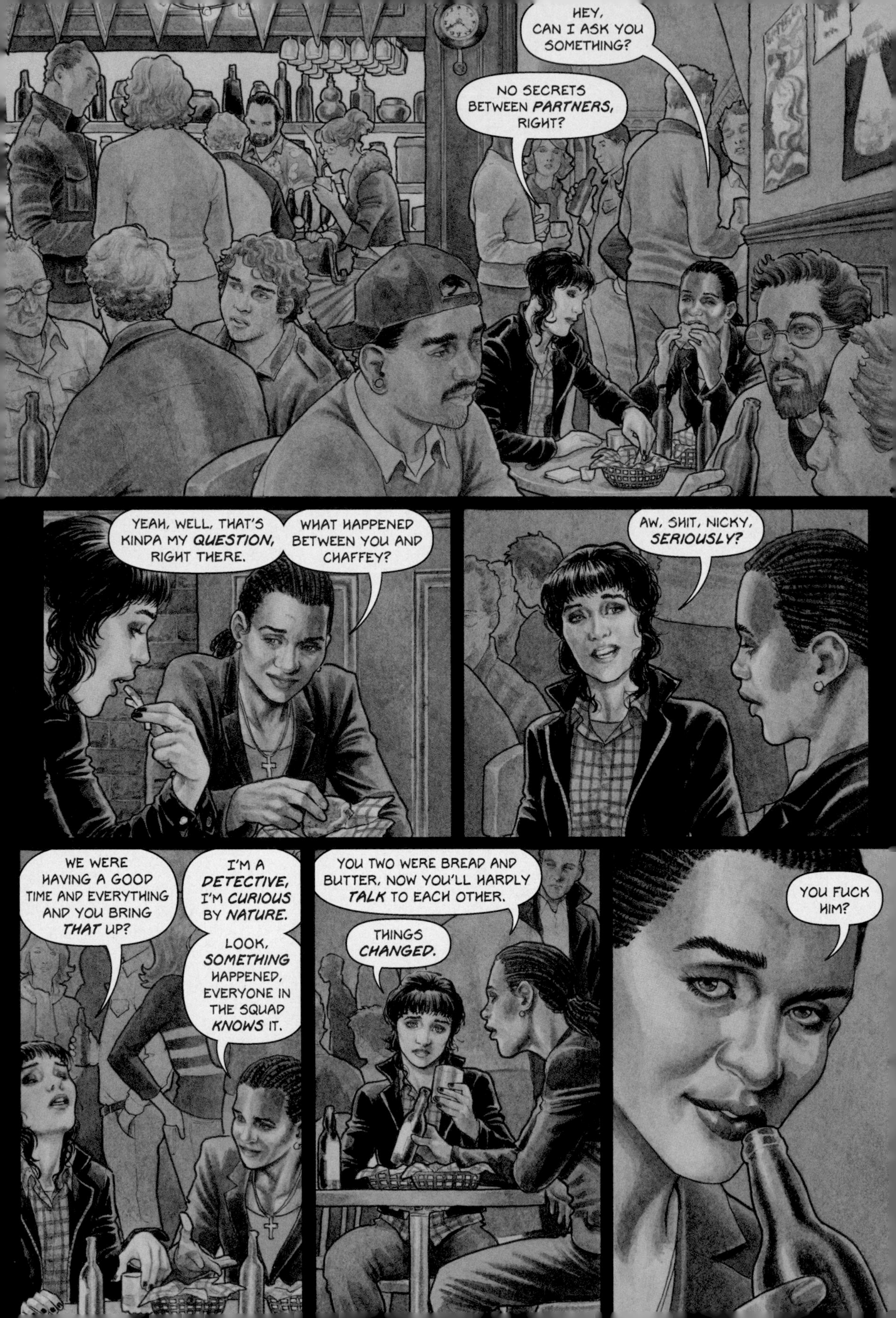
HEY, CAN I ASK YOU SOMETHING?
NO SECRETS BETWEEN PARTNERS, RIGHT?
YEAH, WELL, THAT'S KINDA MY QUESTION, RIGHT THERE.
WHAT HAPPENED BETWEEN YOU AND CHAFFEY?
AW, SHIT, NICKY, SERIOUSLY?
WE WERE HAVING A GOOD TIME AND EVERYTHING AND YOU BRING THAT UP?
I'M A DETECTIVE, I'M CURIOUS BY NATURE.
LOOK, SOMETHING HAPPENED, EVERYONE IN THE SQUAD KNOWS IT.
YOU TWO WERE BREAD AND BUTTER, NOW YOU'LL HARDLY TALK TO EACH OTHER.
THINGS CHANGED.
YOU FUCK HIM?

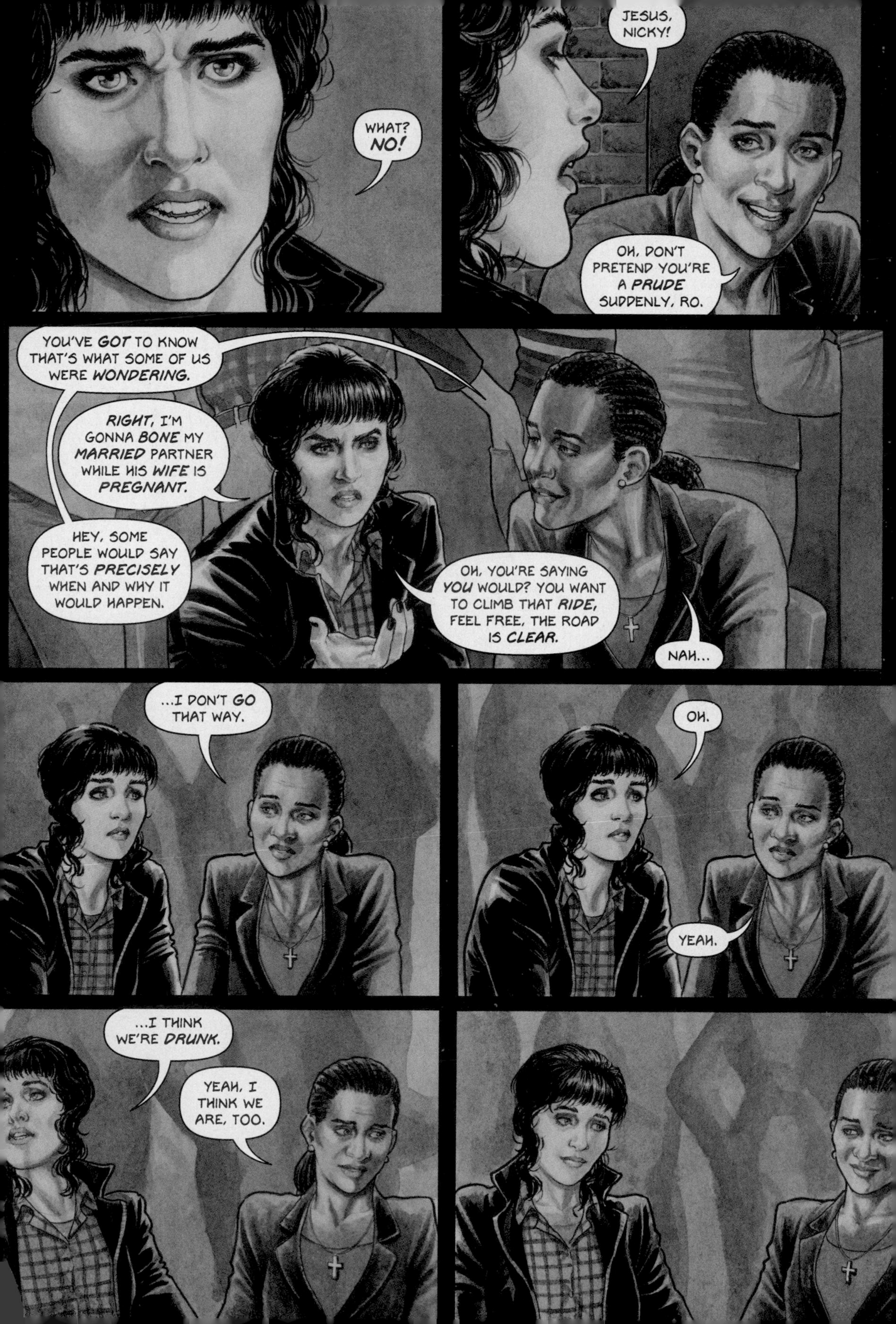
WHAT? NO!
JESUS, NICKY!
OH, DON'T PRETEND YOU'RE A PRUDE SUDDENLY, RO.
YOU'VE GOT TO KNOW THAT'S WHAT SOME OF US WERE WONDERING.
RIGHT, I'M GONNA BONE MY MARRIED PARTNER WHILE HIS WIFE IS PREGNANT.
HEY, SOME PEOPLE WOULD SAY THAT'S PRECISELY WHEN AND WHY IT WOULD HAPPEN.
OH, YOU'RE SAYING YOU WOULD? YOU WANT TO CLIMB THAT RIDE, FEEL FREE, THE ROAD IS CLEAR.
NAH...
...I DON'T GO THAT WAY.
OH.
YEAH.
...I THINK WE'RE DRUNK.
YEAH, I THINK WE ARE, TOO.

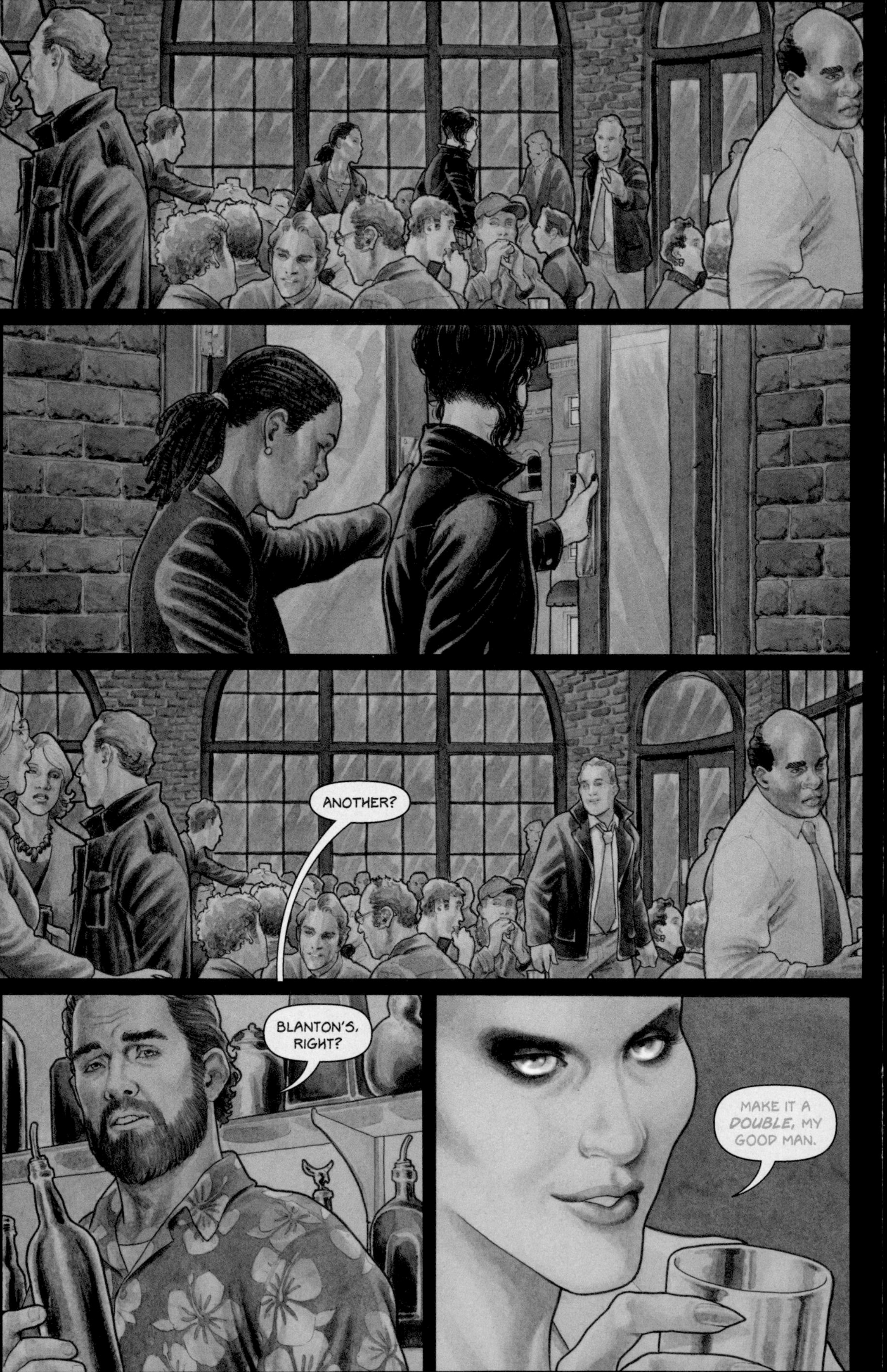
ANOTHER?
BLANTON'S, RIGHT?
MAKE IT A *DOUBLE*, MY GOOD MAN.

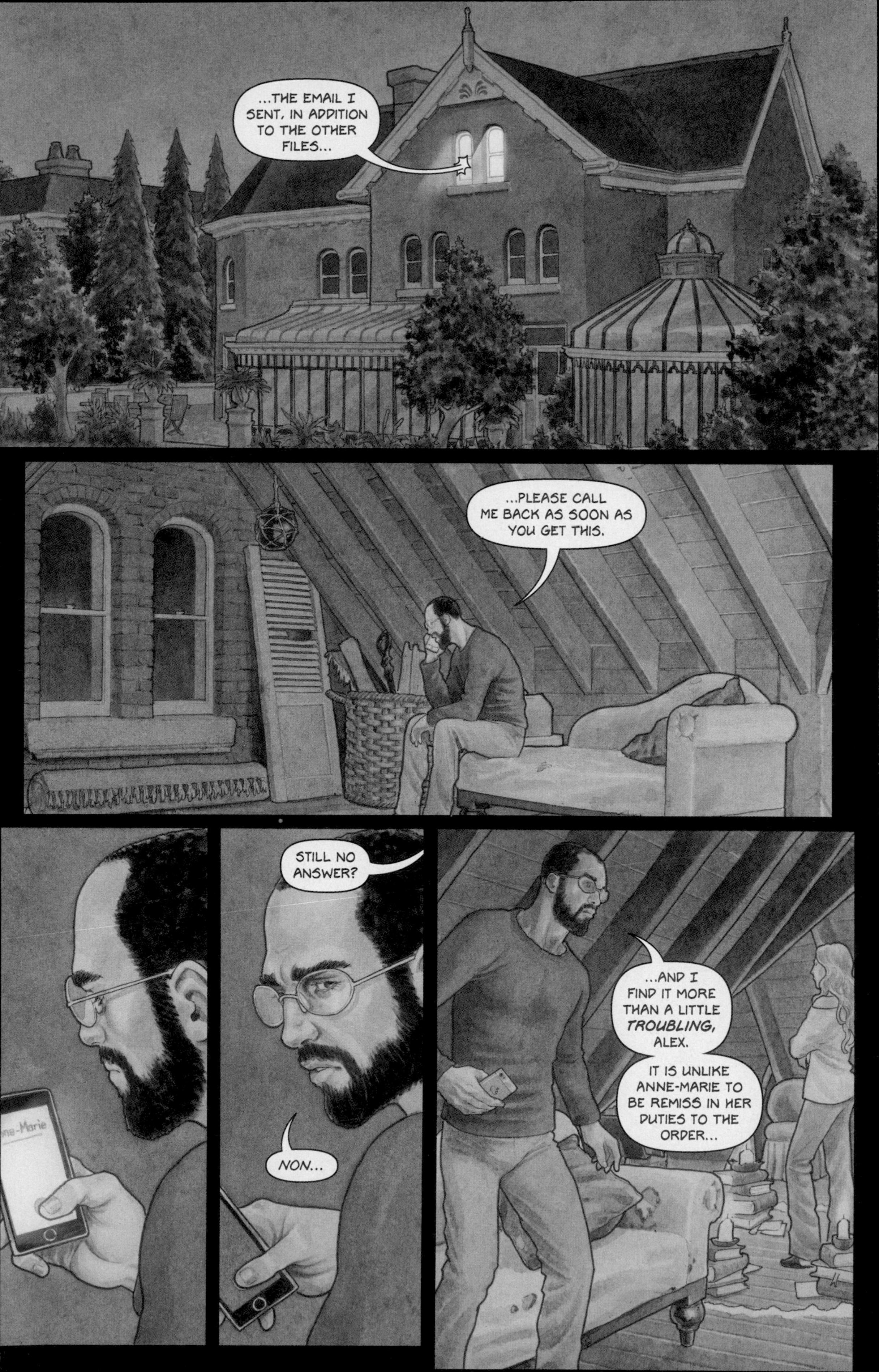
...THE EMAIL I SENT, IN ADDITION TO THE OTHER FILES...
...PLEASE CALL ME BACK AS SOON AS YOU GET THIS.
STILL NO ANSWER?
NON...
...AND I FIND IT MORE THAN A LITTLE *TROUBLING,* ALEX.
IT IS UNLIKE ANNE-MARIE TO BE REMISS IN HER DUTIES TO THE ORDER...

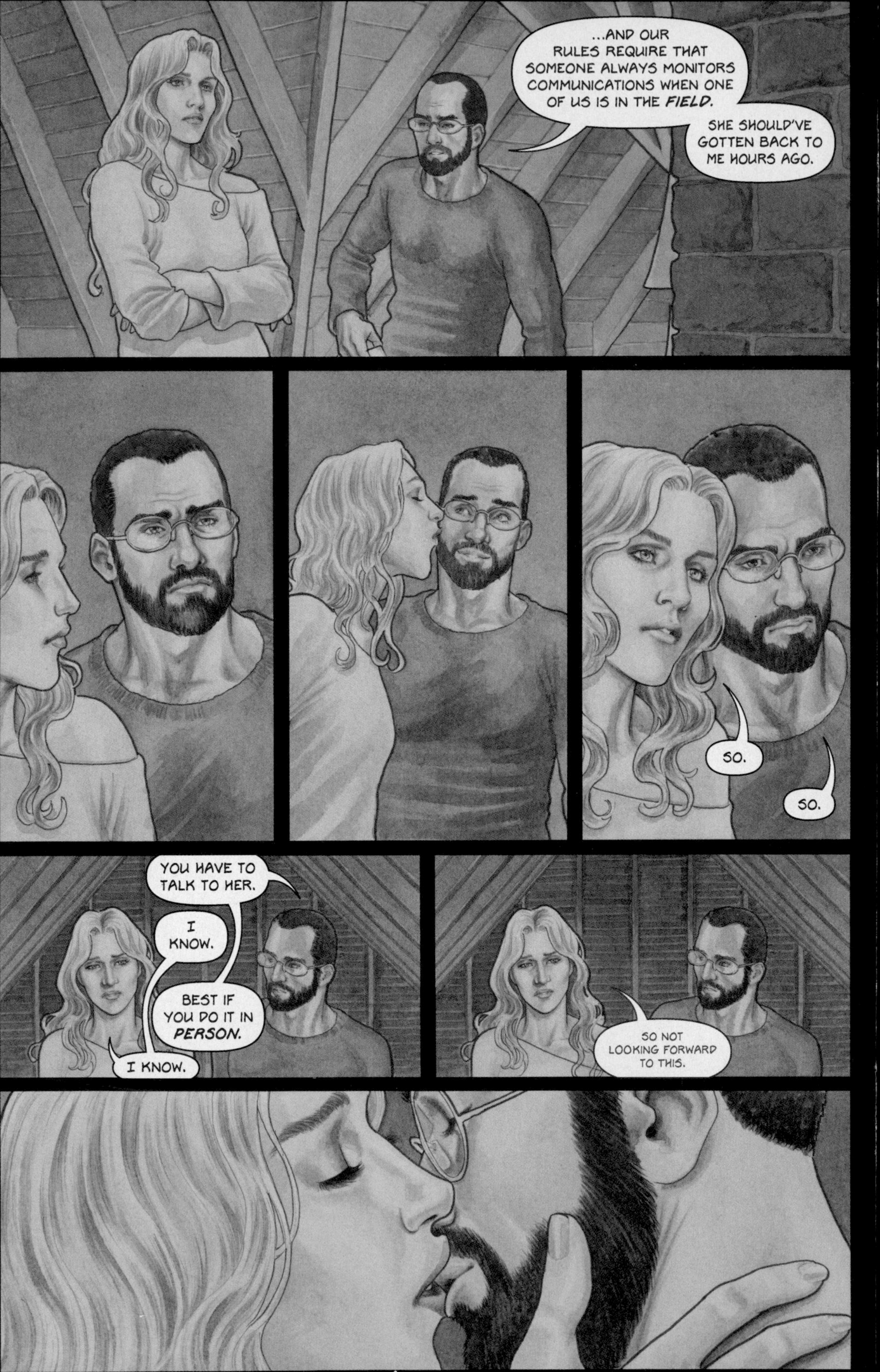
...AND OUR RULES REQUIRE THAT SOMEONE ALWAYS MONITORS COMMUNICATIONS WHEN ONE OF US IS IN THE *FIELD*.
SHE SHOULD'VE GOTTEN BACK TO ME HOURS AGO.
SO.
SO.
YOU HAVE TO TALK TO HER.
I KNOW.
BEST IF YOU DO IT IN *PERSON*.
I KNOW.
SO NOT LOOKING FORWARD TO THIS.

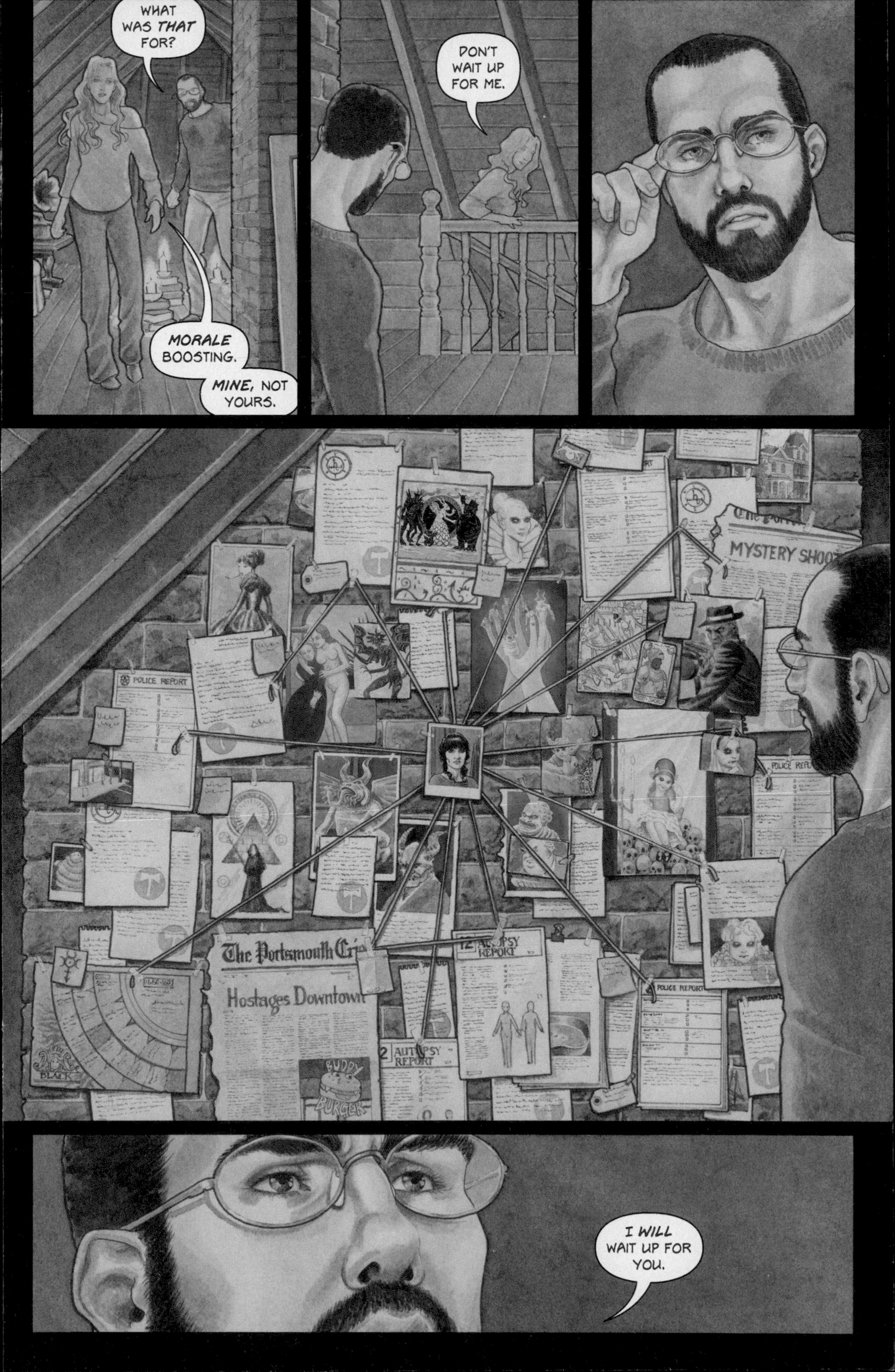
WHAT WAS *THAT* FOR?
MORALE BOOSTING.
MINE, NOT YOURS.
DON'T WAIT UP FOR ME.
POLICE REPORT
MYSTERY SHOO
POLICE REPORT
Hostages Downtown
POLICE REPORT
BUDDY BURGER
I WILL WAIT UP FOR YOU.

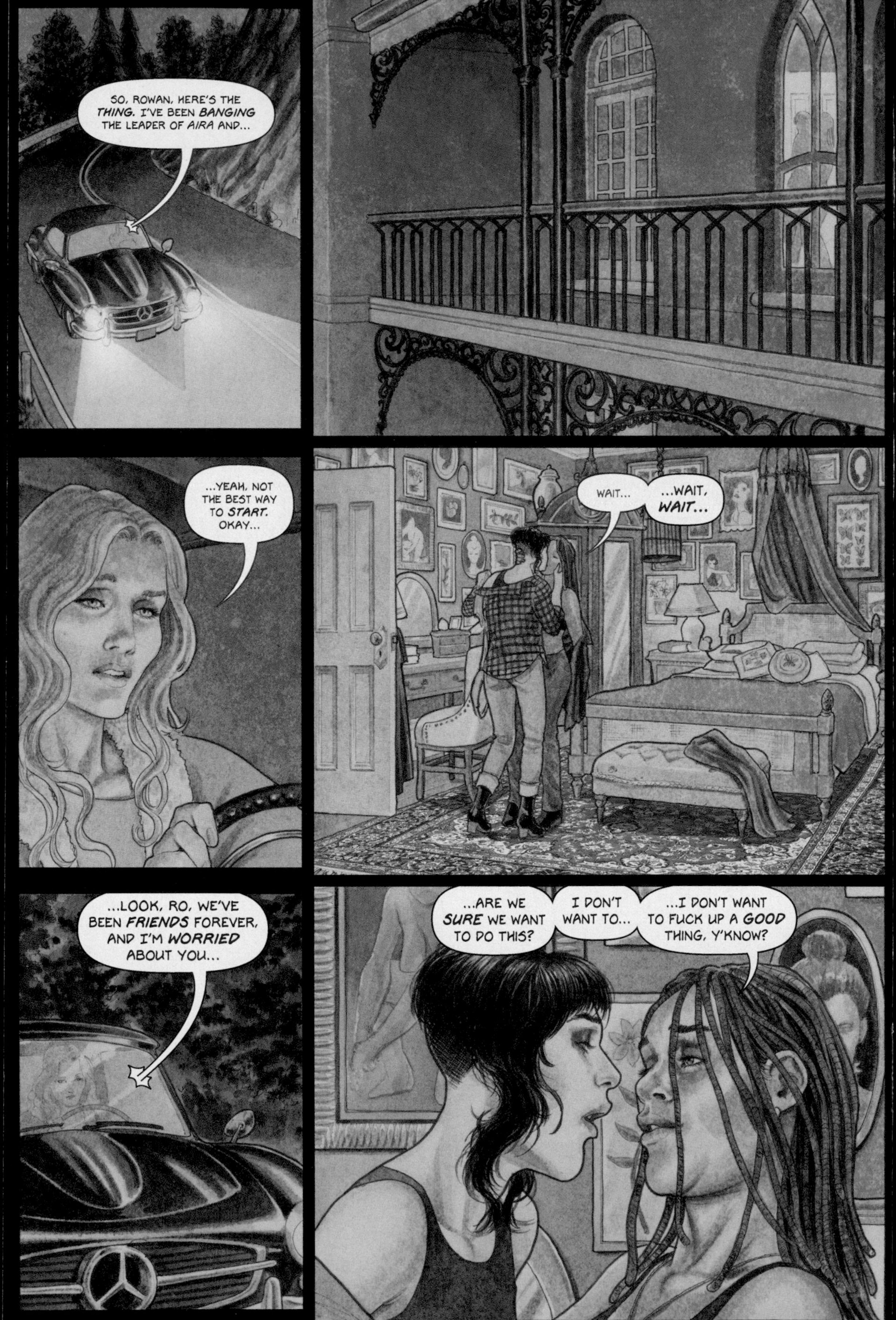
SO, ROWAN, HERE'S THE THING. I'VE BEEN BANGING THE LEADER OF AIRA AND...
...YEAH, NOT THE BEST WAY TO START. OKAY...
WAIT...
...WAIT, WAIT...
...LOOK, RO, WE'VE BEEN FRIENDS FOREVER, AND I'M WORRIED ABOUT YOU...
...ARE WE SURE WE WANT TO DO THIS?
I DON'T WANT TO...
...I DON'T WANT TO FUCK UP A GOOD THING, Y'KNOW?

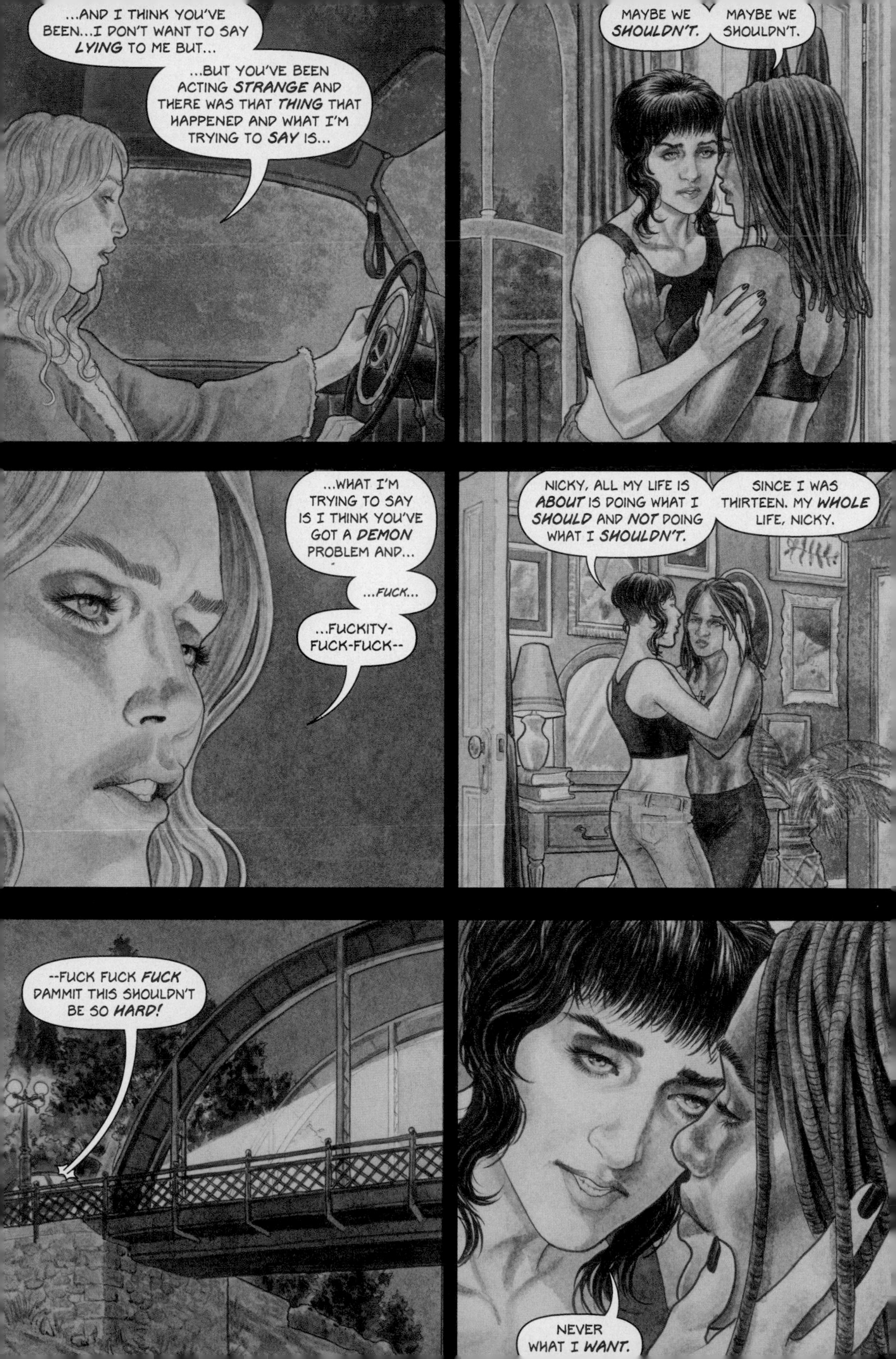
...AND I THINK YOU'VE BEEN...I DON'T WANT TO SAY LYING TO ME BUT...
...BUT YOU'VE BEEN ACTING STRANGE AND THERE WAS THAT THING THAT HAPPENED AND WHAT I'M TRYING TO SAY IS...
MAYBE WE SHOULDN'T.
MAYBE WE SHOULDN'T.
...WHAT I'M TRYING TO SAY IS I THINK YOU'VE GOT A DEMON PROBLEM AND...
...FUCK...
...FUCKITY-FUCK-FUCK--
NICKY, ALL MY LIFE IS ABOUT IS DOING WHAT I SHOULD AND NOT DOING WHAT I SHOULDN'T.
SINCE I WAS THIRTEEN. MY WHOLE LIFE, NICKY.
--FUCK FUCK FUCK DAMMIT THIS SHOULDN'T BE SO HARD!
NEVER WHAT I WANT.

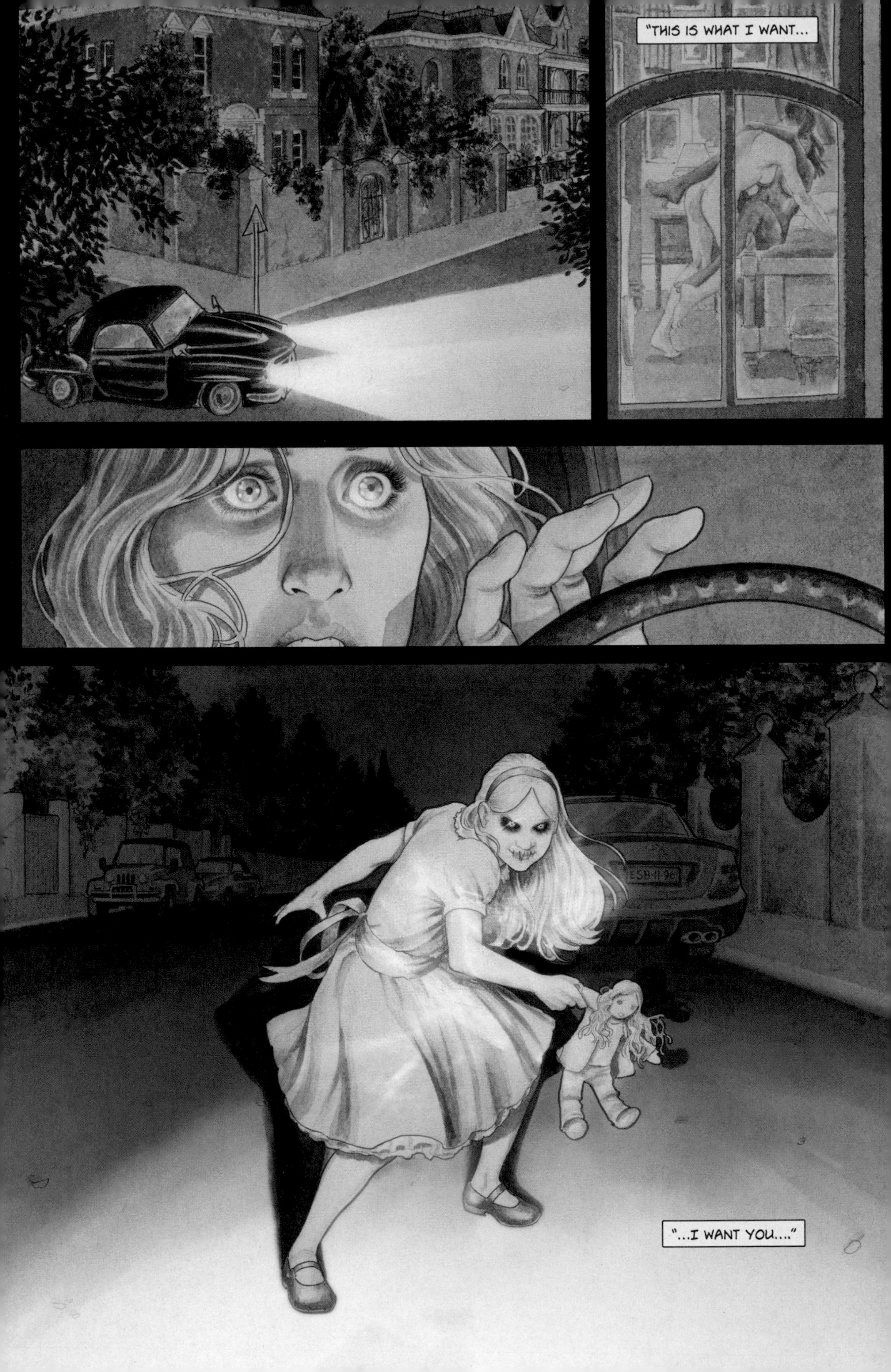
"THIS IS WHAT I WANT...
"...I WANT YOU...."

DEPARTMENT

CITY OF PORTSMO

SON KILLED | FIRST NAME | MIDDLE NAME | RACE SEX AGE | RESIDENCE OF PERSON KILLED | OFFENSE SERIA

TITLE OR RELATIONSHIP | RACE SEX AGE | ADDRESS OF PERSON KILLED | PHONE OF PERS

RED (CRIME) | AFTER INVESTIGATION CHANGED TO

ENCE — STREET AND NUMBER OR INTERSECTION | DIVISION | PLATOON | BEAT | OFFICER MAKING REPORT | I.D. NO. | NAME

ATE OF OCCURENCE | TIME OF DAY | DATE REPORTED | TIME REPORTED | REPORT RECEIVED BY | RECEIVED — TIME — TYPED

DESCRIPTION OF DEAD PERSON

WEIGHT | EYES | HAIR | BEARD | COMPLEXION | DOMESTIC SCARS MARKS, ETC | CLOTHING

NAME OF CORONER | TIME OF ARRIVAL | PROSECUTOR ATTENDING — TIME OF ARRIVAL

D BY PHYSICIAN | PERSON WITH WHOM ACCUSED LIVED OR ASSOCIATED

E (GIVE CIRCUMSTANCES OF OCCURENCE OF ORIME AND ITS INVESTIGATION) | SIDE OF THIS SHEET

CUSTODY | ADDRESS | WITNESS TAKEN INTO CUSTODY | ADDRESS

D OR POSSIBLE MOTIVES

DESCRIPTION OF SUSPECTS OR PERSONS WANTED

ALIAS | ADDRESS | RACE | AGE | HEIGHT | WEIGHT | EYES | HAIR | COMPLEXION

Y | OCCUPATION | DRESS AND OTHER MARKS | CAUSE FOR SUSPICION

ALIAS | ADDRESS | RACE | AGE | HEIGHT | WEIGHT | EYES | HAIR | COMPLEXION

Y | OCCUPATION | DRESS AND OTHER MARKS | CAUSE FOR SUSPICION

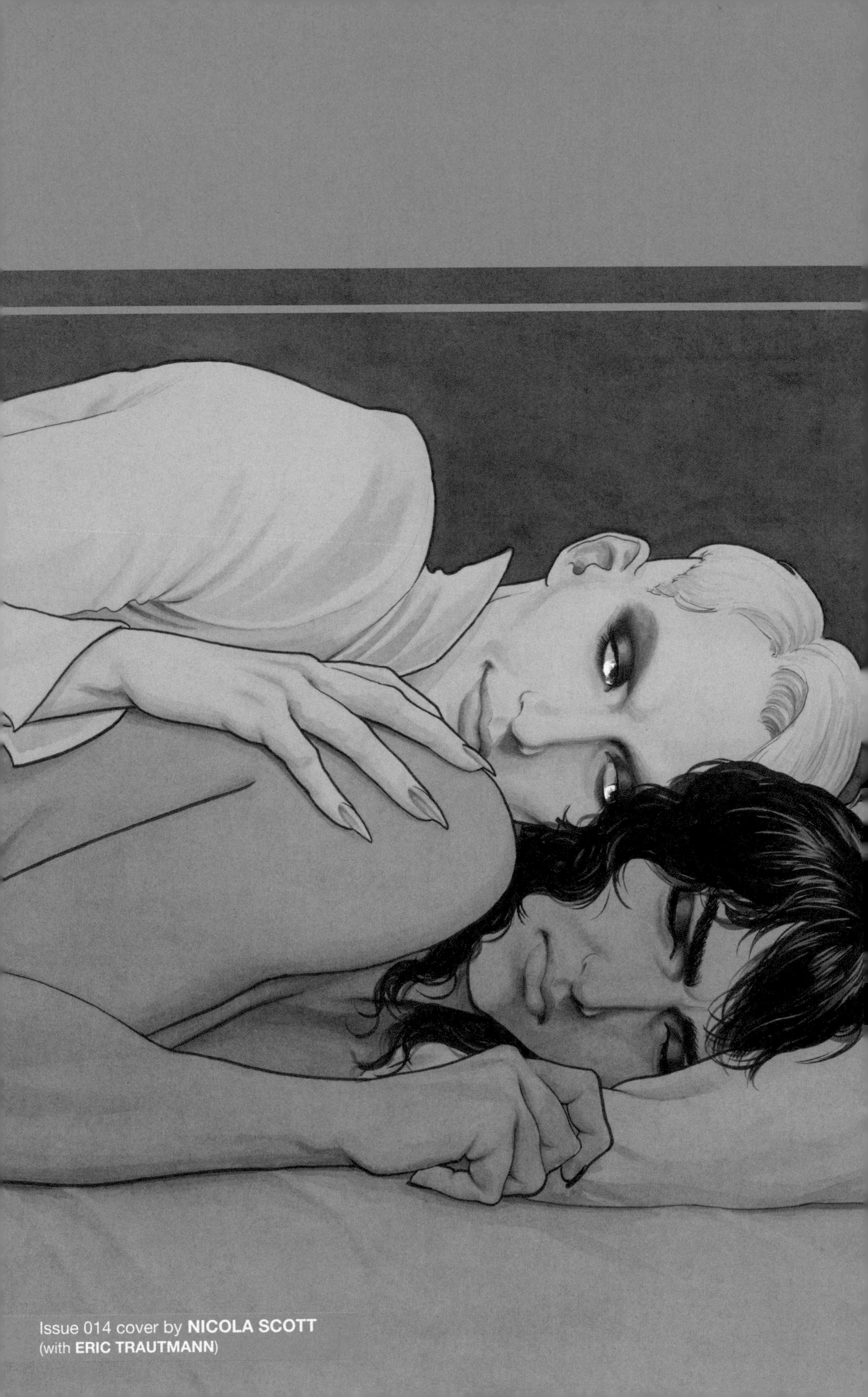

Issue 014 cover by **NICOLA SCOTT**
(with **ERIC TRAUTMANN**)

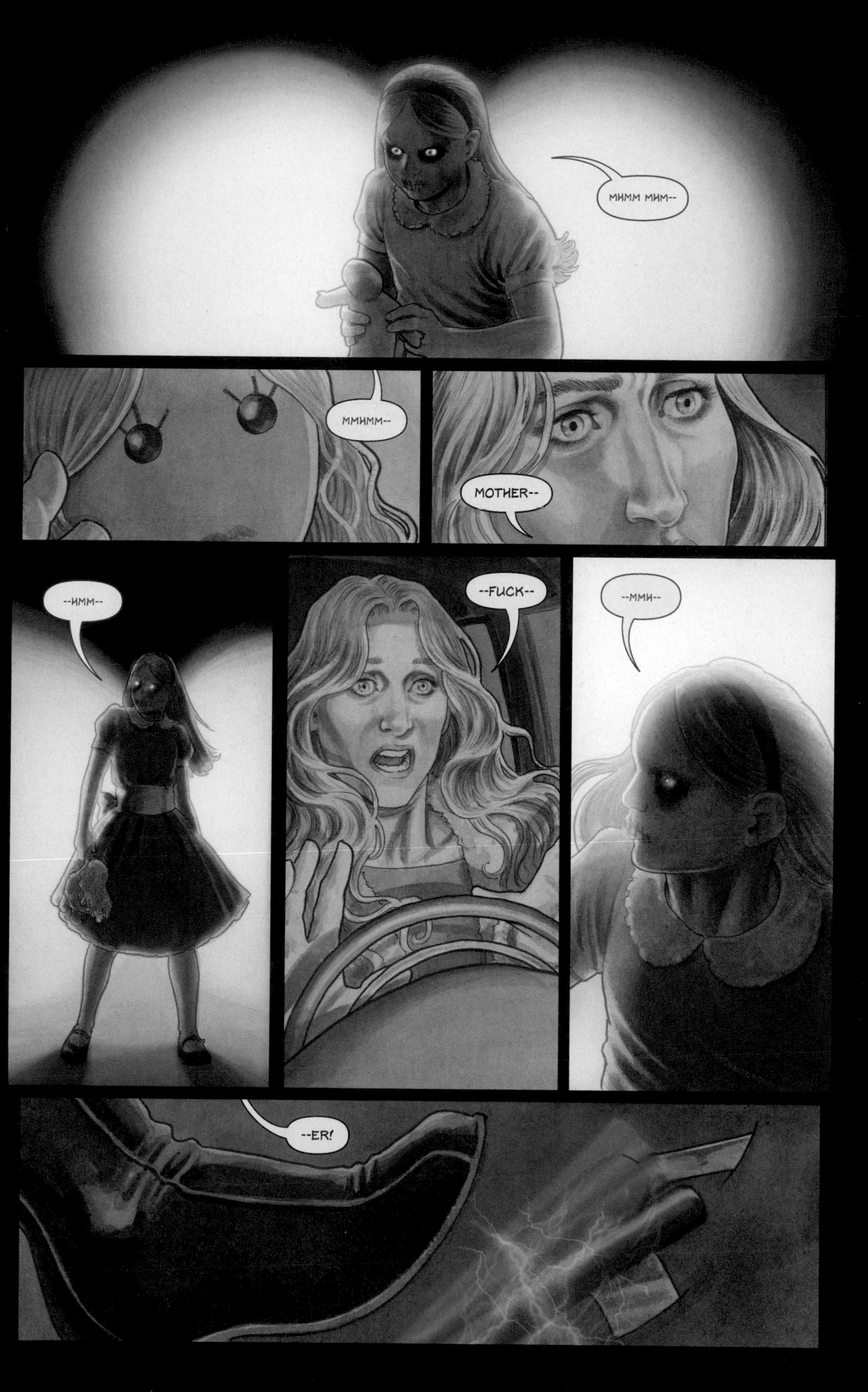
MMMM MMM--
MMMMM--
MOTHER--
--MMM--
--FUCK--
--MMM--
--ER!

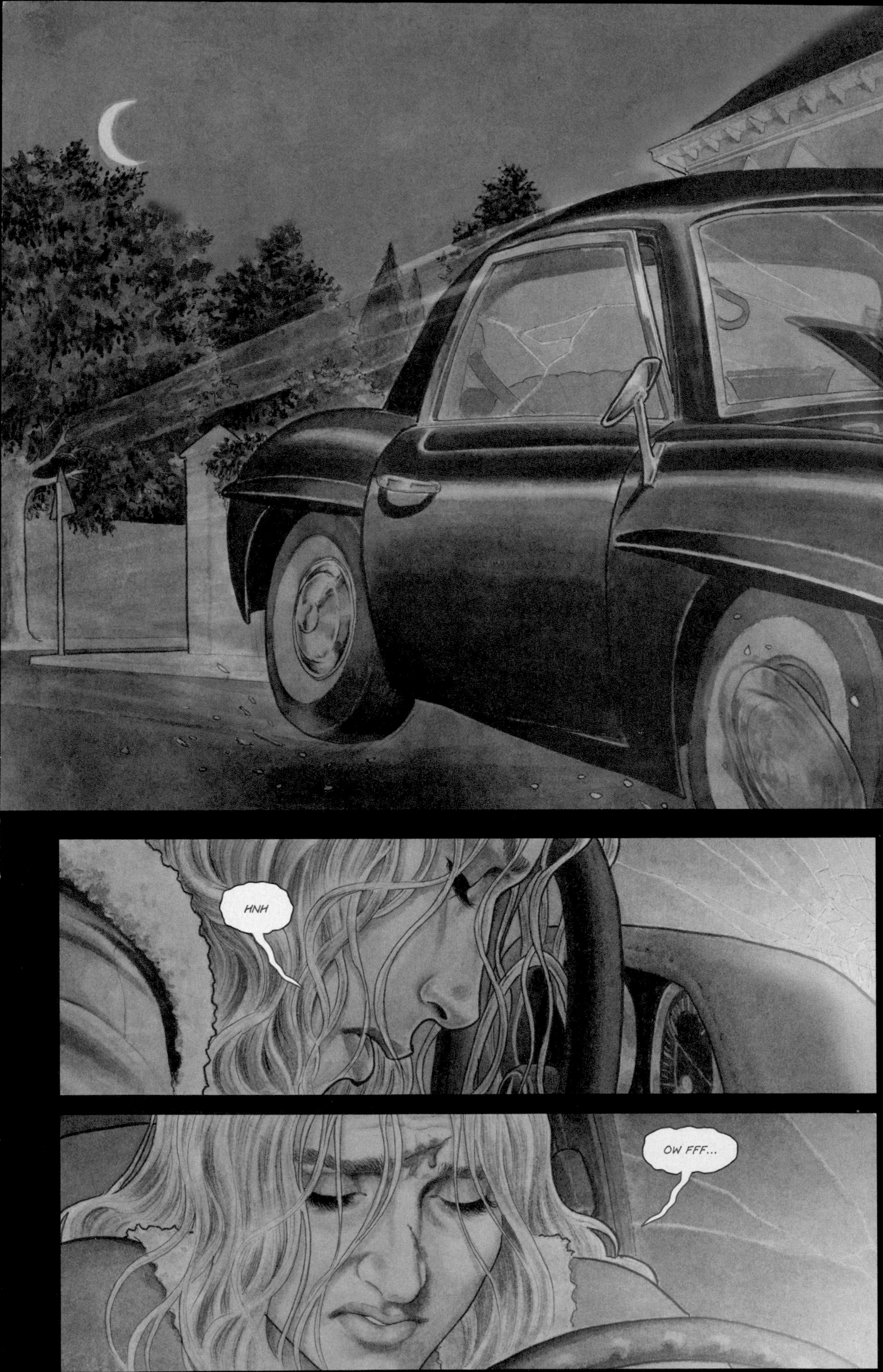
HNH
OW FFF...

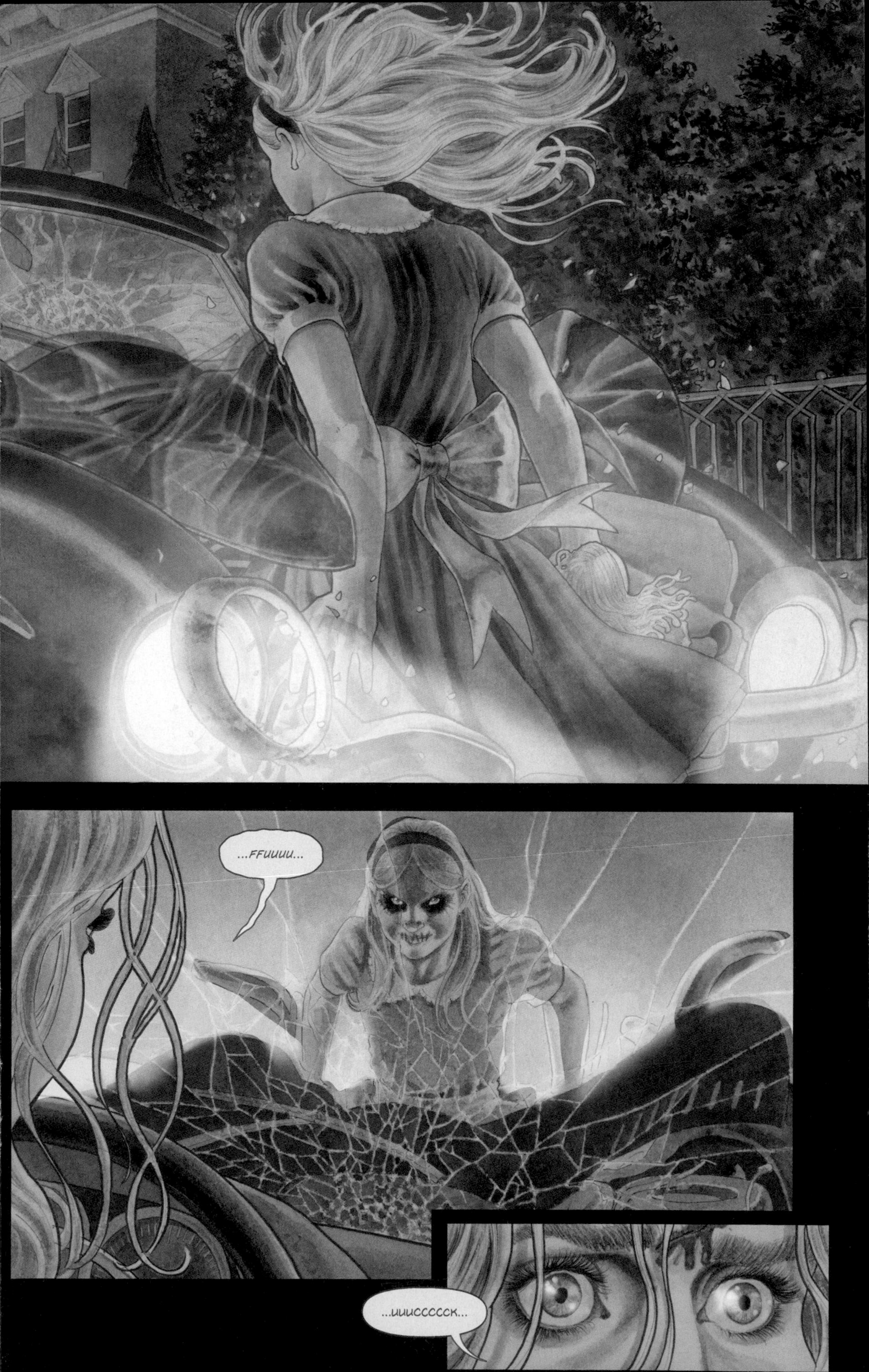
...FFUUUU...
...UUUCCCCCK...

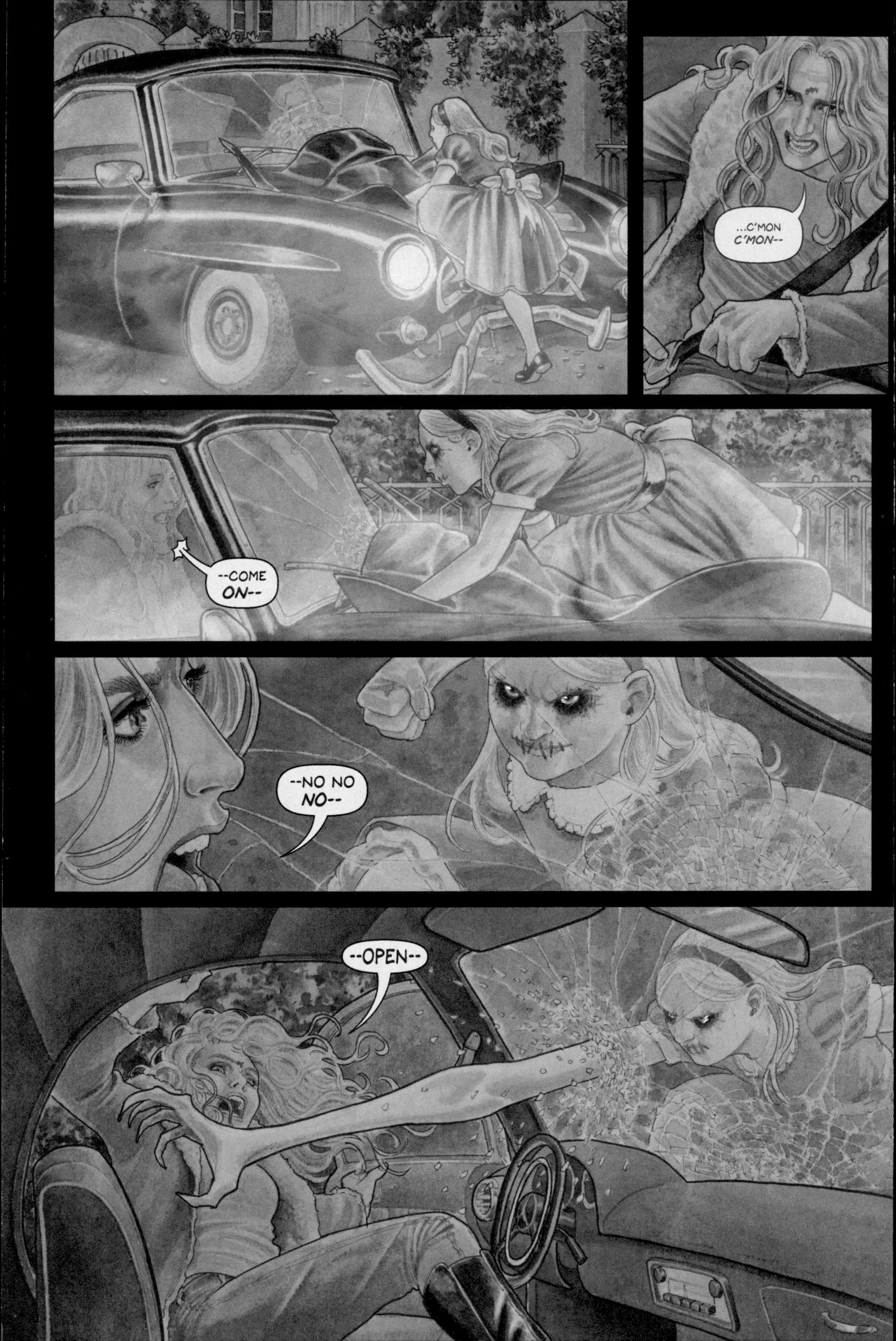
...C'MON C'MON--
--COME ON--
--NO NO NO--
--OPEN--

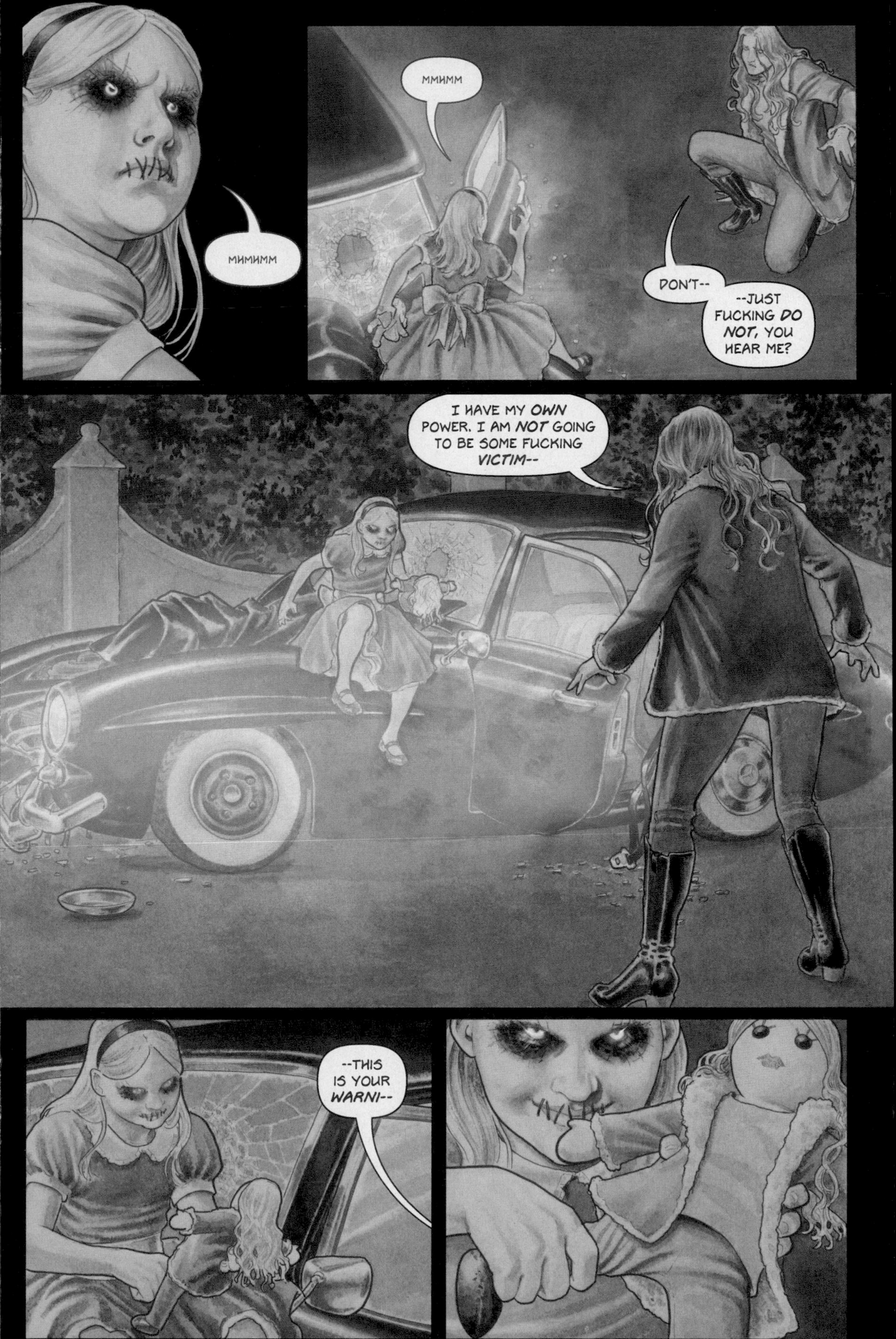
MHMHMM
MMHMM
DON'T--
--JUST FUCKING DO NOT, YOU HEAR ME?
I HAVE MY OWN POWER. I AM NOT GOING TO BE SOME FUCKING VICTIM--
--THIS IS YOUR WARNI--

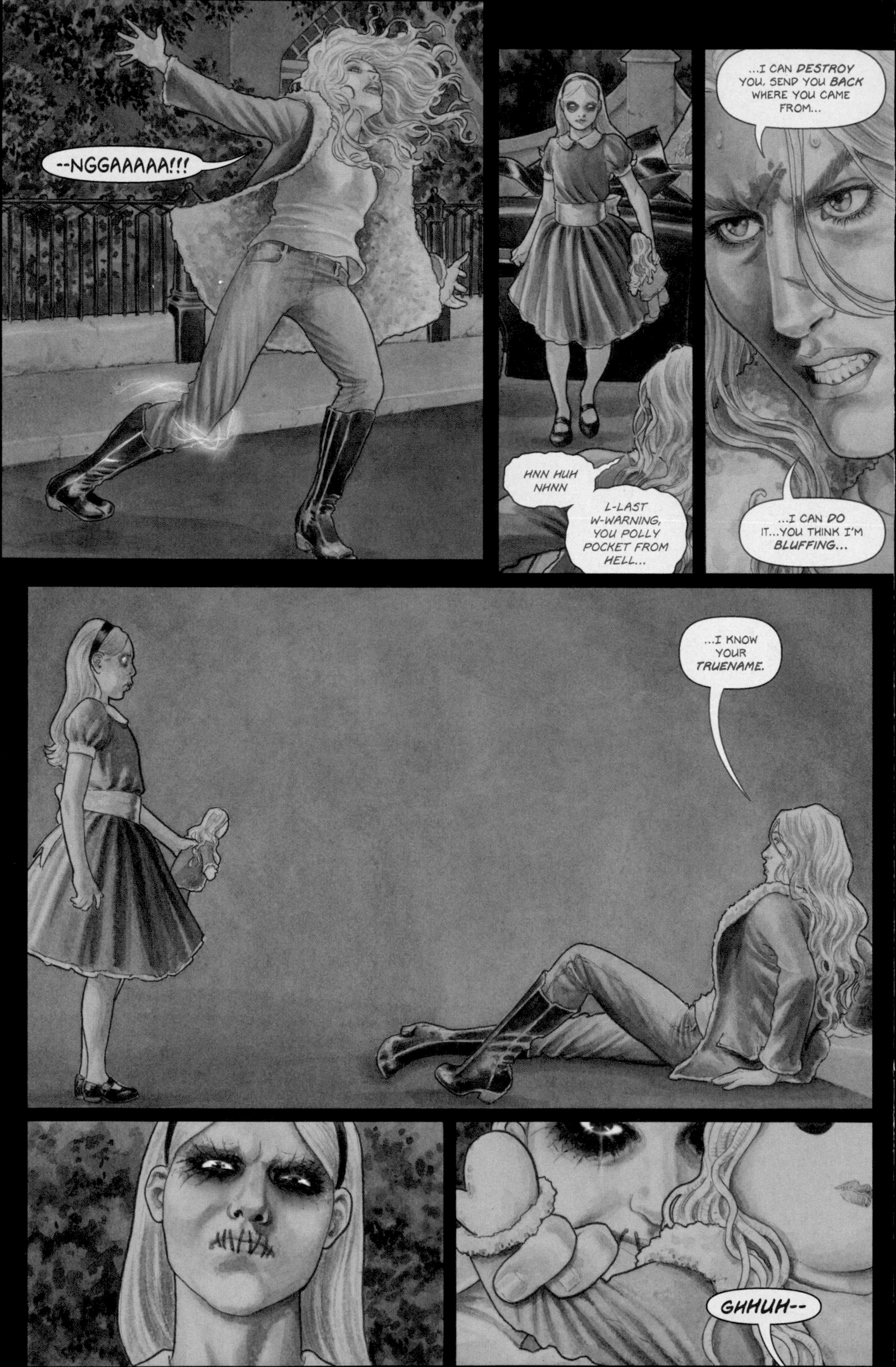
--NGGAAAAA!!!
HNN HUH NHNN
L-LAST W-WARNING, YOU POLLY POCKET FROM HELL...
...I CAN DESTROY YOU. SEND YOU BACK WHERE YOU CAME FROM...
...I CAN DO IT...YOU THINK I'M BLUFFING...
...I KNOW YOUR TRUENAME.
GHHUH--

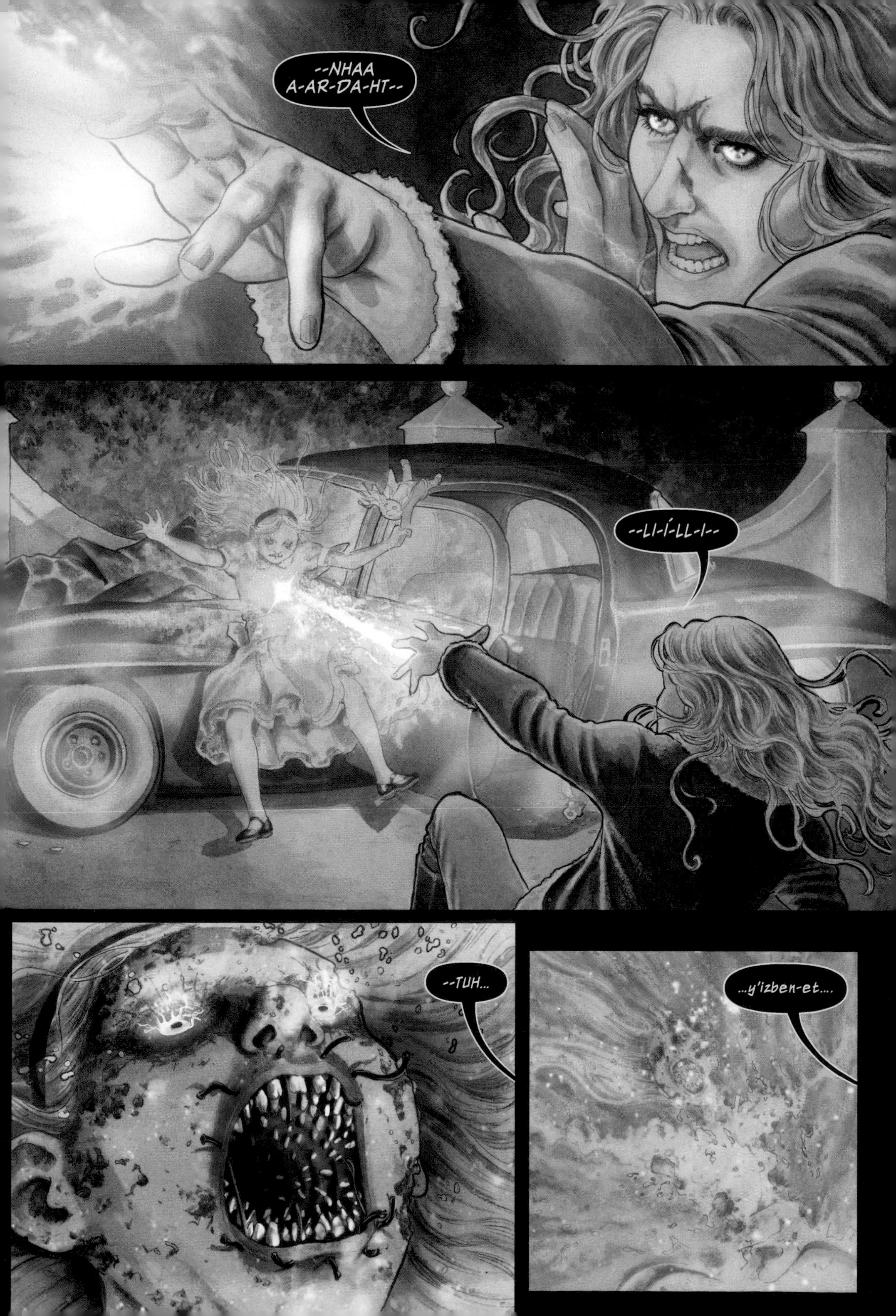
--NHAA A-AR-DA-HT--
--LI-Í-LL-I--
--TUH...
...y'izben-et....

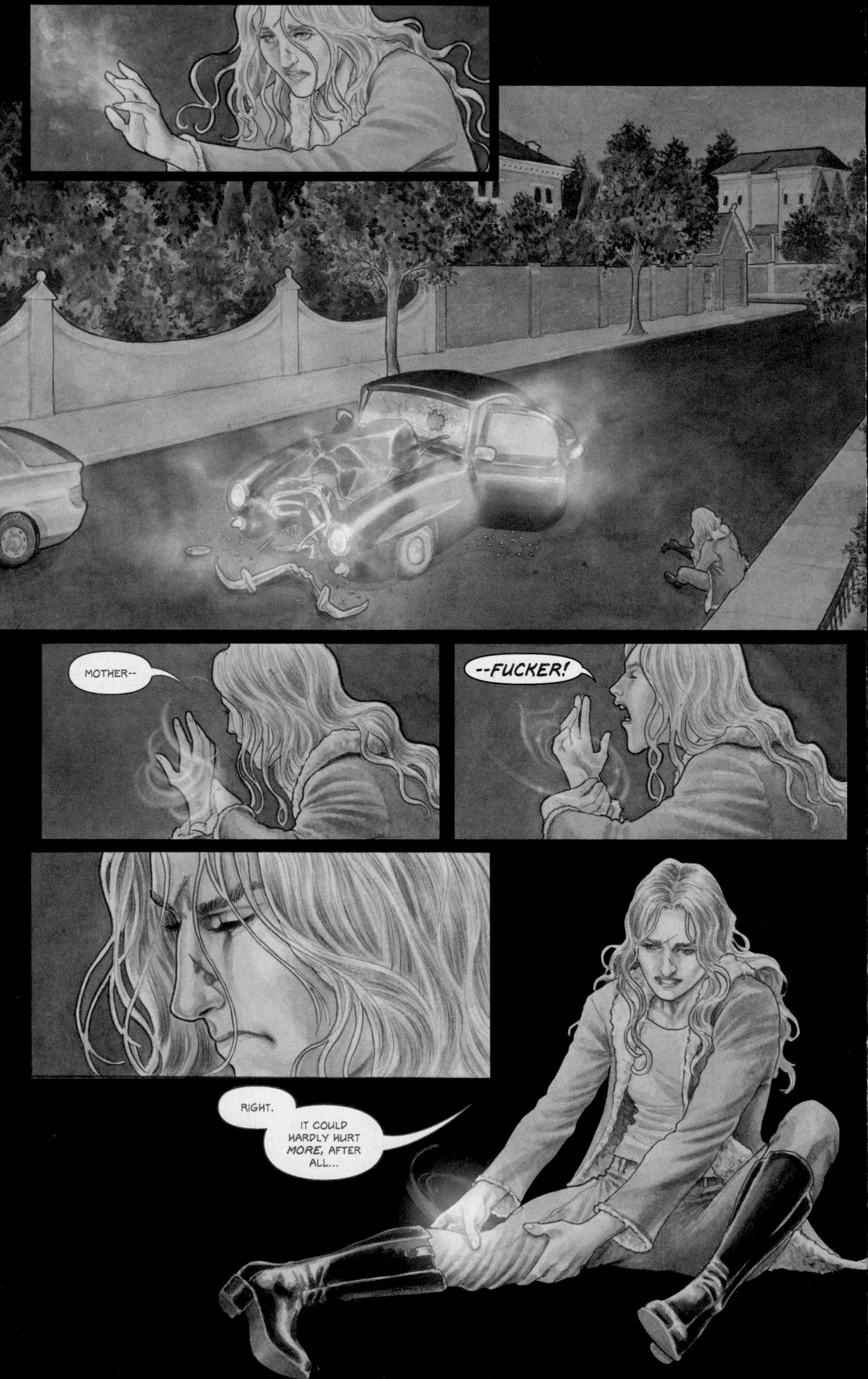
MOTHER--
--FUCKER!
RIGHT.
IT COULD HARDLY HURT MORE, AFTER ALL...

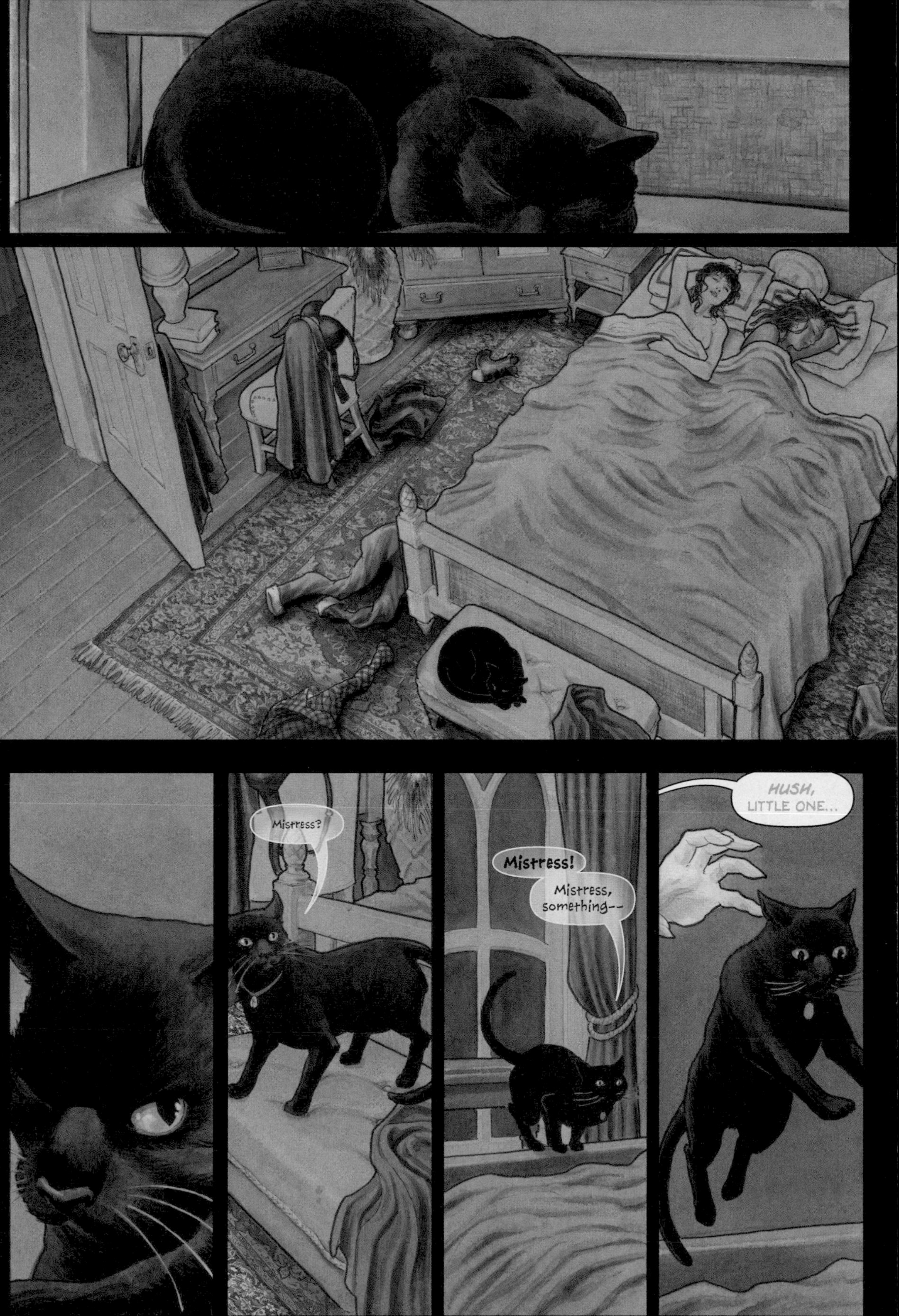
Mistress?
Mistress!
Mistress, something--
HUSH, LITTLE ONE...

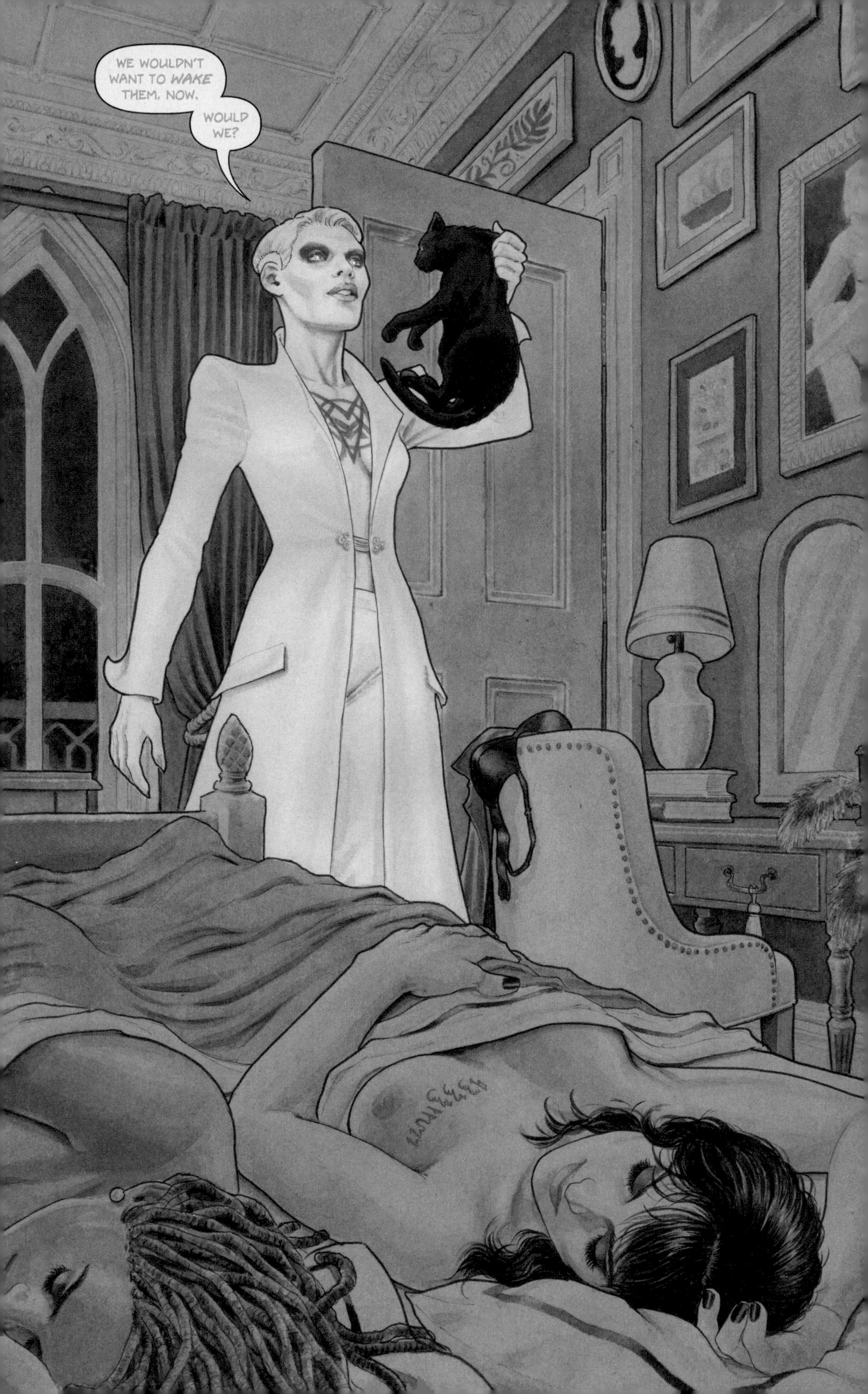
WE WOULDN'T WANT TO *WAKE* THEM, NOW.
WOULD WE?

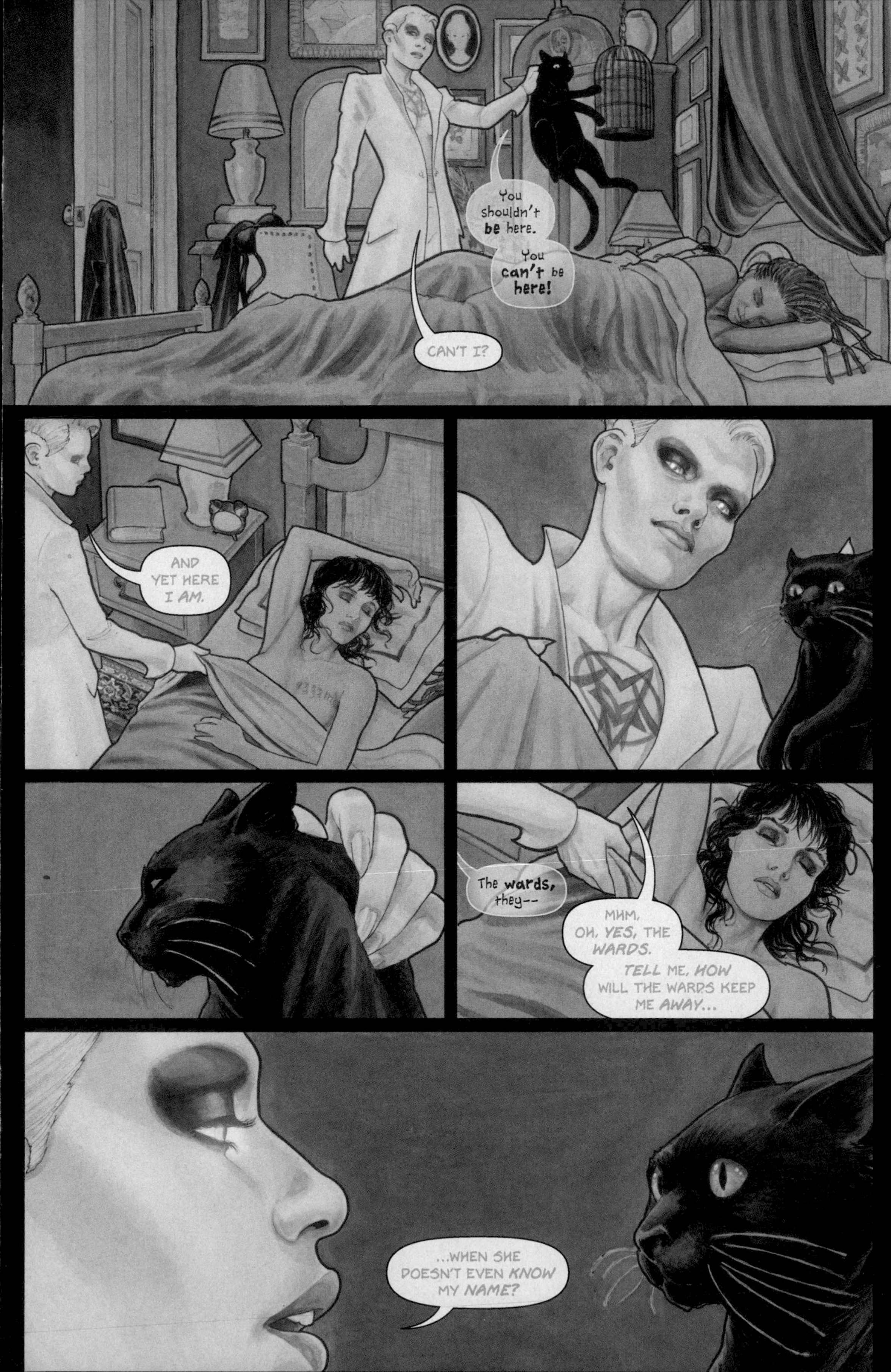
You shouldn't be here.
You can't be here!
CAN'T I?
AND YET HERE I AM.
The wards, they--
MMM, OH, YES, THE WARDS.
TELL ME, HOW WILL THE WARDS KEEP ME AWAY...
...WHEN SHE DOESN'T EVEN KNOW MY NAME?

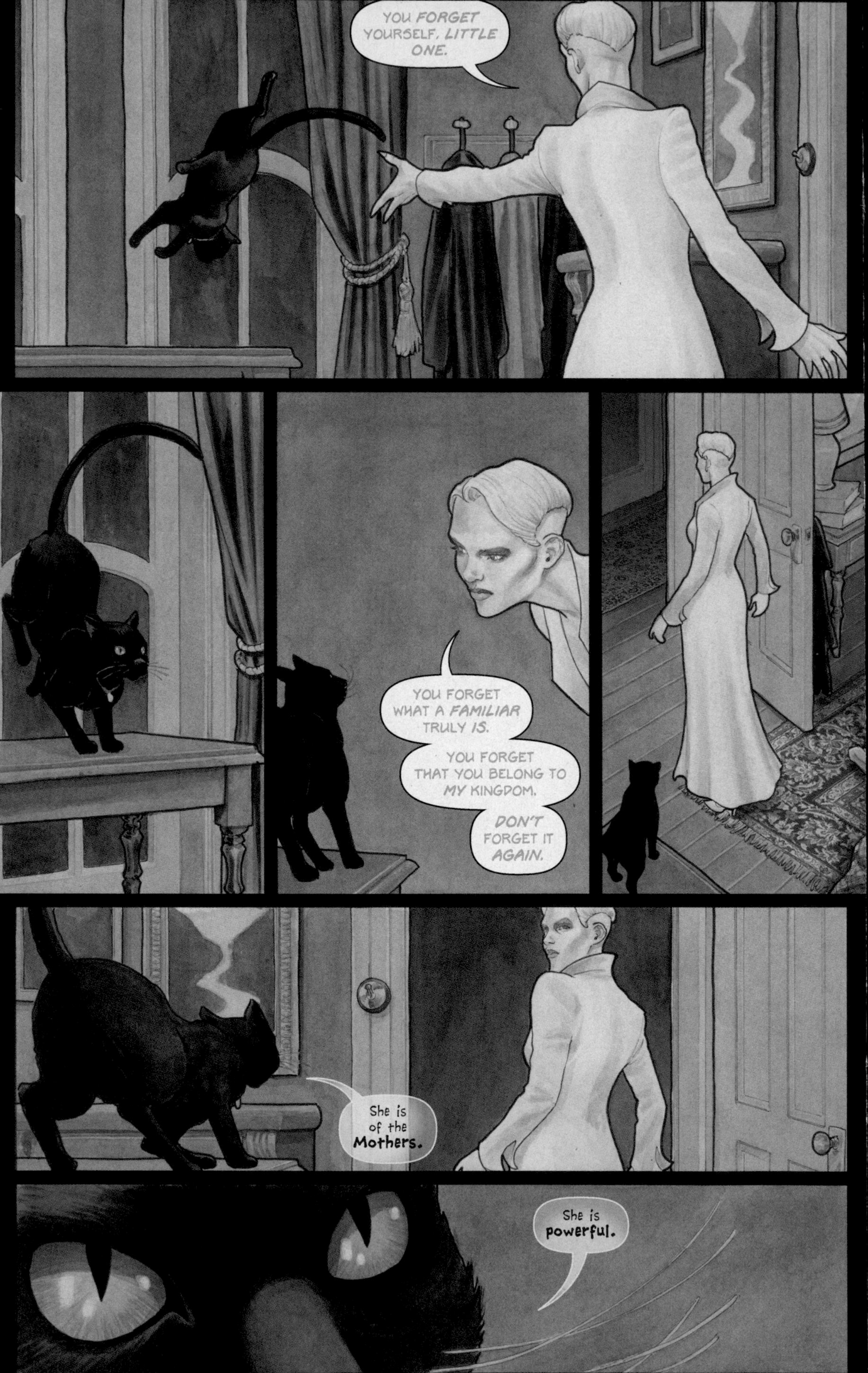
YOU *FORGET* YOURSELF, *LITTLE ONE.*
YOU FORGET WHAT A *FAMILIAR* TRULY *IS.*
YOU FORGET THAT YOU BELONG TO *MY* KINGDOM.
DON'T FORGET IT *AGAIN.*
She is of the **Mothers.**
She is **powerful.**

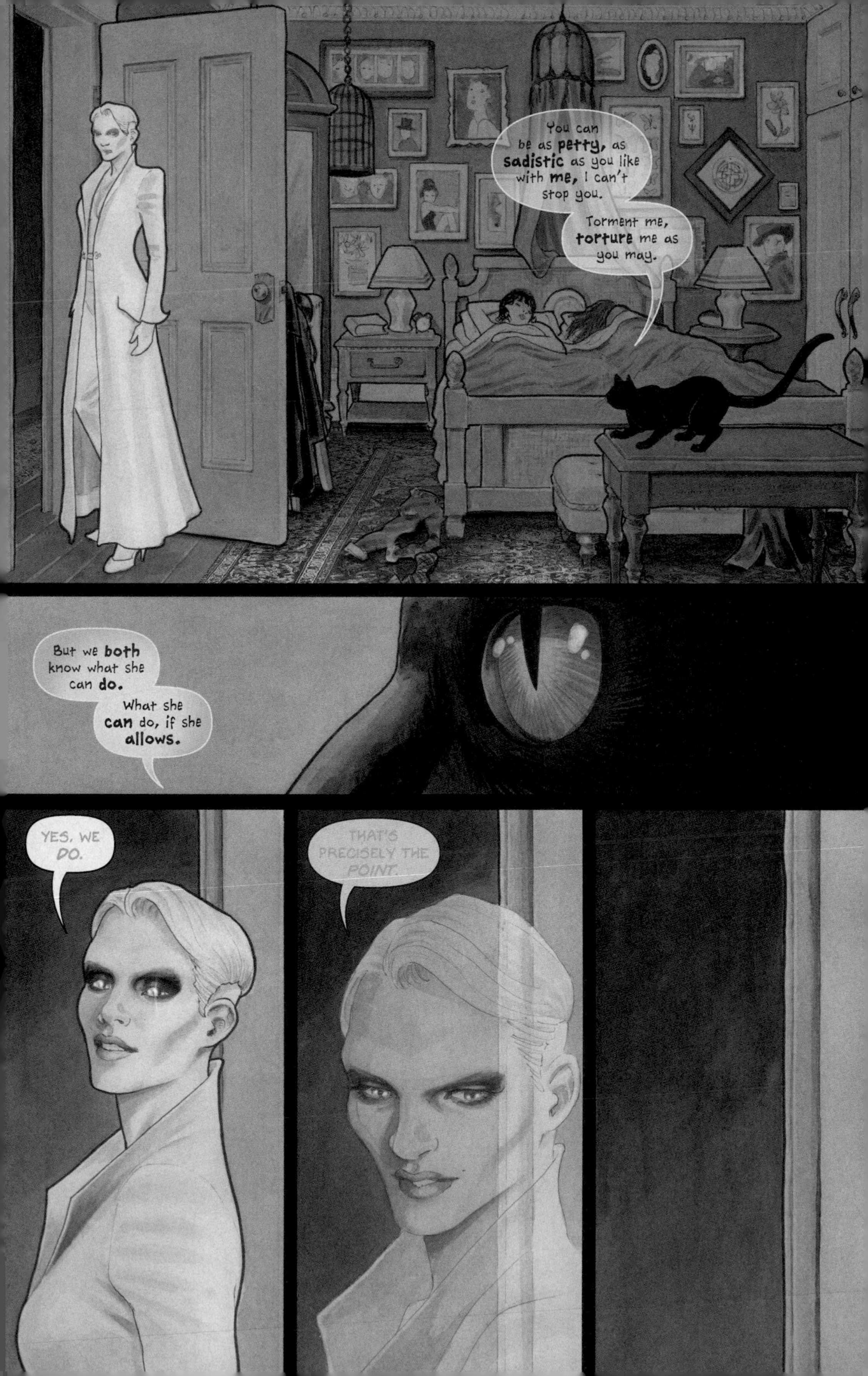
You can be as **petty,** as **sadistic** as you like with **me,** I can't stop you.
Torment me, **torture** me as you may.
But we **both** know what she can **do.**
What she **can** do, if she **allows.**
YES. WE *DO.*
THAT'S PRECISELY THE *POINT.*

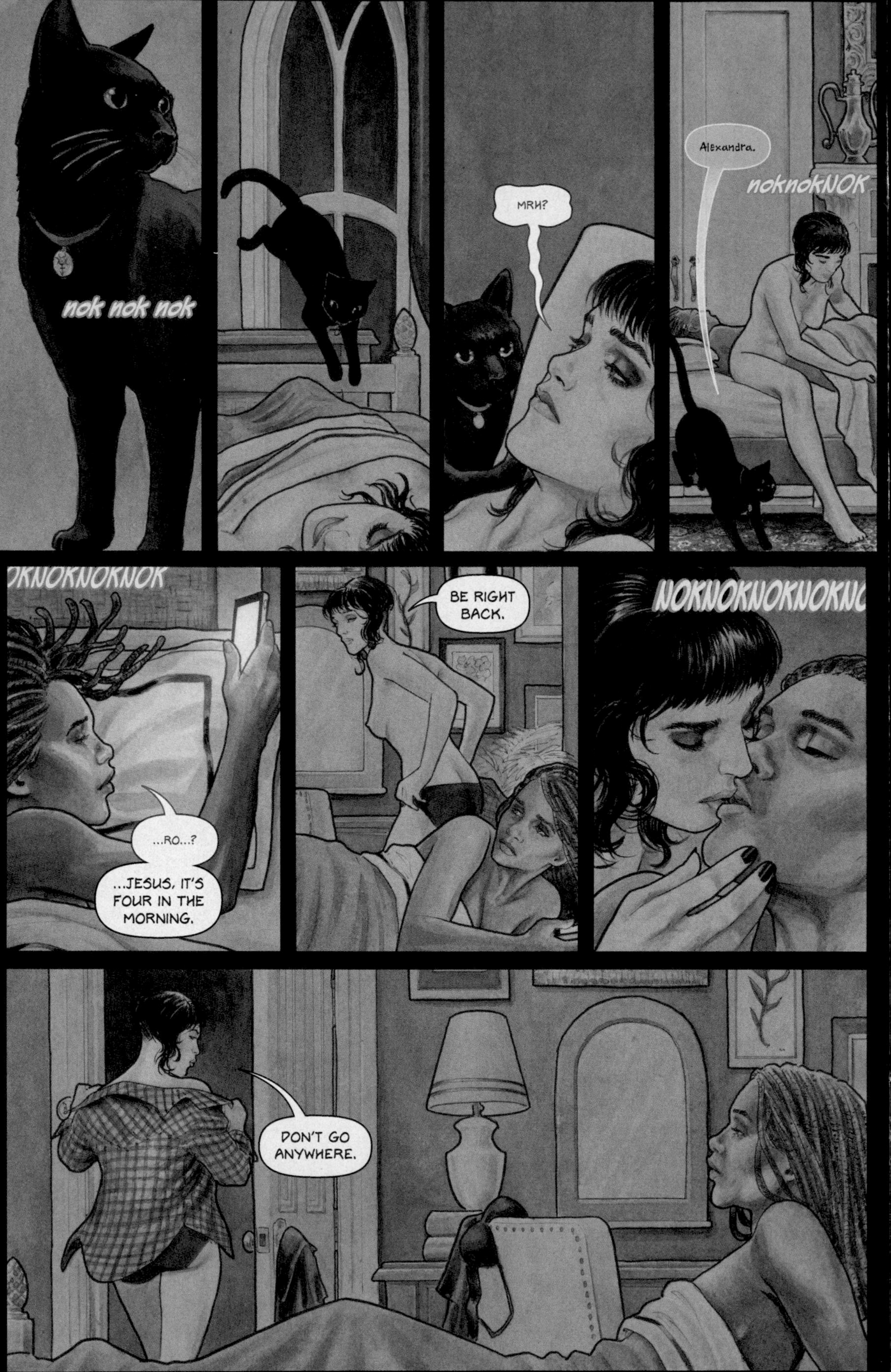
nok nok nok
MRH?
Alexandra.
noknokNOK
NOKNOKNOKNOK
...RO...?
...JESUS, IT'S FOUR IN THE MORNING.
BE RIGHT BACK.
NOKNOKNOKNOKNOKNO
DON'T GO ANYWHERE.

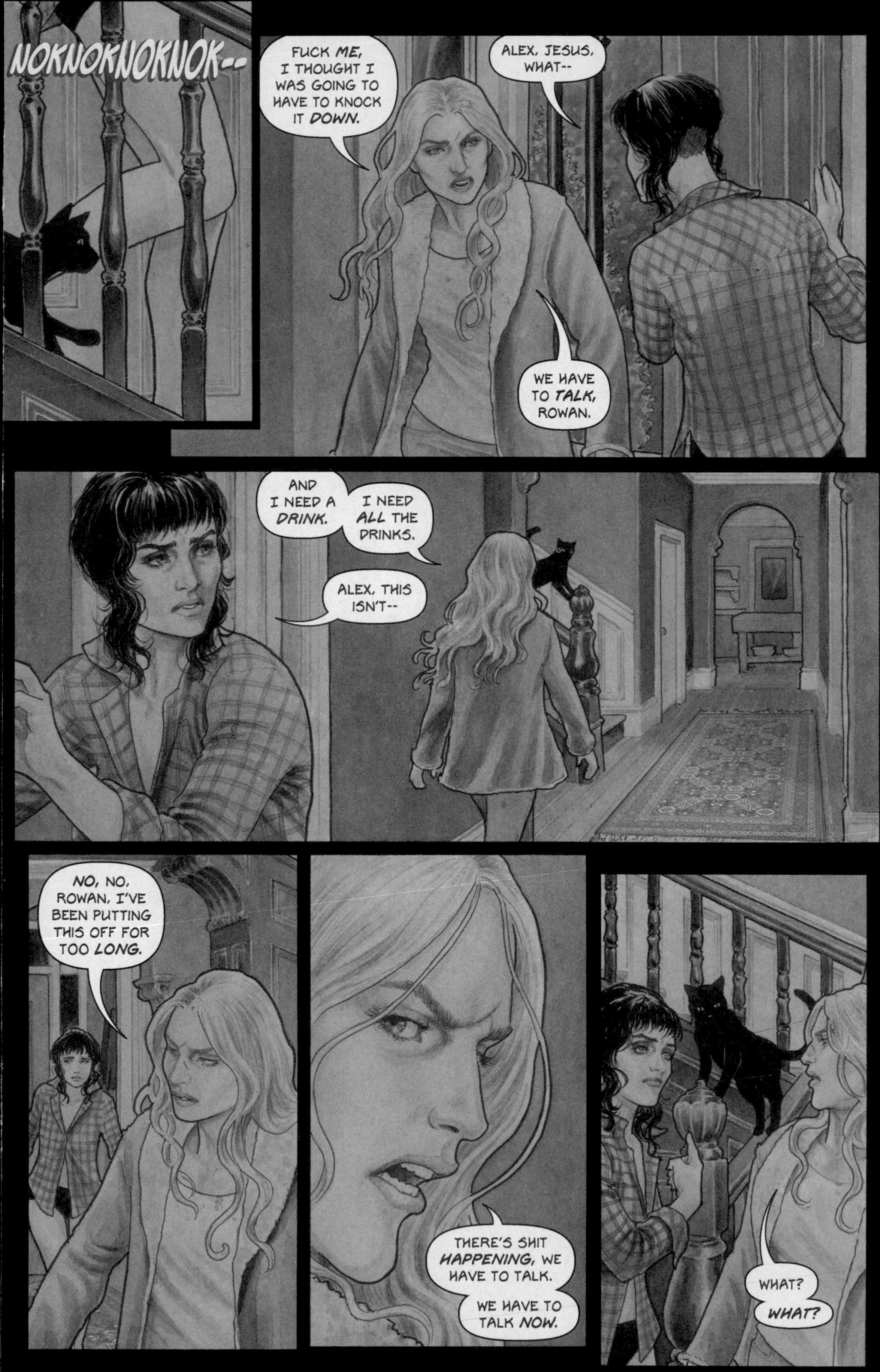
NOKNOKNOKNOK--
FUCK ME, I THOUGHT I WAS GOING TO HAVE TO KNOCK IT DOWN.
ALEX, JESUS, WHAT--
WE HAVE TO TALK, ROWAN.
AND I NEED A DRINK.
I NEED ALL THE DRINKS.
ALEX, THIS ISN'T--
NO, NO, ROWAN, I'VE BEEN PUTTING THIS OFF FOR TOO LONG.
THERE'S SHIT HAPPENING, WE HAVE TO TALK.
WE HAVE TO TALK NOW.
WHAT?
WHAT?

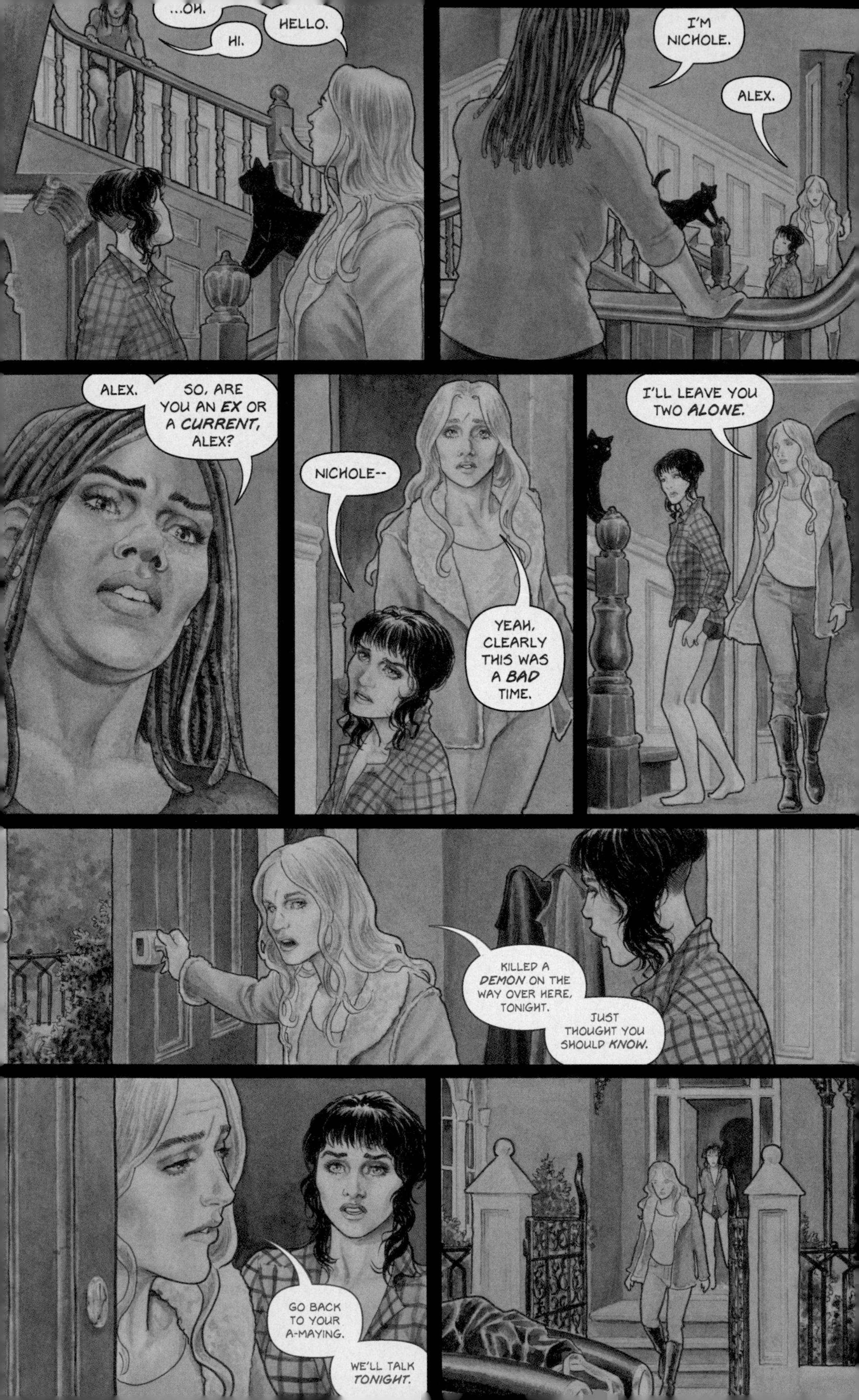

...OH.
HI.
HELLO.
I'M NICHOLE.
ALEX.
ALEX.
SO, ARE YOU AN EX OR A CURRENT, ALEX?
NICHOLE--
YEAH, CLEARLY THIS WAS A BAD TIME.
I'LL LEAVE YOU TWO ALONE.
KILLED A DEMON ON THE WAY OVER HERE, TONIGHT.
JUST THOUGHT YOU SHOULD KNOW.
GO BACK TO YOUR A-MAYING.
WE'LL TALK TONIGHT.

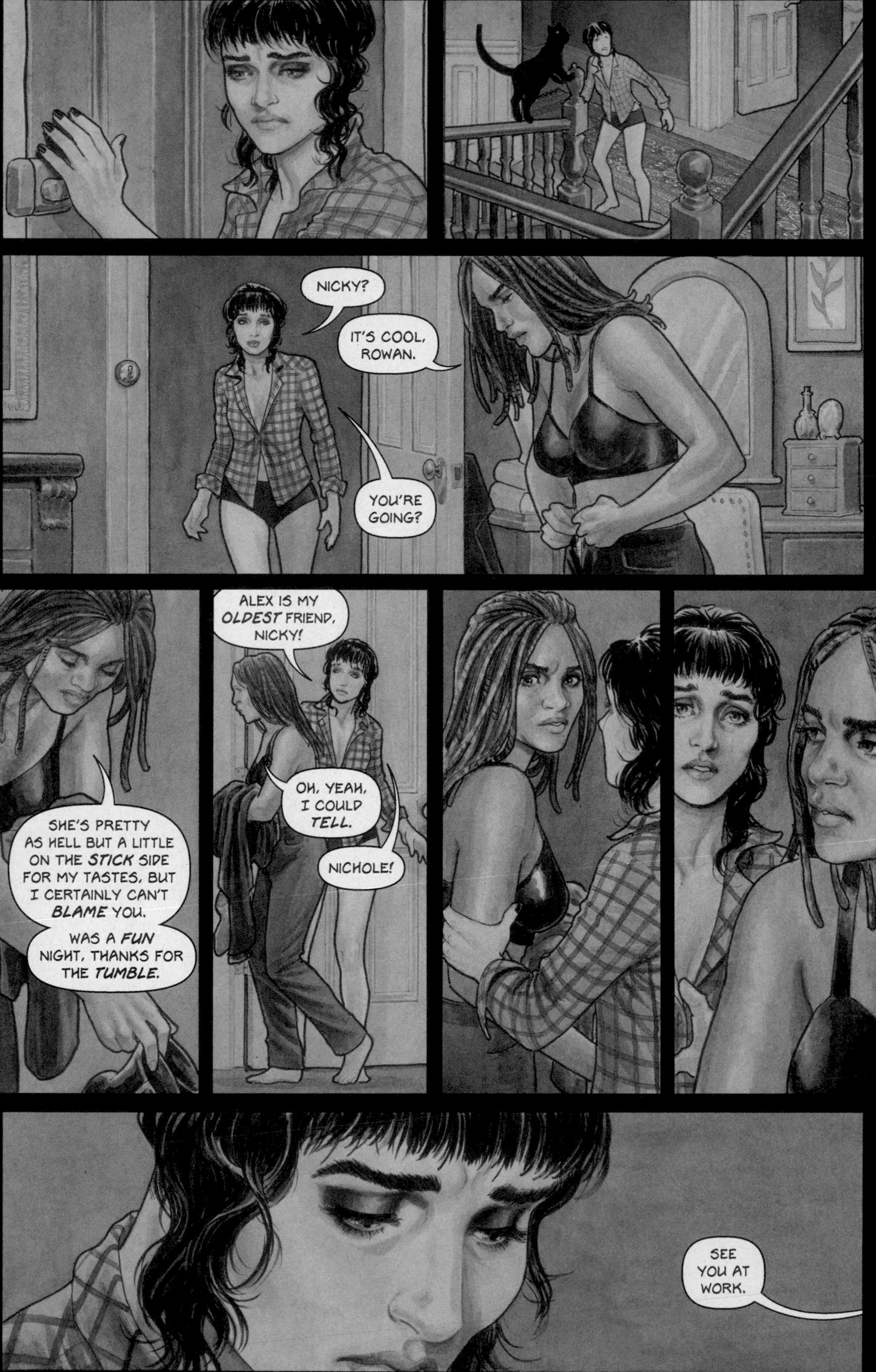
NICKY?
IT'S COOL, ROWAN.
YOU'RE GOING?
SHE'S PRETTY AS HELL BUT A LITTLE ON THE STICK SIDE FOR MY TASTES, BUT I CERTAINLY CAN'T BLAME YOU.
WAS A FUN NIGHT, THANKS FOR THE TUMBLE.
ALEX IS MY OLDEST FRIEND, NICKY!
OH, YEAH, I COULD TELL.
NICHOLE!
SEE YOU AT WORK.

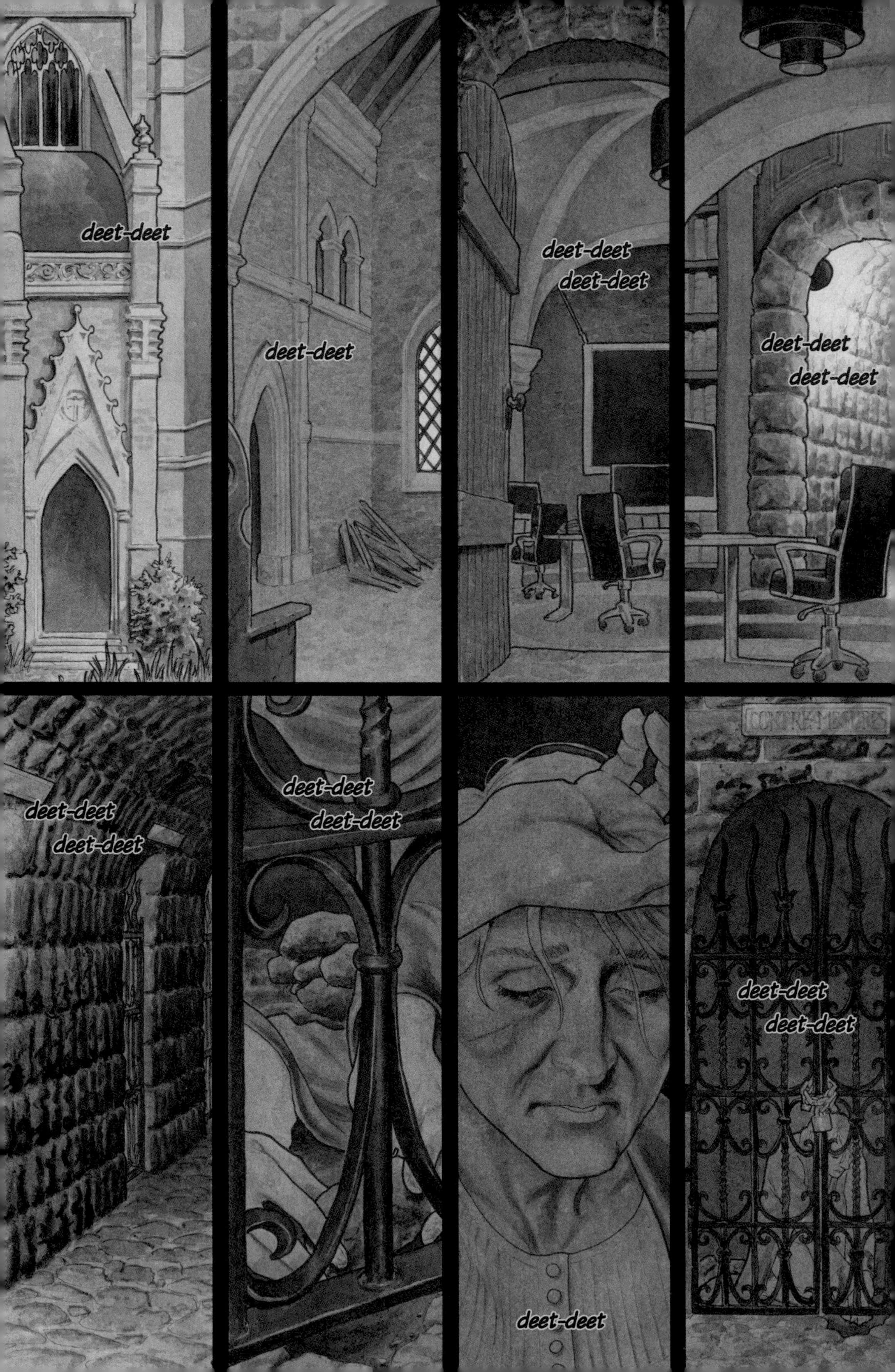
deet-deet
deet-deet
deet-deet
deet-deet
deet-deet
deet-deet
deet-deet
deet-deet
deet-deet
deet-deet
deet-deet
CONTREMESURES
deet-deet
deet-deet

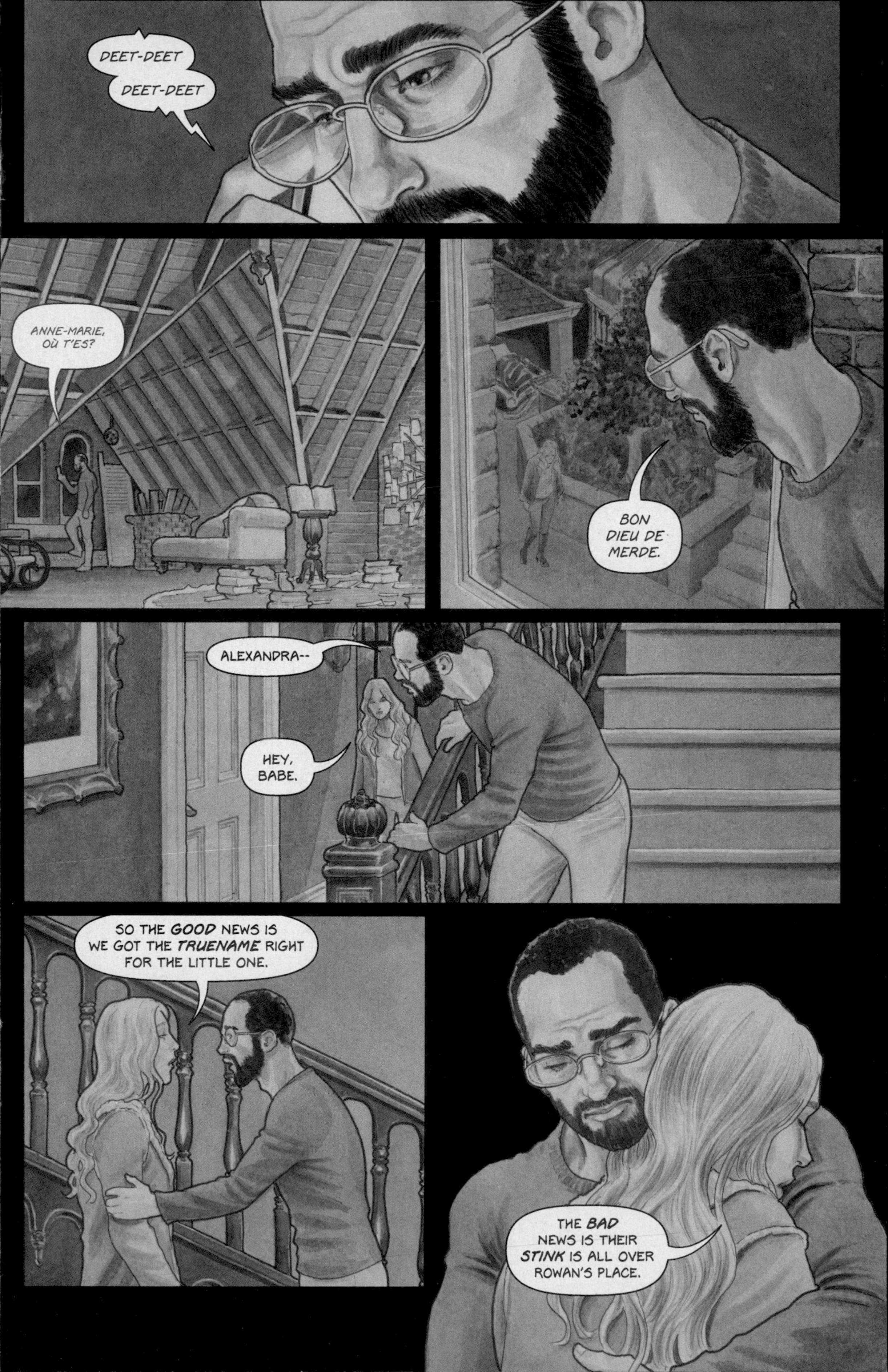
DEET-DEET
DEET-DEET
ANNE-MARIE, OÙ T'ES?
BON DIEU DE MERDE.
ALEXANDRA--
HEY, BABE.
SO THE GOOD NEWS IS WE GOT THE TRUENAME RIGHT FOR THE LITTLE ONE.
THE BAD NEWS IS THEIR STINK IS ALL OVER ROWAN'S PLACE.

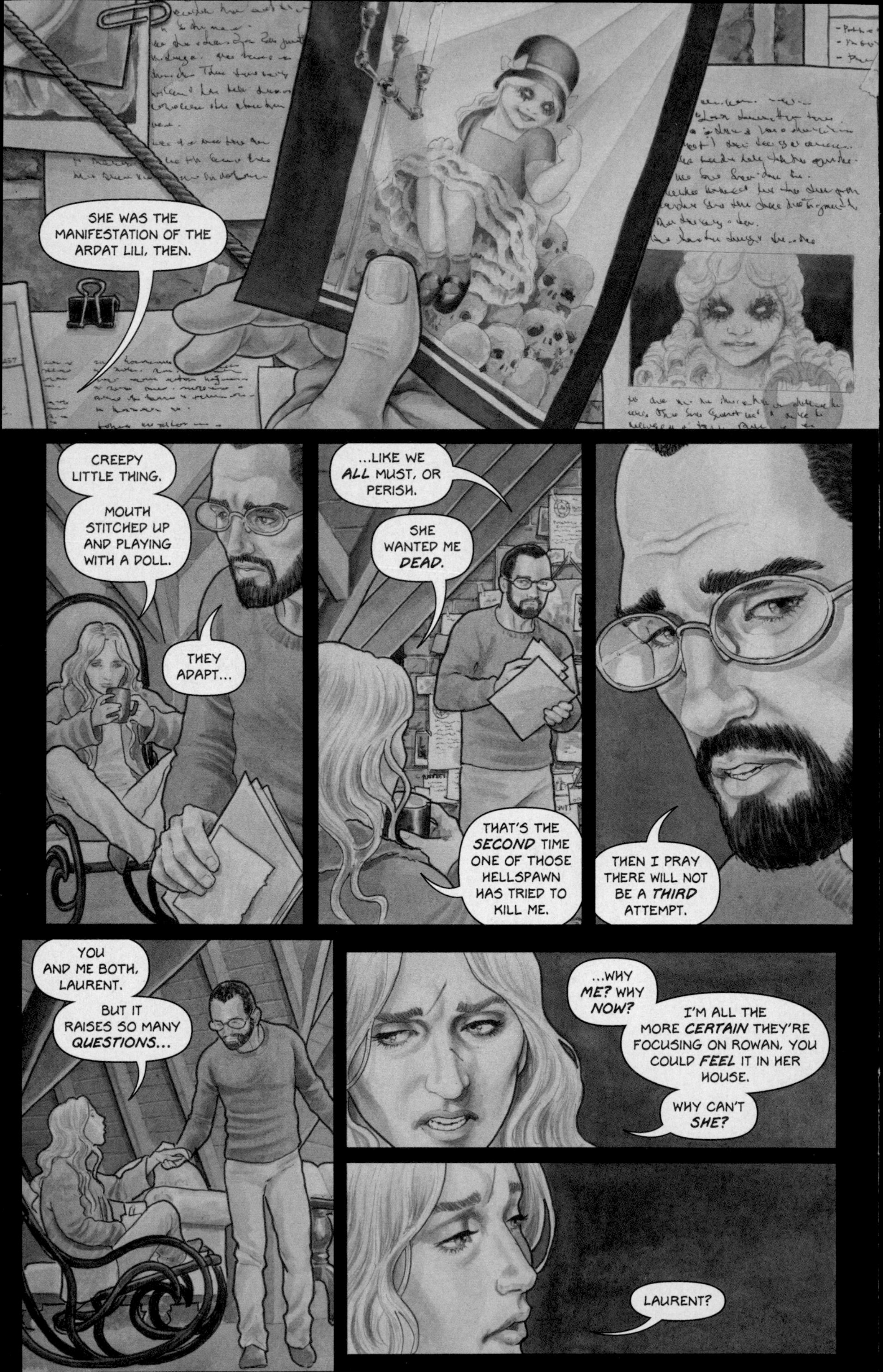
SHE WAS THE MANIFESTATION OF THE ARDAT LILI, THEN.
CREEPY LITTLE THING.
MOUTH STITCHED UP AND PLAYING WITH A DOLL.
THEY ADAPT...
...LIKE WE ALL MUST, OR PERISH.
SHE WANTED ME DEAD.
THAT'S THE SECOND TIME ONE OF THOSE HELLSPAWN HAS TRIED TO KILL ME.
THEN I PRAY THERE WILL NOT BE A THIRD ATTEMPT.
YOU AND ME BOTH, LAURENT.
BUT IT RAISES SO MANY QUESTIONS...
...WHY ME? WHY NOW?
I'M ALL THE MORE CERTAIN THEY'RE FOCUSING ON ROWAN, YOU COULD FEEL IT IN HER HOUSE.
WHY CAN'T SHE?
LAURENT?

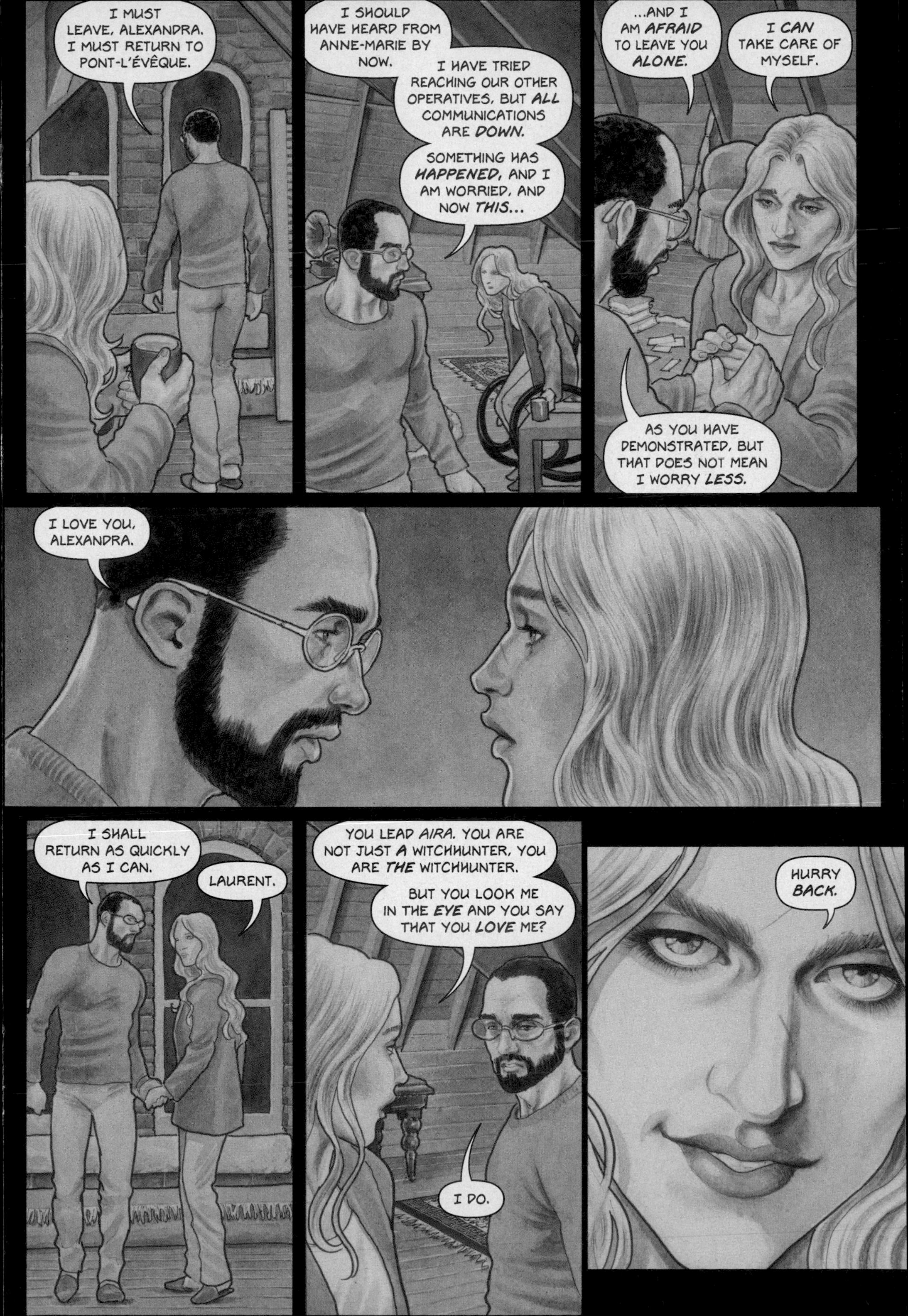
I MUST LEAVE, ALEXANDRA. I MUST RETURN TO PONT-L'ÉVÊQUE.
I SHOULD HAVE HEARD FROM ANNE-MARIE BY NOW.
I HAVE TRIED REACHING OUR OTHER OPERATIVES, BUT *ALL* COMMUNICATIONS ARE *DOWN*.
SOMETHING HAS *HAPPENED*, AND I AM WORRIED, AND NOW *THIS*...
...AND I AM *AFRAID* TO LEAVE YOU *ALONE*.
I *CAN* TAKE CARE OF MYSELF.
AS YOU HAVE DEMONSTRATED, BUT THAT DOES NOT MEAN I WORRY *LESS*.
I LOVE YOU, ALEXANDRA.
I SHALL RETURN AS QUICKLY AS I CAN.
LAURENT.
YOU LEAD *AIRA*. YOU ARE NOT JUST *A* WITCHHUNTER, YOU ARE *THE* WITCHHUNTER.
BUT YOU LOOK ME IN THE *EYE* AND YOU SAY THAT YOU *LOVE* ME?
I DO.
HURRY *BACK*.

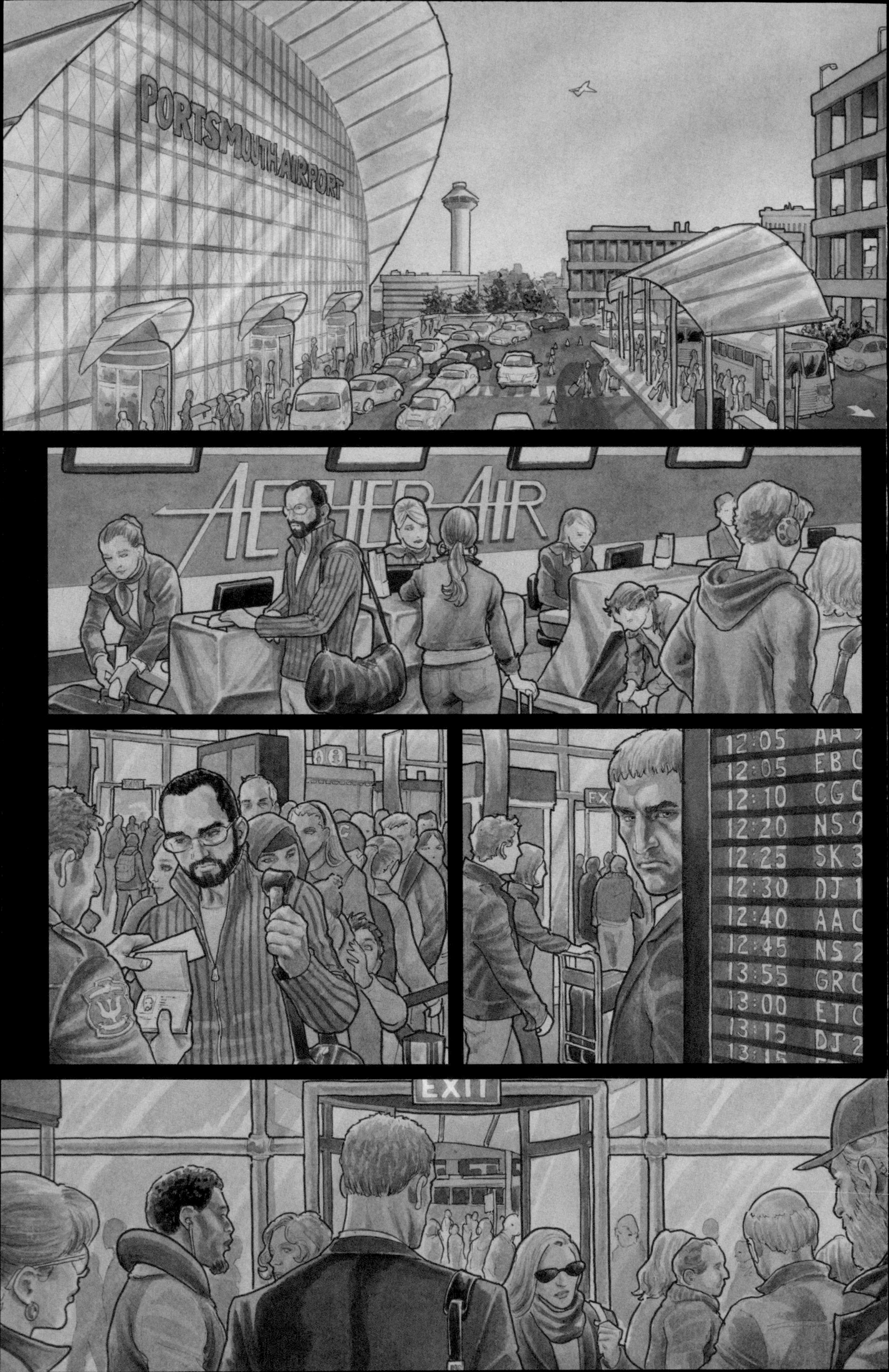
PORTSMOUTH AIRPORT
AETHER AIR
12:05 AA
12:05 EB
12:10 CG
12:20 NS
12:25 SK
12:30 DJ
12:40 AA
12:45 NS
13:55 GR
13:00 ET
13:15 DJ
EXIT

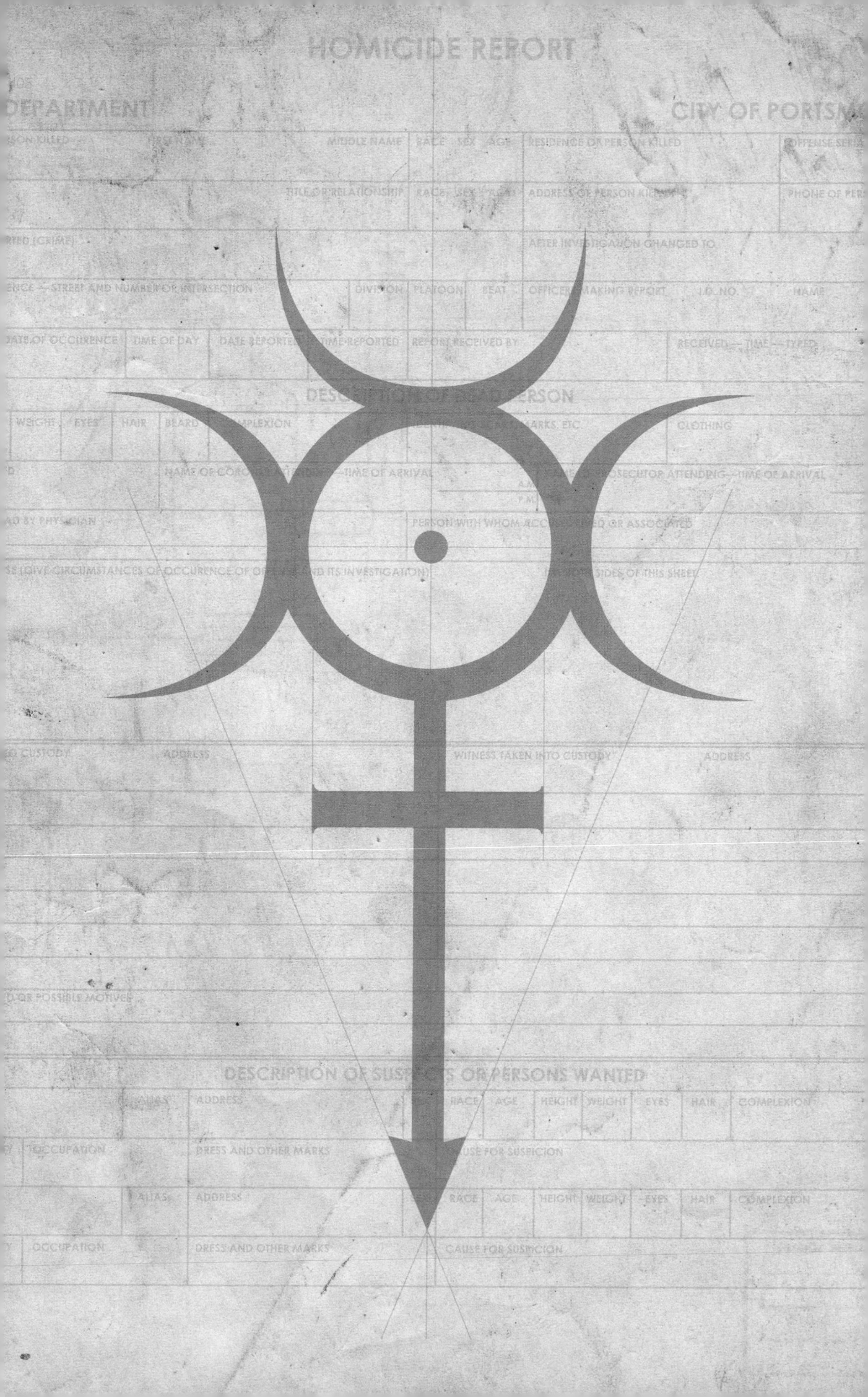
HOMICIDE REPORT
DEPARTMENT
CITY OF PORTSM
DESCRIPTION OF DEAD PERSON
DESCRIPTION OF SUSPECTS OR PERSONS WANTED

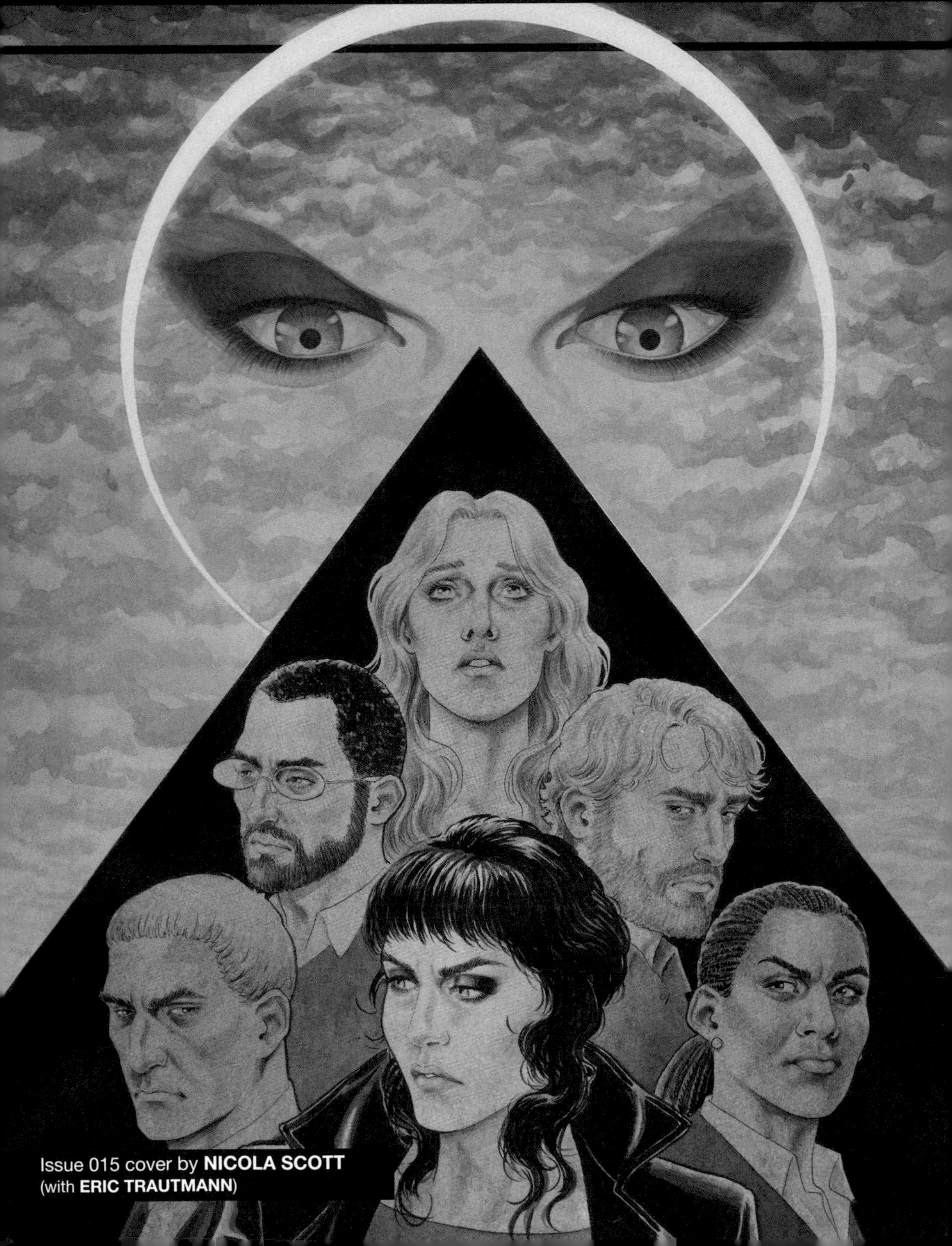

Issue 015 cover by **NICOLA SCOTT**
(with **ERIC TRAUTMANN**)

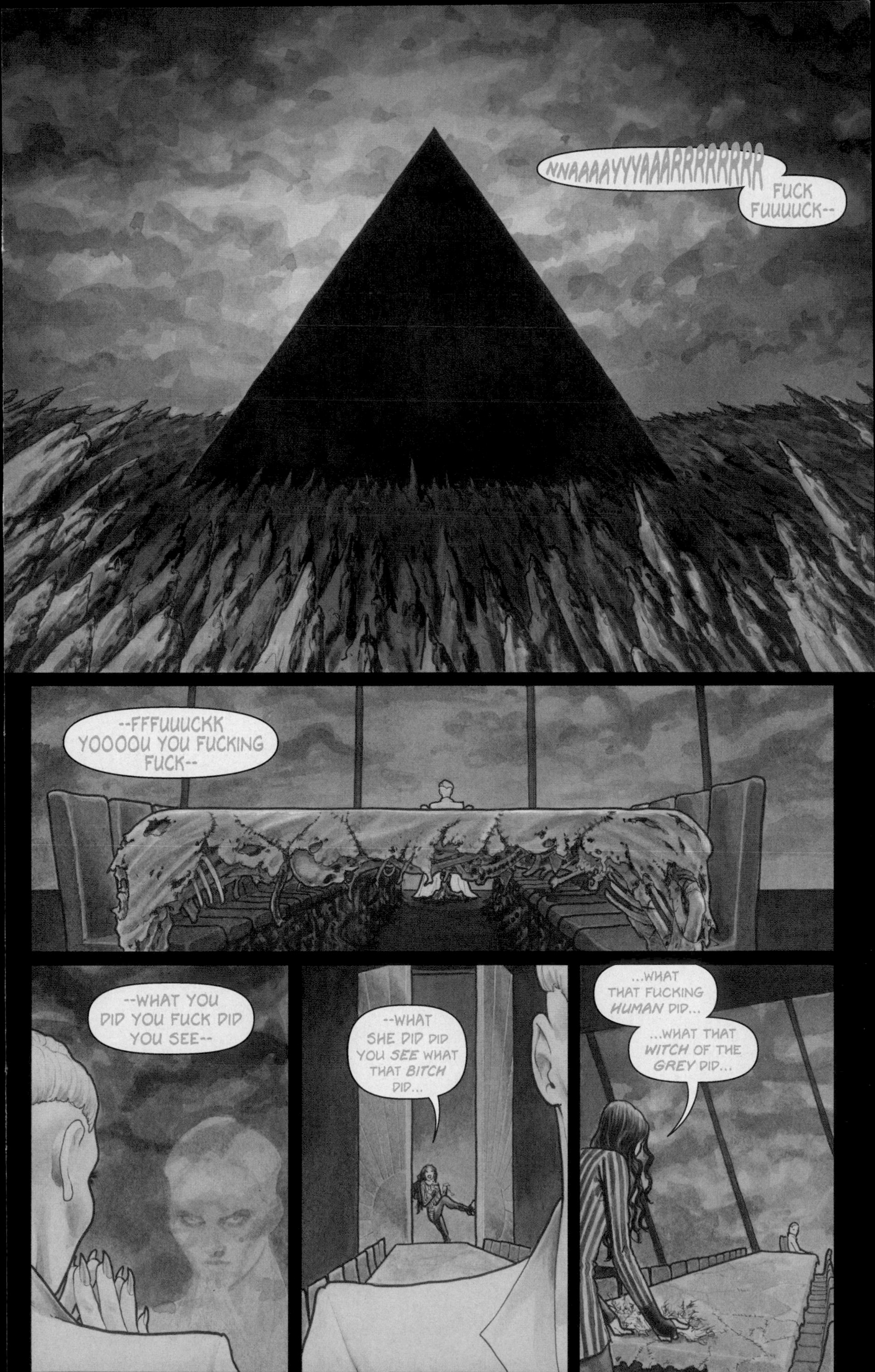
NNAAAAAYYYAAARRRRRRRR
FUCK FUUUUCK--
--FFFUUUCKK YOOOOU YOU FUCKING FUCK--
--WHAT YOU DID YOU FUCK DID YOU SEE--
--WHAT SHE DID DID YOU SEE WHAT THAT BITCH DID...
...WHAT THAT FUCKING HUMAN DID...
...WHAT THAT WITCH OF THE GREY DID...

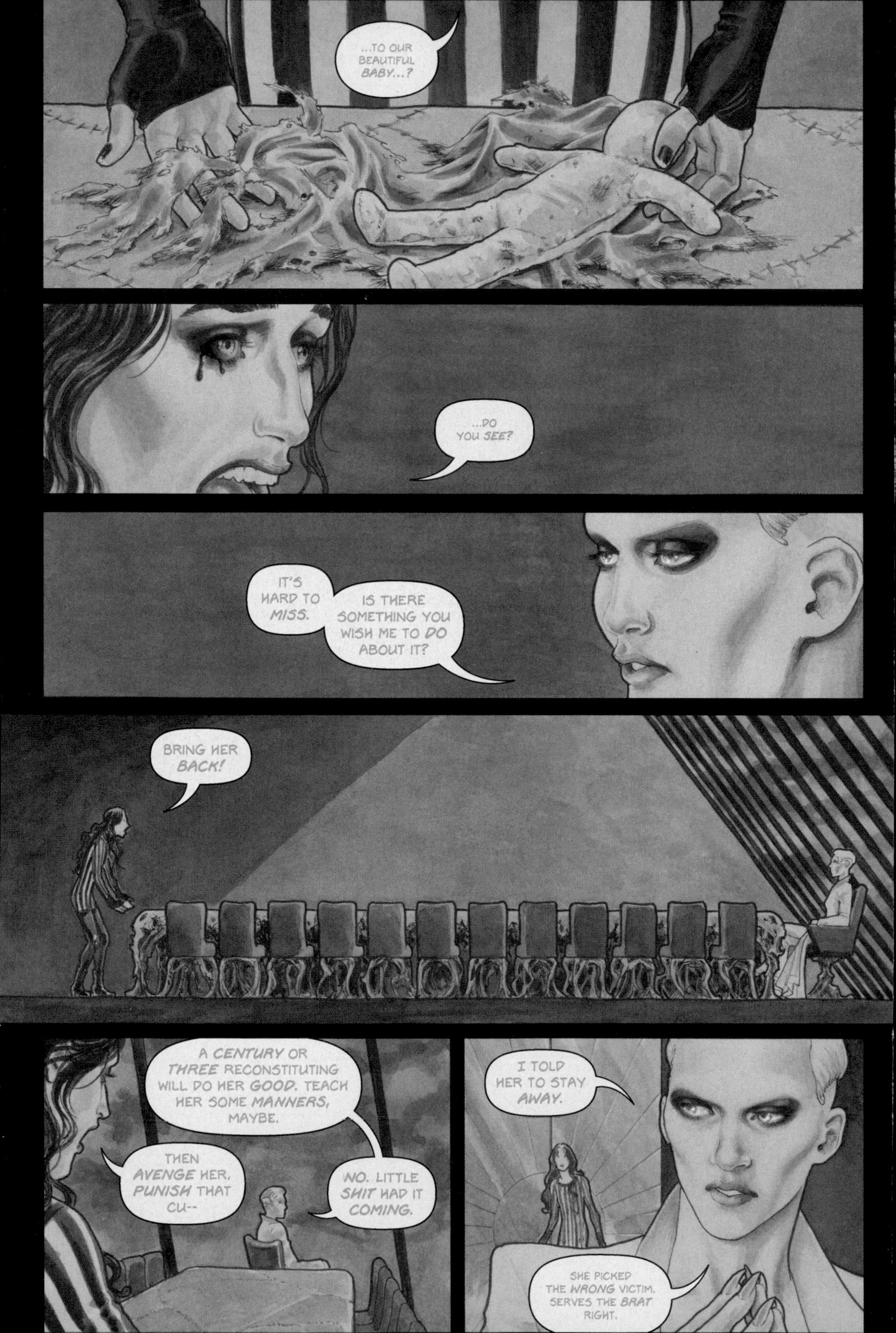
...TO OUR BEAUTIFUL BABY...?
...DO YOU SEE?
IT'S HARD TO MISS.
IS THERE SOMETHING YOU WISH ME TO DO ABOUT IT?
BRING HER BACK!
A CENTURY OR THREE RECONSTITUTING WILL DO HER GOOD. TEACH HER SOME MANNERS, MAYBE.
THEN AVENGE HER, PUNISH THAT CU--
NO. LITTLE SHIT HAD IT COMING.
I TOLD HER TO STAY AWAY.
SHE PICKED THE WRONG VICTIM. SERVES THE BRAT RIGHT.

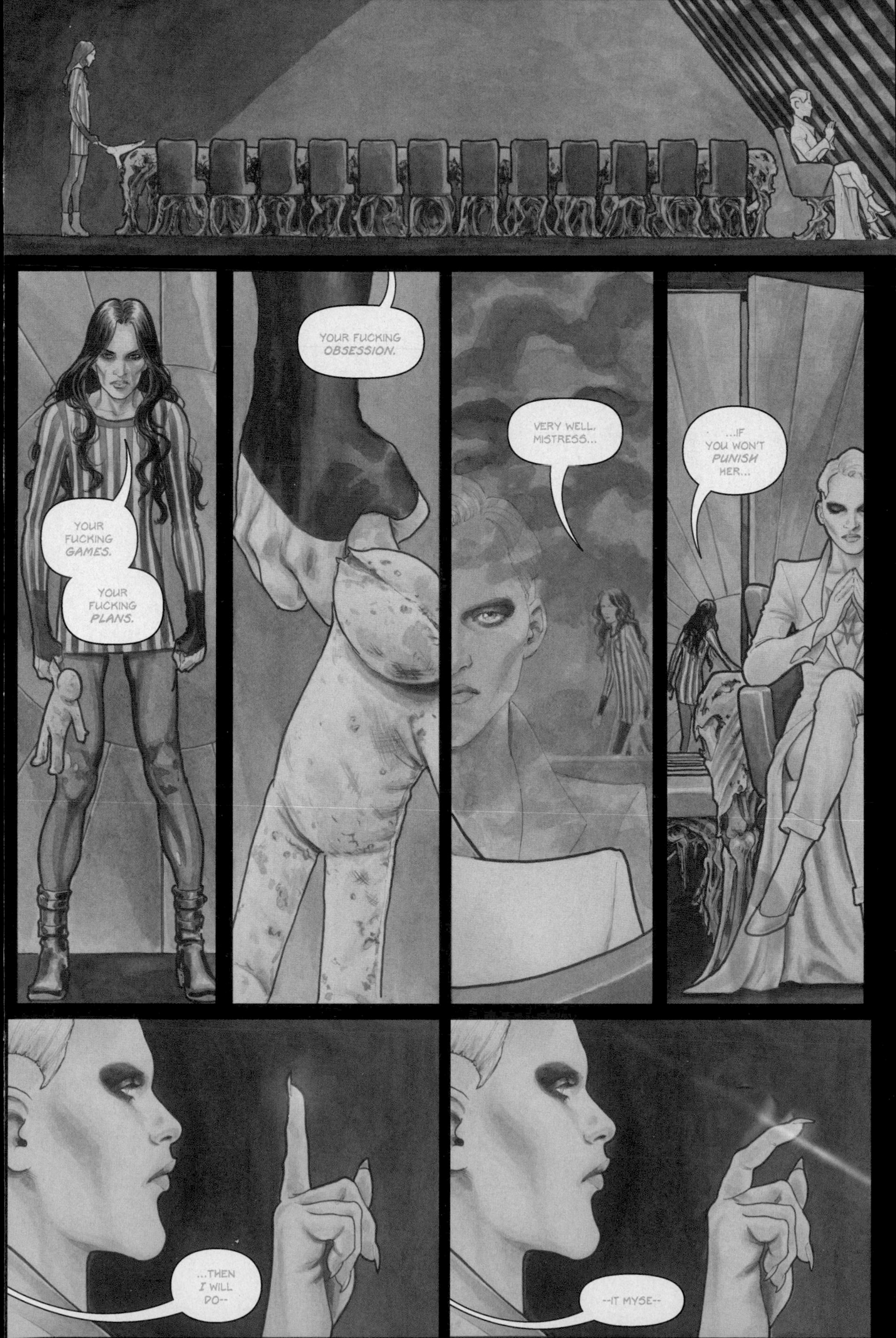
YOUR FUCKING GAMES.
YOUR FUCKING PLANS.
YOUR FUCKING OBSESSION.
VERY WELL, MISTRESS...
...IF YOU WON'T PUNISH HER...
...THEN I WILL DO--
--IT MYSE--

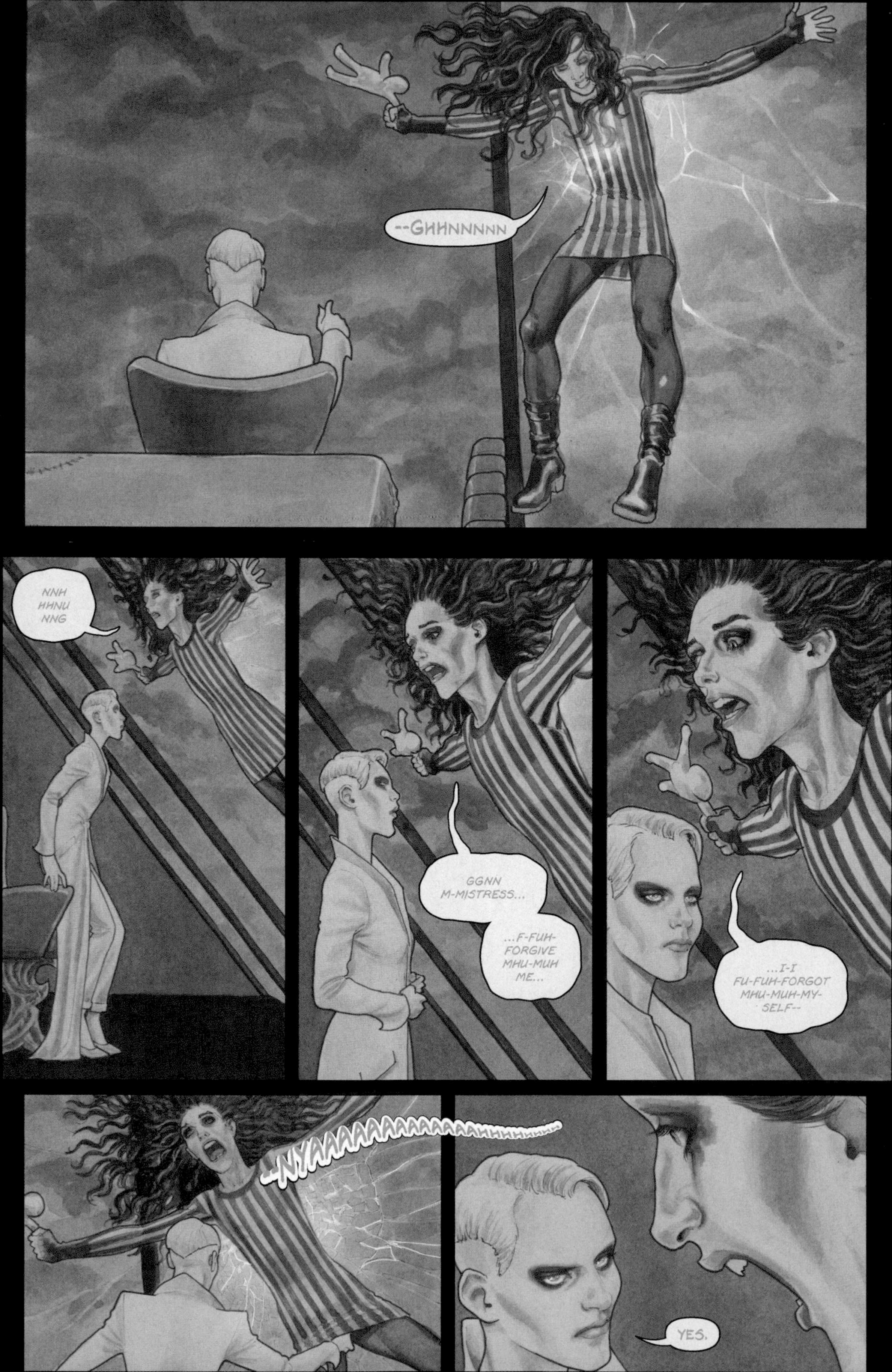
--GHHNNNNN
NNH HHNU NNG
GGNN M-MISTRESS...
...F-FUH-FORGIVE MHU-MUH ME...
...I-I FU-FUH-FORGOT MHU-MUH-MY-SELF--
--NYAAAAAAAAAAAAHHHHH
YES.

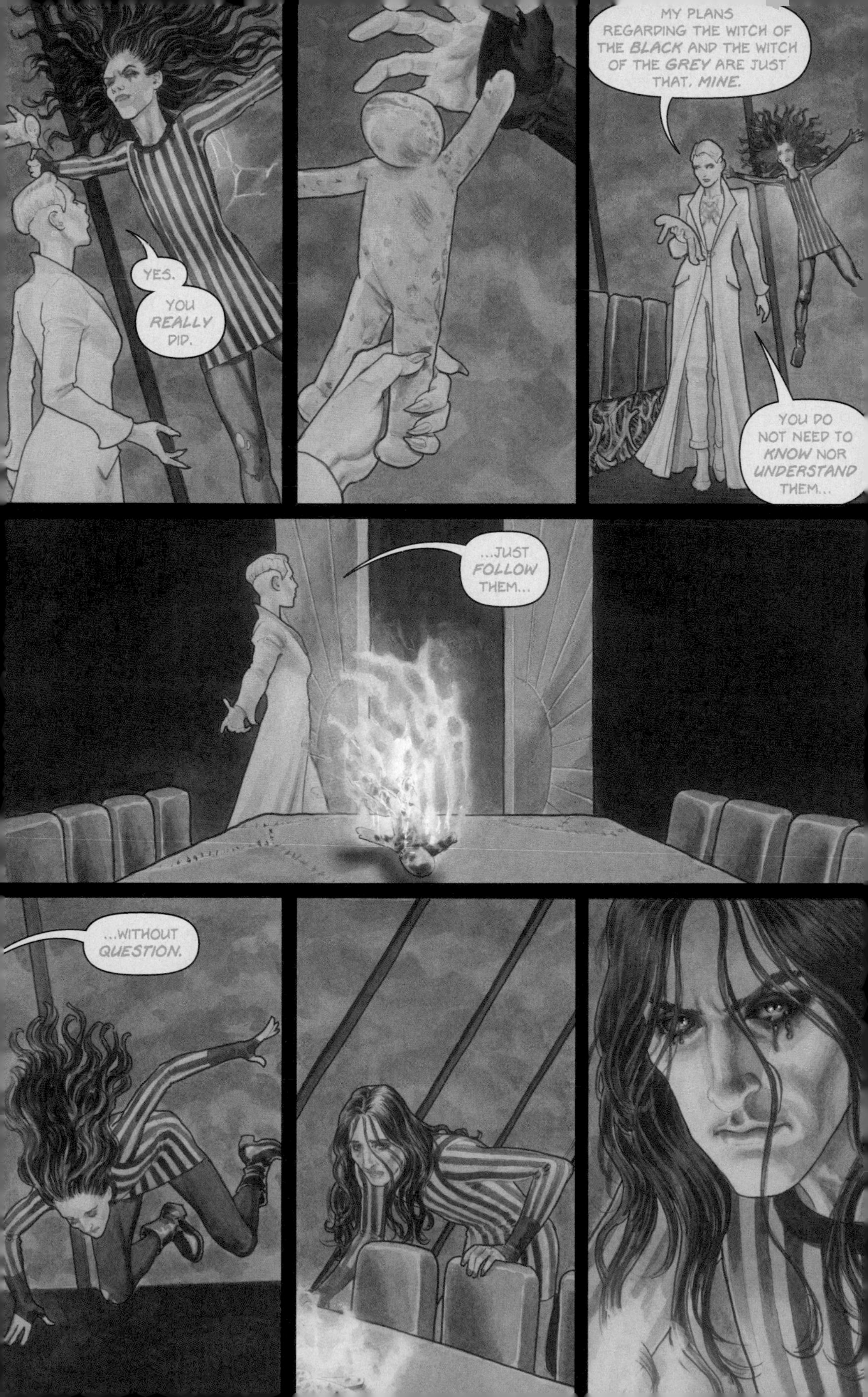
YES.
YOU REALLY DID.
MY PLANS REGARDING THE WITCH OF THE BLACK AND THE WITCH OF THE GREY ARE JUST THAT, MINE.
YOU DO NOT NEED TO KNOW NOR UNDERSTAND THEM...
...JUST FOLLOW THEM...
...WITHOUT QUESTION.

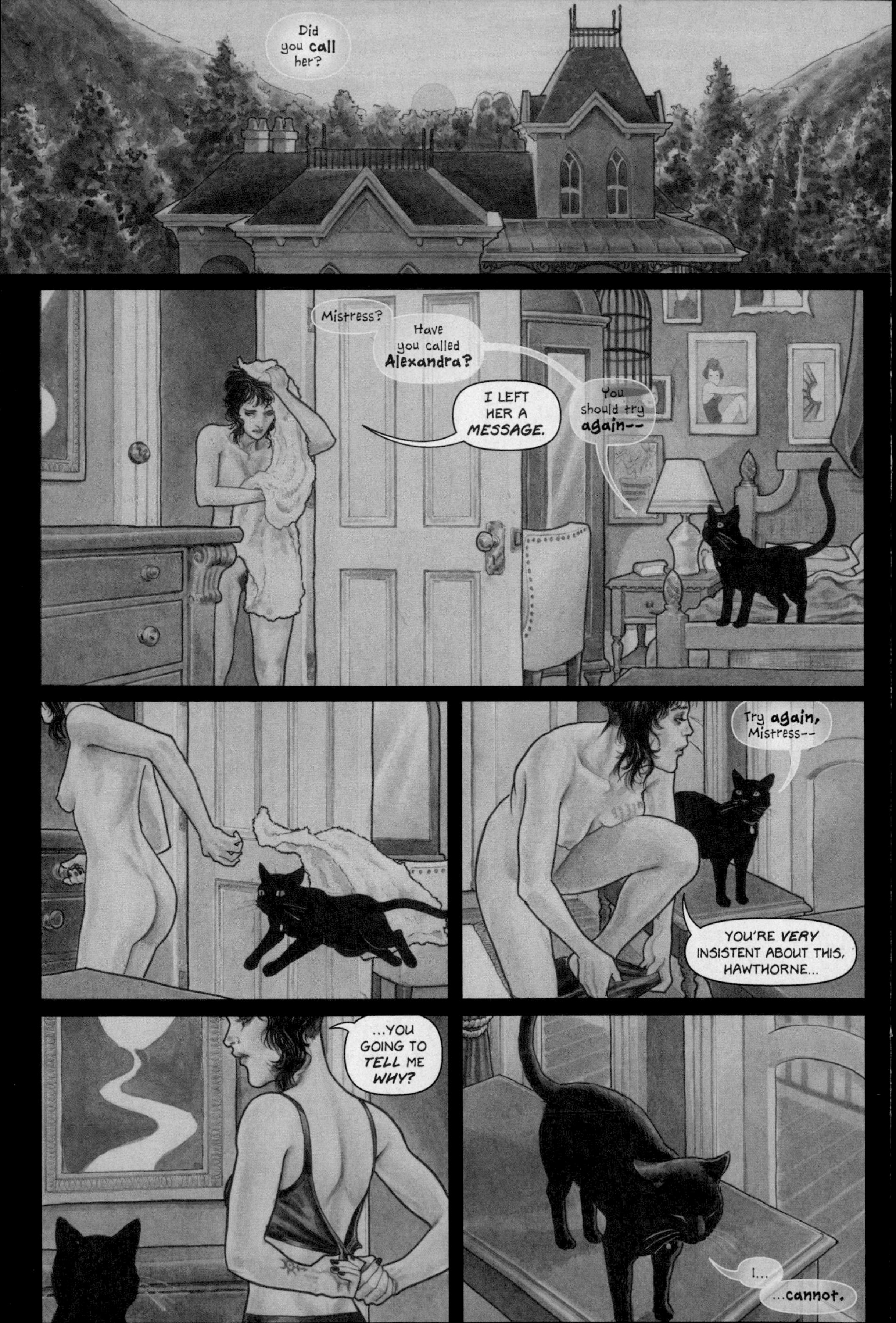
Did you **call** her?
Mistress?
Have you called **Alexandra?**
I LEFT HER A *MESSAGE.*
You should try **again--**
Try **again,** Mistress--
YOU'RE *VERY* INSISTENT ABOUT THIS, HAWTHORNE...
...YOU GOING TO *TELL* ME *WHY?*
I...
...**cannot.**

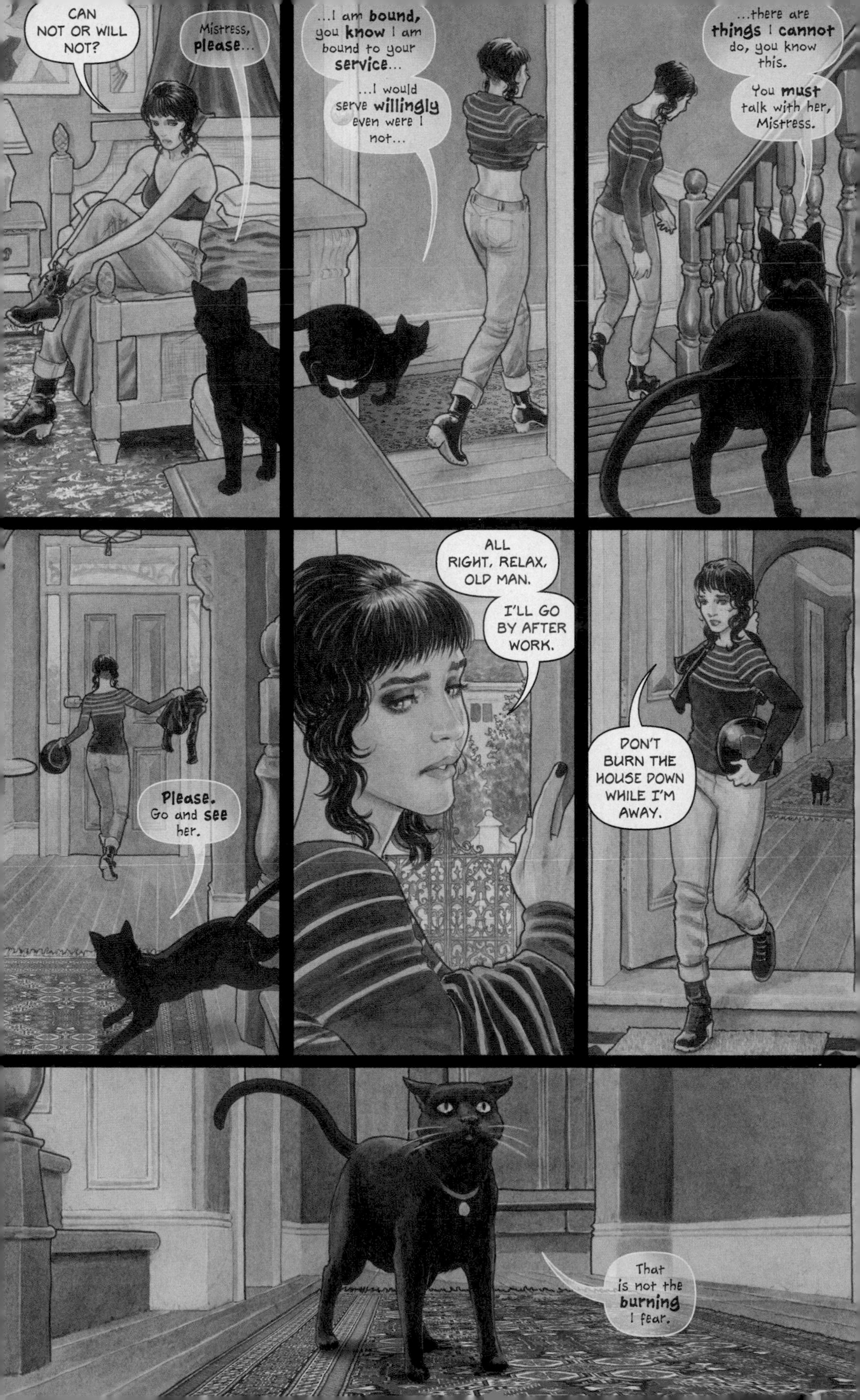

CAN NOT OR WILL NOT?
Mistress, please...
...I am bound, you know I am bound to your service...
...I would serve willingly even were I not...
...there are things I cannot do, you know this.
You must talk with her, Mistress.
Please. Go and see her.
ALL RIGHT, RELAX, OLD MAN.
I'LL GO BY AFTER WORK.
DON'T BURN THE HOUSE DOWN WHILE I'M AWAY.
That is not the burning I fear.

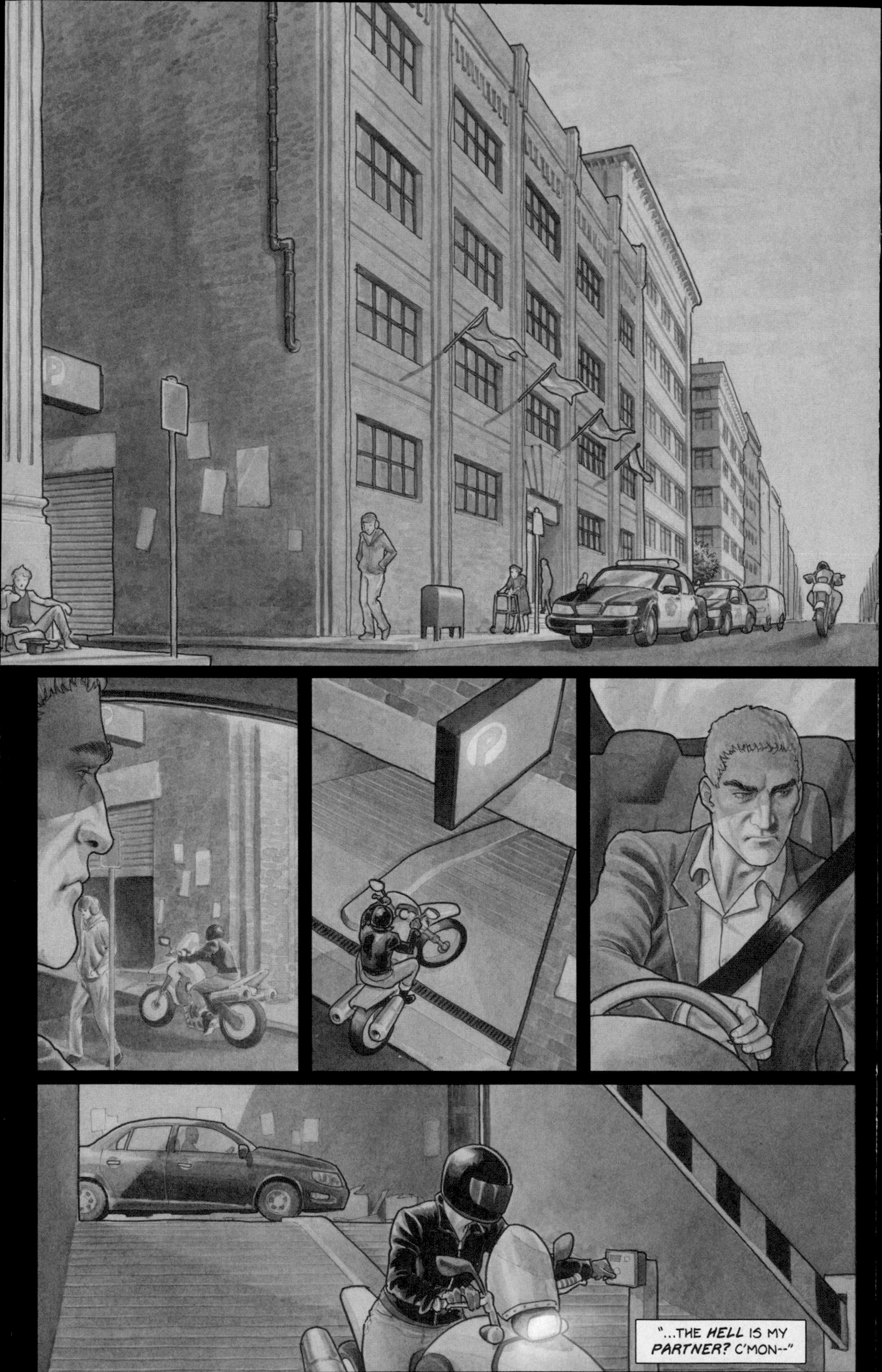
"...THE *HELL* IS MY *PARTNER?* C'MON--"

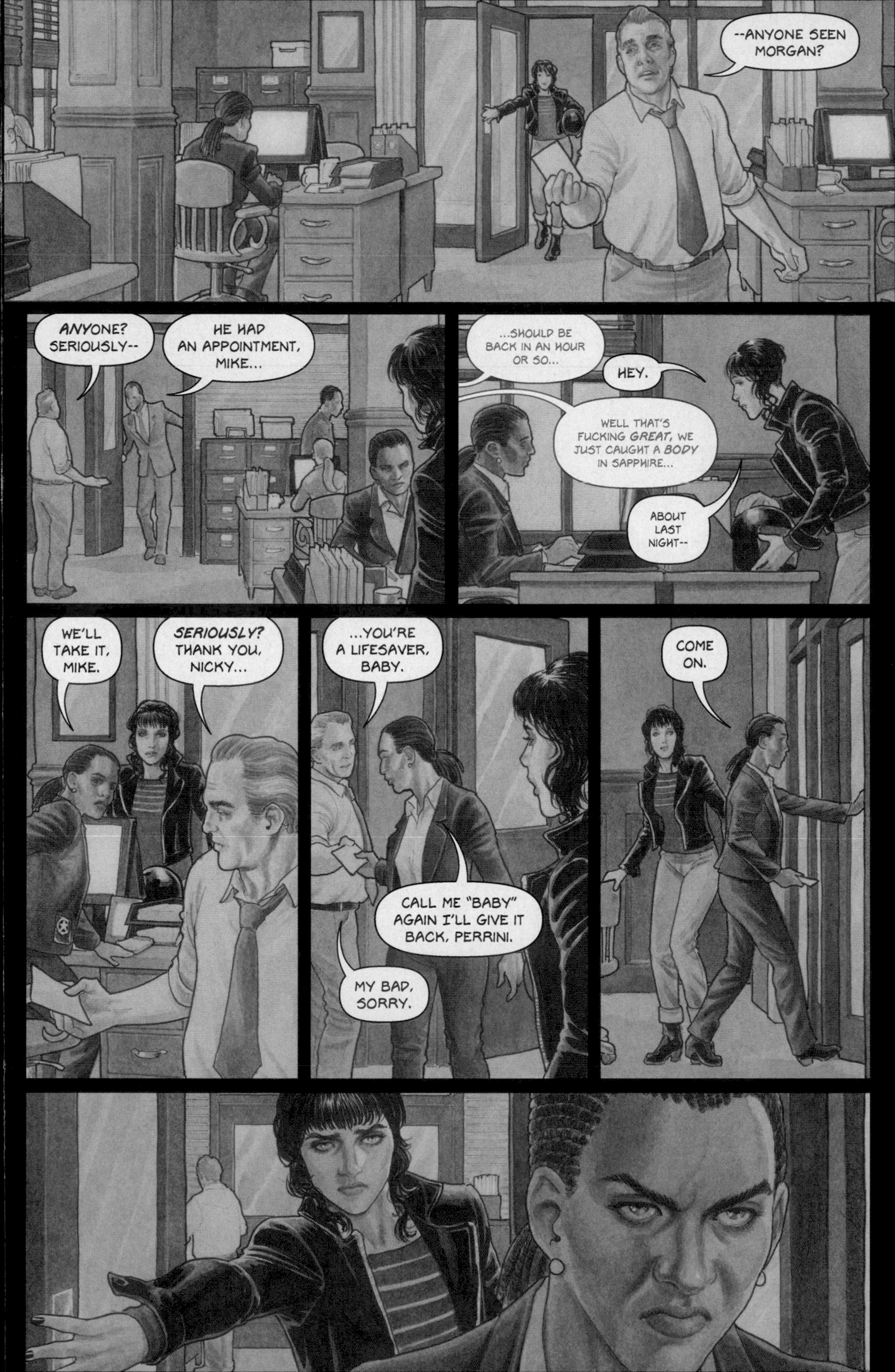
--ANYONE SEEN MORGAN?
ANYONE? SERIOUSLY--
HE HAD AN APPOINTMENT, MIKE...
...SHOULD BE BACK IN AN HOUR OR SO...
HEY.
WELL THAT'S FUCKING GREAT, WE JUST CAUGHT A BODY IN SAPPHIRE...
ABOUT LAST NIGHT--
WE'LL TAKE IT, MIKE.
SERIOUSLY? THANK YOU, NICKY...
...YOU'RE A LIFESAVER, BABY.
CALL ME "BABY" AGAIN I'LL GIVE IT BACK, PERRINI.
MY BAD, SORRY.
COME ON.

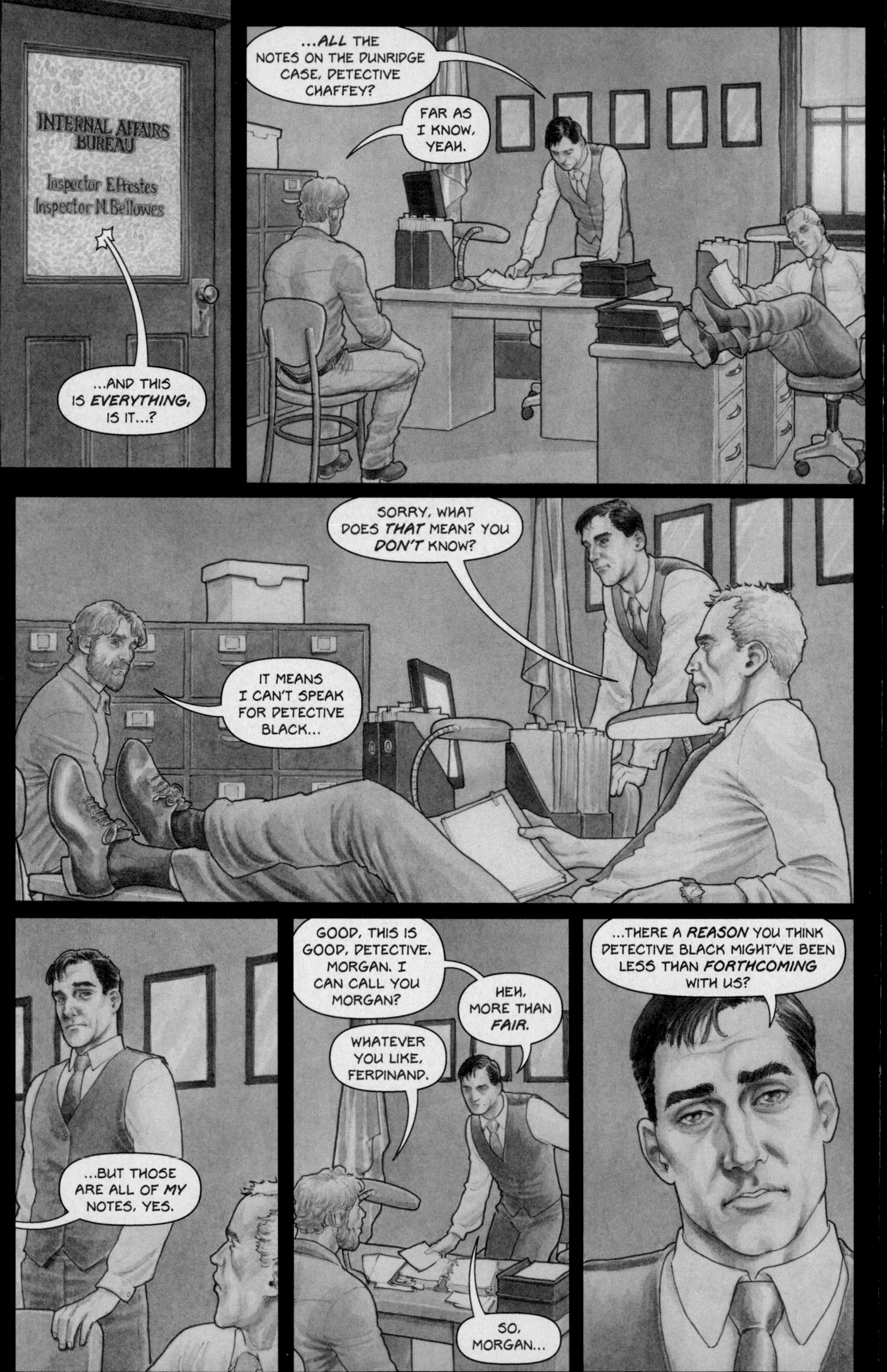
INTERNAL AFFAIRS BUREAU
Inspector E. Prestes
Inspector N. Bellowes
...AND THIS IS EVERYTHING, IS IT...?
...ALL THE NOTES ON THE DUNRIDGE CASE, DETECTIVE CHAFFEY?
FAR AS I KNOW, YEAH.
SORRY, WHAT DOES THAT MEAN? YOU DON'T KNOW?
IT MEANS I CAN'T SPEAK FOR DETECTIVE BLACK...
...BUT THOSE ARE ALL OF MY NOTES, YES.
GOOD, THIS IS GOOD, DETECTIVE. MORGAN. I CAN CALL YOU MORGAN?
HEH, MORE THAN FAIR.
WHATEVER YOU LIKE, FERDINAND.
SO, MORGAN...
...THERE A REASON YOU THINK DETECTIVE BLACK MIGHT'VE BEEN LESS THAN FORTHCOMING WITH US?

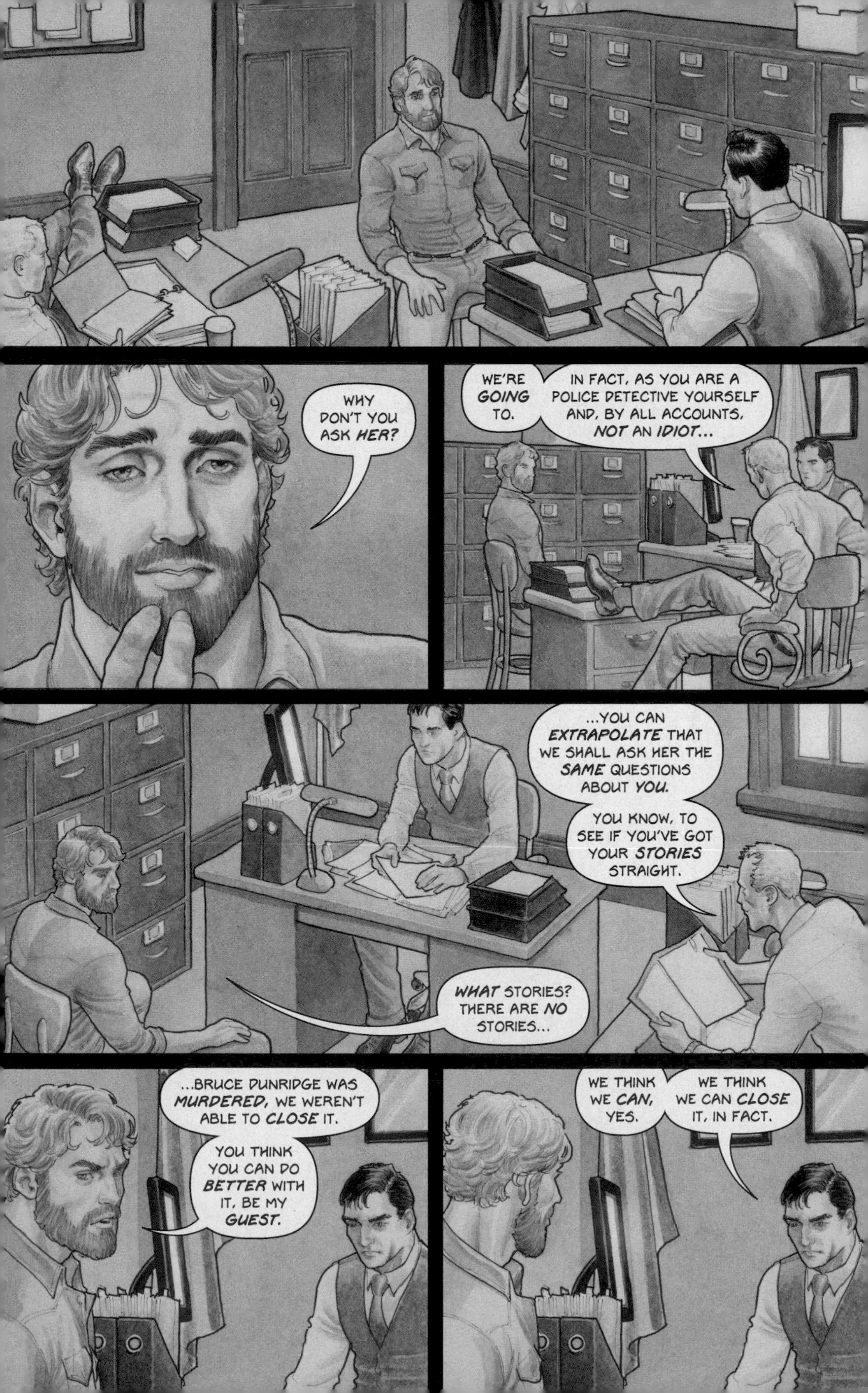
WHY DON'T YOU ASK *HER?*
WE'RE *GOING* TO.
IN FACT, AS YOU ARE A POLICE DETECTIVE YOURSELF AND, BY ALL ACCOUNTS, *NOT* AN *IDIOT*...
...YOU CAN *EXTRAPOLATE* THAT WE SHALL ASK HER THE *SAME* QUESTIONS ABOUT *YOU.*
YOU KNOW, TO SEE IF YOU'VE GOT YOUR *STORIES* STRAIGHT.
WHAT STORIES? THERE ARE *NO* STORIES...
...BRUCE DUNRIDGE WAS *MURDERED,* WE WEREN'T ABLE TO *CLOSE* IT.
YOU THINK YOU CAN DO *BETTER* WITH IT, BE MY *GUEST.*
WE THINK WE *CAN,* YES.
WE THINK WE CAN *CLOSE* IT, IN FACT.

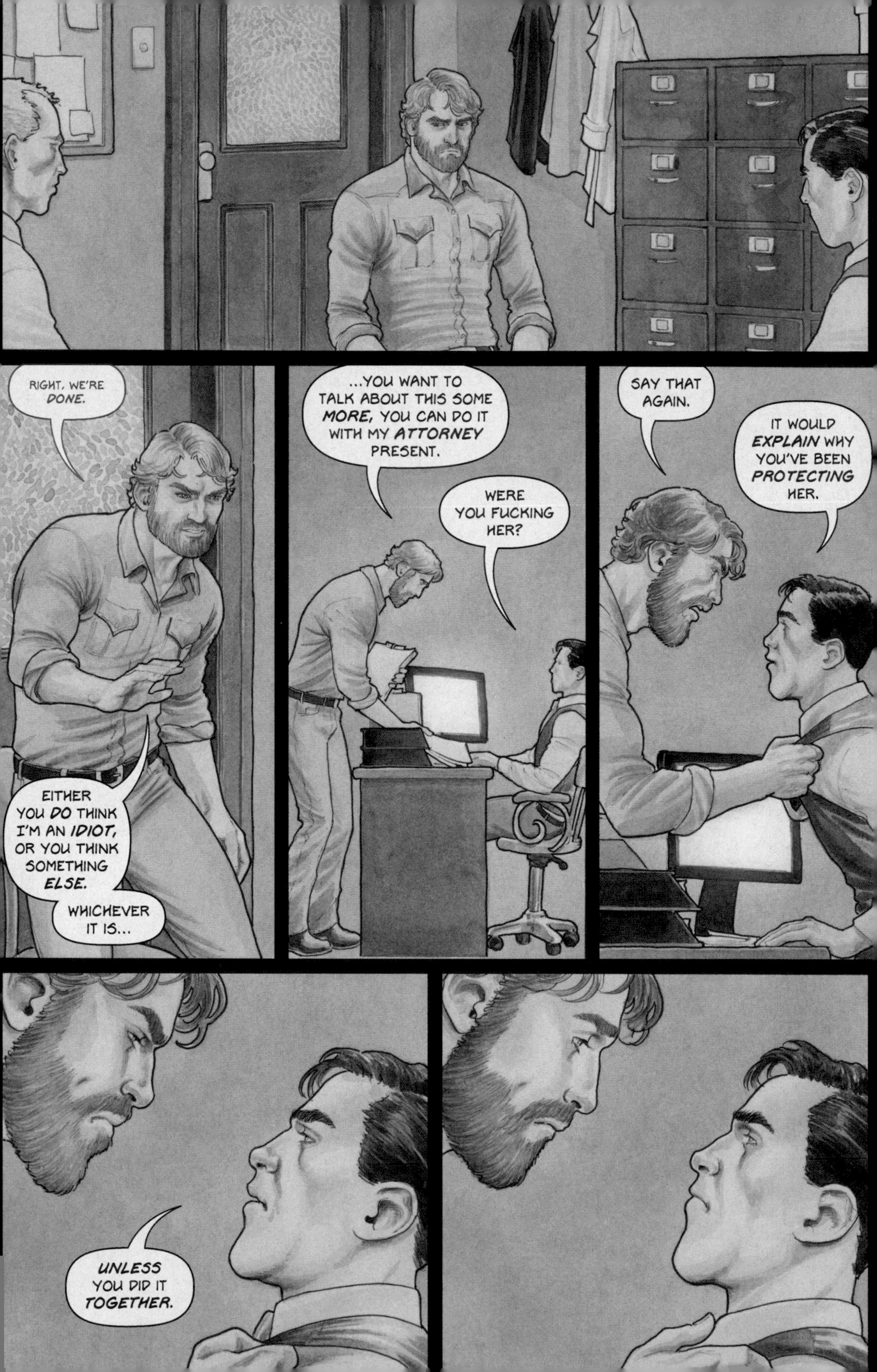
RIGHT, WE'RE DONE.
EITHER YOU DO THINK I'M AN IDIOT, OR YOU THINK SOMETHING ELSE.
WHICHEVER IT IS...
...YOU WANT TO TALK ABOUT THIS SOME MORE, YOU CAN DO IT WITH MY ATTORNEY PRESENT.
WERE YOU FUCKING HER?
SAY THAT AGAIN.
IT WOULD EXPLAIN WHY YOU'VE BEEN PROTECTING HER.
UNLESS YOU DID IT TOGETHER.

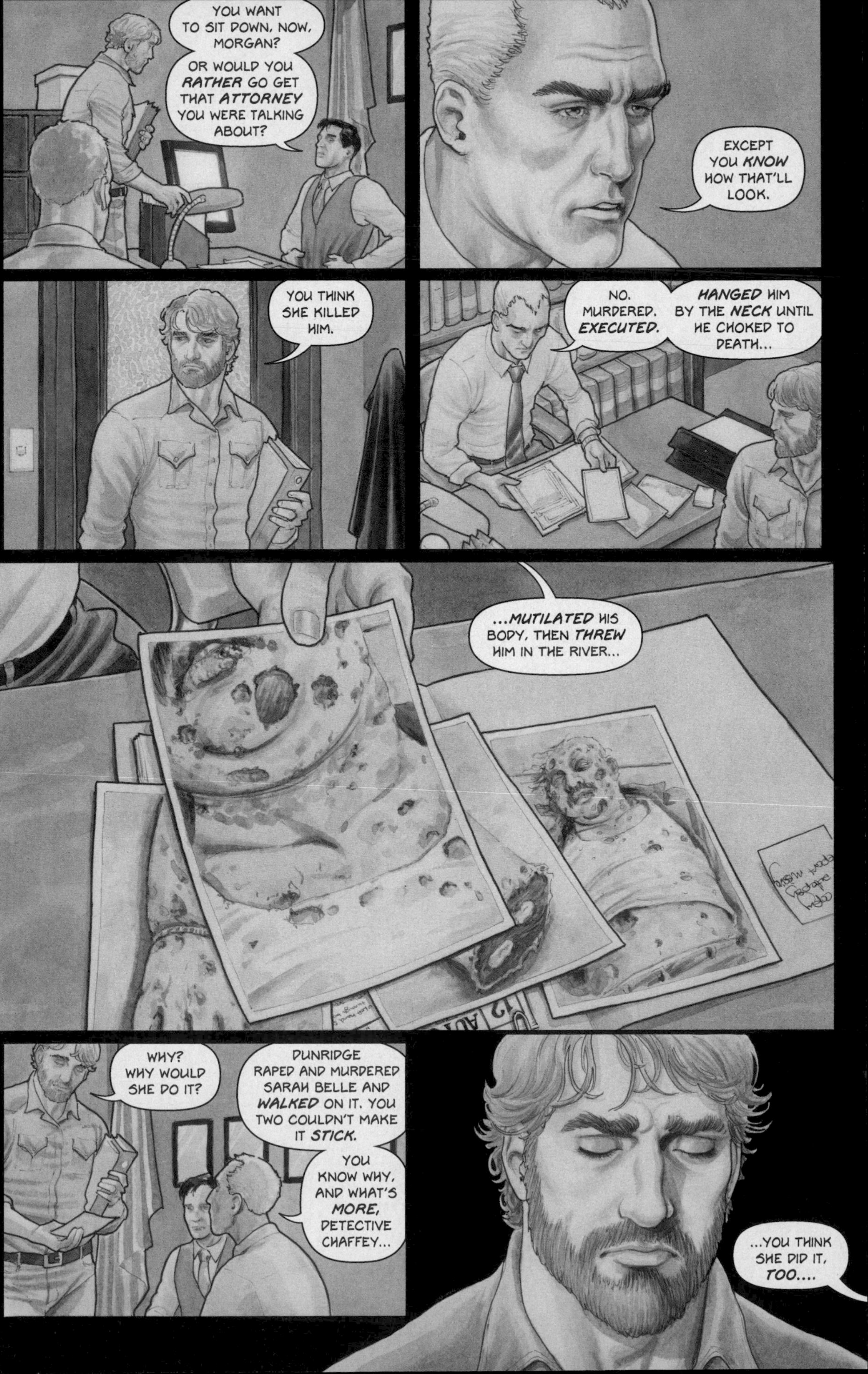
YOU WANT TO SIT DOWN, NOW, MORGAN?
OR WOULD YOU RATHER GO GET THAT ATTORNEY YOU WERE TALKING ABOUT?
EXCEPT YOU KNOW HOW THAT'LL LOOK.
YOU THINK SHE KILLED HIM.
NO. MURDERED. EXECUTED.
HANGED HIM BY THE NECK UNTIL HE CHOKED TO DEATH...
...MUTILATED HIS BODY, THEN THREW HIM IN THE RIVER...
WHY? WHY WOULD SHE DO IT?
DUNRIDGE RAPED AND MURDERED SARAH BELLE AND WALKED ON IT. YOU TWO COULDN'T MAKE IT STICK.
YOU KNOW WHY, AND WHAT'S MORE, DETECTIVE CHAFFEY...
...YOU THINK SHE DID IT, TOO....

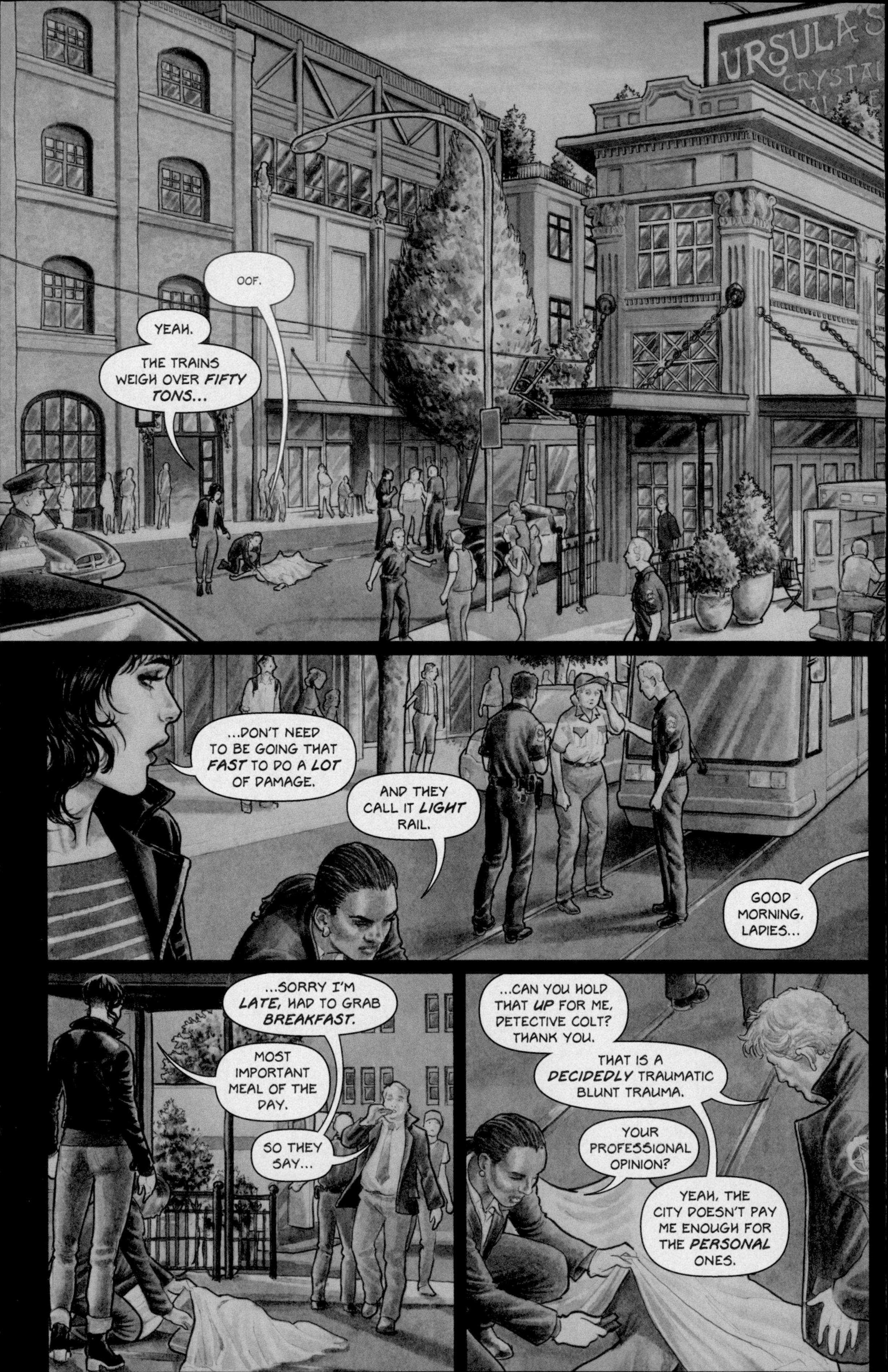
URSULA'S CRYSTAL PALACE
OOF.
YEAH.
THE TRAINS WEIGH OVER *FIFTY TONS*...
...DON'T NEED TO BE GOING THAT *FAST* TO DO A *LOT* OF DAMAGE.
AND THEY CALL IT *LIGHT* RAIL.
GOOD MORNING, LADIES...
...SORRY I'M *LATE*, HAD TO GRAB *BREAKFAST*.
MOST IMPORTANT MEAL OF THE DAY.
SO THEY SAY...
...CAN YOU HOLD THAT *UP* FOR ME, DETECTIVE COLT? THANK YOU.
THAT IS A *DECIDEDLY* TRAUMATIC BLUNT TRAUMA.
YOUR PROFESSIONAL OPINION?
YEAH, THE CITY DOESN'T PAY ME ENOUGH FOR THE *PERSONAL* ONES.

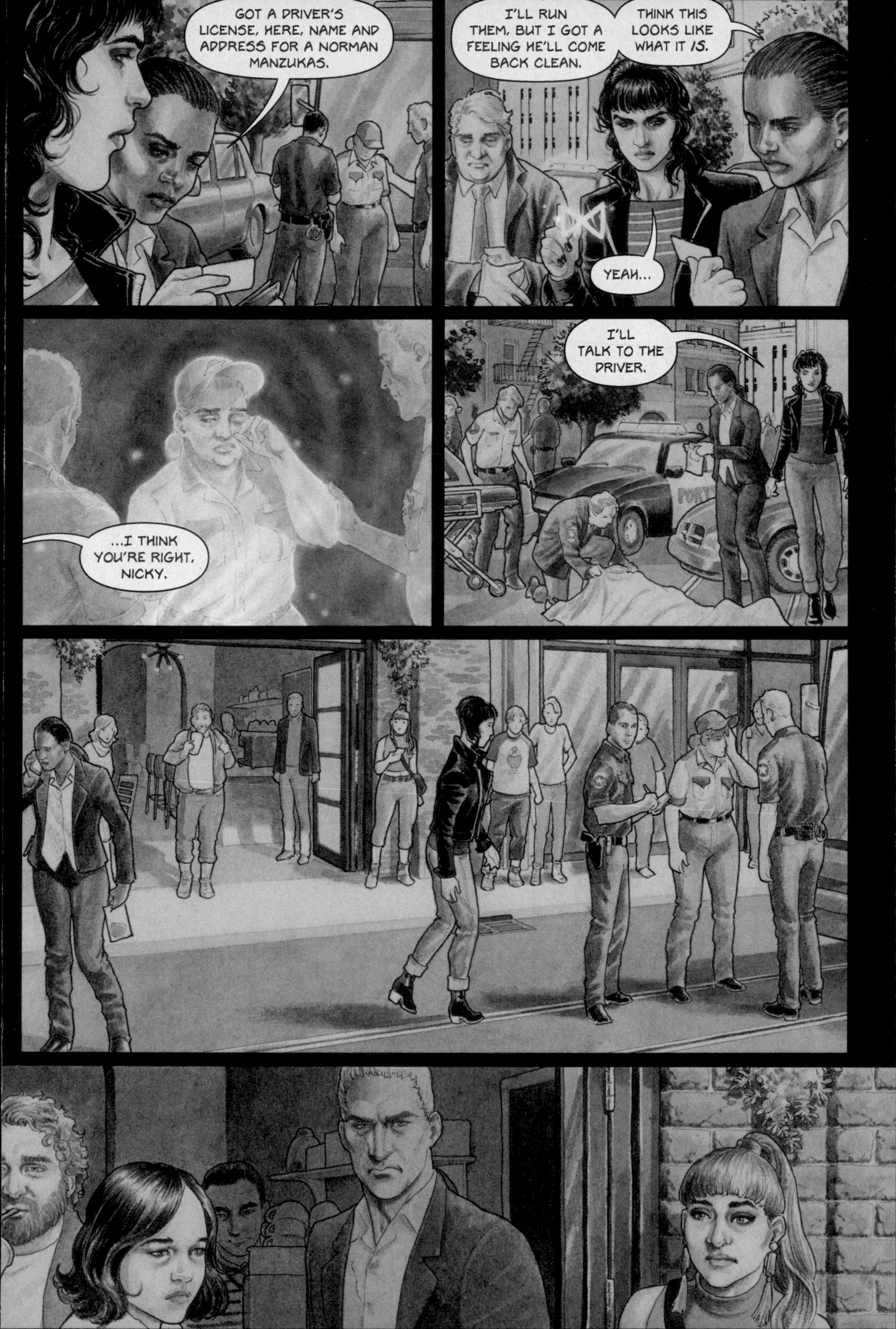
GOT A DRIVER'S LICENSE, HERE, NAME AND ADDRESS FOR A NORMAN MANZUKAS.
I'LL RUN THEM, BUT I GOT A FEELING HE'LL COME BACK CLEAN.
THINK THIS LOOKS LIKE WHAT IT *IS*.
YEAH...
...I THINK YOU'RE RIGHT, NICKY.
I'LL TALK TO THE DRIVER.

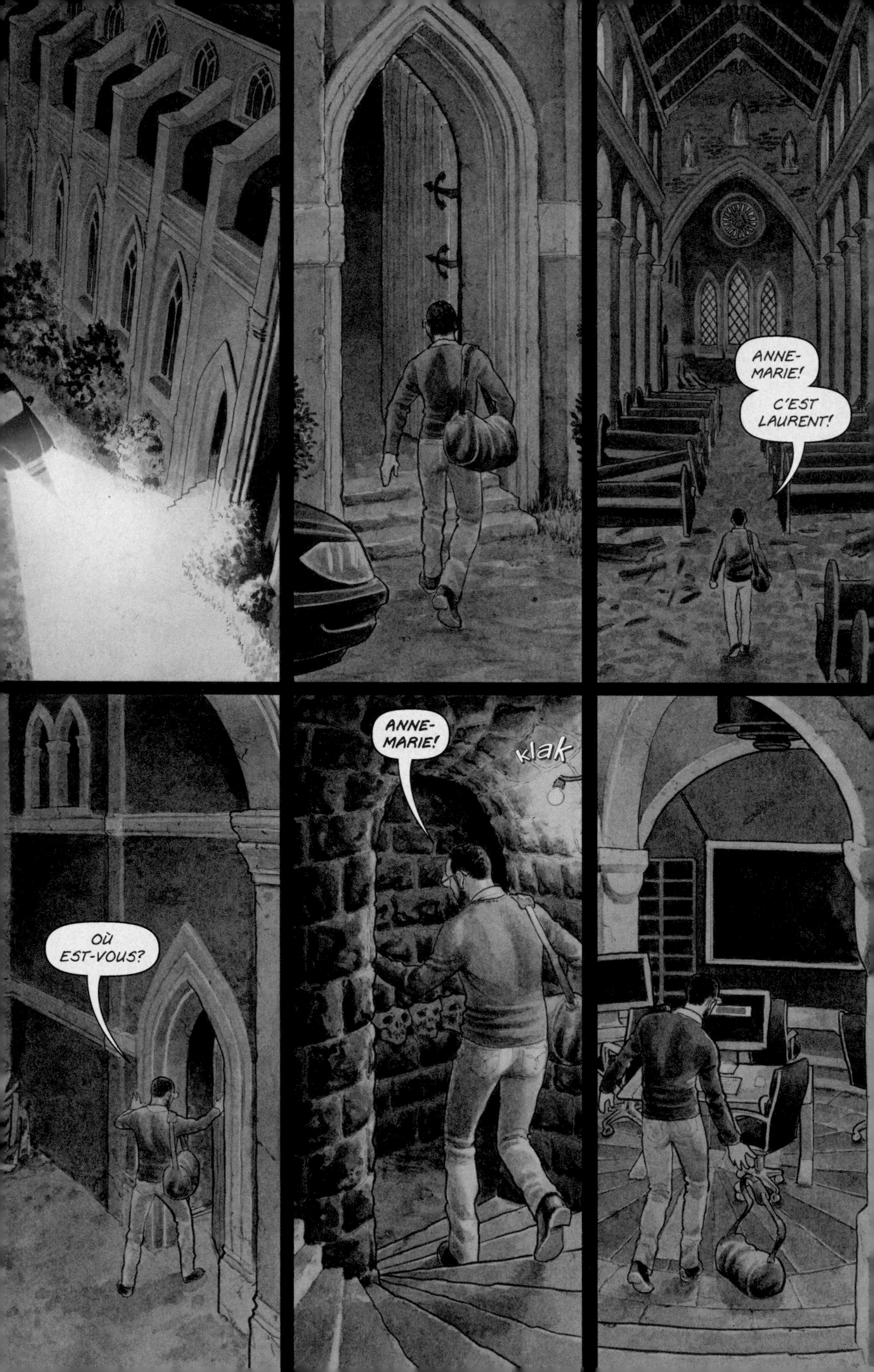
ANNE-MARIE!
C'EST LAURENT!
OÙ EST-VOUS?
ANNE-MARIE!
klak

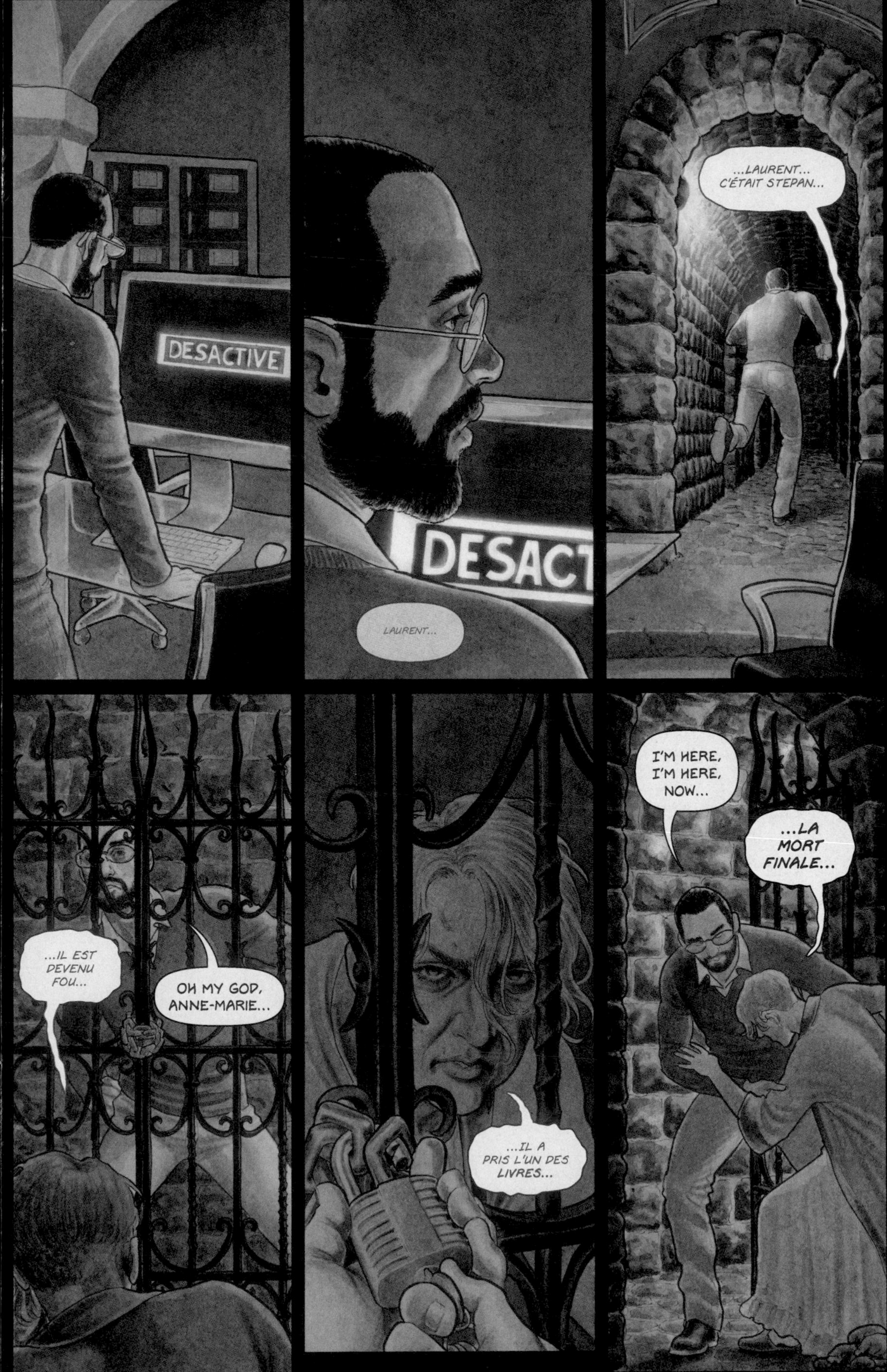
DESACTIVE
DESACT
LAURENT...
...LAURENT... C'ÉTAIT STEPAN...
OH MY GOD, ANNE-MARIE...
...IL EST DEVENU FOU...
...IL A PRIS L'UN DES LIVRES...
I'M HERE, I'M HERE, NOW...
...LA MORT FINALE...

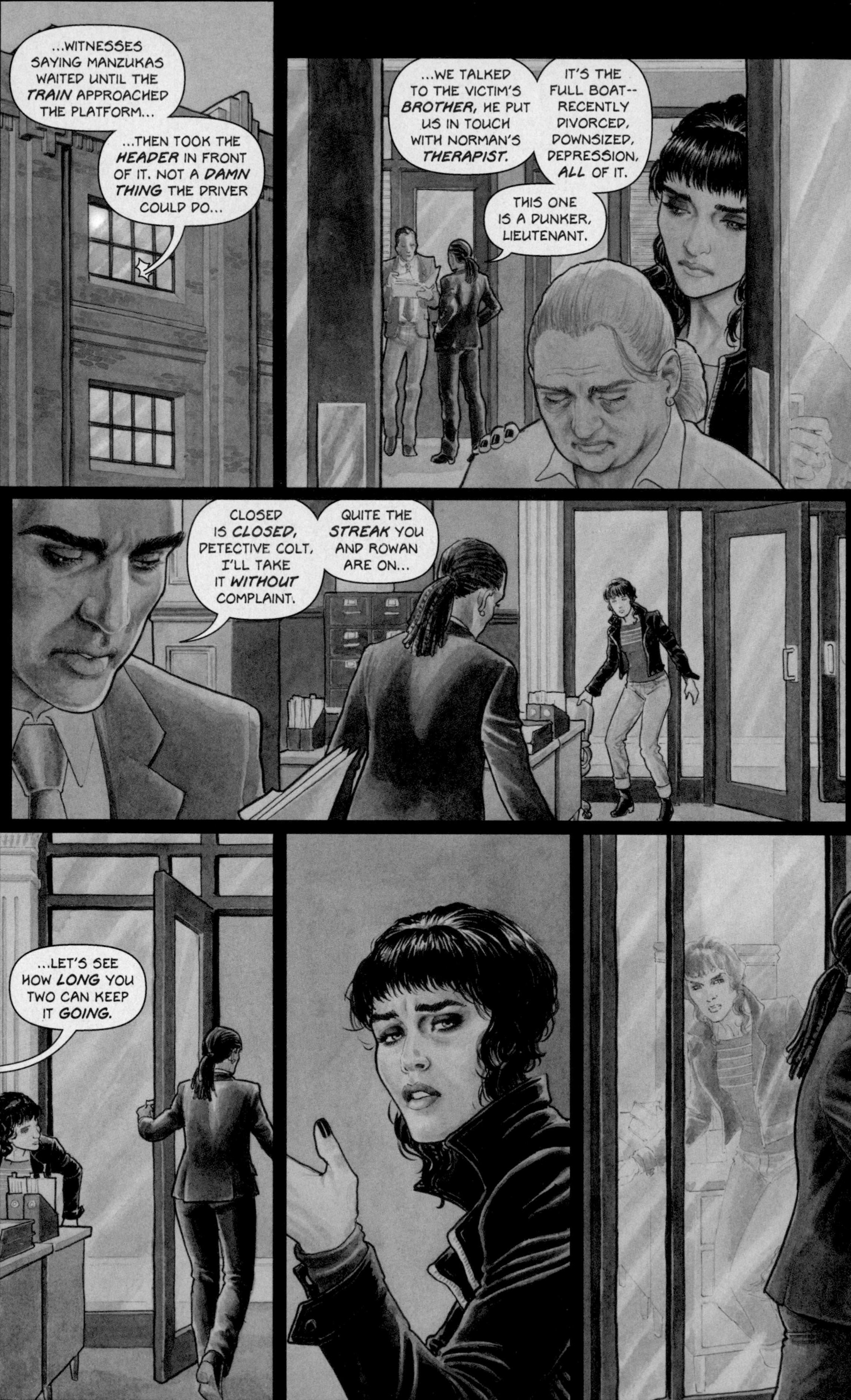
...WITNESSES SAYING MANZUKAS WAITED UNTIL THE TRAIN APPROACHED THE PLATFORM...
...THEN TOOK THE HEADER IN FRONT OF IT. NOT A DAMN THING THE DRIVER COULD DO...
...WE TALKED TO THE VICTIM'S BROTHER, HE PUT US IN TOUCH WITH NORMAN'S THERAPIST.
IT'S THE FULL BOAT-- RECENTLY DIVORCED, DOWNSIZED, DEPRESSION, ALL OF IT.
THIS ONE IS A DUNKER, LIEUTENANT.
CLOSED IS CLOSED, DETECTIVE COLT, I'LL TAKE IT WITHOUT COMPLAINT.
QUITE THE STREAK YOU AND ROWAN ARE ON...
...LET'S SEE HOW LONG YOU TWO CAN KEEP IT GOING.

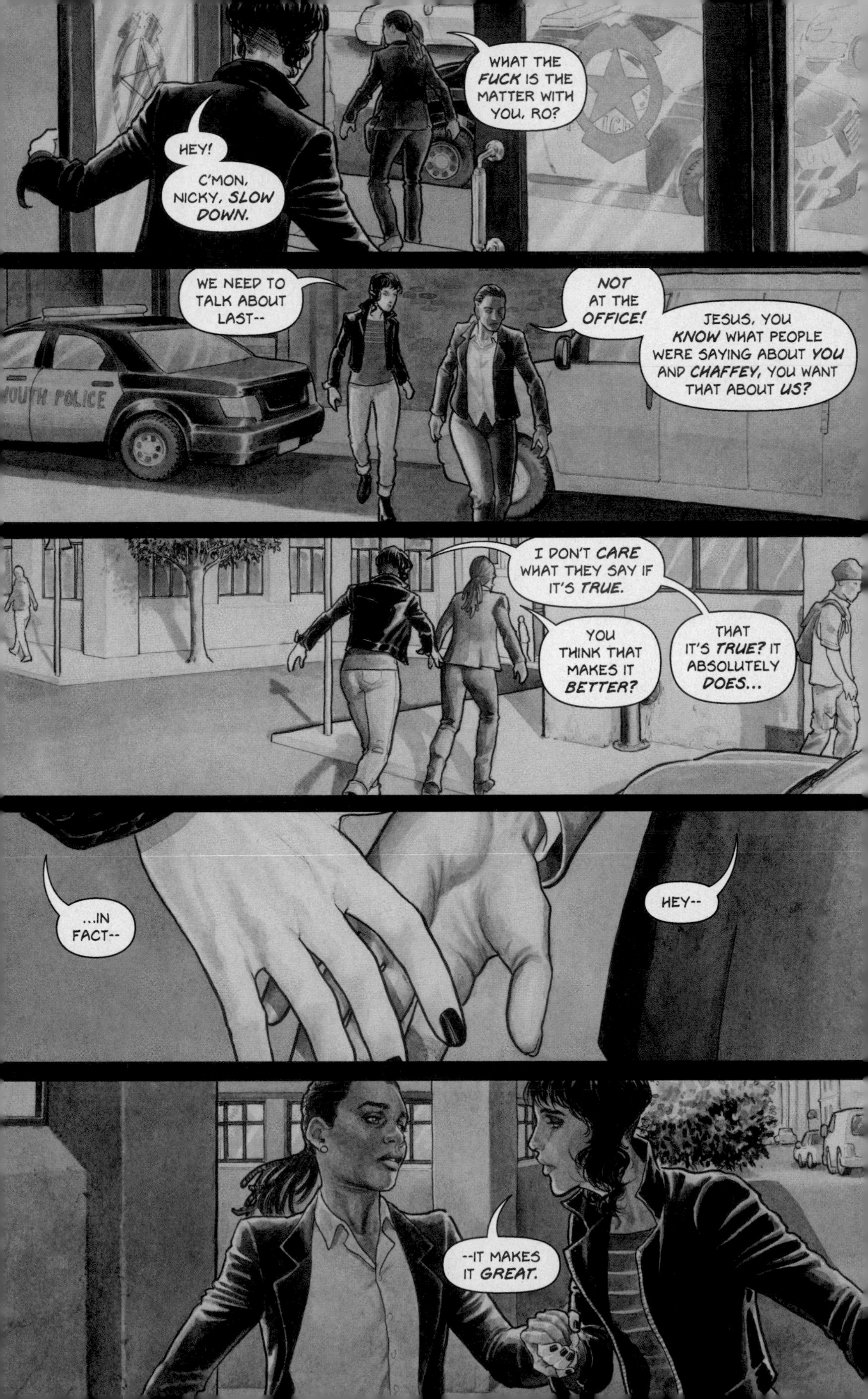
HEY!
C'MON, NICKY, SLOW DOWN.
WHAT THE FUCK IS THE MATTER WITH YOU, RO?
WE NEED TO TALK ABOUT LAST--
NOT AT THE OFFICE!
JESUS, YOU KNOW WHAT PEOPLE WERE SAYING ABOUT YOU AND CHAFFEY, YOU WANT THAT ABOUT US?
I DON'T CARE WHAT THEY SAY IF IT'S TRUE.
YOU THINK THAT MAKES IT BETTER?
THAT IT'S TRUE? IT ABSOLUTELY DOES...
...IN FACT--
HEY--
--IT MAKES IT GREAT.

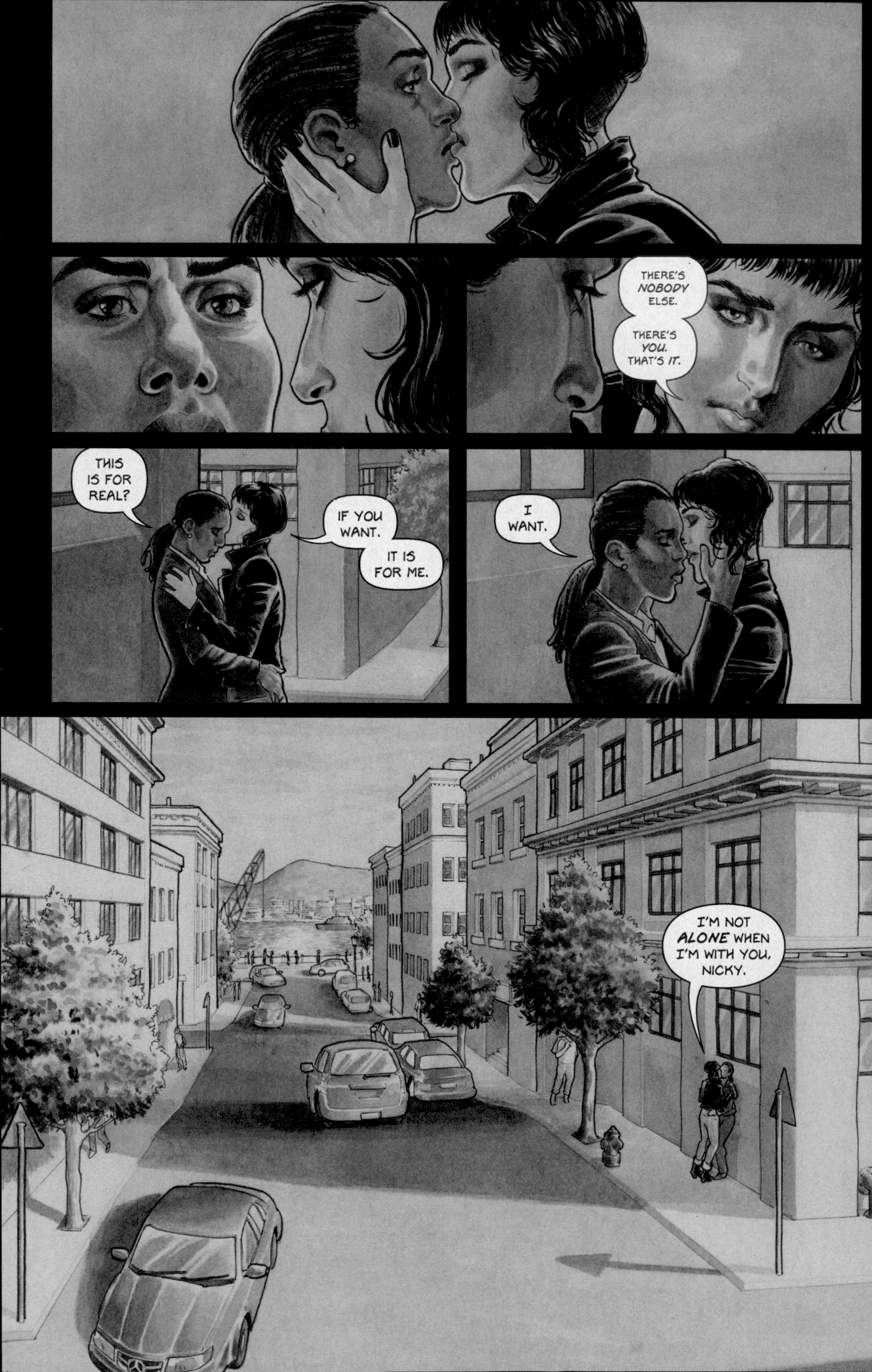

THERE'S NOBODY ELSE.
THERE'S YOU. THAT'S IT.
THIS IS FOR REAL?
IF YOU WANT.
IT IS FOR ME.
I WANT.
I'M NOT ALONE WHEN I'M WITH YOU, NICKY.

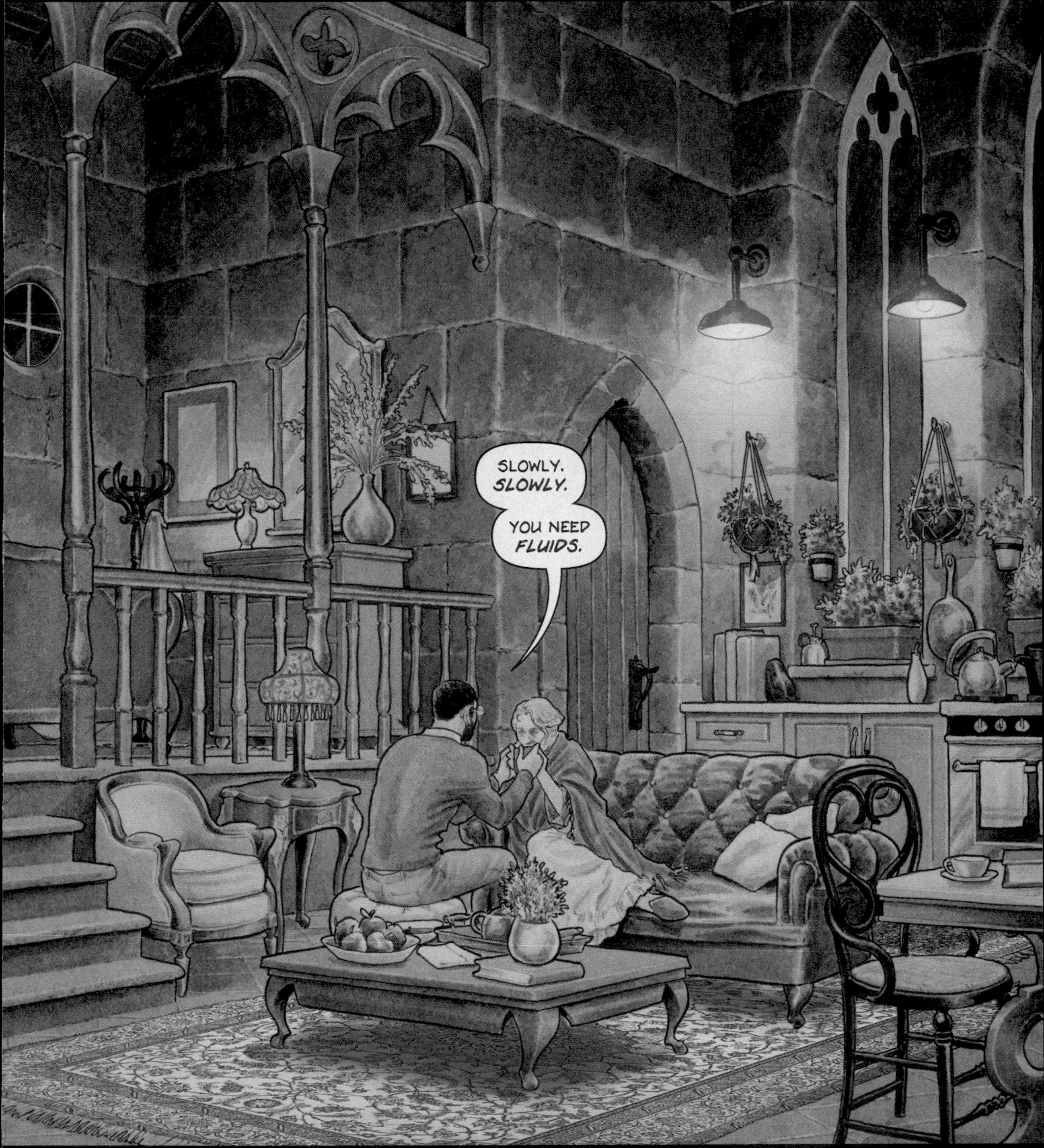
SLOWLY. SLOWLY.
YOU NEED FLUIDS.

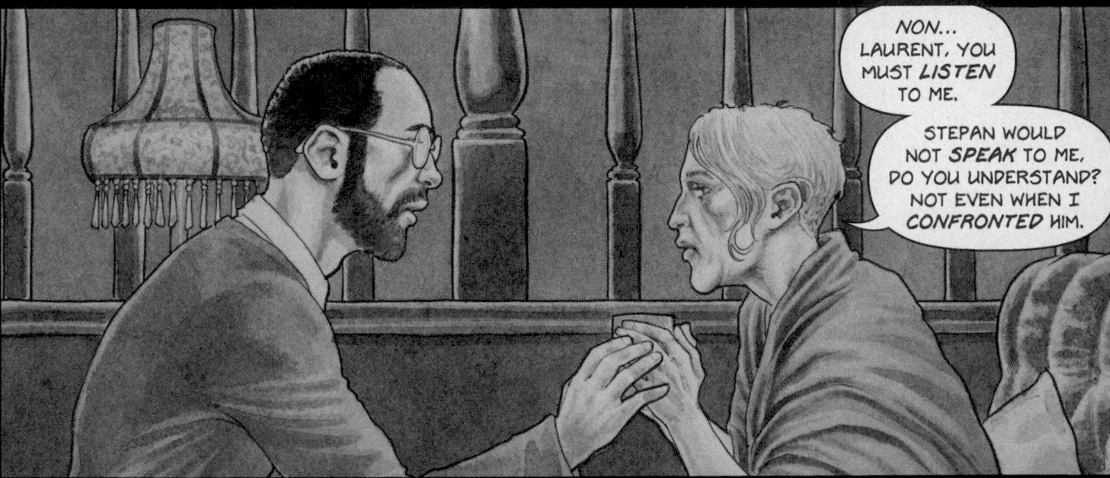
NON... LAURENT, YOU MUST LISTEN TO ME.
STEPAN WOULD NOT SPEAK TO ME, DO YOU UNDERSTAND? NOT EVEN WHEN I CONFRONTED HIM.

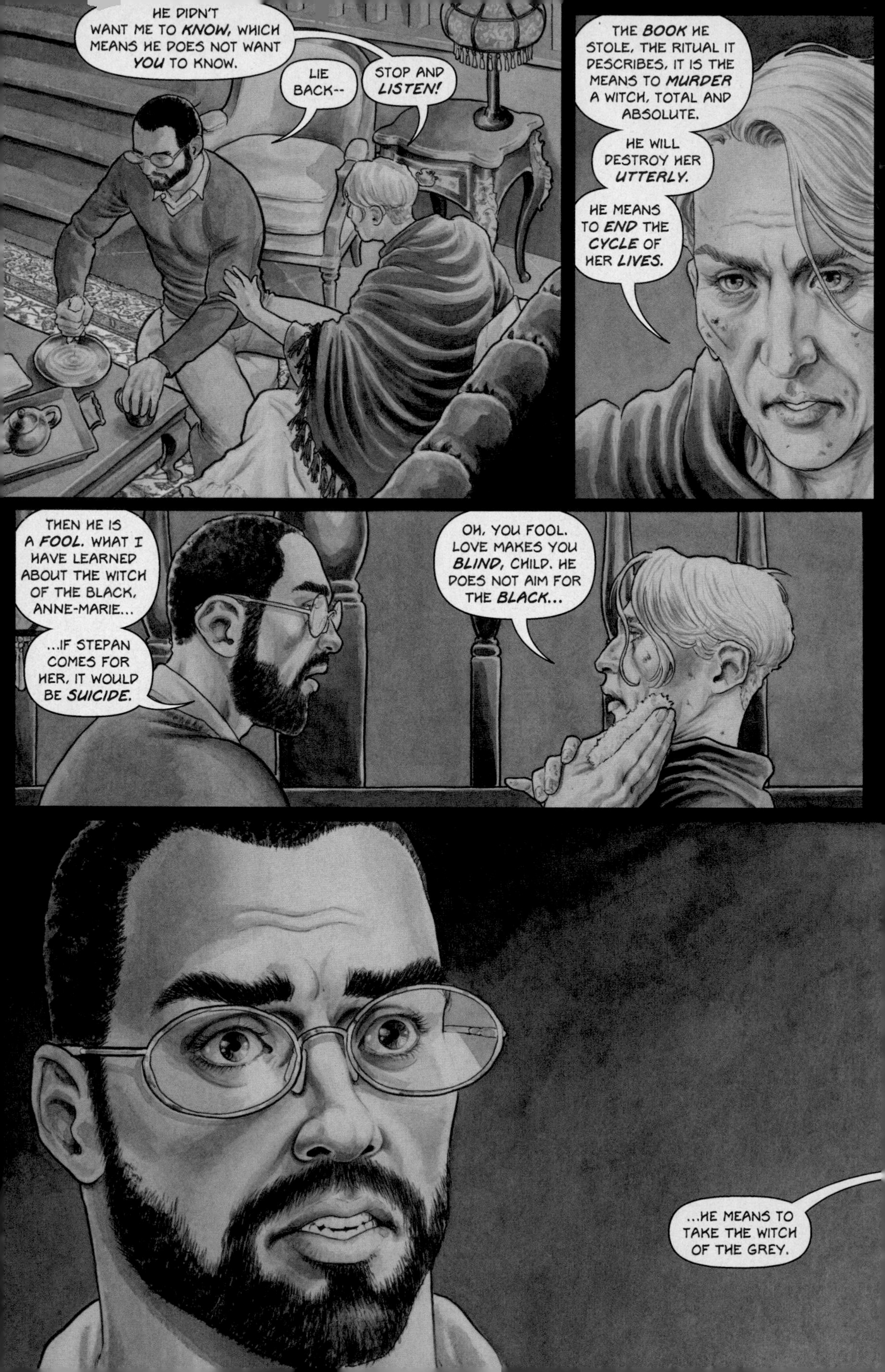
HE DIDN'T WANT ME TO KNOW, WHICH MEANS HE DOES NOT WANT YOU TO KNOW.
LIE BACK--
STOP AND LISTEN!
THE BOOK HE STOLE, THE RITUAL IT DESCRIBES, IT IS THE MEANS TO MURDER A WITCH, TOTAL AND ABSOLUTE.
HE WILL DESTROY HER UTTERLY.
HE MEANS TO END THE CYCLE OF HER LIVES.
THEN HE IS A FOOL. WHAT I HAVE LEARNED ABOUT THE WITCH OF THE BLACK, ANNE-MARIE...
...IF STEPAN COMES FOR HER, IT WOULD BE SUICIDE.
OH, YOU FOOL. LOVE MAKES YOU BLIND, CHILD. HE DOES NOT AIM FOR THE BLACK...
...HE MEANS TO TAKE THE WITCH OF THE GREY.

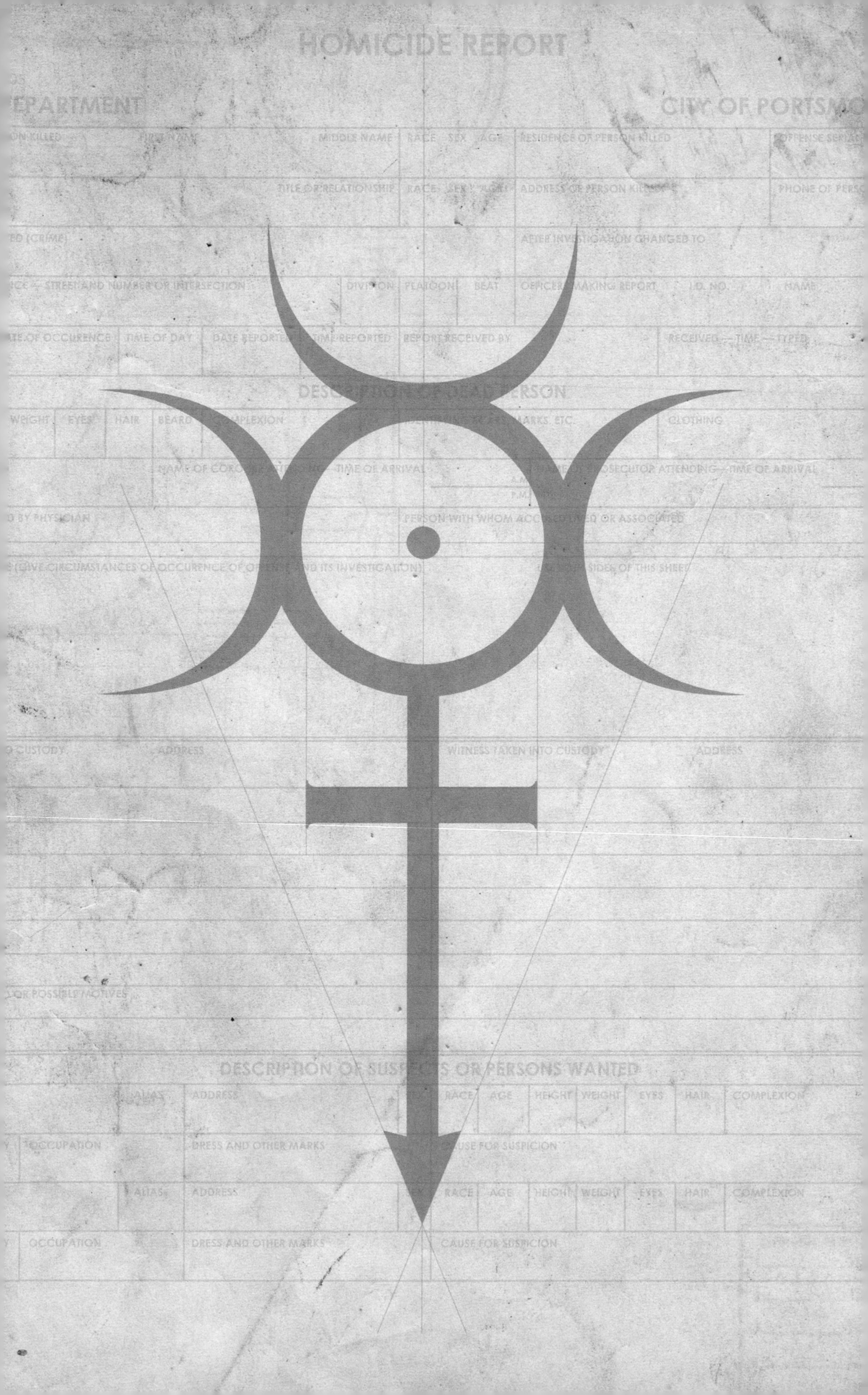
HOMICIDE REPORT
EPARTMENT
CITY OF PORTSMO
MIDDLE NAME
RACE
SEX
AGE
RESIDENCE OF PERSON KILLED
TITLE OF RELATIONSHIP
ADDRESS OF PERSON KILLED
PHONE OF PERS
AFTER INVESTIGATION CHANGED TO
DIVISION
PLATOON
BEAT
OFFICERS MAKING REPORT
I.D. NO.
NAME
TIME OF DAY
DATE REPORTED
TIME REPORTED
REPORT RECEIVED BY
RECEIVED — TIME — TYPED
WEIGHT
EYES
HAIR
BEARD
CLOTHING
PERSON WITH WHOM ACCUSED LIVED OR ASSOCIATED
ADDRESS
WITNESS TAKEN INTO CUSTODY
ADDRESS
DESCRIPTION OF SUSPECTS OR PERSONS WANTED
ALIAS
ADDRESS
RACE
AGE
HEIGHT
WEIGHT
EYES
HAIR
COMPLEXION
OCCUPATION
DRESS AND OTHER MARKS
CAUSE FOR SUSPICION
ALIAS
ADDRESS
RACE
AGE
HEIGHT
WEIGHT
EYES
HAIR
COMPLEXION
OCCUPATION
DRESS AND OTHER MARKS
CAUSE FOR SUSPICION

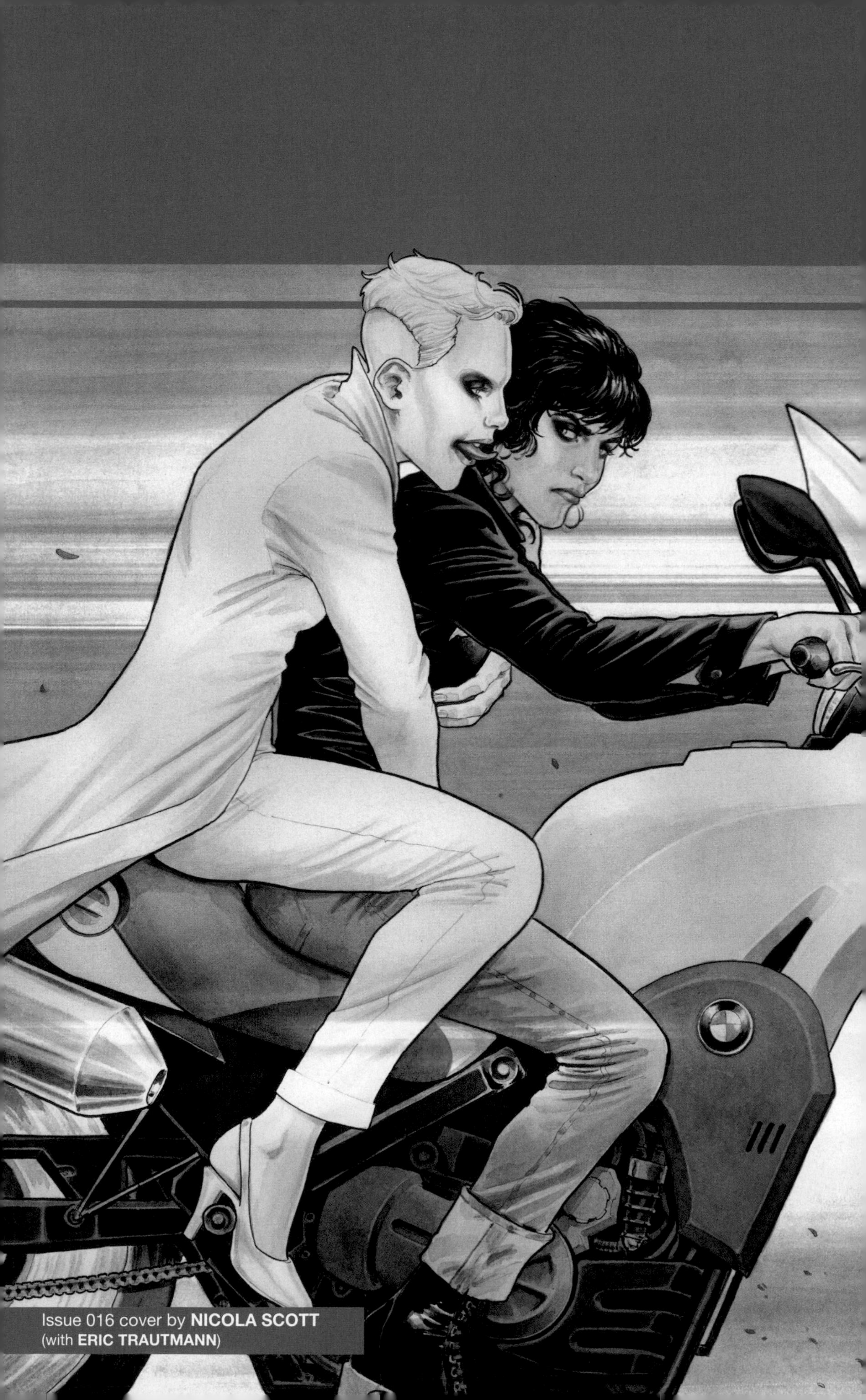

Issue 016 cover by **NICOLA SCOTT**
(with **ERIC TRAUTMANN**)

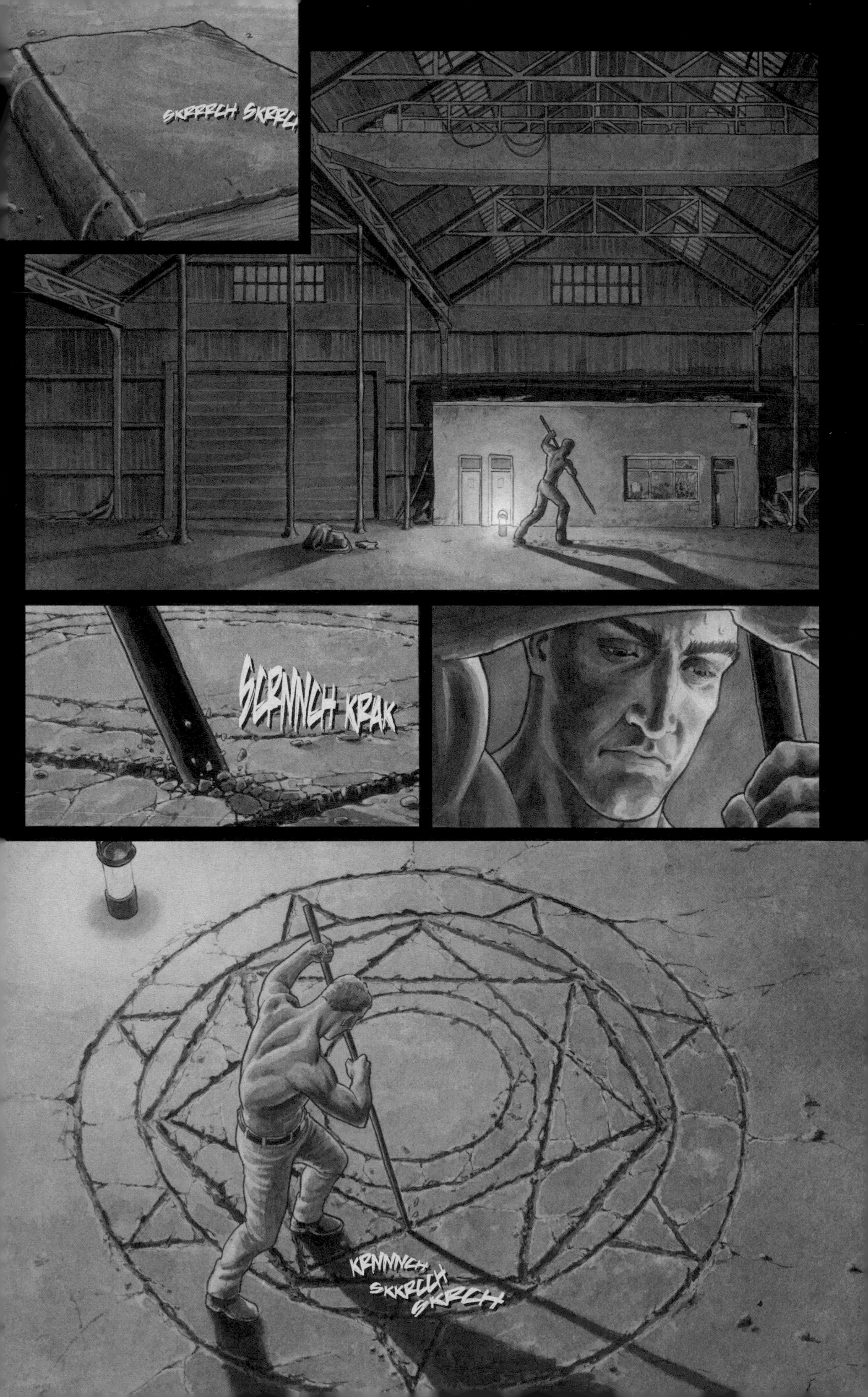
SKRRRCH SKRRC
SCRNNCH KRAK
KRNNNCH
SKKRCCH
SKRCH

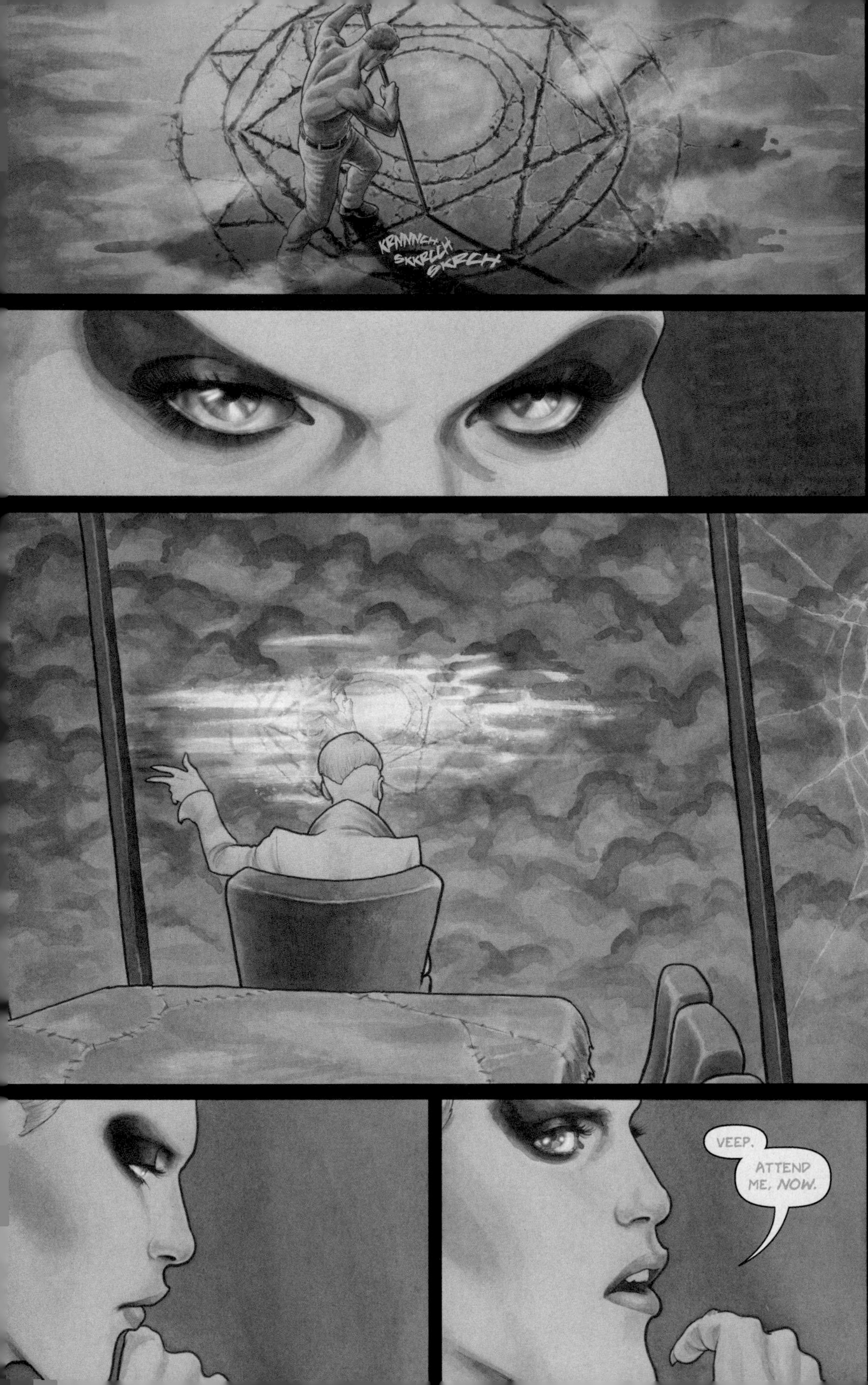
KRNNNCH
SKKRCCH
SKRCH
VEEP.
ATTEND ME, NOW.

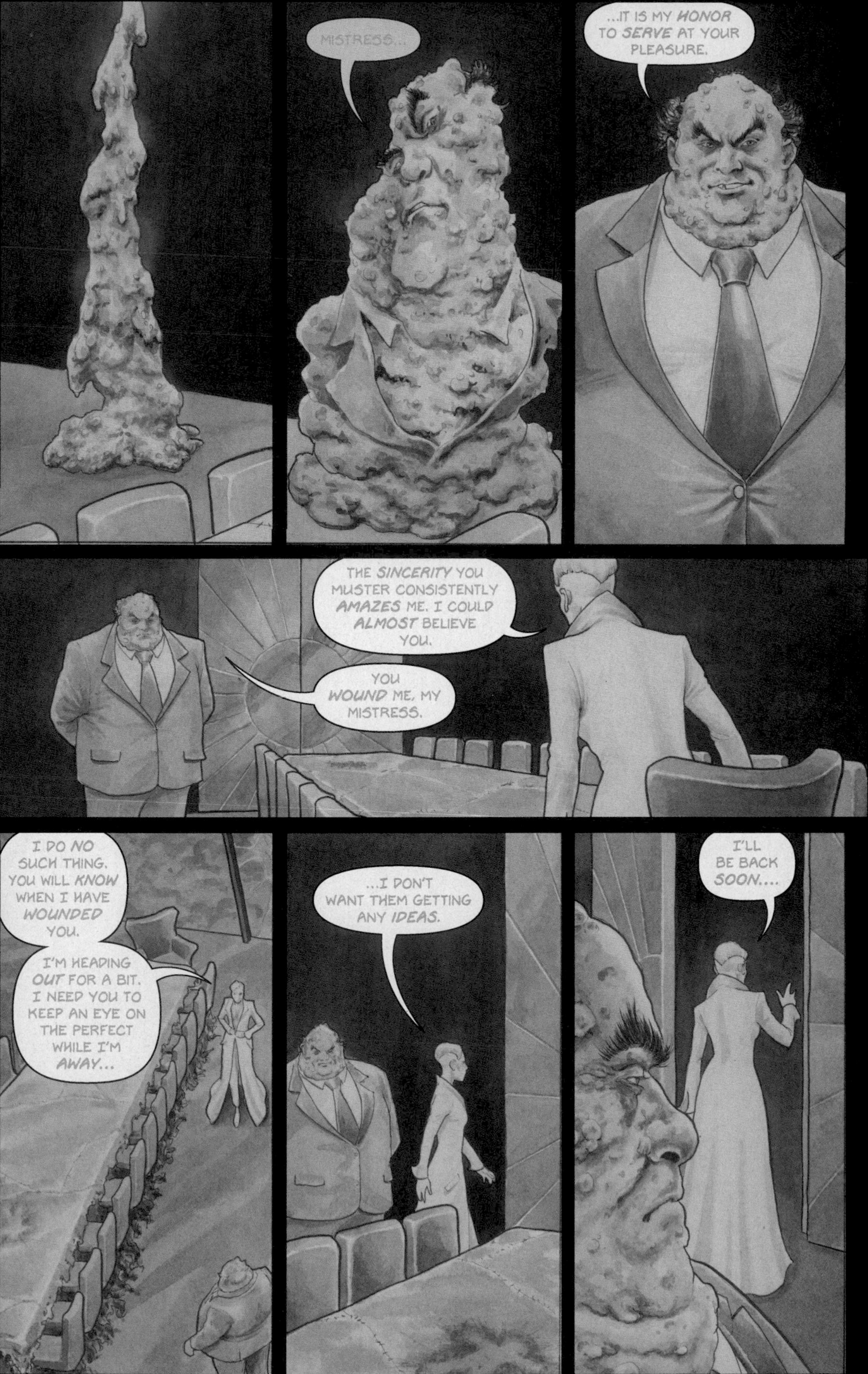
MISTRESS...
...IT IS MY HONOR TO SERVE AT YOUR PLEASURE.
THE SINCERITY YOU MUSTER CONSISTENTLY AMAZES ME. I COULD ALMOST BELIEVE YOU.
YOU WOUND ME, MY MISTRESS.
I DO NO SUCH THING. YOU WILL KNOW WHEN I HAVE WOUNDED YOU.
I'M HEADING OUT FOR A BIT. I NEED YOU TO KEEP AN EYE ON THE PERFECT WHILE I'M AWAY...
...I DON'T WANT THEM GETTING ANY IDEAS.
I'LL BE BACK SOON....

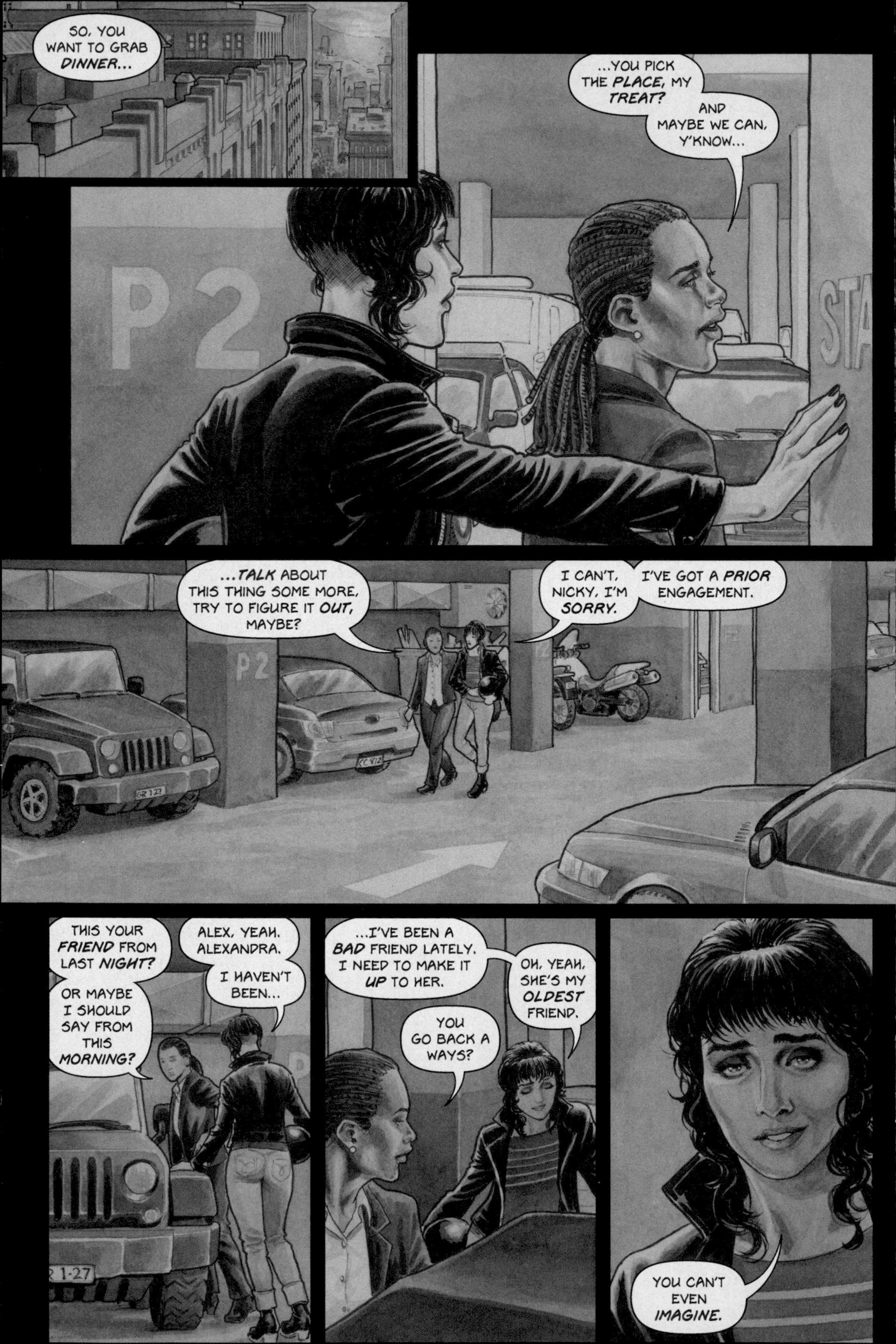

SO, YOU WANT TO GRAB DINNER...
...YOU PICK THE PLACE, MY TREAT?
AND MAYBE WE CAN, Y'KNOW...
STA
P2
...TALK ABOUT THIS THING SOME MORE, TRY TO FIGURE IT OUT, MAYBE?
I CAN'T, NICKY, I'M SORRY.
I'VE GOT A PRIOR ENGAGEMENT.
P2
THIS YOUR FRIEND FROM LAST NIGHT?
OR MAYBE I SHOULD SAY FROM THIS MORNING?
ALEX, YEAH. ALEXANDRA.
I HAVEN'T BEEN...
...I'VE BEEN A BAD FRIEND LATELY. I NEED TO MAKE IT UP TO HER.
OH, YEAH, SHE'S MY OLDEST FRIEND.
YOU GO BACK A WAYS?
YOU CAN'T EVEN IMAGINE.

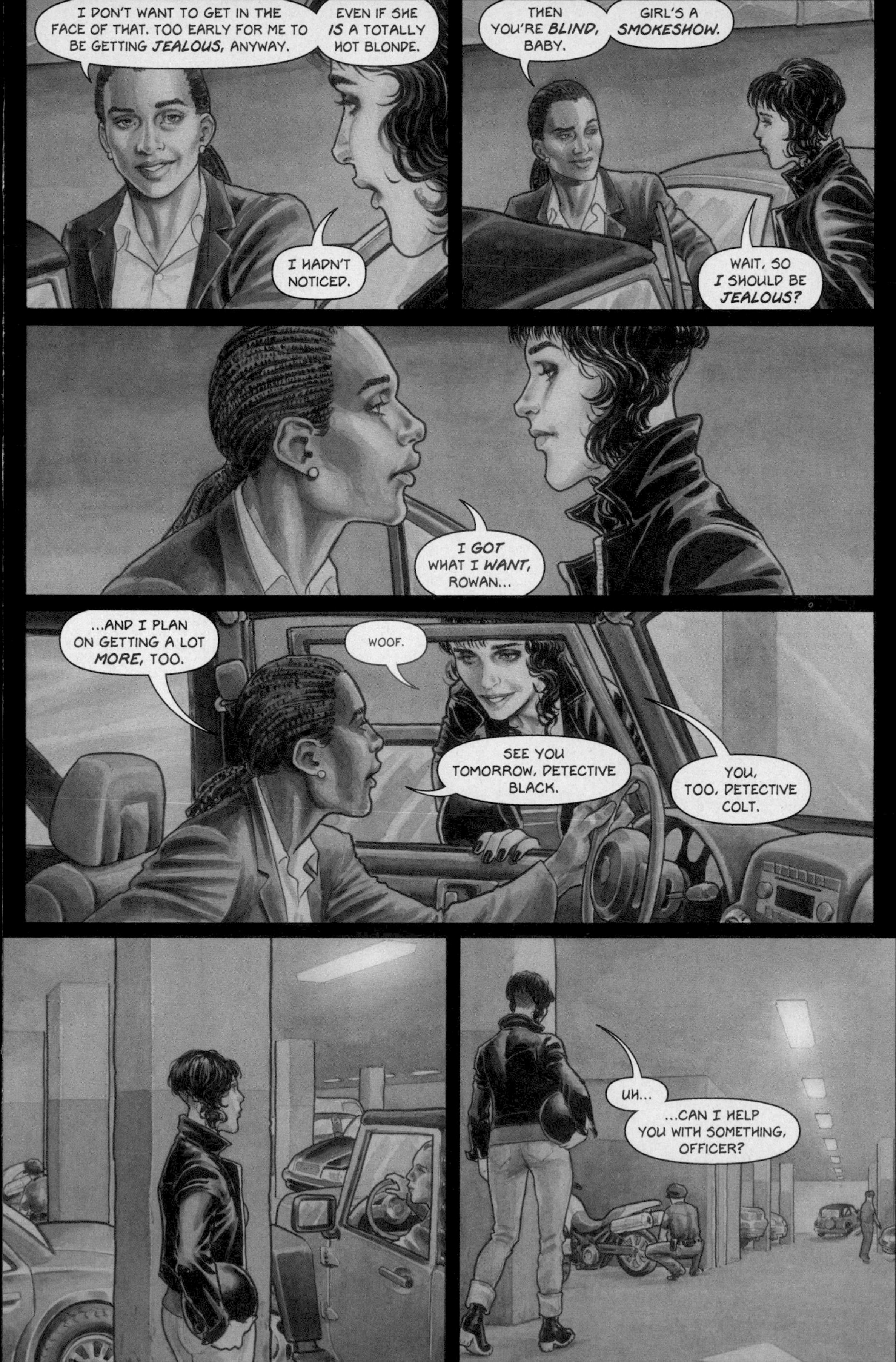
I DON'T WANT TO GET IN THE FACE OF THAT. TOO EARLY FOR ME TO BE GETTING *JEALOUS*, ANYWAY.
EVEN IF SHE *IS* A TOTALLY HOT BLONDE.
I HADN'T NOTICED.
THEN YOU'RE *BLIND*, BABY.
GIRL'S A *SMOKESHOW*.
WAIT, SO *I* SHOULD BE *JEALOUS?*
I *GOT* WHAT I *WANT*, ROWAN...
...AND I PLAN ON GETTING A LOT *MORE*, TOO.
WOOF.
SEE YOU TOMORROW, DETECTIVE BLACK.
YOU, TOO, DETECTIVE COLT.
UH...
...CAN I HELP YOU WITH SOMETHING, OFFICER?

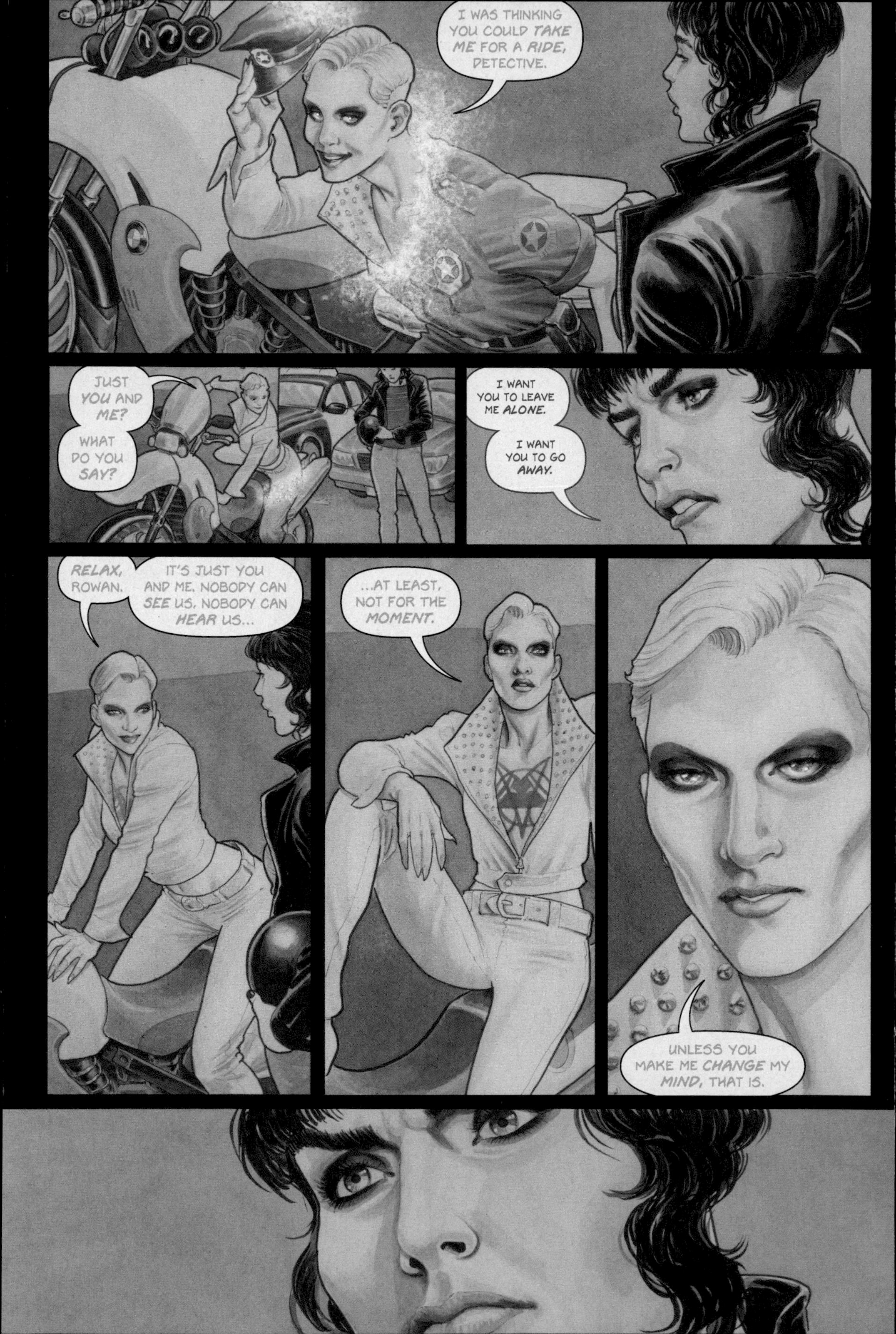
I WAS THINKING YOU COULD TAKE ME FOR A RIDE, DETECTIVE.
JUST YOU AND ME?
WHAT DO YOU SAY?
I WANT YOU TO LEAVE ME ALONE.
I WANT YOU TO GO AWAY.
RELAX, ROWAN.
IT'S JUST YOU AND ME. NOBODY CAN SEE US. NOBODY CAN HEAR US...
...AT LEAST, NOT FOR THE MOMENT.
UNLESS YOU MAKE ME CHANGE MY MIND, THAT IS.

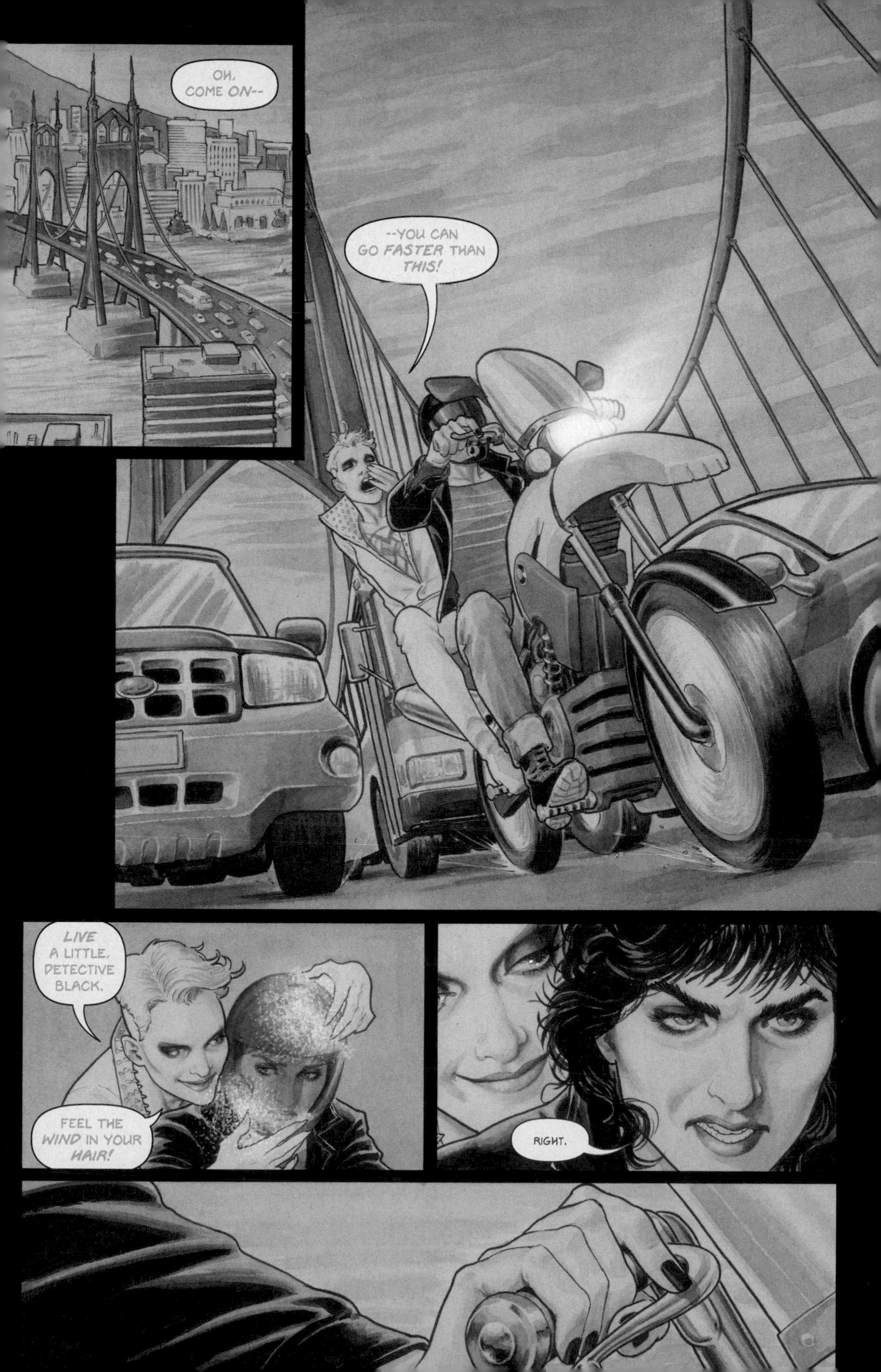
OH, COME ON--
--YOU CAN GO FASTER THAN THIS!
LIVE A LITTLE, DETECTIVE BLACK.
FEEL THE WIND IN YOUR HAIR!
RIGHT.

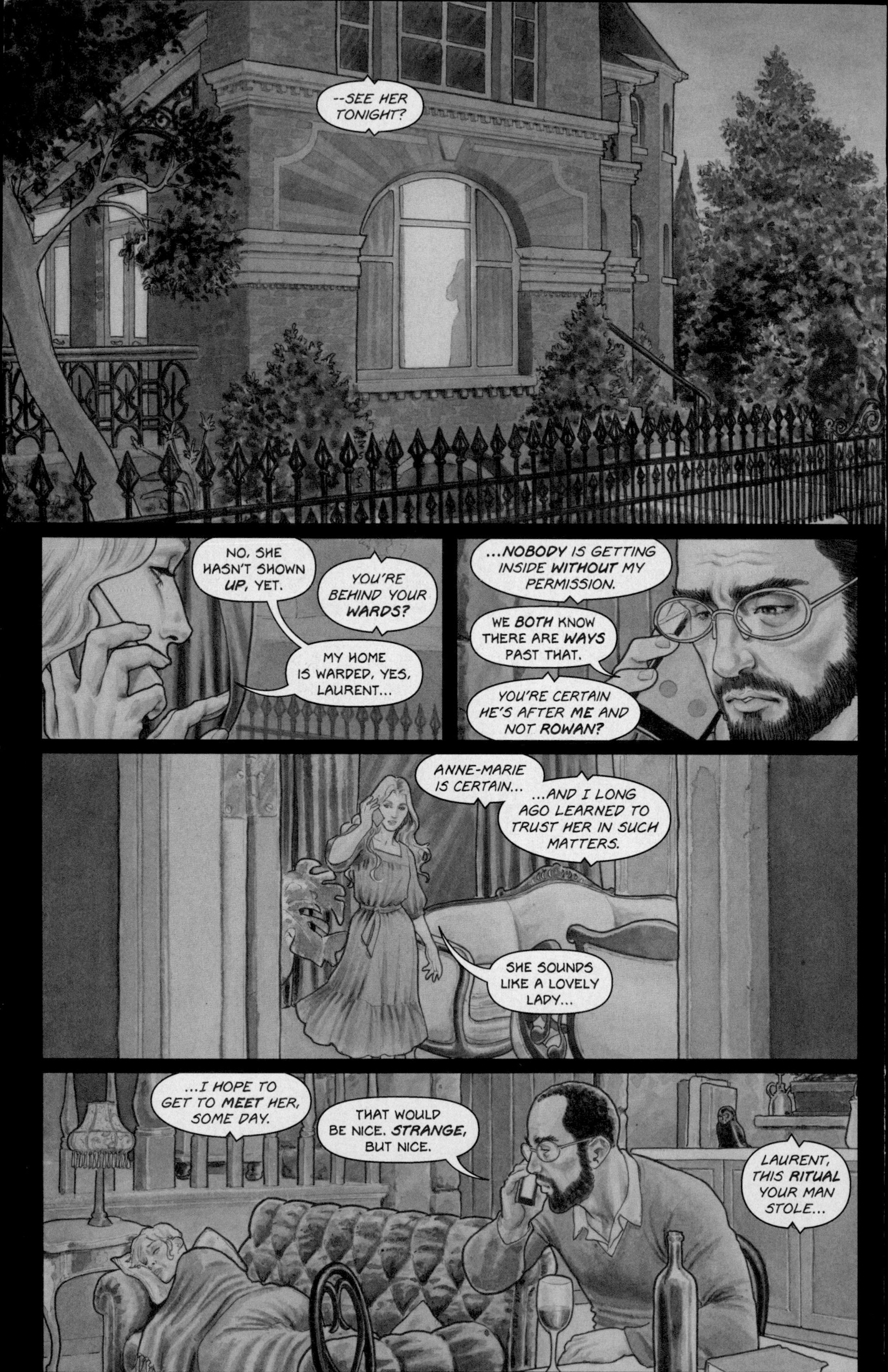
--SEE HER TONIGHT?
NO, SHE HASN'T SHOWN UP, YET.
YOU'RE BEHIND YOUR WARDS?
MY HOME IS WARDED, YES, LAURENT...
...NOBODY IS GETTING INSIDE WITHOUT MY PERMISSION.
WE BOTH KNOW THERE ARE WAYS PAST THAT.
YOU'RE CERTAIN HE'S AFTER ME AND NOT ROWAN?
ANNE-MARIE IS CERTAIN...
...AND I LONG AGO LEARNED TO TRUST HER IN SUCH MATTERS.
SHE SOUNDS LIKE A LOVELY LADY...
...I HOPE TO GET TO MEET HER, SOME DAY.
THAT WOULD BE NICE. STRANGE, BUT NICE.
LAURENT, THIS RITUAL YOUR MAN STOLE...

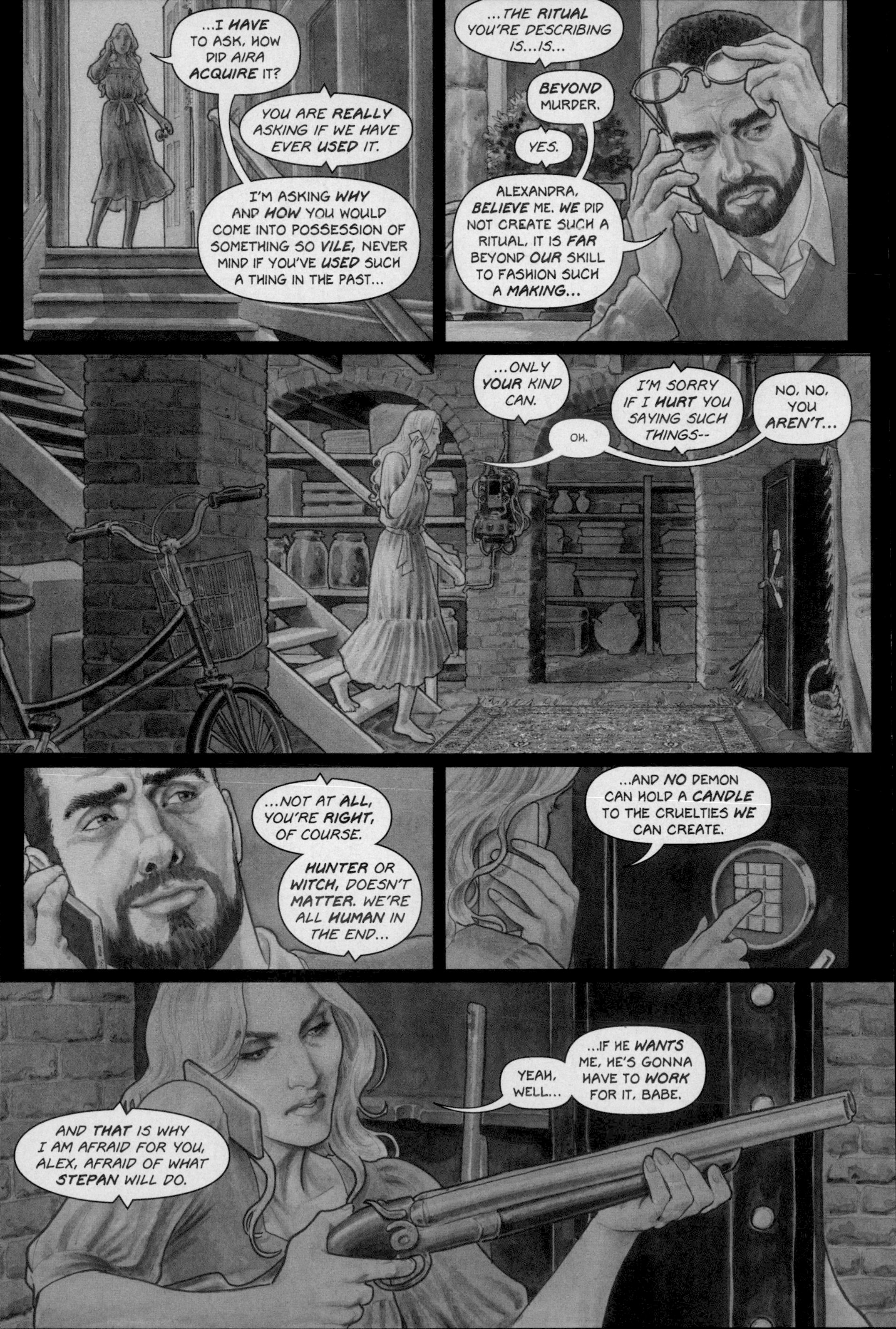
...I HAVE TO ASK, HOW DID AIRA ACQUIRE IT?
YOU ARE REALLY ASKING IF WE HAVE EVER USED IT.
I'M ASKING WHY AND HOW YOU WOULD COME INTO POSSESSION OF SOMETHING SO VILE, NEVER MIND IF YOU'VE USED SUCH A THING IN THE PAST...
...THE RITUAL YOU'RE DESCRIBING IS...IS...
BEYOND MURDER.
YES.
ALEXANDRA, BELIEVE ME. WE DID NOT CREATE SUCH A RITUAL, IT IS FAR BEYOND OUR SKILL TO FASHION SUCH A MAKING...
...ONLY YOUR KIND CAN.
OH.
I'M SORRY IF I HURT YOU SAYING SUCH THINGS--
NO, NO, YOU AREN'T...
...NOT AT ALL, YOU'RE RIGHT, OF COURSE.
HUNTER OR WITCH, DOESN'T MATTER. WE'RE ALL HUMAN IN THE END...
...AND NO DEMON CAN HOLD A CANDLE TO THE CRUELTIES WE CAN CREATE.
AND THAT IS WHY I AM AFRAID FOR YOU, ALEX, AFRAID OF WHAT STEPAN WILL DO.
YEAH, WELL...
...IF HE WANTS ME, HE'S GONNA HAVE TO WORK FOR IT, BABE.

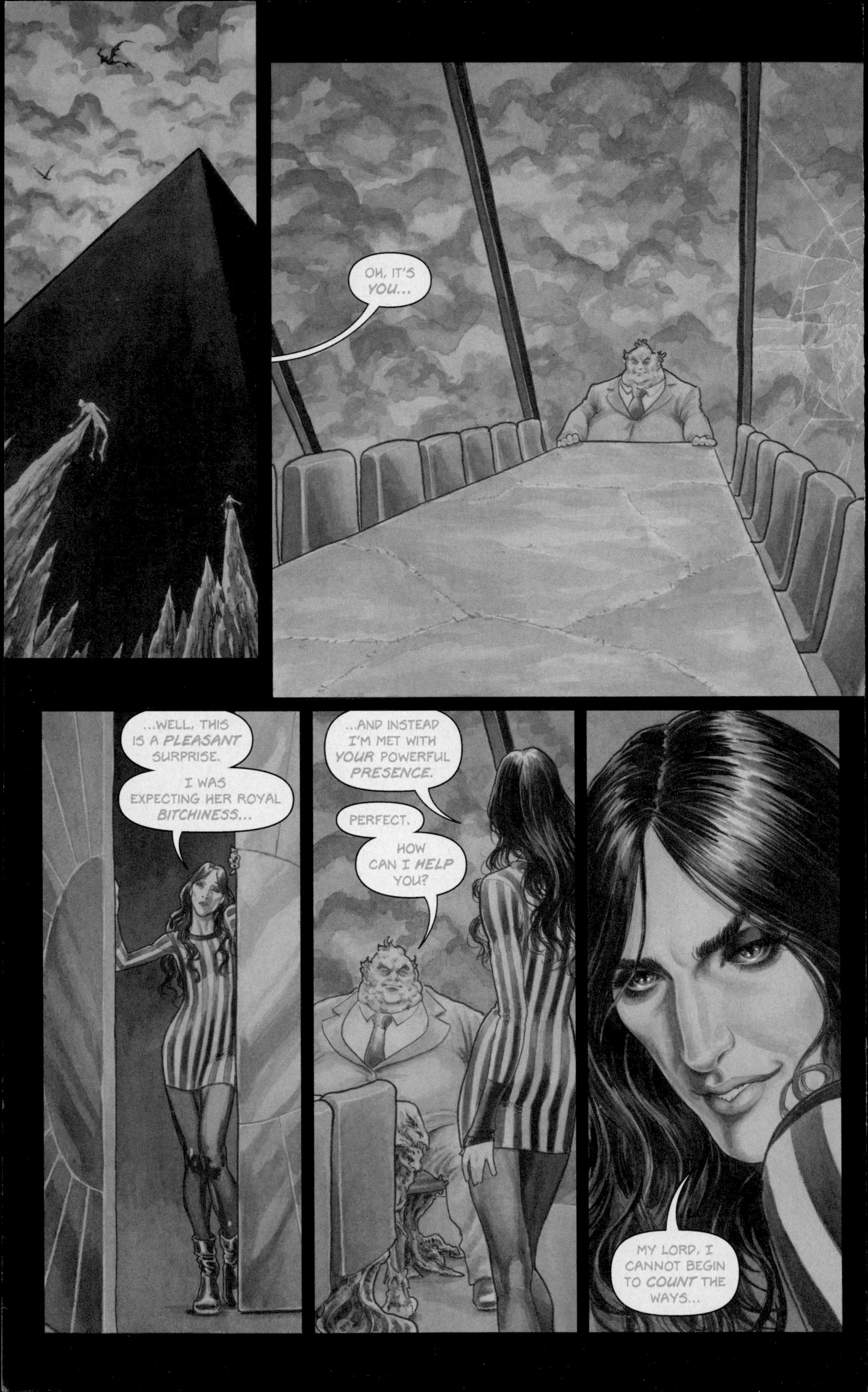
OH, IT'S YOU...
...WELL, THIS IS A PLEASANT SURPRISE.
I WAS EXPECTING HER ROYAL BITCHINESS...
...AND INSTEAD I'M MET WITH YOUR POWERFUL PRESENCE.
PERFECT.
HOW CAN I HELP YOU?
MY LORD, I CANNOT BEGIN TO COUNT THE WAYS...

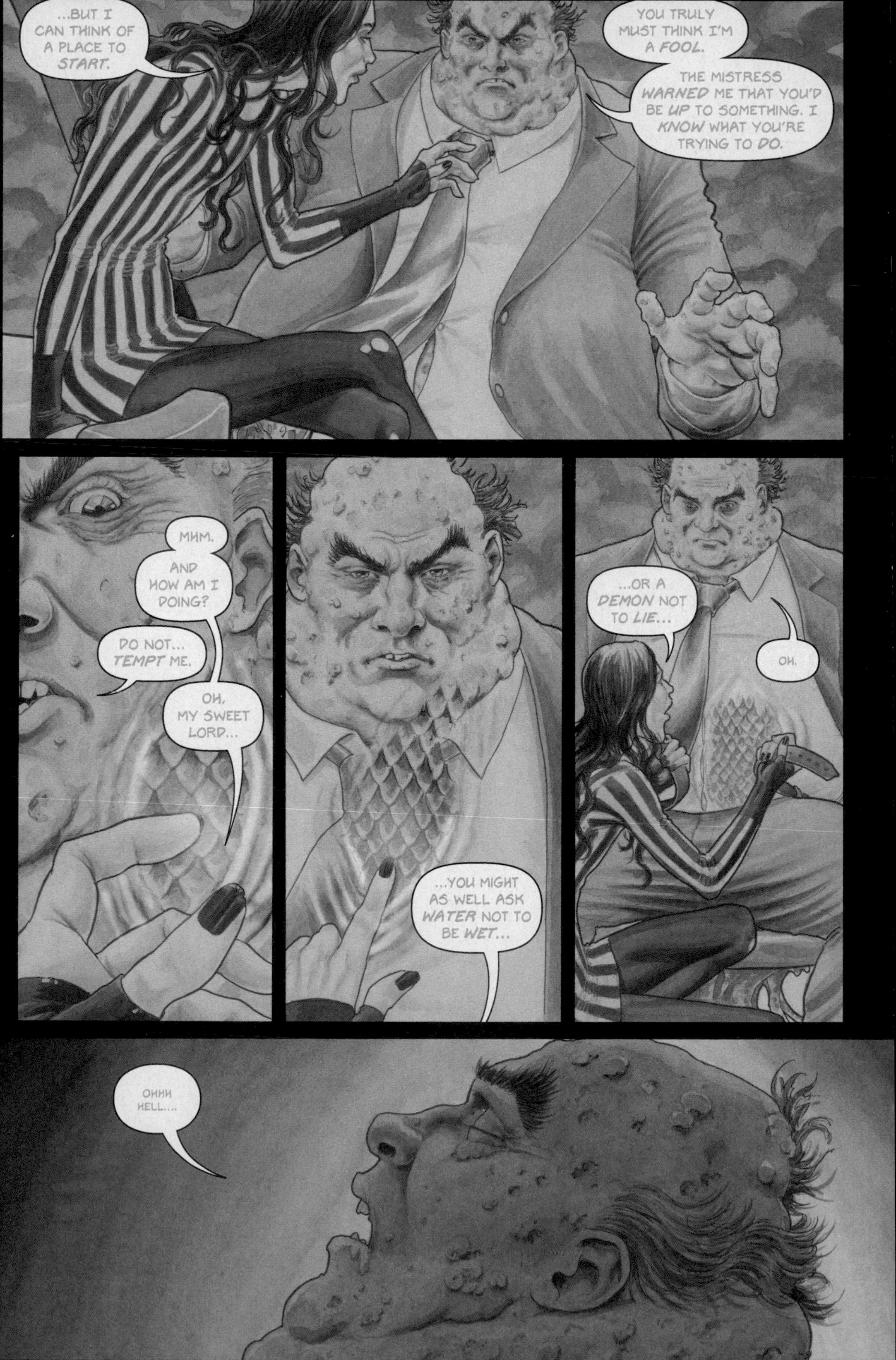
...BUT I CAN THINK OF A PLACE TO START.
YOU TRULY MUST THINK I'M A FOOL.
THE MISTRESS WARNED ME THAT YOU'D BE UP TO SOMETHING. I KNOW WHAT YOU'RE TRYING TO DO.
MHM.
AND HOW AM I DOING?
DO NOT... TEMPT ME.
OH, MY SWEET LORD...
...YOU MIGHT AS WELL ASK WATER NOT TO BE WET...
...OR A DEMON NOT TO LIE...
OH.
OHHH HELL....

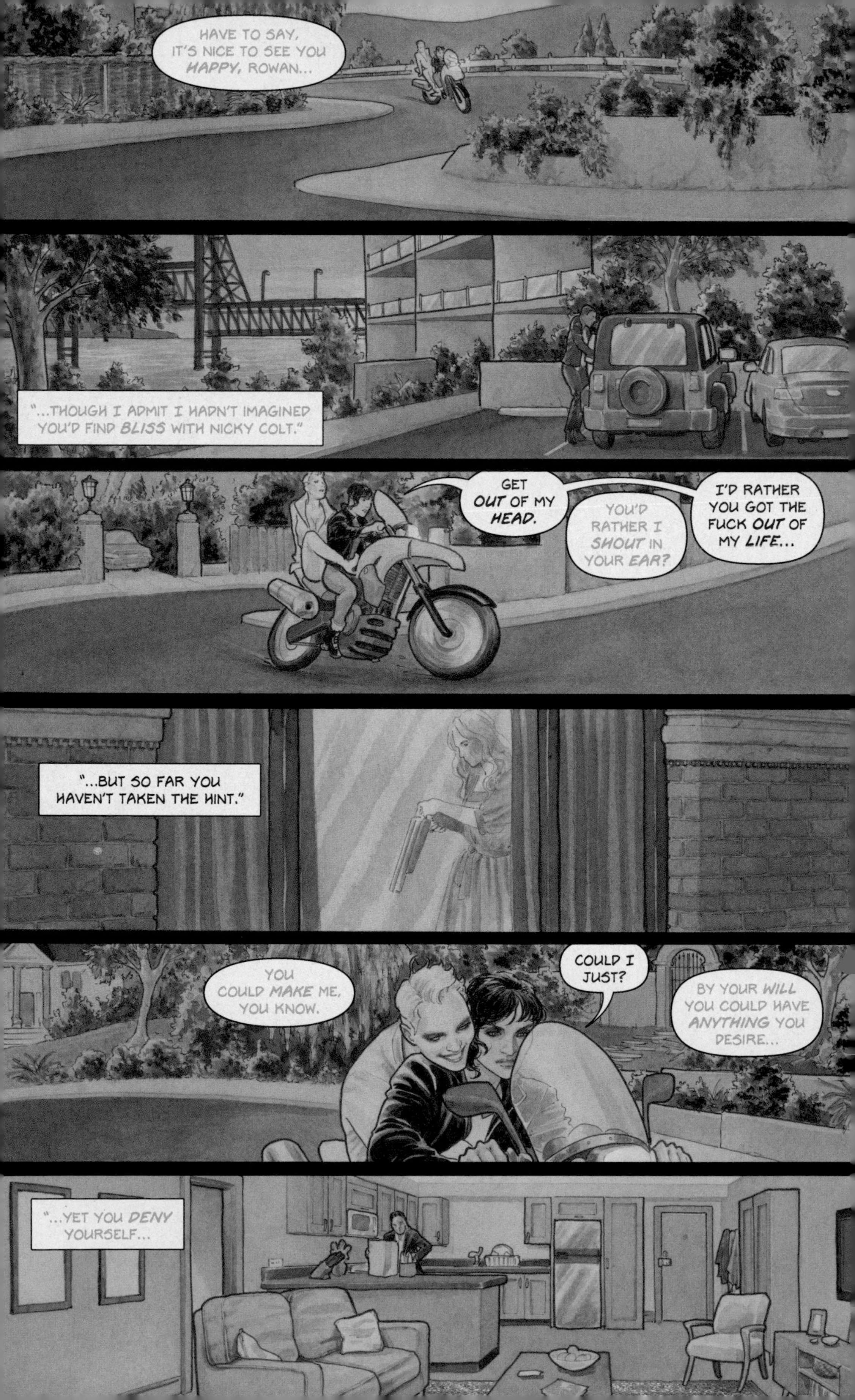

HAVE TO SAY, IT'S NICE TO SEE YOU HAPPY, ROWAN...
"...THOUGH I ADMIT I HADN'T IMAGINED YOU'D FIND BLISS WITH NICKY COLT."
GET OUT OF MY HEAD.
YOU'D RATHER I SHOUT IN YOUR EAR?
I'D RATHER YOU GOT THE FUCK OUT OF MY LIFE...
"...BUT SO FAR YOU HAVEN'T TAKEN THE HINT."
YOU COULD MAKE ME, YOU KNOW.
COULD I JUST?
BY YOUR WILL YOU COULD HAVE ANYTHING YOU DESIRE...
"...YET YOU DENY YOURSELF...

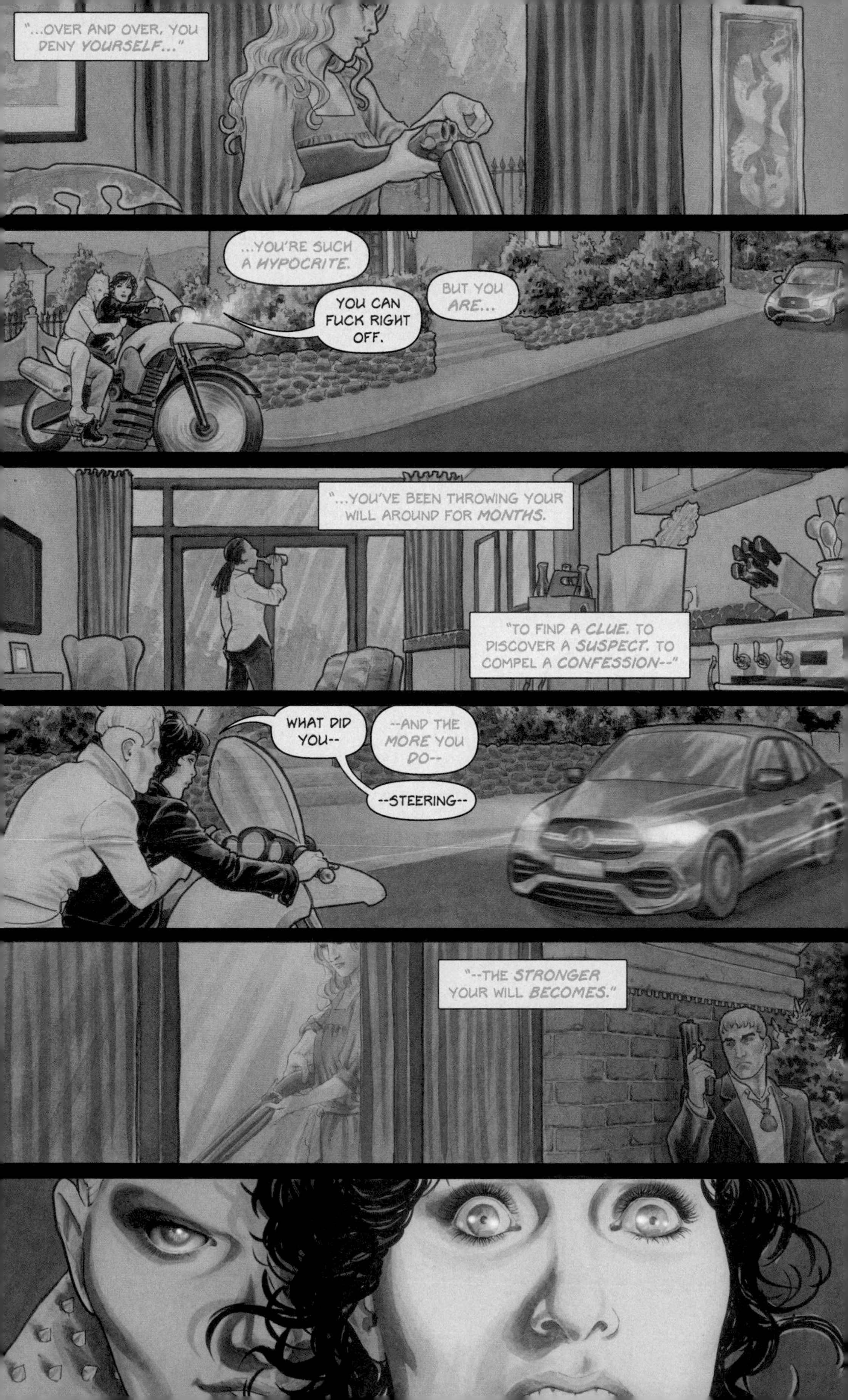
"...OVER AND OVER, YOU DENY YOURSELF..."
...YOU'RE SUCH A HYPOCRITE.
YOU CAN FUCK RIGHT OFF.
BUT YOU ARE...
"...YOU'VE BEEN THROWING YOUR WILL AROUND FOR MONTHS.
"TO FIND A CLUE. TO DISCOVER A SUSPECT. TO COMPEL A CONFESSION--"
WHAT DID YOU--
--AND THE MORE YOU DO--
--STEERING--
"--THE STRONGER YOUR WILL BECOMES."

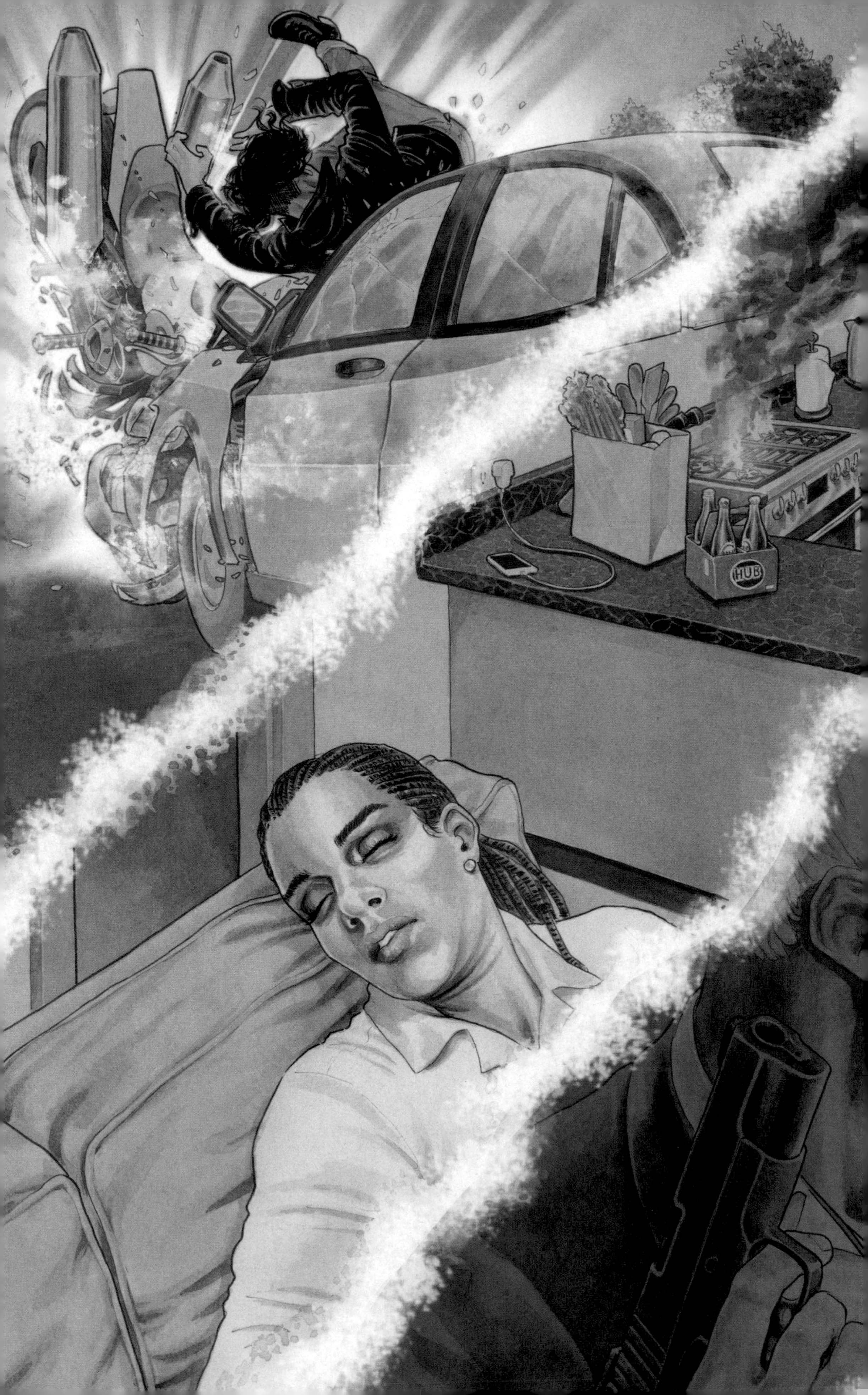
HUB

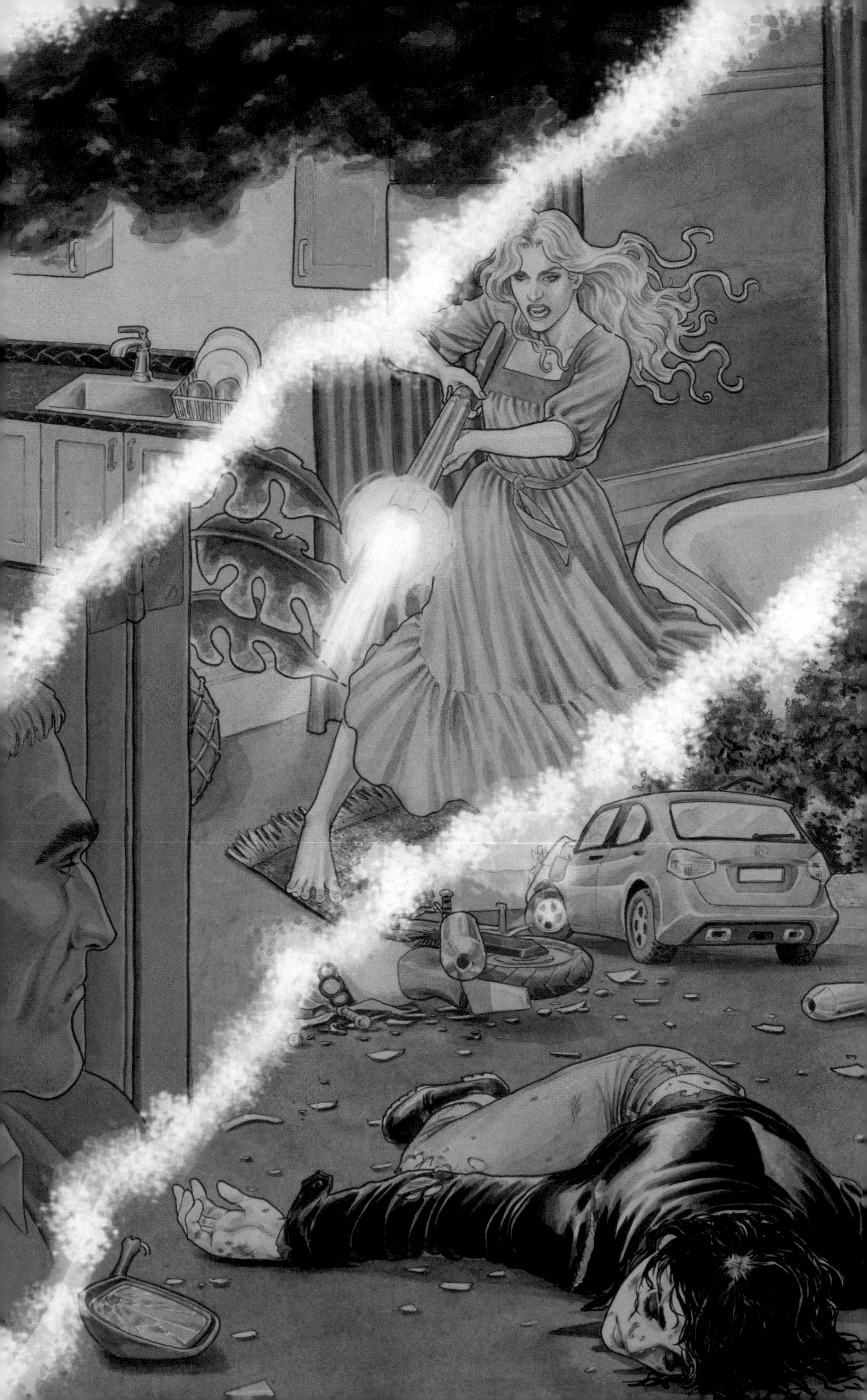

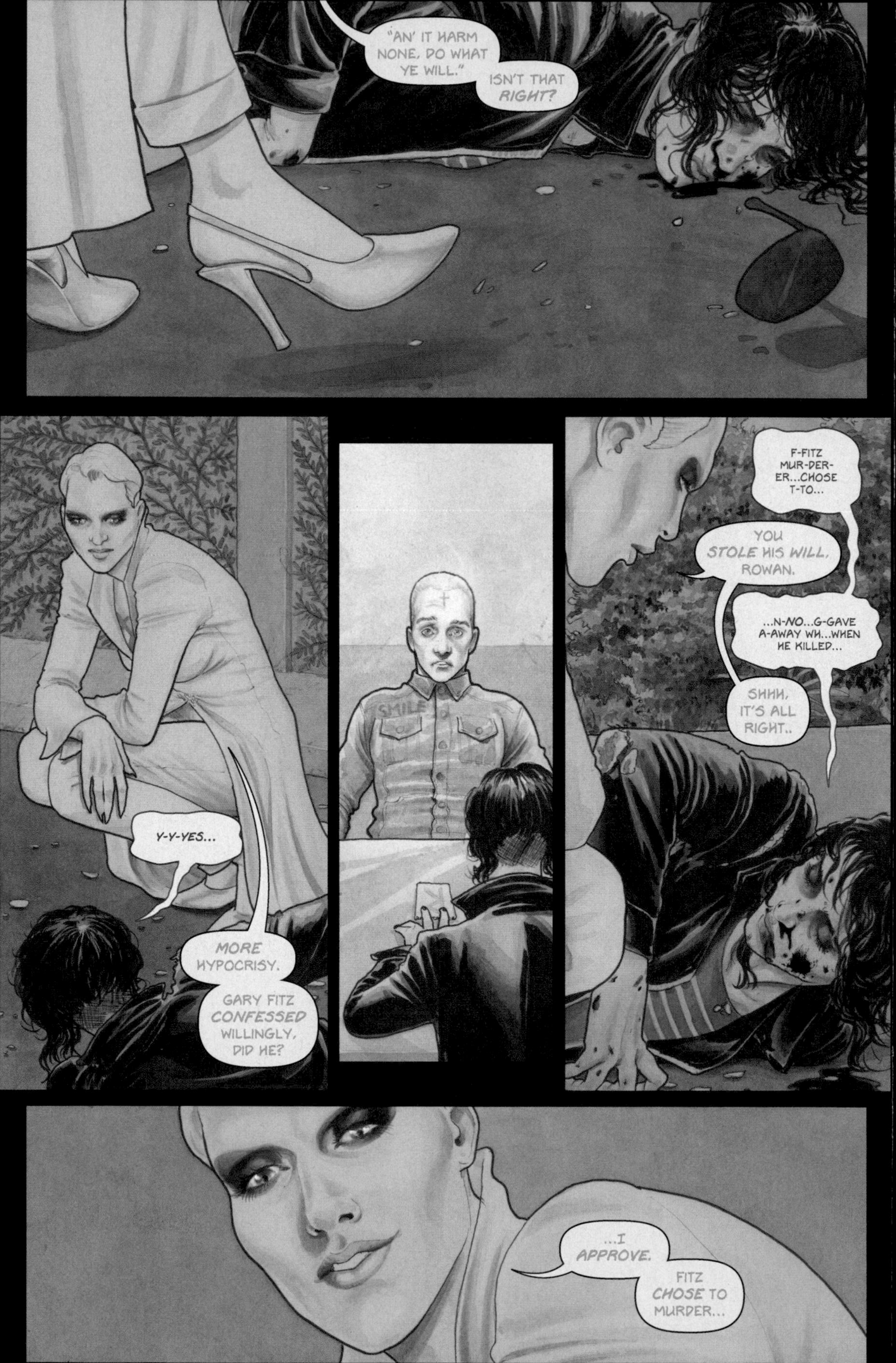
"AN' IT HARM NONE, DO WHAT YE WILL."
ISN'T THAT RIGHT?
Y-Y-YES...
MORE HYPOCRISY.
GARY FITZ CONFESSED WILLINGLY, DID HE?
SMILE
F-FITZ MUR-DER-ER...CHOSE T-TO...
YOU STOLE HIS WILL, ROWAN.
...N-NO...G-GAVE A-AWAY WH...WHEN HE KILLED...
SHHH, IT'S ALL RIGHT..
...I APPROVE.
FITZ CHOSE TO MURDER...

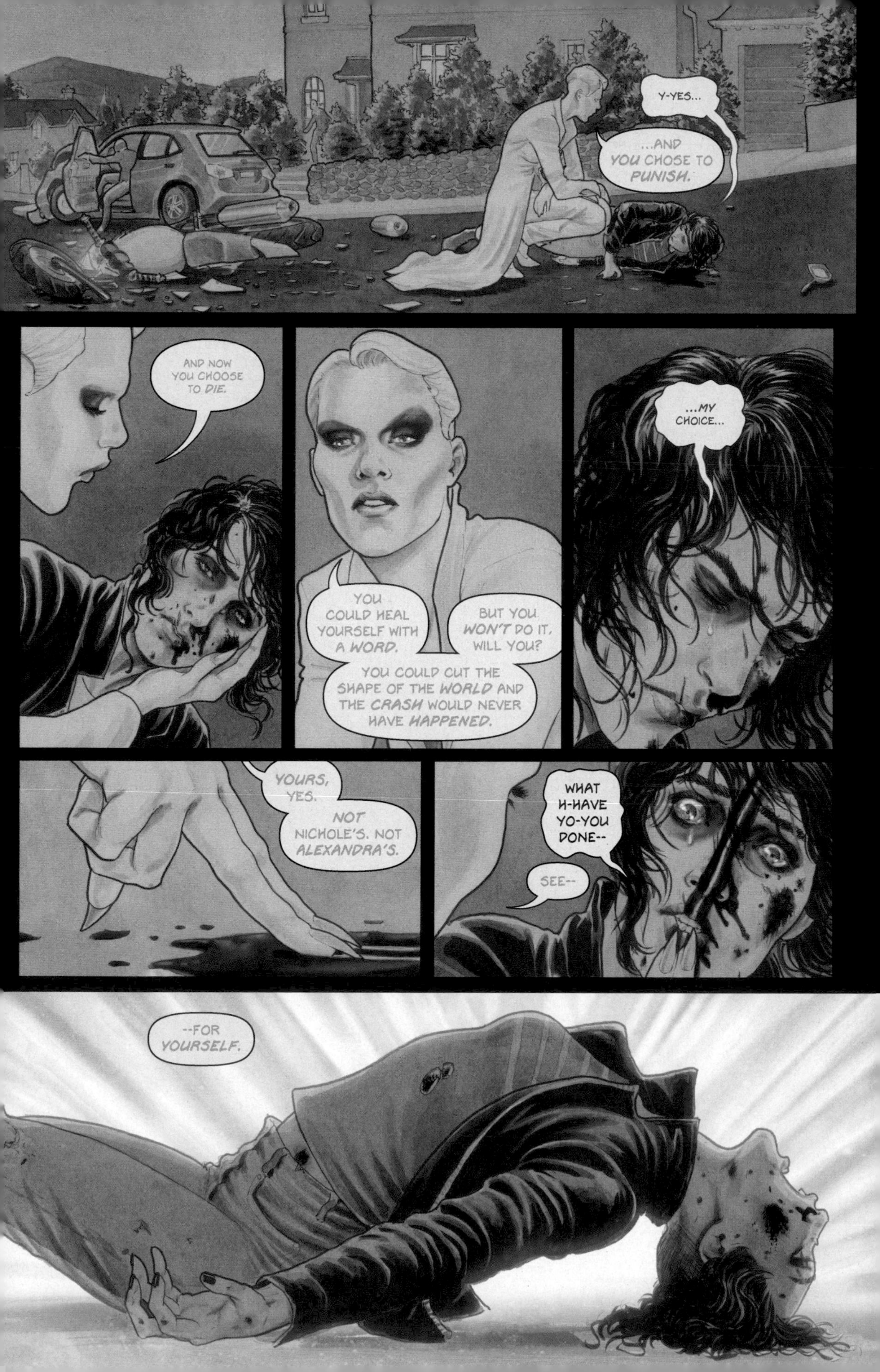
Y-YES...
...AND YOU CHOSE TO PUNISH.
AND NOW YOU CHOOSE TO DIE.
YOU COULD HEAL YOURSELF WITH A WORD.
BUT YOU WON'T DO IT, WILL YOU?
YOU COULD CUT THE SHAPE OF THE WORLD AND THE CRASH WOULD NEVER HAVE HAPPENED.
...MY CHOICE...
YOURS, YES.
NOT NICHOLE'S. NOT ALEXANDRA'S.
WHAT H-HAVE YO-YOU DONE--
SEE--
--FOR YOURSELF.

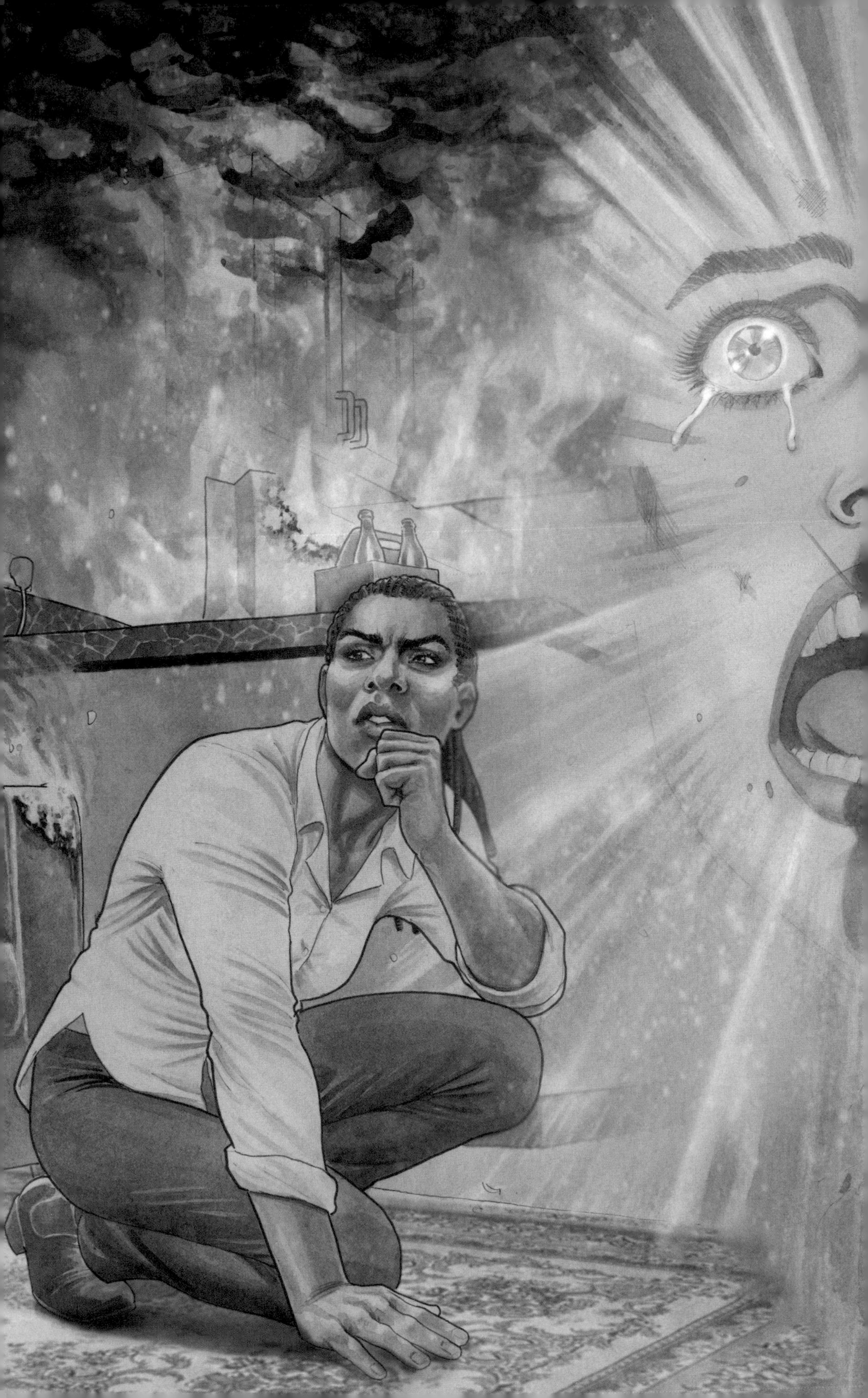

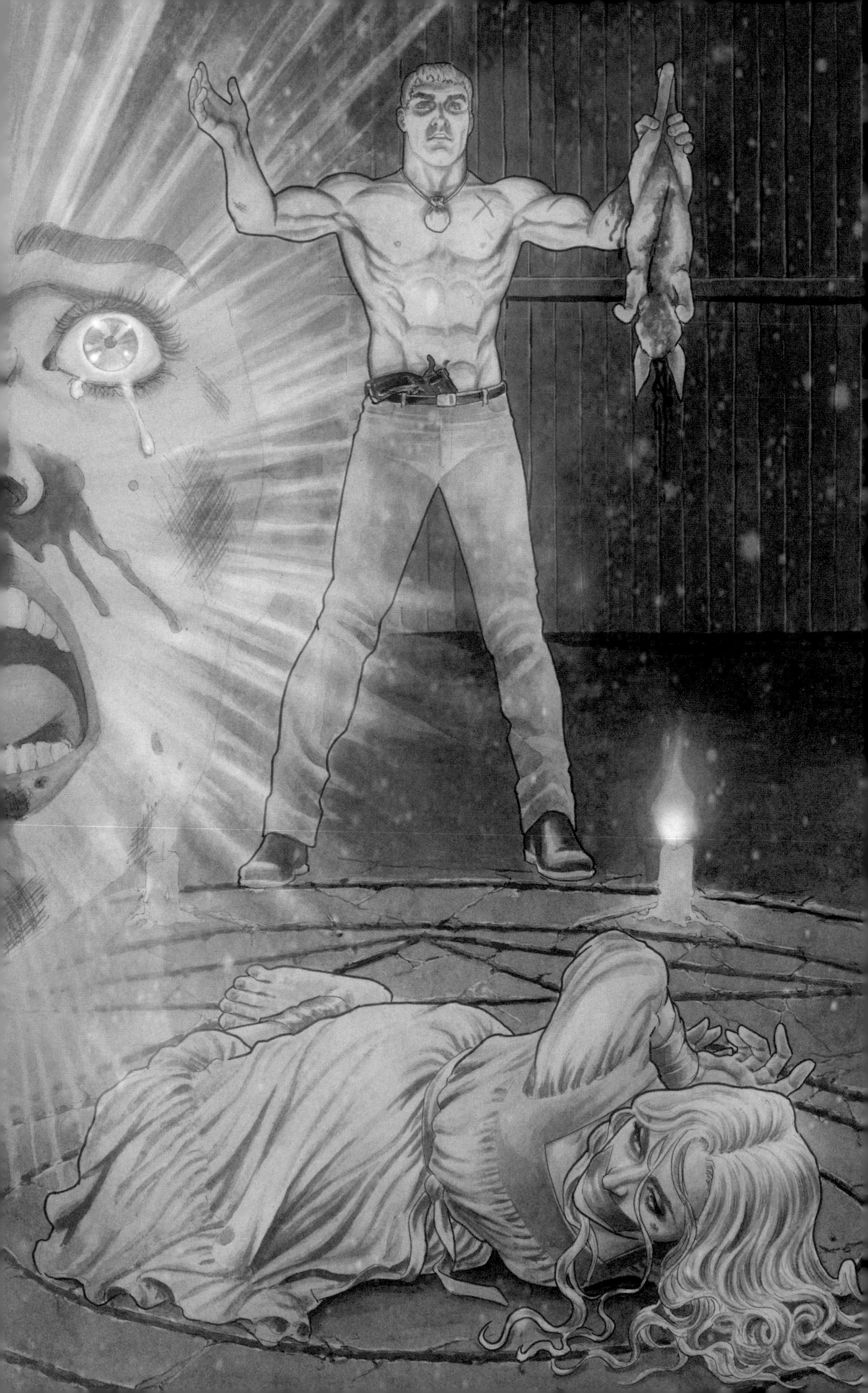

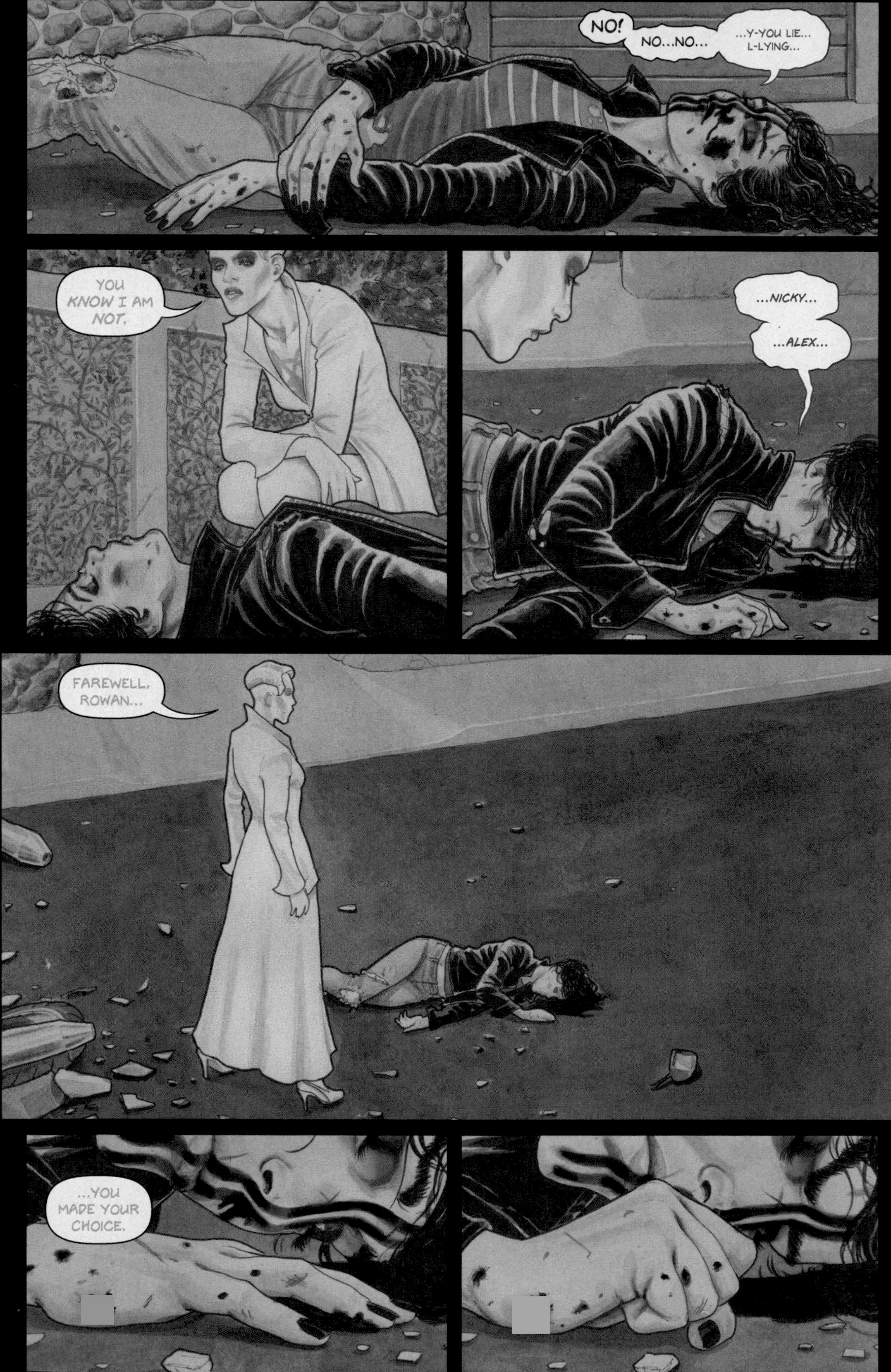
NO!
NO...NO...
...Y-YOU LIE... L-LYING...
YOU KNOW I AM NOT.
...NICKY...
...ALEX...
FAREWELL, ROWAN...
...YOU MADE YOUR CHOICE.

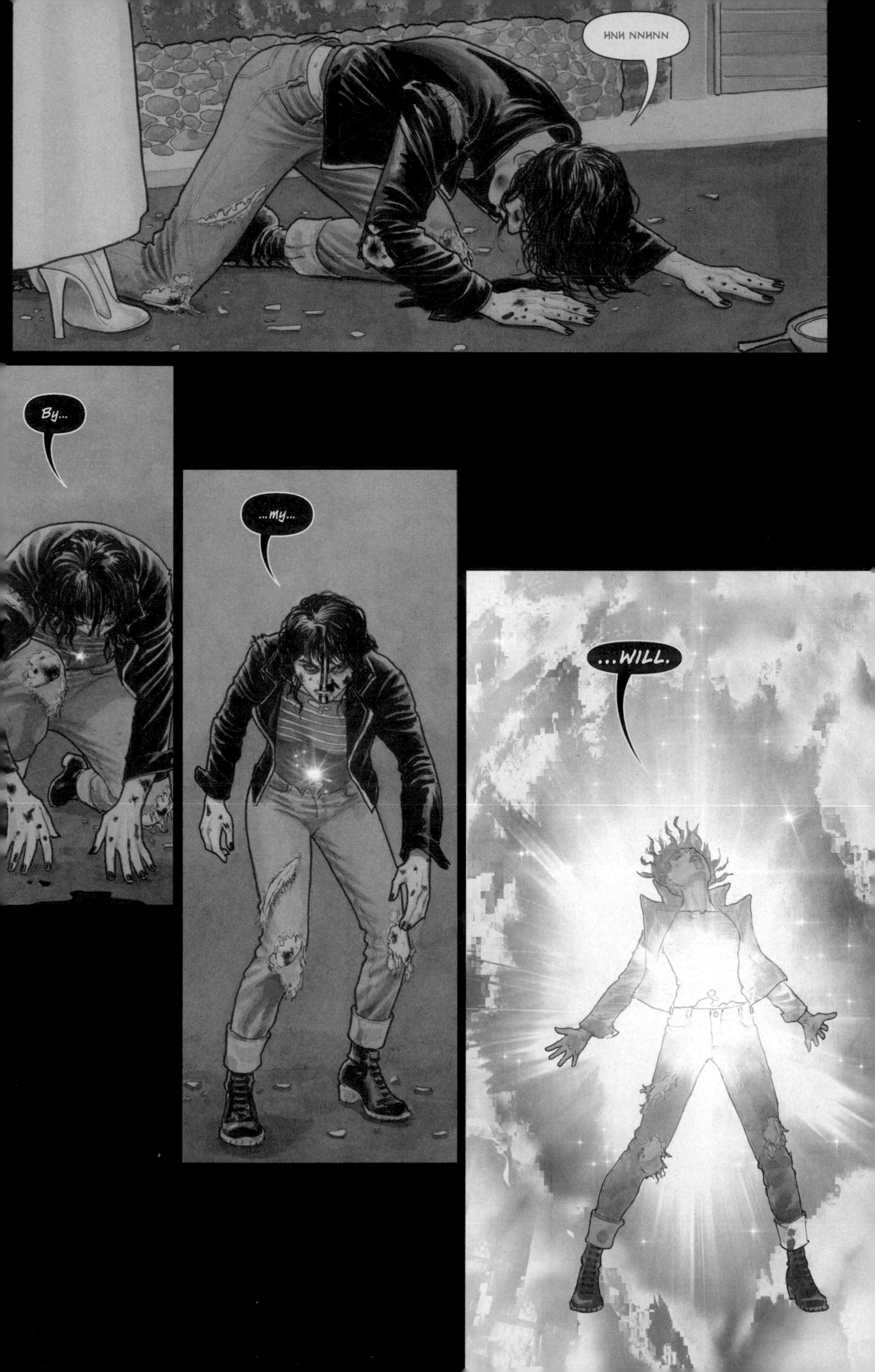
ИNИ NNИNN
By...
...my...
...WILL.

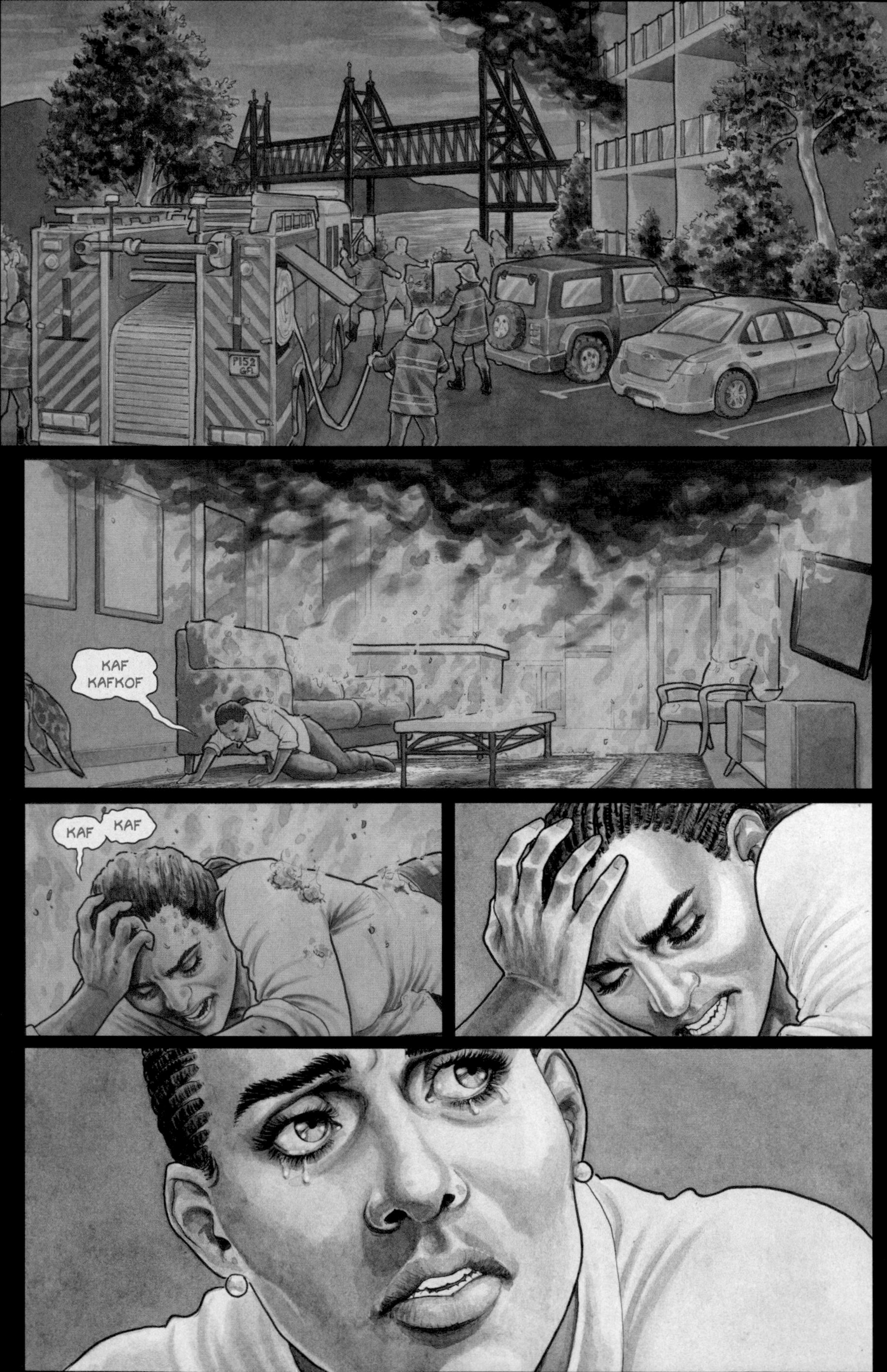
KAF
KAFKOF
KAF
KAF

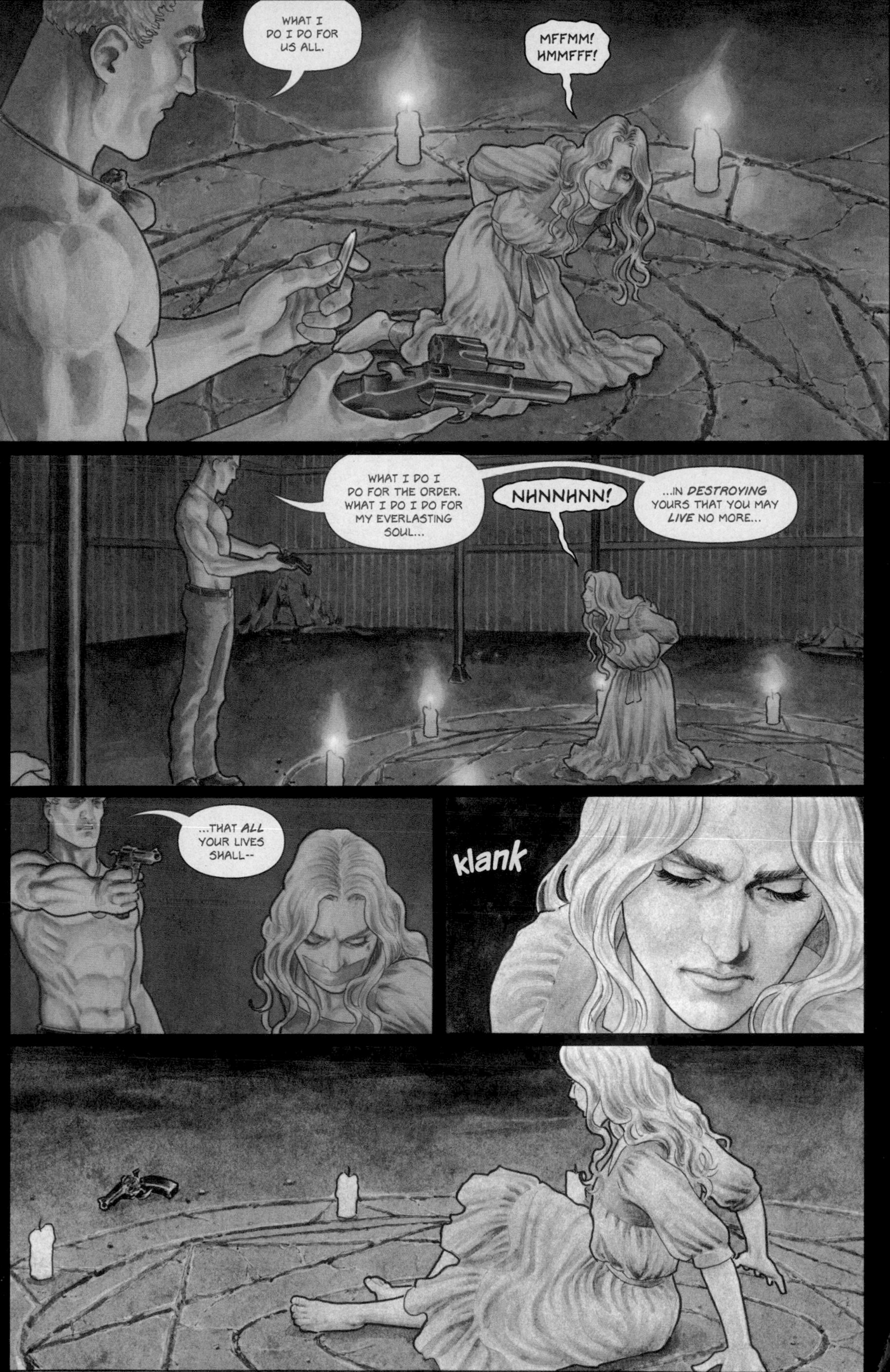

WHAT I DO I DO FOR US ALL.
MFFMM! HMMFFF!
WHAT I DO I DO FOR THE ORDER. WHAT I DO I DO FOR MY EVERLASTING SOUL...
NHNNHNN!
...IN DESTROYING YOURS THAT YOU MAY LIVE NO MORE...
...THAT ALL YOUR LIVES SHALL--
klank

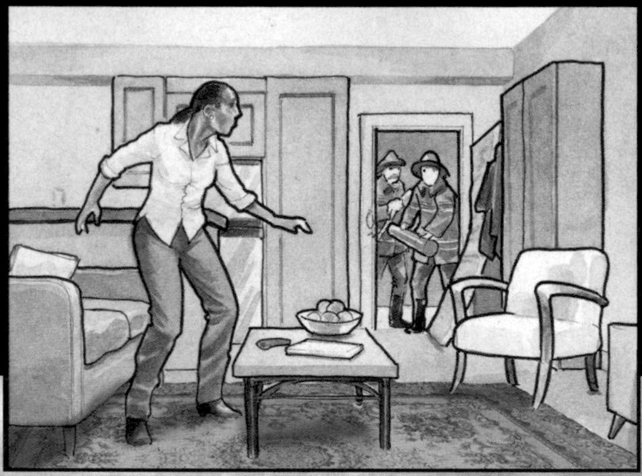
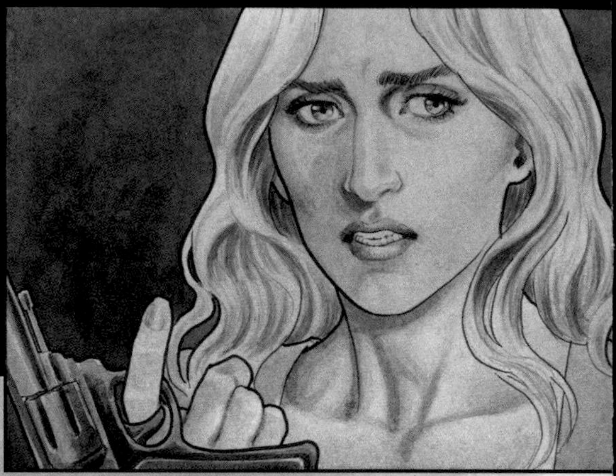
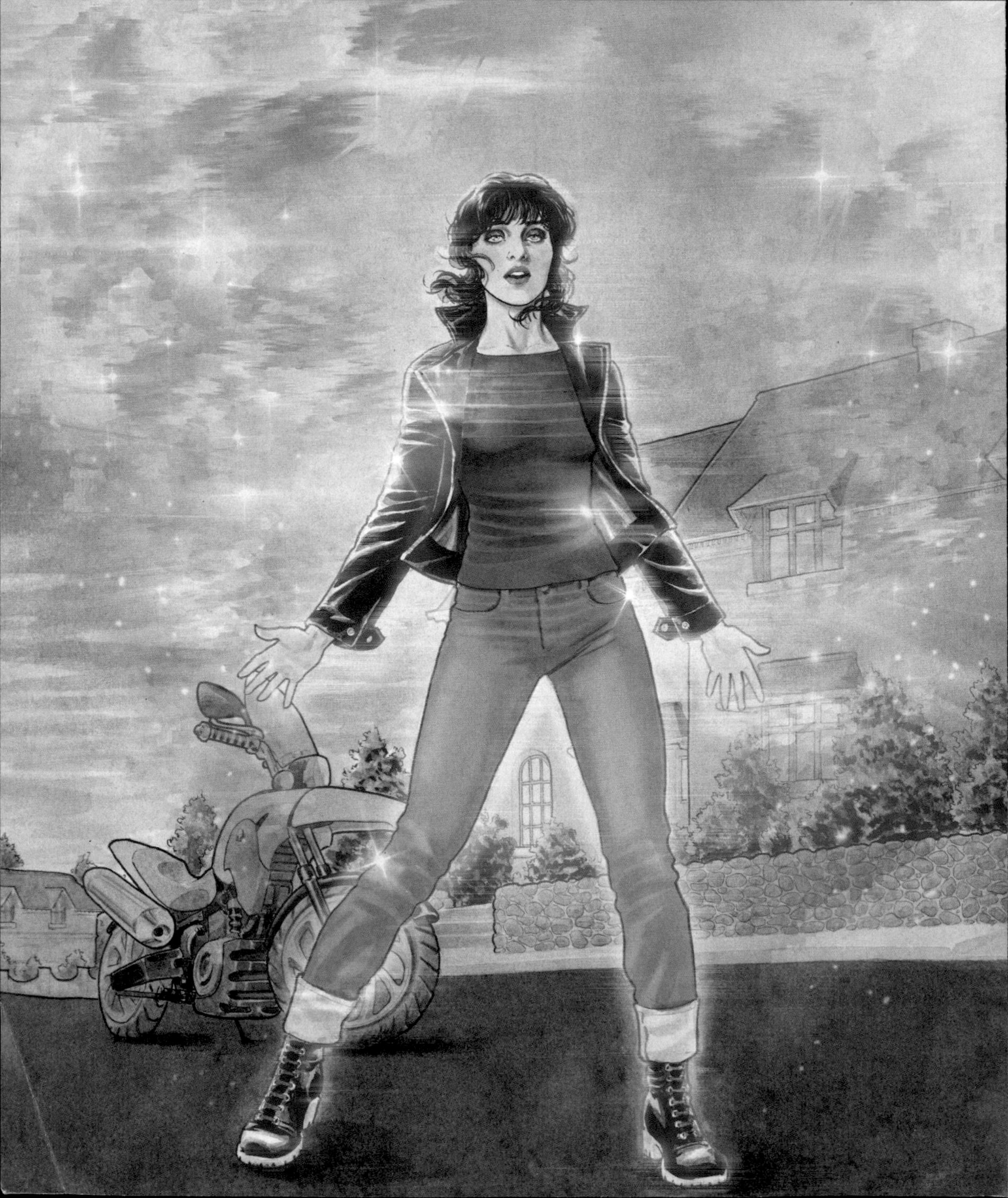

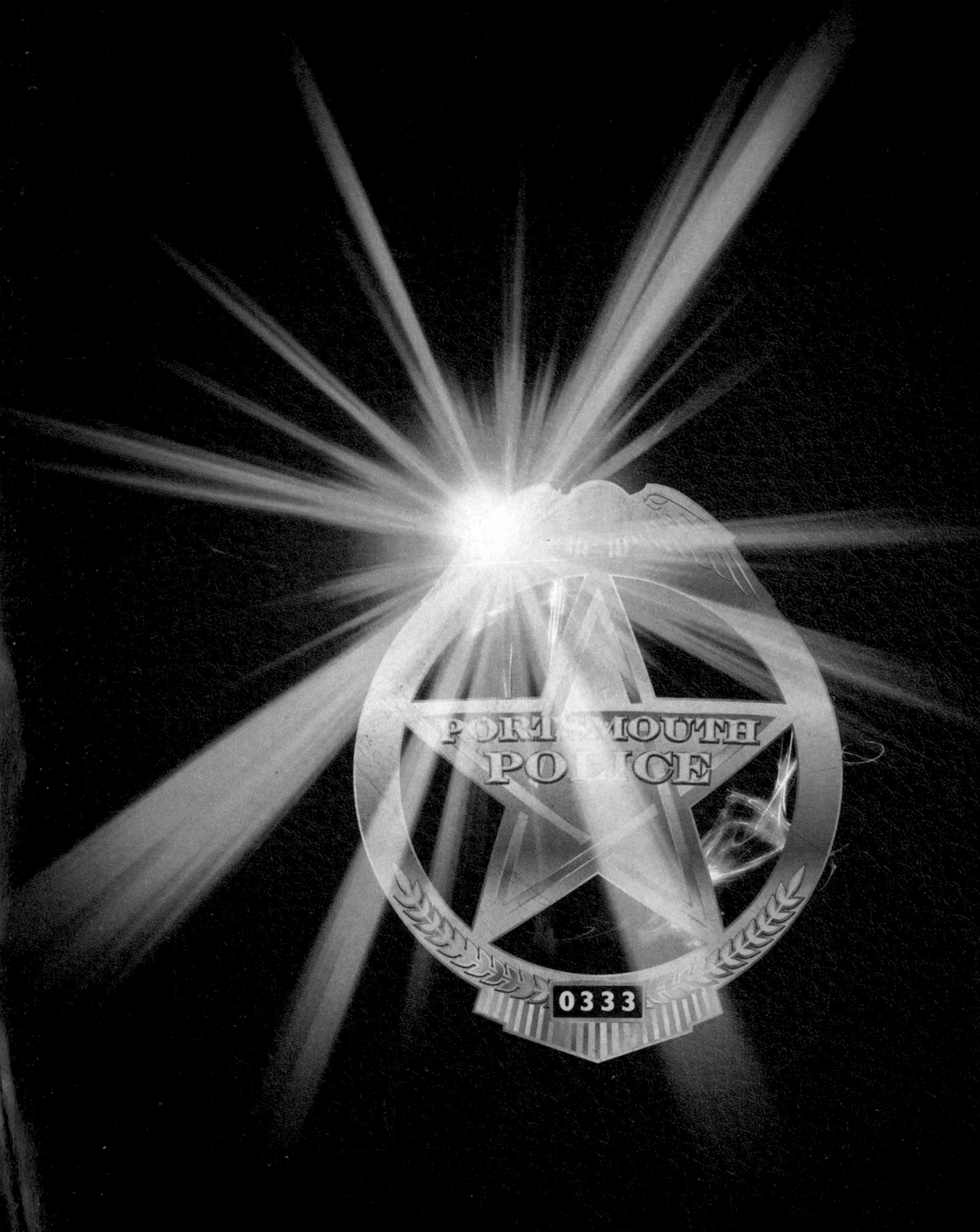
PORTSMOUTH
POLICE
0333